ADIRONDACK
DETECTIVE
A NEW BEGINNING

JOHN H. BRIANT

Chalet Publishing
P.O. Box 1154
Old Forge, New York

ADIRONDACK DETECTIVE A NEW BEGINNING

Library of Congress Catalog Control Number 99-96188

ISBN 978-0-9648327-6-3

VOLUME V

Graphics and book design
by
John D. Mahaffy

Printed in the United States of America

Chalet Publishing
P.O. Box 1154
Old Forge, New York 13420-1154

John A. Briant

Dedication

*To all the Adirondack People who reside within the Blue Line.
And to all the people, who love and visit this special
place on earth known as
The Adirondack Park.*

and

*To my devoted wife, Margaret,
who continually inspires me to keep the oil lamp lit.*

and

To my reading audience, who make it all possible.

ACKNOWLEDGEMENT

I wish to extend thanks to John D. Mahaffy for steering the Adirondack guide boat and Lydia Maltzan for paddling it.

And, to Margaret, my wife, for her untiring patience, understanding, insight, and opinion and keeping the oil lamp flickering.

To my many fans, a special thanks, for making it all possible.

The Path

The place we love, our home
set in the pines we often roam.
Shall we leave or shall we stay?
Or wait until another day.

The path we follow we hope and pray,
will be the one to show our way,
over the mountains to another home.
Looking ahead to whatever we face
we know the Adirondacks are our place.

...John H. Briant

FOREWORD

Jason Black and his lovely wife, Patty, returned to the Adirondack Mountains of northern New York State from Arizona. Jason had been called to Phoenix by his close friend, Jack Flynn, to work on a case involving a missing student from the University of Arizona, who he had finally located.

Patty, who is pregnant, and Jason, are now looking forward to the birth, and the continuation of their life in the mountains they love. However, events occur when Bernard Draper, escapes from a Michigan correctional facility, bent on avenging his apprehension by making threats against the authorities including private detective JASON BLACK. The situation becomes tense and dangerous.

Jason, during this time of turmoil, is offered a position at the lodge by his close friend, Tom Huston, owner of the Breakshire Lodge of Lake Placid, New York. Huston, with his health slowly failing, has created the Loggers' Museum near Tupper Lake and has plans for his private detective friend. With the impending threats, the forthcoming birth of their child, a new job offer, and the decision of a move to Lake Placid or not to move, have placed indescribable pressure on their shoulders. What lies ahead? Danger lurks in the mountains.

Other books by the Author
One Cop's Story: A Life Remembered 1995
Adirondack Detective 2000
Adirondack Detective Returns 2002
Adirondack Detective III 2004
Adirondack Detective Goes West 2005

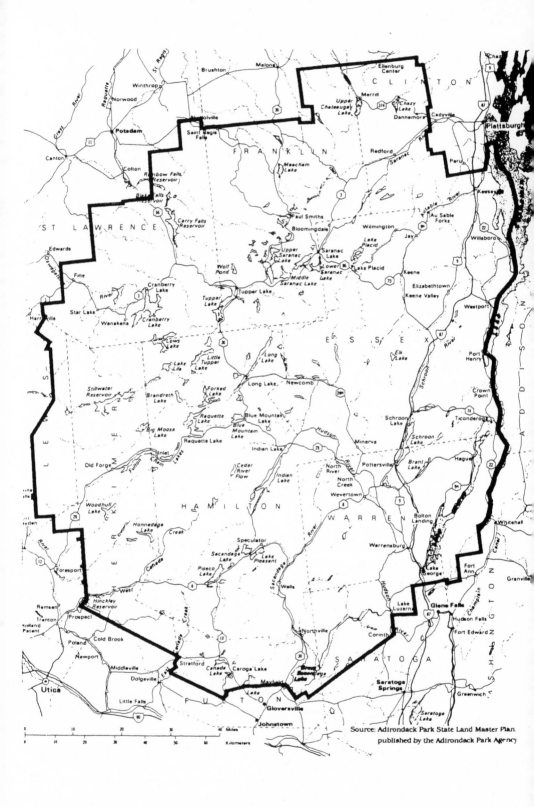

Source: Adirondack Park State Land Master Plan,
published by the Adirondack Park Agency.

CHAPTER ONE

Who would have perceived all the changes in my life since my retirement to my home in the Adirondacks from the New York State Police. I had become private investigator, Jason Black, to supplement my pension and to occupy my idle hours. During one of my cases I became involved with Patty Olson, a waitress, who had somehow captured my heart and led me to break my vow never to remarry: two divorces had taken their toll.

My most recent case had taken us to the southwest state of Arizona to assist my good friend, Jack Flynn, also a private investigator, with an abduction of a wealthy photo-journalist student from the University of Arizona, which I was able to bring to a successful conclusion, and our return home.

After our exciting Arizona escapade, Patty and I adjusted to our beloved Adirondack routine: me to my private investigative work, and Patty to her waitress position at John's Diner. As the days progressed we'd already begun to reminisce about the welcome back surprise party that our group of friends had held at the Hard Times Café upon our return.

It meant so much to us to see their genuine expressions of friendship. The gathering of our friends and the comments across the dining room had welcomed us back to the place we loved and adored—the mountains, lakes, and animals that we were accustomed to seeing. It was great to be back home.

1

In the almost two months since we had returned, our friends Wilt Chambers, Jack Falsey, Dale Rush, and Jim Jenny had been busy on the weekends with the new addition to our log home for the baby's nursery. Charlie Perkins delivered most of the lumber, including the logs needed for the outside. The sheetrock, tape, and sealing materials were in place for installation. The added room was progressing well. Each day that the work crew was present I made it a point to have cold cuts, coffee, and plenty of pastries on hand.

Before the project began I had met with our workers to discuss the cost factor. Wilt, as the spokesman for the group, informed me they remained adamant about volunteering their services. I had tried to insist that there should be some money up front. Wilt again stated, "Jason, you take care of the cost of all the materials and we'll take care of the rest." Patty and I were still reluctant to go along with Wilt's suggestion, but after considering the whole picture we decided not to upset these dedicated friends of ours who wanted to give to us in this way. We finally decided that it would be wise to refrain from pressing the issue any further for now.

Since our return from Arizona, Patty had visited her doctor's office on several occasions and on each visit had received good news that the pregnancy was progressing normally without any medical problems. The doctor advised Patty that if she felt like continuing her work she could do so, leaving that decision up to her. Happily she opted to fulfill her obligation to Lila and John at the diner.

I promised myself that after the baby was born I would initiate an appreciation party for everyone in town. In the meantime, I had some work ahead of me. Fortunately, the missing-person case in Arizona, with the sizable check from Jack Flynn for my participation, had been a Godsend, especially with Patty expecting our child in a few months. Aside from my own set of books for my investigative work, Patty was still maintaining her bookkeeping system for her tips and any added waitress work for special parties or banquets. She kept envelopes for all the individual bills that normally come in the mail each month. I, of course, resumed my duties of preparing dinner for us, but today was different.

It was about 5:00 p.m. when Patty arrived home from the diner. She had called me to let me know that she was bringing home dinner and that it was going to be a surprise. "Jason, honey, just set the table and put on a pot of decaf," she had said, then continued, "No, Jason, on second thought, you had better make a pot of green tea. See you in about fifteen minutes, sweetheart!" She had then hung up.

I could tell by a rhythm resounding through her words that she was happy.

Before she arrived I finished filing some bad-check cases and entered some dollar amounts in my ledger concerning several served process papers. These were of a civil nature, as often I'm called upon to act as a process server. When I left my office, Ruben rose from his air mattress and followed me down the hall. I stopped at the bathroom entrance and told him, "Back to your mattress, Ruben." He turned and went back to his bed and laid down. I continued on into the bathroom and washed my hands.

I then went to the kitchen, opened up the linen drawer of the cabinet, and took out a tablecloth. Patty had sounded so jubilant over the telephone that I had a feeling the supper was going to be a special treat. I placed the blue cloth on the table. It was very special to us because it pictured several mountains with stands of maple trees and several blue spruce. A mountain stream curled around flat circular rocks that protruded above the water. We used this particular tablecloth only for birthdays and holidays, but tonight we'd make an exception. After setting the silverware at each place I went to the china cabinet and took out two unused candles. I placed them in the center of the table. As I finished, the teakettle began its eerie whistle. Steam shot out of the spout. I turned the flame low under the pot and could hear the bubbling of hot water boiling. Ruben was becoming uneasy, and in a flash he headed towards the door. I looked out of the window and saw nothing, but I knew that Patty and her red Jeep would soon pull up to our log home.

"Sure enough, here she comes, Ruben!"

After she parked I opened the door and let Ruben out. I followed. Ruben hurried, with tail wagging, to the Jeep. Patty opened the door and got out.

"Jason, will you help me, my darling? I have some hot dishes. Please bring out a couple of potholders," she said excitedly. I noticed how very lovely she looked; her facial expression appeared soft and relaxed.

I went to the cupboard and opened the top drawer reaching inside for two holders. "I'll be right there, sweetheart," I called through the door. "By the way, what's in the hot dishes?" I asked.

"I can't tell you right now. You just wait until I get it served, Jason. After all, it's a surprise. Don't you like surprises, big guy?"

I approached her and kissed her cheek. "Okay, you win. I'll be surprised. Whatever it is, it sure smells good. You're making me hungry, Patty, I believe I smell a scent of garlic."

Ruben, evidently feeling neglected, began to bark and jumped up. "Settle down, boy," I shouted.

Patty had the rear gate open on her red Jeep. I reached down with a potholder in each hand and picked up a hot platter that was wrapped in aluminum foil. Patty carried in two extra dishes. I proceeded inside and placed the platter on the stove. I wanted to remove the foil to see what this big surprise was that Patty had brought home, but respecting my wife's wishes I decided to let her do the honors.

"Jason, I'll be right with you." Patty went into the bathroom to wash her hands and get ready to serve the big surprise. She said in a commanding voice from the bathroom, "Honey, you can uncover the smaller dishes and place them in the toaster oven. They are probably warm enough, but I know how you like your food hot!"

I proceeded to remove the foil from two of the dishes: one was stuffing; the other was candied sweet potatoes. My taste buds must have been teased as my mouth began to water. I had just closed the oven door when Patty joined me in the kitchen.

I noticed she was wearing a bright-colored apron, which I had never seen before, maroon and white. "Where did you get the apron from, honey? I don't believe you've ever worn it," I said, jokingly.

"Lila had given it to me as a welcome-back present. I thought I had shown it to you before. Do you like it, Jason?"

"It's very nice, sweetheart. That was very thoughtful of Lila."

"Yes, it was. She and John are so good to me, Jason."

"I know they are, but always remember, beautiful, you bring a lot of customers into the diner just about every day of the week. John and Lila appreciate you and your efforts and, besides that, mommy-to-be, they both love you. After all, you are thought of as part of their family, too."

"I know that, honey. Are you all ready for supper?" she asked gleefully.

"Ready, babe," I said.

I went to the bathroom to wash up. When I returned, Patty told me to sit because she would do the serving. I went to my place following her instructions. I reached in my trouser pocket for a pack of safety matches and proceeded to light the two candles. They flickered, casting shimmering shadows on the wall. "Close your eyes, Jason," she commanded. I complied, heard her approach, and felt her arm rub against me as she set something in front of me. "Okay, sweetheart, open them."

My curiosity was satisfied. Before me was a well-garnished boneless roast of pork, with slivers of garlic imbedded in the glaze. Patty had placed a carving knife and a large bone-handled fork next to the platter.

"Sweetheart, your surprise is wonderful. Tell me, how did this come about?" I was puzzled.

"They had a sale on roast pork at the grocery store and Lila, knowing how much you love pork, picked up an extra one and roasted it just for you as she was preparing her family meal. It was a slow afternoon giving us time to work together on all the extras. So, honey, this is your surprise."

"Please thank her for this, Patty, until I see her myself. It looks delicious."

I took the sharp knife in hand and drove the fork into the roast. The juices flowed past the fork tines and trickled down the side of the roast. I cut four slices, placing two on Patty's plate along with pork dressing, candied-sweet potatoes, dark rich pork gravy, and a scoop of cabbage salad. I placed her plate in front of her, returned to my side of the table, and served myself. Before starting I said grace and thanked God for the gifts we were about to receive.

I looked over at Patty through the flickering candlelight with the shadows dancing on the wall.

"I love you, Jason," she said, smiling at me.

"I love you, too, my darling," I replied, as I looked at her beautiful face. "But right now we had better get back to dinner or our wonderful meal will be cold."

I looked down at my plate and cut the first bite size piece of pork roast. It was so tender, and flavored with the garlic and pepper I savor. The candied sweet potatoes were equally as tasty. As always the sweetness of the cabbage salad blended well, and my taste buds were jubilant with satisfaction. I told Patty again to thank Lila for this fine gesture and great surprise.

"There is one more surprise, which is still in the Jeep, Jason. I didn't bring it in, so my darling you'll have to go out for it. It's in a white box on the rear seat. I kept it there so you would be further surprised."

I excused myself from the table to go get it. Ruben decided that he wanted to go with me, so I let him out first. He took off for the woods. I went to the Jeep, removed the mysterious white box from the rear seat, and brought it in to the table. Before I sat back down I went over to the sink and rewashed my hands. I then opened up the box: to my great glee there before me was my favorite pie, mincemeat.

Patty sat watching me happily. I immediately went over to her and gave her a kiss.

"Honey, thank you! Mincemeat pie! I can remember back to the many holiday meals at my grandparents' house. I've told you how mincemeat and pumpkin were the desserts. That was when I was first introduced to my favorite pie."

"Jason, just remember, only one piece of pie tonight. You've said how you want to keep your weight in check," she cautioned.

"I know, darling. You're right again."

"I love this pie. The crust is just right and the mincemeat, so tasty. It's wonderful, Patty."

"I knew you'd enjoy it, Jason," she said.

After enjoying my piece of pie, I blew out the candles and cleared the table. I suggested to Patty that she might take Ruben for a short walk if she felt up to it while I did the dishes and cleaned up the kitchen. She agreed. As she bundled up for the cool temperatures of the early April evening, Ruben realized what was in the offing. He paced back and forth near the door. I had just started washing the glasses when Patty came over and planted a kiss on my cheek. "How are you feeling, Patty?" I asked.

"I feel pretty good, Jason," she replied, giving me another kiss.

"You two have a nice walk. Give me about twenty minutes and I'll have the kitchen back to normal." I was in the process of wiping the chrome on the refrigerator door handle when the cabin door opened again. My family had returned. Ruben came in first and went directly to his air mattress.

"It's going to be a cold one tonight, Jason. The water may freeze. You'd better let the faucets drip."

"Good idea." I immediately opened up the faucets in the kitchen and bathroom just enough for them to drip.

We retired to the living room and read until almost 10:00 p.m. I could tell that Patty was tired, as she dozed off a few times. I removed her book from her lap and kissed her forehead lightly. She put her arms around my shoulders and we held each other for a minute or two. "Are you ready for bed?" I asked.

"Yes, I'm ready, sweetheart."

I let Ruben out for a few minutes. He soon returned and

went directly to his air mattress. He is a loyal canine and we both love him dearly. He looked good for almost nine years old. I checked the doors and found them to be locked. When I looked out the window, one of our motion security lights came on. A large buck had entered our yard and activated the sensor. I watched until the deer entered the nearby woods, and then I turned the lights off. Patty and I continued to believe that motion-activated lights were a good investment.

When I entered the bedroom, Patty was standing sideways in front of the mirror. I went to her and gently embraced her. I gently put a hand on her belly.

"I love you, Jason," she said, looking up into my eyes.

"Patty, you have brought so much happiness into my life. I love you so very much, and our child will have the love of us both," I said.

"Yes, dearest," she agreed.

I pulled the covers back on her side of the bed and she lay down. I then went around to my side and slipped between the covers. Patty fell off to sleep right away, while I read for a while till I began to doze.

CHAPTER TWO

I heard a bell in the distance and saw Ruben and a small child running across our front lawn. I then awoke and realized that the alarm on the clock was going off. I was just about to touch Patty's shoulder when I saw her arm reach over to turn the alarm off. The room was now silent. She turned toward me and slid over into my arms. We embraced, not uttering a word. Just as I felt as though I were going to drift back off to sleep, Patty pushed the covers back and got out of bed.

"Jason, darling, I've got to get ready for work. You can stay in bed and sleep for a while," she said groggily.

"No, honey. I've got some things to accomplish today."

Patty went to the bathroom to shower and prepare herself for work. I went into the kitchen with Ruben at my feet. Before I started the coffee I let him outside for his early morning run to the woods. I went over to the sink, washed my hands, dried them, and turned the faucet on to fill the teakettle with water. I then placed the teakettle over the burner. When I turned the burner on I noticed the flame seemed lower than usual. I surmised that the propane gas was in need of replenishing.

While the water was heating for our coffee I went into the bathroom. When I came out I met Patty in the hallway. She looked beautiful in a newly purchased blue maternity pantsuit. Her blond hair was done up in a bun.

"Jason, I'll make the coffee while you're dressing," she

offered.

"Thanks, honey," I replied.

When I entered the bedroom I quickly made the bed, then went to the closet for a fresh shirt and a pair of trousers. It didn't take me long to dress. I returned to the kitchen just as Patty was letting Ruben back inside. The K-9's tail was wagging as Patty gave him a dog biscuit. I noticed that two cups of coffee were on the table along with four toasted slices of sourdough bread. Patty had put some grape jelly in a small saucer. We both sat down and sipped our coffee—mine full-strength and hers without caffeine. I buttered and spread grape jelly on the toast.

"I love sourdough toast, Jason, especially with grape jelly," Patty said with a giggle.

"Me, too, sweetheart. By the way, I'd like to drive you to work today with your Jeep. I'd like to take it to Dr. Don's garage and have the oil changed and a lube job, if that's alright with you. I checked with Don yesterday, but I forgot to mention it to you."

"Yes, dear, thanks. And you'd better have Dr. Don check the tailpipe while you're there. It has developed a rattling noise. Before it gets any worse, it probably should be checked. I'll make out a list."

"Okay, I'll do that. By the way, as long as we have a couple of minutes, Patty, let's talk. We've got to sit down someday soon and discuss our financial picture. You know as I've told you before, I'd rather have you stay at home after the baby is born."

"Honey, I will for a while, but I would like to continue working. Do you mind?" she asked as she waited for my reaction.

"You know if you want to work I certainly won't stand in your way, but I'm thinking about our child. I realize, in our society today, many mothers return to the work force soon after the baby is born."

"Jason, while I'm breast feeding the baby I won't go to work at least for a while after the birth. You're right that we'll discuss this more. Right now we'd better get ready to leave for the diner," she said with her winning smile.

I told Patty to stay inside until I had the Jeep started and warmed up. When I went outside Ruben followed me and sped off toward the woods. I went to the Jeep and started it up. In a short while I could feel the heat from the heater. The light coat of frost on the windshield rapidly melted when I turned on the defroster. I got out of the Jeep and went to Ruben's gate to open it for him. He entered the fenced area into his doghouse. His water and food dish were still full. I patted him on the head. "Be good, Ruben. I'll be back in a while." He wagged his tail, looking up at me.

Patty was now in the doorway. She was wearing her maroon ski jacket with the collar pulled up around her neck. I noticed she was wearing mittens, as the temperature had dipped below freezing. Fortunately there was no wind, which would have lowered the chill factor even more. As she stepped out of the log home, I went over to lock the door. We walked to the Jeep and I opened the passenger side door for her. She climbed in; I closed the door, went around to the driver's side, and got in. The interior of the Jeep was warm and comfortable. I leaned over and gave her a kiss on her cheek. She grasped my right hand and gently squeezed it. "I love you, Jason," she said looking into my eyes. "I love you, too, sweetheart," I replied.

As we started toward the road, about halfway out of the driveway a large snowshoe rabbit jumped out of our way. The rabbit was a part of our neighborhood of assorted wild animals. The joy of seeing the animals from time to time is an Adirondack experience that we look forward to, and we can only hope the feeling is reciprocal. After all, the animal inhabitants of these mountains were here before humankind lay down their first footprints.

There was very little traffic on Route 28 with the exception of three or four pickup trucks heading out early to an out-of-town construction project. As we pulled into the parking lot at John's Diner, John and Lila were just entering through their office door. I pulled as close as I could to the diner entrance and let Patty out. "See you later, honey," she said, squeezing my hand as she left the Jeep. "Oh, Jason, I almost forgot. Please ask Dr. Don to check the right-side headlamp. It seems to be aiming the beam too far to the left."

"I will, sweetheart. And I'll stop by later for a cup of green tea."

"Okay. Be careful driving, Jason," she said, closing the passenger side door.

I watched her as she cautiously climbed the frost-slippery steps to the diner entrance. She turned and gave me a wave. I tooted the horn and continued on to the rear of the parking lot to make a U-turn. I waited for a Town of Webb highway department truck to pass by before I drove onto Route 28 toward Dr. Don's garage. I knew that he would already be at the garage because he always liked to begin his workday early. I was right. I found him in his parking lot jockeying vehicles around to allow more room. I pulled up in front of the main door, turned the ignition switch to the off position, and exited the Jeep. I walked around to the edge of the parking lot as Dr. Don was parking a pickup in line. He spotted me and gave me a wave. I walked toward him as he climbed out of the truck.

"Good morning, Dr. Don. I see you're on the job."

"Hello, Jason. What can I do for you this early part of the morning?" he asked with a chuckle.

"Patty made out a small list of things she'd like you to do." I handed over the piece of paper. Dr. Don took it, shifted his glasses on his slender face, and looked at the items Patty had listed.

"Well, Jason, she wants me to change the oil and filter, adjust the brakes, check the air filter, rotate the tires, check the tailpipe, and adjust the right front headlight. Whew, that's a big list, Jason. I'll get right on it. Maybe I can complete this in about an hour or two. Do you want me to drop you off some place?"

"No, that won't be necessary. I'll walk down to the diner and have a cup of tea."

"Let's see, Jason, it's almost seven. Why don't you come

back at around eight and it should be about ready for you," he said, removing his glasses and wiping them with his handkerchief.

"Okay, Dr. Don, see you around eight."

I pulled up the collar of my jacket and fastened the top button. It was almost a mile to the diner and the air was brisk. I knew I could use the exercise. I crossed Route 28 and headed toward Old Forge. A couple of cars heading south passed me and tooted their horns. I recognized the cars as belonging to workers headed to Utica to their places of employment. I was about halfway to the diner when I heard a vehicle pull up behind me. The white pickup belonged to Wilt Chambers. He rolled his window down.

"Jason, get over here and climb in. I'm headed to the diner," he shouted in a booming voice.

I crossed back over Route 28 and climbed into the big white Dodge pickup. Wilt extended his hand to shake mine. "What are you doing out here this morning without your Bronco, Jason?" Wilt asked.

"I took Patty's Jeep down to Dr. Don's for a few adjustments and an oil change and grease job," I answered.

"Oh! That explains it. How's Patty, Jason?" he asked, showing his usual fatherly concern.

"She's doing fine, Wilt. We have a few more months ahead of us, and the pregnancy seems to be normal. But you know I can't help but worry a little."

"I understand how you feel. You know, we'll probably put the finishing touches on the addition soon and then you can furnish it with things for the baby," Wilt said, almost tearing up with happiness for the new mom-and-pop-to-be. This big, rough and tough logger and woodsman was truly a gentle, sensitive person under that crusty facade. He was just a softy at heart, yet I knew by experience that he could handle himself very well in any altercation that might come up. Going through my mind as we pulled into the diner parking lot was the time I was with Wilt when he had confronted three deer poachers who had wandered onto his posted land. When Wilt approached them, one of them sarcastically asked, "What do you want, fat man?"

"What I want, mister, is for you and your friends to get off my land," Wilt had said with stern calmness. "This is posted property."

"Why don't you try to make us leave, fat man?" the poacher had responded.

Wilt, without another word, had charged the three hunters, grabbed the collars of their jackets with his huge hands, and knocked their heads together. Wilt and I had watched their weapons fall to the ground. Completely ignoring me, the third man had attempted to strike Wilt from behind. Wilt had turned and put the assaulting man to sleep with a haymaker.

Now I watched as Wilt gently shut the Dodge off. He looked over at me and asked, "Are you hungry, Jason Black?"

"Well, I could sure use a cup of hot green tea," I replied.

"Green tea, Jason? Shucks, that's not enough for a big man like you. Breakfast is on me."

I knew that Wilt wouldn't take no for an answer, so I followed him into the diner. Most of the tables were already occupied, but the larger table in the corner was available. I could see Patty as she hurried to take an order from some of her steady customers. She was the only waitress on duty. A few of the patrons nodded to us when Wilt and I sat down. Lila must have seen us right away, for she came over with a cup of coffee for Wilt.

"Good morning, Wilt and Jason," she said, wearing a big smile. "Jason, I've got your tea water on," she added.

"Thanks, Lila. By the way, thank you for that wonderful pork dinner. We really enjoyed it," I told her.

"I'm pleased that you liked it. Don't forget, Patty helped me with it, too," she replied.

In a short while Patty appeared at our table. "Good morning, Wilt. I see that Sherlock caught up with you."

"Good morning, Patty. Yes, I found him walking along the highway."

"What would you gentlemen like for breakfast?" she asked,

readying her pencil to take the order.

Wilt spoke first. "Patty, I'll have a large orange juice, a stack of buckwheat pancakes, three slices of crisp bacon, and a refill on the coffee."

"Patty, you know I had toast and jelly earlier this morning. I'll have one buckwheat pancake with a sunny side egg on top and, of course, my cup of green tea that is already on its way."

Patty efficiently took our order and went to the kitchen to place it.

"It's good to see you, Wilt. I want you to know how much we appreciate all the work that you and your crew are doing. It really looks wonderful," I added.

"We know you do, Jason. I've been doing some thinking about you and Patty. I'm not trying to pry, but I consider you both a part of my family. With the baby being born in a few months, I'm concerned." I could tell that Wilt was somewhat uncomfortable about approaching me on this subject.

"What do you mean?" I asked.

"Jason, I know that your investigative work is sometimes lacking, and with the baby coming and Patty not working for a while after the child is born, well, it may be a little rough on you getting by financially."

I sighed. "Yes, Wilt, in truth that's crossed my mind more than once. I've been thinking about the situation very seriously."

"Jason, you've told me how your friend Tom Huston would put you to work tomorrow at the Breakshire overseeing his operation and his properties. But it would be quite a distance to travel every day."

"That's all true. But what are you getting at, Wilt?" I asked, puzzled.

"Jason, it boils down to this. Charlie Perkins and I are going into the wood products business. I'm putting up most of the capital. Charlie and I have been good friends for many years. He is a hard working fellow and a darn good family man. We've been pondering who we could hire on a part-time basis to handle security issues that might come up. So, Jason, would you consider taking the job?"

I mulled over his question before giving my answer. "I don't know, Wilt. I'll have to give it some thought. You know how it is that sometimes close friends have problems when it comes to one working for the other. I would never want anything jeopardizing the friendship that you, Charlie, Dale, Jack Falsey, Jim Jenny, and I have."

"You know better than that, Jason. The six of us are truly good friends. In this instance I'm just thinking of you and Patty and your forthcoming child."

"Well, I appreciate your offer, but I'll have to think it over before I can give you an answer." I gave Wilt a full warm smile.

Patty arrived at our table. She set Wilt's plate of steaming buckwheat pancakes with the crisp bacon and warm syrup in front of him, along with a glass of orange juice for each of us. Then she placed in front of me a plate holding one buckwheat pancake with a sunny-side-egg on top. She rushed away to pick up the coffeepot and a pot of hot water, then returned to refill our cups.

"Golly, Jason, these buckwheat cakes are mighty tasty. And the bacon has a flavor that just makes you want more."

"I agree," I said. "And this orange juice is the best I've tasted in a long time."

"It is," Wilt agreed.

"Jason, in a couple of weekends we'll complete the work on the baby's room."

"Patty and I certainly appreciate all the efforts that you fellows have put forth with the addition. I'm sorry I haven't been more help to you, but when it comes to carpentry, that's not one of my attributes. Are there any other supplies that you'll need, Wilt?" I asked.

"No, I believe we have everything. You've paid for all the materials. We like knowing that our work on the project is our gift to the forthcoming baby. We'll expect lots of pictures of the little one in his or her new surroundings."

"Wilt, I definitely want to compensate you and the fellows

in the near future."

"Don't worry about it. We wanted to do this or we wouldn't have. Remember, my friend, we are Adirondackers, we may be stubborn sometimes, but our word is golden."

"I know, I know."

Wilt and I finished our breakfast, and after another refill of coffee and green tea we left the diner. Patty was busy, but she waved at us as we departed. Wilt told me that he'd drop me off at Dr. Don Norton's garage. On the way he told me that he had acquired three two-man saws for my collection. An elderly man in his mid-eighties had had an estate sale, and Wilt had picked them up for seven dollars apiece.

The big Dodge pulled up in front of Dr. Don's, and I got out.

"Thanks for breakfast, Wilt," I said.

"You think about what we were discussing, Jason."

"I will—I promise." I watched him as he left.

"Hello, Dr. Don. How's the Jeep doing?"

"Jason, all the work is completed. I checked the brakes and they won't need replacement for another ten thousand miles. The Jeep, even though it has high mileage, is still in good condition. By the way, I adjusted the front seat a little so Patty will be more comfortable."

"Well, Dr. Don, that's why we bring it back to you all the time. Patty wouldn't let anyone else work on it. You know how loyal she is."

"Patty's a darn good customer, Jason. You know, you're a lucky fellow—and very shortly we'll be calling you 'daddy'," he said with a chuckle.

"You're right on that. I am a fortunate person," I answered, also chuckling.

I paid the reasonable bill and told Dr. Don that I would be bringing the Bronco in for service in a few days. We shook hands and I left the garage.

I stopped at the post office on the way home to pick up the mail. As I opened our box a letter dropped onto the floor. I reached down and picked it up. The return address on the business envelope, in English lettering, was that of The Breakshire Lodge, Lake Placid. I gathered the rest of the mail and went inside to the desk. The post office staff was busy preparing for afternoon pick-up. The mail clerk came over. I purchased two books of stamps and left the office, then sat in the Jeep for a few minutes looking over the mail. From the assortment of letters and magazines, the first piece of mail I opened was that of the Breakshire Lodge.

I read the letter. It was from my friend Tom Huston. He started out with Dear Patty and Jason. He went on to ask how we were doing and how Patty was feeling. Tom indicated in the letter that he would like me to stop by the lodge when I was in the Lake Placid area. He failed to go into any detail about what he wanted to see me about. I reread the letter, folded it, and slid it back into the envelope. I placed the mail on the passenger side seat and started the engine. As I was backing out of the parking space I noticed Jack Falsey pull in with his pickup. He must have seen me, as he tooted the horn. I was going to pull back into the parking space to talk with him, but another vehicle was waiting for me to leave. I quickly decided I would call Jack later. I knew that I would see all the fellows over the weekend at the log home as they worked to complete the addition. Again I thought gratefully of Jack Flynn and the sizable check he had issued to me for the Arizona investigation. Going through the mail I had noticed some letters from banks, undoubtedly containing bad checks; following up on them for the banks would be another welcome piece of income. I continued my swing out of the parking lot and drove onto Route 28, heading home.

When I passed the Old Forge Hardware and Furniture Store I noticed Linda, one of the owners, coming out of the front door. I tooted the horn and she displayed a gracious smile and waved. I had many memories of this popular business place, which "has it all." It was definitely a favorite tourist attraction. It brought to my mind how each community in the Adirondacks has a good selection of offerings for all visitors and residents. Patty and I are most fortunate to reside in this region, where Mother Nature's beauty is always prevalent and civility appears to be alive and well.

I stopped for an oncoming truck before I turned into the driveway and pulled the Jeep up to the house. There was my faithful dog Ruben standing up with his front paws braced on the wire fence. His tail was gyrating like a propeller. The ears were at attention. I went over to the dog run and opened the gate. Ruben then came out and ran toward me. I could tell he wanted to play. I rubbed his head and back, opened the gate, and let him out. Playful, he ran in a circle and then off into the woods. I walked back to the passenger side of the Jeep, opened the door, and took out our mail.

When I went up the stairs to the entrance, Ruben was again by my side. I opened the door and he slid past me into the house, right to his air mattress. The temperature outside was a bit chilly, so the warmth of the house must have felt good to the big fellow.

I went through the rest of the mail in my office. Around noon I went into the kitchen to cut up some lettuce, cucumbers, tomatoes, and red onions. I mixed in some balsamic vinegar dressing, then sprinkled on some blue cheese. I poured myself some ice tea and went to the table. After that roast pork dinner it was about time that I measured my intake. It was fine for Patty to be putting on pounds with the baby, but my waistline didn't need widening.

After lunch I cleared the table and took some chicken breasts out of the freezer for that night's dinner. I looked over at Ruben. He was lying on his right side and appeared to be asleep. I completed the kitchen work and went into the office.

I took out Tom Huston's letter and reread it. The sense of humor usually present throughout his letters was absent. From the unusual tone, I wondered if everything were all right with him. I again returned the letter to the envelope and put it aside. I went on to open up several letters containing bad checks from the Mountain Bank. I processed them, made some telephone calls, and prepared several of my form letters to be sent to the writers of the bad checks. I had just completed the task when the telephone rang.

"Hello," I answered.

"Hi, honey, what are you doing? Did you have lunch?" Patty asked affectionately.

"Hello, sweetheart. Yes, I made myself a nice fresh salad. And what am I doing? I just finished processing some bad checks. Say! I'm going to ask you a question."

"What's that, honey?"

"I know you have just returned to work, but do you think you could take tomorrow off so we could go to Lake Placid for the day? We received a letter from Tom this morning saying that he would like to see us at our convenience, but he didn't indicate any reason."

"Maybe.... I'll have to talk with Lila. I'll ask her and let you know. I don't really look forward to the long drive, but if he wants to see us, we'll go. Is that alright, sweetheart?"

"Sure, that'll be fine," I replied.

"Well, I'd better get to work. I love you, Jason."

"I love you, too, darling. I hope you're feeling all right."

"I'm fine, honey. Please don't worry so much. See you later."

"Bye."

I couldn't help but worry about Patty. She had gone through so much in the last few years. I still shuddered about how cruelly her first husband had treated her during their marriage. I was determined to make her life easier.

I reached for Brady's book on checks. I reviewed the section on stale dated ones to refresh my knowledge. I continued work by closing out some old cases and shredded a file drawer of outdated material. I cleaned off the desk and with a cloth dusted the case files and the two bookcases. I heard Ruben moving around, and when I looked up he was standing in the doorway.

"Come here, Ruben," I commanded.

Ruben came over and rubbed his big head against my pant leg. I reached down and rubbed his neck. "You're about ready for a good bath and some grooming," I told him. I thought of how I had missed him while we were in Arizona.

With Ruben beside me I went outside. He ran off toward the woods while I continued on to my woodpile in back of the house. I decided to split some chunks of wood, for exercise and to add some kindling to my pile. The outside thermometer showed a temperature of 52 degrees. Swinging the ten-pound sledgehammer against the wedge buried in the block of wood, soon worked up a sweat. I had to remove my handkerchief from my trouser pocket several times to wipe away the perspiration. "Ruben, you have the life, just lying there rolling your eyes back and forth, while I'm splitting the wood," I told the K-9, feeling somewhat envious. But even though it was hard work, I felt good getting some exercise. I continued to split wood till late afternoon. When I finished, I added the new cords to the woodpile. After putting my tools away, I took Ruben for a walk where he had run to the edge of the woods to explore. The big dog was casting an all-seeing eye toward the brush piles, probably looking for one of the many chipmunks that lived in the area. Chasing the scampering chippies was one of his favorite things to do.

Ruben and I returned to the log home after spending about an hour's time in the woods. I let him into the dog run and proceeded to go inside. After I washed up I took three chicken breasts out of the refrigerator to finish thawing in the microwave for my recipe of Maryland oven-fried chicken, which would be the highlight of our dinner menu. I broke two eggs, added a little milk, beat them to make a batter, then dipped the breasts into the batter and then the peppered flour, returning them to the batter and into the flour for a second coating. I added some more pepper, then covered them and placed them in the refrigerator. I then scraped several medium-size carrots and was in the process of peeling some potatoes when the telephone rang. I glanced at my watch. It was a little after four.

"Hello."

"Jason, Lila has given me the day off tomorrow. Have you started dinner yet?" she asked.

"That's great, honey. Yes, I have the chicken ready for the oven. I'll be right outside of the diner at five to pick you up," I replied.

"See you soon, sweetheart."

Setting the table for two was never difficult. We always sat at opposite sides, affording us a good position to carry on our sometimes lengthy conversations, which we always looked forward to. I laid our napkins and silverware at each place and decided to use our tall water glasses.

I finished peeling the potatoes, then cut up some cabbage for coleslaw.

I placed the chicken in the oven, having preheated it to 350 degrees. I then placed the potatoes and carrots on the burners, turning them down to low. It was time to leave to pick up Patty at the diner. I quickly checked the kitchen and left.

"Ruben, keep an eye on things. We'll be back shortly!" I called to him humorously as I entered the Jeep.

As I pulled into the parking lot of John's Diner I could see that the dinner crowd was beginning to form. Patty gave me a wave from the porch. I pulled as close as I could to the steps. She opened the passenger side door and climbed in.

"Hello, my darling," I said, leaning over to kiss her on the cheek.

"Jason, you're right on time," she replied, giving me a quick kiss.

"How was your day, Patty?" I inquired.

"All my steady customers seemed to visit the diner today. Several of them asked for you, Jason," she offered. "What was your day like, honey?"

"I caught up on reports, wrote some letters to the usual check passers, cleaned up the office a little, and then split some wood. Afterwards, Ruben and I went to the woods. And I started supper. That's about it."

"That sounds like a day's work to me. You must be exhausted," she said.

When we pulled into the driveway, we observed Ruben standing up against his dog run's fence. His tail was spinning like a propeller on a model airplane. I stopped the Jeep by the door and Patty got out. She walked over to Ruben as I backed the Jeep up and parked it next to the Bronco.

I joined Patty at the run and both of us made a fuss over Ruben. The K-9 loved the attention. Then Patty and I went inside where the aroma of Maryland fried chicken was wafting throughout the house.

"Something smells mighty good, Jason," my wife said, removing her coat.

I took her coat and hung it in the closet. "I thought you might like chicken tonight, darling."

"I love everything you cook, my dearest. By the way, wasn't that wonderful of Lila to give me the day off, especially when we had all that time off for our trip to Arizona?"

"Yes, Patty, that was very decent of Lila," I acknowledged.

"Is Tom Huston all right, Jason?" she asked curiously, with a suspicious glance at my face.

"I'm not sure, Patty. His letter does seem serious in tone. But why do you ask?"

"I just have a feeling that something may be amiss. Maybe it's pregnant woman's intuition."

"As far as I <u>know</u>, everything is alright at the Breakshire Lodge. But I'm glad we're going there tomorrow. Thank you for taking the day off, Patty. It will feel good to have you riding with me. And maybe if we time it right we can stop at Gertie's for some breakfast."

"I'd love that, Jason."

While Patty prepared for dinner, I checked the potatoes and the carrots on the burners to make sure they hadn't burned. Then I quickly mixed the coleslaw and sweetened it with a teaspoon of sugar. I made a mixture of cornstarch and orange juice to glaze the carrots.

When the potatoes were cooked I drained off the water, then added butter and milk before whipping them into mashed potatoes, which I garnished with parsley and paprika. After I removed the aromatic, crispy Maryland fried chicken from the oven, I placed the breasts on an oven-safe platter so I could make my chicken gravy by adding the potato water to the pan of drippings and some flour. My culinary chores were now complete.

Patty joined me in the kitchen and lit the two candles for me. We set the hot and cold dishes on the table. When everything was ready I seated Patty and went to my side of the table. I asked Patty to hand me her plate.

I served Patty by placing a chicken breast on her plate, with mashed potatoes and carrots, then gravy. I handed the plate back to her, then served myself. The pepper in the crusty covering of the chicken enhanced the flavor. Patty's appetite was good, but mine was even better after my wood-chopping afternoon. We were quiet during supper as we enjoyed the Maryland fried chicken, one of Patty's favorites among my culinary efforts.

After dinner I cleared the table, washed the dishes, and cleaned up the kitchen. While I finished, Patty took Ruben for a short walk. They returned in a few minutes.

"Did you and Ruben have a good outing?" I asked.

"Yes, honey, we certainly did. I've noticed that now when I take Ruben for his walks he doesn't run ahead of me. He heels close to me, as though he's trying to protect me. What do you think of that, Jason?"

"Ruben is a smart dog. He's sensitive and very protective."

"Do you think he knows that we're going to have a child?" she asked.

"I can't answer that definitely, my dear," I replied.

All I knew was that this K-9 loved us both and hopefully would love our baby as well. Through the years I had heard of several incidents of family dogs growing jealous of the newcomer in the home, many involving German Shepherds. I knew I would have to monitor him closely for a while.

Patty retired to the living room to do some knitting, while I picked up a book that I had started to read before we had left for Arizona. I hoped to finally finish it.

We went to bed around 9:30 and talked about our forthcoming day trip to Lake Placid and how nice it would be to see Tom Huston and possibly Bob and Gertie at the diner in Long Lake. It had been a long time since we had seen them and we were looking forward to it. Patty fell off to sleep before I did. Feeling a bit restless, I got up to check the doors to ensure that they were locked. Ruben, sprawled out on his air mattress, appeared to be sound asleep. I returned to the bedroom, said my nightly prayers, and crawled in between the covers. Just before I fell off to sleep, I could hear rain hitting the roof.

CHAPTER THREE

Awakening to the sound of the shower running in the bathroom wasn't new to me. However, this morning I heard Patty singing in the shower. It made me happy to hear her in such a good mood. I was a fortunate person to have such a lovely, caring wife. I pushed the blankets back and got out of bed. I went directly to the kitchen door and let Ruben out, watching as he scurried off toward the woods. Just as I closed the door, Patty came out of the bathroom wearing her cream-colored robe. I noticed that the sash did not reach around quite as far as it used to. I went over to her for a morning hug.

"Jason, I'm certain that I felt the baby move this morning. Oh, honey! I'm so happy that we're going to have a child," she said excitedly.

"I am, too, sweetheart. Just a few more months," I responded.

Patty continued to the bedroom to get dressed and I went to the bathroom. She had laid out a fresh towel and washcloth for me. I took off my robe and pajamas and went into the shower. The hot water felt good on my back and neck. After soaping and rinsing I turned the ice cold water on and experienced Adirondack well water at its best. I was now fully awake and alert. I donned my robe, went to the sink, lathered up, and shaved. I splashed some after-shave lotion on, tidied up the bathroom, and went into the bedroom to dress. Patty was already dressed in a stylish maternity shirt and slacks, a rosy color, which looked lovely on her. She had placed my slacks, shirt, and sweater out on the bed along with fresh underwear.

I had not driven the Bronco in a while and I was happy that it fired up right away when I first engaged the starter. I let it warm up for a few minutes while I went back inside the house. Ruben, returned from the woods, was inside his run.

"Patty, I think we'll drop Ruben off at the Eagle Bay Kennel on the way. He is due for a bath and some grooming."

"That's a good idea, honey," Patty agreed. "I fixed us a quick cup of decaf and a slice of toast to tide us over until breakfast."

After our snack we secured the log home and I opened the rear gate of the Bronco. Ruben came charging out of the dog run and jumped up into the rear of the vehicle. He was always happy to go for a ride. When I closed the gate I looked up at the sky. The overnight rain had subsided and the bright sun was peering over the mountaintops. It looked as though we'd have a good trip north.

The passenger side door stuck a little as I opened the door for Patty. She climbed in and I closed the door. Ruben was sitting alert and ready for a ride. After rechecking the door of the house I joined Patty and Ruben and we headed to Eagle Bay.

Lynn greeted Ruben and me from her desk as we entered the kennel.

"Where have you been, Jason? I heard you were in Arizona working on an important case," she said.

"Yes, my friend Jack Flynn had some trouble, so Patty and I went out west to give a hand," I replied, wondering how Lynn had heard. I guessed that Dale Rush or one of my other friends had mentioned it.

"I understand that Wilt looked after Ruben while you were away. That's a good friend you have there, Jason."

"Yes, he did. Wilt is a good friend, and not only to me, Lynn. He's that way with everyone. I think you agree that he's a fine person who believes in helping out his fellow man or woman."

"Of course I do. Now what can I do for you today, Jason?"

"Patty and I have to go up north, and I'm hoping you can give the big guy a much deserved bath and a little grooming."

"I think we can handle that alright. Will you be back by 5:00 p.m.?"

"No, probably not, but if it's okay with you I'll pick Ruben up tomorrow."

"That'll be fine, Jason. And be sure to say hello to Patty for me. How is she feeling?" Her face showed kind concern.

"Good so far, Lynn. Thanks for asking."

"I'm so happy for you both."

"Yes, Lynn, God has been good to us."

When I turned the leashed Ruben over to Lynn, he seemed to hesitate for a moment and his tail no longer wagged, but he finally settled down and went with her. "Be a good dog," I said.

I bid farewell to Lynn and joined Patty in the Bronco. We hungrily passed a couple of our local restaurants that were serving breakfast, but we hadn't seen Bob and Gertie in a while, so wanted to stop there on our way through Long Lake.

Spring was coming on, we could see by the buds on the trees. The smell of pine was in the air. Traffic was light. It was the time of year between snowmobiling season and the heavier tourist traffic to this special place on earth known as the Adirondack Park of northern New York State. Developers yearned and angled to build houses and condos in the wilds of the great Adirondacks; however, uncontrolled growth was kept at a minimum by the "Forever Wild" legislation enacted by concerned lawmakers in the 1890's who wished to keep the region intact for present and future generations. However, a negative result is that the region suffers from the lack of jobs for the younger generation, who find that they have to leave the area for gainful employment. Fewer parents mean fewer children, which has led to the closing of some of the schools in the area.

We met only five or six vehicles between Inlet and Long

Lake. When we made the left-hand turn at Hoss's Country Corner, we noted several cars parked near the store. The lakefront was quiet, with only four cars and two pickup trucks parked at Gertie's Diner.

I pulled in next to a black truck, got out of the Bronco, and went around to open Patty's door. Wafting through the air was the delicious smell of bacon. Stomachs rumbling, we walked to the diner and climbed the steps to the entrance. Gertie spotted us as we entered and immediately came rushing from behind the counter to hug Patty and then me. She was genuinely overjoyed to see us.

"I heard you got back from Arizona. I wondered when I'd be seeing you two. How did it go out there in the wild west?" Gertie asked.

"Everything worked out well," Patty replied. "How have you been?"

"It's so good to see you. You just missed Bob. He went to Tupper Lake for supplies. We're both doing just fine. Where would you two like to sit?" she asked.

"The corner table will be fine, Gertie. We certainly have missed seeing you and Bob."

"Well, now that you're home, don't be strangers," she added good-naturedly.

I pulled the corner table chair out and seated Patty. I went around the table and sat down opposite her. Linda, the waitress, appeared with two menus.

"Would you care for coffee, folks?" she inquired.

"Let's see, Linda. Patty, would you like coffee?"

"No, Jason, I'll just have a cup of decaf." Patty replied.

"Okay, that will be two cups of coffee—one regular and one decaf along with two glasses of water?" Linda asked.

"That'll be fine," Patty responded.

Patty and I looked the menu over. She decided on the French toast and I selected two eggs over medium and three slices of crisp bacon. When Linda returned with our water and coffee we placed our order.

I glanced over at Gertie behind the counter. A true chef she handled the grill work masterfully. A flapjack flipped in mid-air and she caught it on the end of the pancake turner. I admired Gertie and Bob, for they were dedicated workers who went above and beyond to please their many customers. In order to survive in the Adirondacks they had come to the realization that the only way to earn a livable wage was to go into some type of an occupation to make a decent living. At one time, they had opted to leave their beloved mountains, but soon found out that living in the hubbub of urban living was just not for them. They wanted to raise their family where they had grown up. Fortunately for them, their diner thrived.

Linda, the waitress, returned shortly carrying a tray over her right shoulder. Again Gertie had performed her artistry at the grill. Patty's French toast was golden brown with a dollop of sweet butter on top and a miniature pitcher of warmed syrup on the side. My straight-crisp bacon was arranged beside my two eggs, along with two slices of Texas toast. We thanked Linda before she returned to the counter to take an order from a customer.

I said grace quietly and thanked the good Lord for all the blessings He had bestowed upon us. We then sat and enjoyed our breakfast. Patty shared some of her French toast with me and I gave her a piece of my crisp bacon. We each enjoyed a refill of our drinks.

I thought of my many wonderful memories of visits to Gertie's Diner and my numerous conversations with Gertie and Bob. I pictured the straw hat that Bob wore on occasion, especially during the summer. Then there was an Adirondack character, a New York City transplant whose nickname was Zing Zing, the only name I ever knew him by. He always wore green duck-back shirts. I always revisited these images upon my many returns to the Long Lake area.

"Jason, are you okay? You're so quiet," Patty asked with some concern.

"Oh? Oh, honey, I'm sorry. I'm fine. I was just thinking about times gone by and how they've passed too quickly."

"I know, dear, I know," Patty said, with tears forming in

her eyes.

"Here, honey, use my clean handkerchief to dry your eyes," I said. She took it and wiped the forming tears away. "What did I say or do to make you cry?"

"Nothing, dear. Your comment brought back many childhood memories, I guess." She sniffled. "I'm okay now."

I again saw Gertie flip a flapjack, which landed on one of her warmed-up plates. It was her policy to serve her customers hot food, and that she always did.

Patty and I finished our breakfast. I paid the check after leaving a tip on the table for Linda. Gertie came around from behind the counter and embraced Patty. She wished us well and told us to be sure to stay in touch.

"Jason, I'm sorry that Bob isn't here to see you and Patty, but someday we'll all get together, even if it can't be until after the birth of the baby."

"Don't worry. I'm very much aware of the fact that Bob is a very busy man," I replied.

"I don't know what I would do without him, Jason. We both bounce off each other. This diner business isn't easy. It takes both of us to keep our heads above water. We try to keep our prices in a moderate range in order to accommodate our steady customers and to attract the summer tourists and the snowmobile enthusiasts during the winter months," she said.

"We know how hard you both work, Gertie. We're not here on a day-to-day basis, but you and Bob are always in our thoughts and prayers. Tell him we said hello."

"I will, Jason. You take good care of Patty," she added, embracing Patty again.

We left the diner. On the way to the Bronco, Patty and I stood for a while near the edge of Long Lake looking off at the mountains. We spotted a flock of Canada geese high in the sky making their way north. Looking down toward the lake again, we saw a mechanic checking one of the two seaplanes at the shoreline, probably getting ready for the summer season.

It was a little too early for the Long Lake kids to be playing softball, but my many memories of watching them engaged in this sport was still very clear in my mind. I couldn't remember many of their names. There was one very dedicated participant whom Patty and I had met recently—Linda from Long Lake. I was sure I would always remember her love of softball.

Before we entered the Bronco to continue our trip to Lake Placid, we decided to take a short walk along the shoreline. Early spring brought us clean fresh air in our precious Adirondack Mountains. The temperature was not too cold, and walking was good exercise for Patty. Her pregnancy was clearly progressing well, with the exception of some occasional normal discomfort. She had to avoid certain foods, and yet she craved others. After our refreshing walk we returned to the Bronco.

In a few minutes we were headed toward Tupper Lake en route to the Breakshire Lodge. We were both eager, yet a little anxious, to see our friend Tom. As Patty nodded off into a nap, I found myself wondering again about why Tom wanted to see me. We had developed a strong bond as friends over the past few years. I had a sense of uneasiness about his request. Hopefully, I would find out soon why he had written that letter.

I had first met him on a case involving a suspicious guest at the lodge. Our business relationship had grown into a mutual respect for each other as I continued working on other cases for him. We had become close friends, and through the years I had introduced him to some of my other friends and associates. I recalled how I had introduced him to Wilt, who was so impressed with the lodge and Tom that he had presented him with one of his carved black bears, now a much admired fixture in the lobby of the Breakshire. Tom, in turn, had spread the word about the unique carvings Wilt skillfully created. This endorsement brought Wilt in contact with some of Tom's elite acquaintances, people of means who desired to have Wilt's bears in several business places as well as hunting camps and palatial residences.

On one of my cases, Dale flew me to Lake Placid, where I introduced him to Tom. Over lunch, Dale had explained to Tom how much he enjoyed flying avid fishermen and hunters into the remote regions of the Adirondacks. From this encounter, Tom decided how much this availability would mean to some of his guests. As a result, Dale gained much business transporting fishermen and hunters into lesser-traveled areas of the mountains. He also began to fly Tom to Maine and New Hampshire. All this additional income had become a boom for Dale.

Always ready to help people, Tom was a thoughtful, caring person, of whom I came to think very highly. And now I would see him again, very soon, after a few months, I realized as we neared the Breakshire Lodge.

"Patty, darling, I hate to wake you, but we're here," I said gently. I knew she must need the extra sleep.

We pulled into the tree-lined driveway of the impressive Breakshire Lodge. I observed several workers cleaning out brush and debris. I pulled the Bronco into the nearest parking space to the front entrance. Several vehicles were parked along the front of this stately-looking lodge. I told Patty, still trying to wake fully, that I would open her door for her.

There was a chill in the air as we made our way up the front steps. When we entered the lodge I didn't recognize the desk clerk. I approached the desk, identified myself, and advised the clerk that I would like to see Mr. Huston.

"Just a moment sir, I'll tell Mr. Huston you're here."

"Thank you."

"Mr. Huston will be right with you, sir," the clerk told me after a brief call.

I turned around and saw that Patty, after excusing herself to go to the ladies room, was standing close to one of Wilt's carved bears, which she was admiring in the center of the lobby. I walked over to her.

"Jason, this large bear looks so real," she said. "I'm always overwhelmed when I see it."

"Honey, it certainly does. As you know, Wilt is a master carver, able to create bears that seem to have stepped right out of the wild. Tom has received so many positive comments on Wilt's artistry."

Just then we heard a familiar voice.

"Patty and Jason, how are you two?" Tom asked happily.

We turned to greet him with warm happy smiles. He wore a blue three-piece business suit, with a blue-checkered tie and white starched shirt that matched perfectly and complemented his well-groomed gray hair.

"Hello, Tom," Patty spoke first, looking up at the owner of the stately Breakshire Lodge.

Tom came over to Patty and embraced her warmly.

"Patty, how are you feeling?" he asked with genuine concern.

"I feel wonderful," she responded. "Thank you for asking."

"I am glad that everything is going well for you. You look wonderful." He turned to me and extended his hand.

"Jason, it is so good of you to make the trip to Lake Placid."

We shook hands. I noticed that his palm was uncustomarily sweaty. Tom looked a little pale. I began to worry that there was something wrong with his general health.

"Likewise, Tom. It's so good to see you. It's been awhile. As you know, Patty and I were away in Arizona."

"Yes, I'm aware of that. Your friends Wilt and Lieutenant Jack Doyle keep me posted on your activities. I'm just glad you're here now. Would you and Patty mind following me to my office? I have a call holding."

Patty and I followed Tom down a lushly carpeted hallway to his office.

"I'll only be a minute or two, folks. Please make yourselves comfortable."

Patty and I seated ourselves in the room's soft leather chairs. I glanced at my wristwatch and saw that noon was fast approaching. Patty picked up a magazine from a rack of them and began reading. In a few minutes Tom completed his telephone conversation and joined us in front of his desk. He sat down next to us as Patty returned the magazine to the rack.

"Tell us, Tom, how have you been?" I asked, concerned over his pale appearance.

"I want you to know that I have been thinking about you and the new addition that you're expecting in a few months. It was more than nice of you both to drive up here to Lake Placid. I have to be honest with you: I've missed you. The old saying that it is lonely at the top of any organization is true."

"I'm very much aware of the feeling, Tom. Although my role as station commander in the troopers a few years ago was nothing compared to operating a lodge, I still at times felt lonely in that position. But you have surrounded yourself with good people and over the past few years you have developed such a wonderful organization here at the lodge."

"I know. I know, Jason. But it is hard work, and I'm not getting any younger. The only heirs that I have are Matthew and Brenton, whom you met a while ago."

"Yes, your nephews, I remember them well, two very sharp-looking young men. How are they doing?" I asked.

"They are both very busy in their professions in the health care arena, so I don't get to see them very often."

"The health care profession is so important," Patty commented.

"Yes, it is," Tom agreed. "But it does keep them occupied away from here." He paused. "Jason, I had you stop by for a special purpose. I know you remember well the matter involving Morey Harris."

"Very well, Tom, why do you ask?" How could I have forgotten the young man that had sought revenge against Tom over his father's dismissal. I was curious.

"You remember his father worked for me here at the lodge and left Morey to shift on his own and, well, you know the rest of the sad story."

"Indeed, I do." I had worked on that case. "Patty knows about it, too."

Tom nodded regretfully. "His father had been a good worker up to the time that he became dishonest and that, as you know, was the time I discharged him."

My jaw tightened. "Yes, I recall the situation involving Morey's father."

"Jason, what you don't know is that I took it upon myself to obtain counseling for Morey. Consequently, he is now employed here at the lodge as the head groundskeeper."

"Are you kidding me, Tom?" I was more than surprised. I was shocked. I could see that Patty, too, was taken aback.

"No, I'm not kidding. I felt very sorry for him. In fact, along with the counseling I suggested he go on a properly maintained diet, and my personal physician created one for him. As far as the courts are concerned the matter is closed. I am taking a small amount of money from each of his paychecks to cover the tools he stole from me that he had sold in Utica. I took it upon myself to give this fellow human a decent chance at life." Tom paused again, and added proudly, "I might add that he is also attending night school a couple of evenings a week."

This was so typical of him. Tom's generosity, I realized. "Where is he living, Tom?" I was pretty sure I knew the answer.

"I have furnished him with a room here at the lodge. Believe me, you will not recognize the Morey Harris you dealt with," Tom said with satisfaction.

"Will we be seeing him today?" I asked. I was curious about this young fellow for whom I myself had felt sorry.

"No. Not today. He and one of his men have gone to Burlington to pick up some piping for the lawn-watering system."

The news of Morey surprised both of us, but knowing the kind of person Tom Huston was, we could understand. Tom believed that there was good in everybody; one just had to find those qualities in people. Tom's vast experience as a lodge owner positioned him in life to seek out certain attributes in people, and he had taken it upon himself to give young Morey Harris another chance. Patty and I, at first taken aback, soon understood Tom's kind compassion for it reflected him.

The three of us chatted for a while in Tom's office. We talked about the upcoming birth of our child and the new baby's nursery at our Old Forge home. I could tell during our conversation that Tom felt true concern about Patty. After some time talking about the expected arrival of our new addition to the family in a few months, the conversation changed. Tom offered a different subject.

"Since I've been here in Lake Placid I have always attempted to do things for the region that would carry on the tradition of the Adirondack Mountains. In doing so, I have met with little opposition; however, once in a while it is necessary to explain my ideas for the future with the citizens. I have recently acquired an abandoned logging camp in the Tupper Lake area. When I mentioned my idea for it at a recent meeting with area businesses my plan met with much enthusiasm."

"What are you going to do with the camp, Tom?" I asked with interest.

"My plans are to create a woodsman museum. The purpose is to keep alive the past, present, and future of the logging industry. As you both know, these precious mountains and woodlands were, and still are, important to the Adirondacks. They are a major factor in the growth of this area. I do not profess to have all the answers; however, I have formed a board of active and former timber-men and women to oversee the project. Wilt Chambers does not know it yet, but I'm considering him for the position of chairman of the group, if he'll be willing to assume it."

Patty spoke up first. "Tom, what a wonderful plan you have! Can you tell us what type of items will be on display? I'm certain that Wilt would be so honored to be involved in your project. Do you agree, Jason?" Patty was obviously excited about what Tom had shared with us.

"It's a terrific idea," I said. "Much needed!"

"I thought you'd both be pleased. I wanted to tell you about it several weeks ago, but I wanted to complete the real estate transaction first. This good news was one of the reasons I wanted to meet with you."

"Tom, Patty and I are honored to be privy to your museum plan. It will certainly generate a great deal of interest throughout the region. You are to be congratulated for your creativity," I said, admiringly.

"Well, you both know that the community has been good to me. It's my way of giving back something to the people who reside here and who visit this region."

"Tom, you've always given part of yourself to the Adirondacks. You've furnished jobs to many, contributed to important causes, and represented the Breakshire Lodge in the highest traditions in serving the public."

"Jason, I agree wholeheartedly," Patty said.

"Now that we've discussed this item, how about some fine cuisine for lunch you two?" Tom offered with a winning smile.

We could see how pleased he was with our reception to his future museum. "We never turn down an invitation from you for lunch," Patty replied, also smiling.

Tom went around behind his desk and made some notes on a pad. When he had finished, Patty and I left the office with him following close behind. We reached the lobby and the desk clerk gave us a smile as we passed en route to the dining room. The noon hostess met us at the entrance. Several guests were partaking of lunch. The hostess seated us at a large table in a private section of the dining area. Tom seated Patty. I took the chair to Patty's left and Tom seated himself across from her. As we examined our menus the waitress appeared with a pitcher of ice water flavored with lemon slices. After pouring our waters, she set the pitcher down on a nearby serving cart and returned to the table for our drink orders. Patty and Tom ordered decaf and I ordered a cup of regular coffee. As the waitress went to bring us our drinks, we continued to scan the menus. There were several specials listed, but at Tom's recommendation we all selected the broiled haddock, baked potato, slivered carrots, and coleslaw.

The waitress soon returned with our steaming hot drinks. While Tom conversed with Patty, I gazed around the dining area and noticed some changes in the décor. New beige decorative lampshades appeared on the lamps in the room. The matching beige window drapes were also new. When Patty and Tom had finished their topic of conversation, I asked Tom about the changes. He told me his dining room manager had approached him to suggest the changes for the purpose of allowing more natural light into the room. He indicated that some of the steady lodge customers had recommended such a change with the notes dropped into the suggestion box near the cashier's desk.

"Jason, I check that box once a week, personally. Some of the ideas are excellent, so I'm willing to put up with reading the ones that are rather outlandish," he explained.

"The changes that you've made certainly brighten up the dining room, Tom, I agree wholeheartedly," I said.

Our orders soon arrived and were placed on the table before us. The cuisine was garnished with parsley and a touch of paprika appeared on the broiled fish.

During our meal little was discussed. We chose instead to enjoy the good food. The waitress appeared as needed to refill our water glasses.

Upon our completion of the main course, she returned to clear our dinner plates, refill our cups, and leave the dessert menu. After we perused it, she returned to ask what we had decided. We all selected the bread pudding with a tangy lemon sauce. Feeling very full, Patty requested a smaller portion for herself.

When the dessert arrived, the waitress asked if we would like any more refills of our coffee. We all declined. The bread pudding with the lemon sauce was delicious. Tom told us that his pastry chef was one of the best in the Adirondack region. Patty and I both agreed. Neither of us had ever tasted lemon sauce so good.

Patty excused herself and went to the ladies room to freshen up. Tom and I remained at the table and chatted.

"Tom, your acquisition of the old logging camp is a wonderful idea. I do believe it is important to preserve some of the past, especially the once-all important phenomenon of the logging camp and some of the dynamics of a logger's life during that era when the two-man saw and double bladed axes were used in the harvesting of timber, along with memorabilia of the time period. People need to remember the lifestyle that existed then."

"I fully agree with you. Jason, you surprise me: you seem to be familiar with that part of history in the Adirondacks."

"Yes, I am, Tom. My father was involved in logging and pulping in the late 1920's and the early 1930's. In his later life he shared with me stories about some of those experiences. I do not possess all the information about that way of life, but just enough to stir my continual curiosity about a hearty time of hard work by men who worked and lived in those camps. Tom, your logging camp museum will join other museums that will keep alive the traditions of the woodsman and their way of life."

"Thank you, Jason, for your comments. The board that I'm forming will seek out individuals who may have articles that they would like to donate for display. We have already received contributions of antiquated tools that the loggers of yesterday used in the performance of their daily tasks."

Patty returned, and the three of us continued to converse. She and I expressed surprise when Tom mentioned the fact that he was going to New York City to have a complete physical examination. He didn't explain why he was going, but told us that he was very fatigued and thought it best to have a doctor friend of his perform the exam. This news bothered me. I had noticed that Tom just didn't seem to be his old self, and now I feared he might be suffering serious illness. We both wished him good luck with the examination and asked him to let us know of the results. I wondered to myself if this was the true reason for his letter.

"Jason, before you and Patty leave, I have some bad checks for you to look into. Would you mind?" he asked.

"Not at all. I'll be happy to work on them for you."

I offered to pay for the lunch, but Tom insisted that we were his guests and lunch was on the Breakshire Lodge. He told me that next time it could be my treat. I assured him that it would be. Patty and I thanked our host for his generosity.

We followed Tom to his office. He walked along with

Patty and I trailed behind them. I heard him tell Patty that if there was anything she needed she should just have me call on him. I sensed that Tom's caring for Patty was that of a father for the daughter he never had. I knew that Tom Huston loved his two nephews very much, and that he considered Patty and me part of his family.

We entered the office and seated ourselves in the comfortable leather chairs. Tom went around to the rear of his desk, opened up one of the drawers, and took out a manila envelope. He removed the several checks in question, placed them in another smaller envelope, and handed it to me.

"Tom, I'll work on them as soon as we return to Old Forge. By the way, I was very interested to learn that Morey Harris is now in your employ. I hope that everything works out for him. You are to be commended for helping this young man."

"I know. I know, Jason. Hopefully it will work out. He received some excellent counseling and is trying to better himself. And he also knows that if he should step out of line, Lieutenant Jack Doyle of the New York State Troopers will be talking with him. Jason, I have my ways of keeping track of my employees."

"I know you do, Tom. I think what you have done for this young man is very commendable. You are a caring person."

"I believe that everyone deserves a second chance. Morey Harris didn't have a good family environment, and when his father left him he was devastated. The harm he attempted to the Breakshire Lodge and to me was a result of his father's actions at the time. Anyway, I feared that this young man would eventually end up in prison or some other punitive institution. I know I'm probably taking a chance, but I've done it and so far it has worked out well."

My heart went out to Tom. "It is inspiring to know that there are people like you who care enough to go that extra mile to help someone. I myself believe that there is good in Morey Harris, and now we'll see if this young man possesses the true grit to walk the good path through the rest of his life's journey." I paused, then queried, "Do you see Lieutenant

Doyle once in a while?"

"Yes, Jack stops by for lunch from time to time. Usually he is with some of his personnel."

"That's great! I don't have to tell you what a fine member of Troop S he is."

"No, Jason, I have you to thank for making this contact for us here at the Breakshire. All the troopers who dine and visit here are fine representatives of the force."

I began to feel our visit should come to a close. "Tom, I wish we could stay longer, but I believe that it's about time for Patty and me to start back to Old Forge. We both thank you for the wonderful lunch and the good conversation. I do sincerely hope that Morey appreciates what you have done for him. Please say hello to him for me. I look forward to seeing him sometime in the future."

"I will, Jason. And when you see Wilt Chambers, kindly tell him that I will be in touch with him soon. Oh, and give my regards to Dale Rush and his bride-to-be! When is the wedding?"

"We believe it will be in the summer, Tom," Patty said.

"Thanks, Patty. I thought it might be this summer." Tom smiled benevolently at us. "Jason, you and Patty be careful on the drive to Old Forge," he cautioned.

"We will, Tom. And you take care of yourself."

Tom gave Patty a hug and we left the office. I told the desk clerk as we passed that we hoped he would have a good rest of the day.

Before Patty and I left the lobby, we looked over at the bears that Wilt had created. Their life-like eyes and strong-clawed paws impressed us. Several of the guests at the lodge gathered nearby to view the bears. They seemed to be in awe of the carved animals. One of the group took pictures of the bears.

I held the door open for Patty and followed her out.

The thought of Morey Harris working here at the Breakshire Lodge as the head groundskeeper was a little troublesome for me to digest. I remembered well the night when private investigator Gordy Whigham and I had apprehended Morey on the grounds of the Breakshire Lodge and the struggle that had ensued in removing him from the rusty old car. It was difficult for me to fathom why Tom would risk trying to rehabilitate Morey. I was too well acquainted with the recidivism rate of the criminal element. I could only hope that Harris wouldn't disappoint Tom Huston. I guess my former occupation as a trooper made me a little cynical.

I opened the passenger door of the Bronco and Patty climbed in. I went around to the driver's side and entered. I started the vehicle and let it warm up before we pulled out of the parking space. The lot was half full. We were both surprised that there were that many cars there this early in the season.

During our return trip we discussed how pale Tom had appeared and we spoke with concern about his forthcoming trip to visit a doctor in New York City. Tom Huston was a godsend to the Adirondack region. Himself a shrewd businessman, he possessed a soft spot in his heart for the less fortunate people of our society. He was known for having Christmas baskets delivered to needy families in the region, making sure they contained a turkey and an assorted variety of foods needed for the holidays. However, there were those who possessed professional jealousy toward Tom. Patty and I knew Tom was steadfast in his charitable generosity toward the needy as he shared his success.

The signs of spring were all around us as we made our way across the bridge entering Long Lake. No vehicles were parked at Gertie's Diner. It appeared they might have closed early.

"Jason, honey, would you mind if we stop at Hoss's Country Corner?" Patty asked. The pleading look on her beautiful face was followed by her winsome smile.

"Certainly, darling," I replied. "Your wish is my command."

I pulled up next to Hoss's and turned the ignition switch off. The vintage Bronco coughed and then died. Apparently the timing needed to be adjusted. That would be a job for Dr. Don, who knew his cars and was an excellent mechanic.

I helped Patty out of the Bronco and we went inside Hoss's Country Corner.

"Jason, I want to look around for a while. Would you purchase a pound of that strong cheese? It is so, so good!" she emphasized.

"I will, honey. You look around the store and I'll pick up the cheese," I replied. We had had that cheese many times. It is delicious, especially when preparing macaroni and cheese.

After making the purchase I joined Patty and we spent about an hour browsing through this unique store. Most of our time was devoted to the clothing department. We made a few purchases of some items on sale: Patty needed gloves and I bought a shirt and some handkerchiefs. The store personnel were friendly and courteous, as usual.

After paying, we left the store. But before leaving Long Lake, we filled up the gas tank at a local service station. The twenty-dollar bill that paid for the fuel turned into sixty-five cents in change.

Traffic was light as we headed south on Route 28, a trip that we had made so many times before. Patty, as usual, was peering out the passenger-side window, marveling at the beauty of Long Lake though the pine trees. The mountains had lost their blanket of snow, and a softening of the crisp air presented the awakening of another season. I glanced over at Patty. She was beautiful with her long blond hair flowing on her shoulders, and with the radiant complexion of an expectant mother. My eyes quickly returned to the highway. A log truck was directly in front of us slowly ascending a hill. We slowed down to a crawl and followed the heavily loaded truck halfway to Blue Mountain Lake before we could safely pass. He gave us a blast on his air horn, apparently his way of thanking us for being patient. It wasn't uncommon for us to see a log truck or two on any given day along Route 28. One could only imagine what it must have been like hauling logs or skidding them to a river, towed by horses. I thought of how Tom Huston's acquisition of the old logging camp and his vision of a museum to represent the logging and timber history was his way of further contributing to the Adirondack region. The mountains had been good to him, and his gratitude was being transformed into the creation of a unique museum for the Adirondackers and for the many visitors to this pristine place. One could visualize people, young and old, taking a look at the saws, the ropes, and the assorted tools that the lumberjacks of the past and present used to harvest the vast forests of our land.

This era of time had already been well represented in other worthwhile places and events, such as the museums at Blue Mountain, the Northern Logger in Old Forge, and the annual Woodsmen's Field Days held at Boonville. Patty and I on our trips to Boonville and the Woodsmen's events always learned something new. We found the energy exerted by the participants fascinating to view.

We pulled up in front of the Eagle Bay Kennels just before closing time. Patty waited in the car while I went inside. Lynn must have seen us drive up; she appeared with Ruben in the hallway. He pulled hard on his leash with his tail spinning like a propeller on a model airplane when he caught sight of me. Lynn was wearing a warm smile.

"Hello, Jason. You're just on time," she said.

"Has he been a good dog?" I asked, watching Ruben strain on the leash trying to get to me. Lynn released him and he came to me. I rubbed his neck and he finally settled down.

"How much do we owe you, Lynn?" I inquired.

"I'll bill you. Is that alright?" she asked.

"Fine. In fact, I'd appreciate it. I just purchased gas at Long Lake and it just about emptied my wallet until I get to the Mountain Bank."

"No problem, Jason. Your credit is good with me. You know that."

"I'll send you a check when I get the bill, Lynn." I was a bit embarrassed that my funds were not sufficient at the moment.

"That'll be fine. Please say hello to Patty for me."

"Sure will," I answered.

Lynn held the door open as the big K-9 lurched forward and pulled me along through the doorway and down the stone steps to the Bronco. When I opened the rear gate he jumped in, spun around twice, and lay down. I closed the gate and climbed in behind the steering wheel next to Patty.

"Ruben looks good. Lynn does a fine job bathing and grooming him," Patty said.

"She certainly does a good job, honey," I agreed.

When we pulled into the driveway, two does ran directly in front of us from behind the pine trees. I quickly braked the Bronco.

"Whew! That was too close, Jason," Patty cried out.

"It's a good thing we weren't going fast," I replied, my own pulse racing.

I pulled up close to the entrance of our log home, got out, went around to the passenger side, and opened the door for Patty. I then let Ruben out of the vehicle, and he dashed toward the woods. He returned shortly and went directly to his dog run. Patty and I went inside. While she went to the bathroom to freshen up, I went into my office. The light on the telephone answering machine was flashing. I pressed the button to listen.

"Jason, Chief Todd Wilson here. When you get in, please give me a call. Thanks."

The second call was from Mountain Bank regarding a check scam. It was too late to contact the bank, but I dialed Chief Wilson's number. He answered politely. "Chief Wilson. Can I be of assistance?" The chief sounded efficient.

"Chief, Jason Black speaking. I'm returning your call."

"Jason, could you stop by the office in about twenty minutes?" he asked.

I wondered what that's about. "Sure, I'll be right down. Is there something wrong?"

"I'll talk with you when you stop by," he replied.

"See you in a few minutes, Todd."

I hung the telephone up.

"What's the matter, Jason?" Patty asked as she entered the kitchen.

"Don't know, honey. Chief Wilson asked me to come down to his office. I'll go down and see what he wants. I'll be back in a few minutes, Patty."

"Sweetheart, do you want me to fix something to eat while you're gone? We had such a large lunch today at the Breakshire Lodge."

"If you'd like to make a club sandwich I'll split it with you, maybe with a cup of green tea."

"Sounds good to me, Jason," she replied.

I walked over to her and held her in my arms. I kissed her passionately.

"I love you, Patty. Are you feeling alright?" I asked.

"Fine, Jason. I love you, too, darling. I'll prepare the things for the club sandwich while you're gone."

I put my jacket on and went out to the Bronco. It was still warm and started on the first engagement of the ignition switch. I let it idle for a minute and then backed around and headed to Old Forge. I wondered what Todd wanted. Why couldn't he tell me over the telephone? I asked myself.

When I pulled into the driveway of the Town of Webb Police Department, the only vehicle parked near the office was Todd's cruiser. It appeared shiny. The chief always kept his police car in tip-top condition, no matter what the weather conditions were like. I pulled my antiquated Bronco up next to the cruiser and shut off the ignition, then got out and went inside the office.

Todd was behind his desk. He looked up and said, "Jason, thanks for stopping by. Sit down. I've got some bad news that I want to share with you. Remember Bernard Draper? He's in a federal institution in Michigan, and some troubling information has been gathered through a snitch who is also doing time there. It seems that Draper wants to get even with all those responsible for his incarceration. You're on his list, Jason!" Todd looked concerned.

"What? That bastard has me on a list, huh!" I could feel my blood pressure rising. It was difficult to hear this information.

"Settle down, Jason. We've got it covered. I had to let you

know, man. For God's sake, relax."

"Listen, Todd, I don't deal with threats very well. Is there any more you have to tell me?"

"I've already contacted your friend, Lieutenant Jack Doyle. He reacted the same way. When Jack heard this he wanted to hop on a plane for Michigan himself to conduct his own investigation. However, he may send an investigator to look into this alleged threat. It may be just talk, but they are not going to take any chances. You've got a good friend in Doyle, Jason."

"I know, I know, Todd. He's one of the finest working field officers on the job, and he's got plenty of intestinal fortitude. He'll follow through with an investigation and find out what is actually going on with Draper."

"I had you stop here at the office because I think it is important and I didn't want to upset Patty."

"I appreciate you letting me know without telling her. At the time of his apprehension on Route 28, I remember that he vowed to get even. I believe you heard him say that after he bit you."

"True, he did utter something under his breath at the time. Speaking of the bite he gave me, I'll always wear that scar." Todd rolled up his sleeve and continued speaking. "Look, Jason. See what I mean? It's ghastly looking!"

"Yes, it is, Todd," I responded sympathetically to the jagged scar on his arm.

"Well, that's all I can tell you. I've alerted my patrols and the local troopers. Lieutenant Doyle indicated that he'd be monitoring this potential threat as he himself directed the operation on the Draper case."

"Thanks for giving me the information. I'd better get home; Patty will be worried."

As I left the office I asked, "Please let me know if you should hear of any further information."

"I will. Don't worry." Todd responded.

I went down the steps of the police station and entered the Bronco. My memories of the Draper case rushed into my thoughts. Here was Draper, confined to a federal institution in Michigan, and now he was planning our demise. What a change from the smooth-talking salesman of the southwestern jewelry store that he once owned in the Adirondacks, where unsuspecting customers believed for a while that Draper was a genuine hardworking entrepreneur! Those same customers had a drastic change of heart after he was arrested on state and federal charges.

Ruben was standing up on the runway fence looking directly toward me. I pulled to the left of the runway and turned the ignition switch to the off position. "What am I going to tell Patty when I get inside?" I asked myself.

I stopped momentarily by the enclosure and petted the loyal K-9. I checked his dishes. They were full. I kept mulling over in my mind what I was going to tell Patty about my visit to Todd's office.

When I opened the door, Patty was standing by the table. She turned and looked up at me.

"Honey, I was getting worried. What did Todd want?" she asked with apprehension.

"Patty, it was something to do with Mr. Draper, the man from Arizona who had the jewelry store west of Tupper Lake."

"Oh, yes! I remember him very well." She shuddered. "I remember that he bit Todd when Todd apprehended him. What's going on with him?" she asked, wrinkling her forehead.

I didn't want to come out too strong, so I soft-pedaled it a little. I wanted to avoid causing her extreme distress because of her pregnancy. But I also didn't want to fib to my precious wife. "It's something to do with Draper threatening people who were involved with his apprehension."

"Are we in danger, honey?" she asked in a light voice.

"We should exercise caution, darling, that's all," I said, still trying to keep it light.

I looked into her eyes. She was beginning to tear up. I placed my arms around her to give her a hug.

"Patty, don't cry. I had to tell you why I went to Todd's office. He just wanted to let us know what's going on with this

Draper character," I said, trying to comfort her.

"Honey, we've gone through so much. We are expecting our child in a few months. I have horrible memories of being abducted, then being stalked by my former husband. And now we have to worry about threats from a person who is presently serving time for his crimes. Jason! What's next? I'm worried!" she exclaimed, with good reason.

"I know, I know, Patty. I'm very concerned about it, too. Todd informed me that Lieutenant Doyle is investigating the information received from a snitch—who, by the way, is probably trying to work out a deal with the authorities for crimes he is involved with, to get a shorter sentence, something like that. It may be bogus or it may be legitimate. Believe me, Jack Doyle will find out if it's actually a threat to be concerned about. Until a determination is made one way or the other, we'll use caution during our day-to-day activities. I'm very worried, dear, but we have to exist and do the very best we can for ourselves and our forthcoming child."

"I agree, Jason, but nevertheless, I don't need any extra strain right now. What are we to do?" she asked with tears welling in her eyes.

I pulled my arms even more tightly around her. Then we separated and, holding hands, went into the living room and sat down on the couch for a few minutes. Neither one of us spoke. Her head lay against my shoulder. When she seemed quieted, I gently got up. Patty relaxed further by placing her head on one of the stuffed pillows, and I went into the kitchen to prepare a club sandwich for us.

Patty had everything ready to go. I placed the wheat bread into the toaster. When it was done I lightly buttered the slices and built the sandwich with lettuce, sliced tomatoes, sliced turkey, ham, and Swiss cheese on one slice. I added mayonnaise and placed the other slice on top. To add to our light evening meal, I heated a can of tomato soup, stirring in some two percent milk. While the soup was heating I set the table with silverware and napkins.

With everything ready I went into the living room. Patty

had dozed off. I leaned down and gently kissed her forehead. She opened her eyes and smiled.

"Everything is ready, sweetheart," I whispered.

"I didn't mean to fall off to sleep, Jason," she said groggily, rubbing her eyes.

I assisted her to her feet and we went into the kitchen and dining area. Patty washed her hands and dried them.

I then pulled Patty's chair out from the table and seated her. I placed the bowls on the table at each of our places and proceeded to pour the hot steaming soup.

"Jason, you did a wonderful job. The soup is hot. And the sandwich looks great. Maybe you should become the sandwich maker at John's Diner."

"Yes, that's all I need now is to become the sandwich chef at John's," I replied, knowing that Patty was pulling my leg.

"Oh, honey! This sandwich is delicious. There is nothing like crisp lettuce, tomatoes, and crunchy bacon along with the taste of turkey and ham. I love it!" she exclaimed, lifting her spoon with hot cream of tomato soup to her beautiful lips.

"I'm glad that you are enjoying our light dinner. Everything seems to be tasty. Honey, would you care for some coffee or tea?" I asked.

"After we finish, would you mind making me a cup of decaf?" she asked.

"Sure, I'll have a cup with you. We can both have decaf. After we've finished eating you go into the living room and turn some music on. I'll clean up the kitchen and then I'll make a pot of decaf with a little cream. And how about a couple of oatmeal cookies, too?" I asked.

"That'll be great, Sherlock!" she agreed. "Jason, you can make me a club sandwich anytime you want to. You've got the right touch."

"I'll take that comment as a compliment. But, my dear, we've both got to watch our weight, especially you in your pregnancy."

"I realize that you're right. I just want you to know I think you could have been a grand chef."

"Thanks, sweetie, but a chef has to spend many hours on his feet. Maybe when I was younger it wouldn't have been difficult. Now it's a different story."

Patty went into the living room and I cleaned up the kitchen, while the decaf was perking. I removed three oatmeal cookies from the cookie jar and placed them on a plate.

Soon we were sitting on the couch sipping coffee and enjoying the cookies. Soft music played in the background. The evening went by rapidly. Ruben went out for his nightly run to the woods and returned to lie contentedly on his air mattress.

I thought about the meeting with Chief Todd Wilson earlier in the day. I knew only too well about the societal issues that affect everyone's life. Take the mailman delivering mail, who has to be aware of a mad dog on the street. Or the school teacher of today, not knowing if someone has brought a weapon into class to act out on a grievance imagined or real. As I continue to ponder the sad reality, I could feel sleep tugging at my mind.

CHAPTER FOUR

The alarm went off at 5:15 a.m. Patty got up first and went into the bathroom. I heard the shower go on. I rolled out of bed and went into the kitchen. Ruben followed me to the door and I let him outside. He sped off toward the woods and he disappeared in the fog. It had rained during the night, and water drizzled off the roof. It appeared to be a damp day ahead of us.

I waited by the door for Ruben to return. When he did I let him in. Patty came out of the bathroom and went directly to the bedroom to dress. I noticed how round she was becoming.

I entered the bathroom and splashed some Adirondack cold water into my face.

It felt refreshing and I came alive. Patty called in to me that she would catch some breakfast at the diner. I could tell she was in a rush.

"Patty, I'll go outside and start the Jeep. It hasn't run for a couple of days, remember." I put a jacket on over my pajamas.

"Thank you, sweetheart. You're precious, Jason," she sang out to me from the bedroom as she finished dressing.

I went outside and unlocked the Jeep. It was cold and damp. I climbed in and pulled out the choke that Dr. Don had installed. I pumped the gas pedal once and engaged the ignition switch. The engine started with a cough and then it smoothed out. I let it idle, set the brake, and went back inside the house.

The rain seemed to have stopped. I helped Patty on with her coat. She no longer tried to button it. She looked gorgeous. Her long blond hair was now pulled back into a neat bun. As always, she wore very little makeup.

"Jason, don't take anything out of the freezer for tonight. I'll be bringing dinner home from the diner."

"That sounds good to me, babe. Be careful driving. As you can see, it is quite foggy outside. And the roads are probably a little slippery because of the rain," I said as a warning.

"I will, Jason. Don't worry so much. Sometimes you drive me crazy," she said jokingly. "What are your plans for the day?"

"I'm going to pay some bills today and do some work in my office. I may stop in today for lunch. I have to make some telephone calls, including touching bases with Jack Doyle. Oh, and I wouldn't mention anything to anyone about the meeting with Todd. Just keep your eyes open."

"Don't worry, honey, I won't. I'll call you later."

We hugged each other and I kissed Patty on the cheek, not wanting to smear her fresh lipstick. She walked to the idling Jeep and got in, then rolled the window down and said, "Honey, thank you! The Jeep is nice and warm for me."

"Okay, Patty. Drive carefully. Oops, there I go again. Sorry. Love you."

"Love you, too, Jason."

I watched her back up the Jeep in a reverse Y and drive toward Route 28.

I glanced at my watch: 5:45 a.m.

The kitchen looked in good shape. I decided to fry two eggs and make a slice of whole-wheat toast. The tomato juice was cold and tasted good with the bit of pepper sprinkled on it. I added a pat of butter to the pan. When it was ready I cracked the two eggs into it. One broke, while the other remained intact. I turned them over and fried them slightly hard. The toast sprang up as I slid the eggs onto a small plate. I poured myself a cup of strong coffee and sat down at the table. Ruben, with his head tucked neatly between his paws, looked up and watched my every move. He knew better than to come to the table to beg. He was an obedient K-9.

After breakfast I dusted and cleaned all through the log home and placed some soiled clothes into the laundry bag. I was pleased to see that the sun was coming up over the mountains as the sky cleared. Sunshine in the Adirondacks helps to bring out the true beauty of the region.

Standing at the south end of First Lake looking north with the sun rising from the east and mist hovering over the water is a quiet experience no one can forget very easily. Such a scene is a painter's or a photographer's setting for a perfect picture. It is not uncommon to sight an artist sitting on a canvas stool in front of an easel, brush in hand, transforming this segment of Mother Nature's beauty onto the canvas. It gives me deep pleasure to observe such creativity occurring before my eyes.

When I took the dust mop outside to shake it, I let Ruben out and put him in the dog run. He immediately entered his doghouse.

With the cleaning completed I went into my office and typed several letters to makers of bad checks. I considered with satisfaction the fact that I had been fairly successful in collecting on many of the checks that had already passed through my office. Mountain Bank never complained, for they knew that eventually the check passer would be contacted diplomatically by me or would receive a visit from an officer of the law. In handling check matters my diplomacy was usually effective, as in our fast-moving society being forgetful about paying bills was not uncommon. The approach taken toward a potential defendant concerning these matters sometimes determined the outcome. Being harsh with people can lead to unpleasant encounters. I always believe that you get back what you send out.

I was sitting at the desk when Patty called. She again reminded me not to take anything out of the freezer for dinner. She indicated that she would have another good surprise for us from the diner. No sooner had we hung up than the phone rang again. It was my good friend Wilt.

"Good morning, Jason," he said in a husky voice.

"Hello, Wilt. Good to hear from you. You got a cold? Your voice sounds raspy!"

"Just my allergies, Jason," he replied.

"Sorry to hear that you're suffering from the sniffles." I knew Wilt was plagued every spring.

"Jason, I had a call from Tom yesterday and I understand that you and Patty had a nice lunch with him. Wish I could have joined you."

"We would have loved to have you with us," I replied.

"Jason, I'm certain you are aware of the museum that Tom is in the process of creating. I called to let you know that he has selected me to head up the committee for the project," he said excitedly.

"Yes, I knew that you were being considered, but I didn't want to spoil Tom's surprise in notifying you. I did highly recommend you for the position. You, Wilt, have the knowledge and the background for this type of program. Do you have any idea who else is on the panel?" I asked.

"Tom will be sending me the list, along with telephone numbers and addresses. I do know that retired forest ranger, Gary Leach, has been selected. I'm looking forward to working with Gary. He's an exceptional person and possesses vast knowledge of the forest industry."

"Gary will definitely be an asset to the project. I'm pleased that he is being selected." This was good news indeed.

"The existing museums in the Adirondacks are wonderful. This one will be especially unique. It will showcase tools and equipment that were used in harvesting timber of the past, along with equipment that is being used currently. Jason, I'm going to ask you to lend us some of your two-man saw collection, if you don't mind."

"I'll be happy to display them for as long as you need them, Wilt. I assume that there will be others?" I replied.

"We'll just use yours for the opening celebration. Yes, I've already got several leads in mind regarding donations of various old tools lying around in barns and garages just taking up space."

Before we ended our conversation, I decided with careful consideration to confide in Wilt about my conversation with Todd. I knew Wilt could keep a secret.

"Wilt, I've got to share some information with you. This is strictly confidential."

"What is it?" he asked with concern in his voice.

"Remember the Bernard Draper case?"

"Yes, I do." His voice was grim.

"Well, Draper wants to get even with everyone who had something to do with his arrest on state and federal charges. A snitch in the federal institution where Draper is serving a life's sentence was able to overhear him talking about it. The snitch wants to get his own sentence reduced, of course, so we can't be sure the information is accurate."

"You'd better be on guard, Jason. It sounds serious to me."

"It is. Draper has many outside contacts. And you know I'm concerned for Patty's welfare as well as myself and the others who worked diligently on the case. I just wanted to share this with you. Before we tell anyone else I had better check with Todd or Lieutenant John Doyle."

"Don't worry, Jason. I won't say anything. But I'll keep my eyes open. I assume Todd and his department are all aware of this threat."

"Oh, yes, they are. Todd is the one who informed me."

"Good! And I assume that your close friend Lieutenant Doyle at Troop S is working on the matter."

"Yes, Todd also said that Doyle's working on it and is taking the information very seriously."

"Good. Glad to hear it. Doyle is one capable trooper, and he's a good man. I know many people in his former patrol district around Pulaski who speak highly of him and his abilities."

"He's one of the best, Wilt."

"Well, Jason, I've got to be going. I have many things to do. Oh! By the way, how would you and Patty like to have dinner on me at Frankie's Restaurant some night next week? I know you agree that Frankie is a wonderful chef."

"We'd love to, Wilt." I knew Patty would be very pleased. "Frank has a great restaurant and wonderful cuisine. We'll look forward to it."

"Okay, Jason, I'd better be going. Take care."

"Take something for that allergy, good friend."

"I will. So long."

With our telephone conversation completed, I finished my paperwork and straightened up the office.

With delight I went into the new nursery and marveled at the wonderful addition that Wilt, Dale, Jack, Charlie and Jim Jenny had spent many hours on. We still had to add a few things for our baby. I tried to look ahead to what it would be like to have our child in the crib. How many things we would have to learn for the raising of a child! Wilt and his volunteers would always be in our thoughts and prayers for the time and effort they were unselfishly putting forth on the addition to our log home. I stood in the nursery for a few more minutes before I returned to the office.

I called Lieutenant Doyle at Troop S Headquarters. The trooper on the desk put me through to Jack without hesitation.

"Lieutenant Doyle. May I be of service?" he asked.

"Good morning, Lieutenant. Jason Black here," I said.

"I was just about ready to call you, my friend. I assume that Chief Wilson gave you some details of what is going on with Bernard Draper. That's why you're calling, right?"

"Right. Yes, Jack, he did. Tell me, how do you feel about this?" I asked.

"I don't like it. Even though he's serving time in Michigan, he should still be considered dangerous. He's cunning and still wields a certain amount of power with some very questionable characters. Remember, Jason, there are several of us that brought this guy down. In other words, through cooperation with other law enforcement agencies, we were able to detect his criminal organization, which led to his apprehension and the cessation of his smuggling operation. Believe me, Jason, it's not only us who are looking into this matter; others are involved in their own investigations. Apparently the snitch is telling the truth. They gave him two polygraphs. So that is where we stand at the moment, waiting for an overt act to take place."

I could not believe what I was hearing. I found it difficult to control my rage. "What overt act, Jack? Hell, no! If Patty and our unborn child or myself are in jeopardy, I'm taking defensive action myself. You know me, Jack. I'll protect my family above anything else!" I couldn't keep the hot anger out of my voice.

"Jason, I hear you, and I know what you mean. But as your friend I've got to remind you that an overt act has to take place before you are justified to proceed with any action. You know that even better than I do."

I felt myself seething. "That's all fine and good, Jack. You know I do understand. But when it comes to my family, including myself, I'll do whatever I feel is necessary, period!"

"I hear you loud and clear. I know exactly how you feel and I feel the same way. Be assured that I'll keep you abreast of any new information. I'll also keep Chief Wilson informed. I did suggest to him that all motels, hotels, and bed and breakfast places should be alerted to keep their eye open for strangers that may act suspicious. And that applies for more than just your area. I've got my investigators out checking our region here as we speak."

I managed to make my voice calm. "Good idea, Jack. You remember how devious Draper was in eluding the patrols."

"Indeed, I do. If it hadn't been for you spotting him on Route 28 and notifying Chief Wilson, he might have made it to New York City. If he had, there is no telling where he would have gone, especially with all the contacts he had."

"And he apparently still has contacts, with this threat looming over us."

"That's right." Jack's tone was grim. "Jason, you know how the system works. It is up to us to try to determine who we have to watch out for. I'll do everything in my power to disseminate this information. I want you to take the necessary precautions, which I know you will do—but don't do anything crazy. I've got a staff meeting now so I have to conclude this call. Take care, and give my very best to Patty. So long, Jason."

"Thanks, Jack, so long—for now."

I hung up the receiver, still feeling great emotion, and went to the kitchen for a glass of water. There was some relief in knowing the lieutenant was actively involved in the case, but I was still seriously worried.

Ruben seemed restless, so I went to the door and let him out. My eye caught a glimpse of a blue jay on a limb overhanging the roof. Ruben didn't waste any time covering the distance from the log home to the edge of the forest. "You're still in good shape, Ruben," I said under my breath. In a short time he returned and I put him in the dog run.

In order to rid myself of some of my turmoil I took the rake and gathered into a pile last autumn's leaves that had blown next to the house. The fresh air felt good as I inhaled deeply into my lungs and exhaled slowly several times. The sun was a real treat for me after some days of heavy cloud cover. What was on my mind inspired me to rake even harder and faster than usual.

Trivial duties around the log home always helped my spirits. Today I could hear the heavy rumble of log trucks on Route 28. The winter harvest had been productive. Logs were plentiful and were now being hauled to their destinations, whether it was to lumber yards, paper mills, or chipping plants.

When I had finished raking I put the tools away. My thoughts drifted back to Patty's and my trip to the Breakshire Lodge. So Tom Huston had gone to bat for Morey Harris. He pitied Morey, whose father had been caught stealing and thus fired from his job as groundskeeper. Now the son had been hired as head groundskeeper, under Tom's watchful eye. I didn't know the complete reasoning behind Tom's decision to help out a young man who had appeared to be on the path of dishonesty. I could make a guess, though. Tom had lost his only son, who had passed away at an early age, and here was

Morey without a father, very much in need of direction. I had been surprised to hear of his decision, but on the other hand I was pleased that Tom, in his own need, had given Morey a chance to prove his self-worth. I certainly hoped Tom would not be disappointed.

I went back inside our log home to call Patty.

"Hello, sweetheart. Sorry to bother you at work. Honey, before you start home, would you mind stopping at the post office to check our mailbox? The late afternoon mail may be in," I said.

"Honey, I will. And you be sure to get ready for another delicious dinner. I'm not going to tell you what it is. I'll see you in an hour, Jason."

Patty hung up before I could respond. She left with only guesses about what the surprise would be. Before I went back to my office I set the table and placed a pitcher of water in the refrigerator. We both enjoyed a glass or two of cold water with our meals. And Patty was taking care to drink plenty of water for the benefit of the growing baby.

I then returned to the office. In order to make additional room in my file cabinet, I purged some of the oldest material. I knew that our accountant had copies and a complete set of all pertinent records. I understood the importance of keeping some necessary data; however, storage space had become a problem.

When I finished my work in the office I went back outside to enjoy the afternoon sun that had warmed the air. It was such a lovely day I decided to take Ruben out of the run for a walk. We ran down to the edge of the woods where I spotted two large early robins on the edge of the adjacent field next to the woods. They didn't even flinch as we dashed by. They were the sure sign of spring. I observed Ruben investigating a brush pile next to a downed elm tree. It appeared he was sniffing for an evasive chipmunk. He soon moved on to another.

Glancing at my watch I was surprised that an hour had passed since my call to Patty. She should be pulling in at any moment. I turned toward the house and had gone about twenty feet when Ruben sped by me directly into his dog run. When I reached the dog run I closed the gate, just as Ruben entered his doghouse, not even waiting for my command. I chuckled: he certainly knew the routine.

I picked up some of the wood that had slipped off my neat pile, placed it on the top of the cord, and then went inside.

When I turned on the hot water to wash my hands, I noticed that some was leaking slightly near the base of the faucet. I'd call Jack Falsey, my plumber, in the morning to advise him. I had just finished drying my hands with the hand towel when I heard the Jeep's horn sounding. Patty was home. I immediately went outside to assist her as she opened her door.

"Hi, honey!" she called happily.

I went over to her with outstretched arms and embraced her.

"Welcome home, sweetheart. How was your day?" I asked, as I brought her lips up to meet mine.

"Fine, dearest," she said. I kissed her warmly.

Patty asked me to bring in the covered foil pan from the rear seat of the Jeep. I opened the door and picked up the pan, which was still very warm to the touch then turned to close the rear door with my shoulder. Patty made her way over to the dog run to pet Ruben's head.

"Just a second. I'll get the door for you," she said.

We met at the door and Patty opened it. I followed her inside and set the warm pan on the stove. I helped Patty off with her coat and hung it in the closet.

"How was your day, Sherlock?" she asked, wearing her usual smile.

"Well, I talked with Jack Doyle and Wilt for a long time on the telephone. I don't want you to worry too much, Patty, but Jack assured me that he is taking the threats concerning the Draper case very seriously. Believe me, sweetheart, Jack will get to the bottom of this," I said strongly.

"Honey, thank goodness we can count on him! I don't need this added stress so far into my pregnancy. And I'm also concerned about you. How I wish now you hadn't ever gotten involved with the Draper mess. It does scare me."

"I know, I know. You are probably right, but you also know I had to. It's in my make-up to ferret out the evil in our society. Long ago in my former career I learned the fact that society does have a dark side. No one will ever be able to stamp out all criminal activity, however when an individual becomes aware of a crime it is his responsibility to notify authorities. The Draper case is a good example. The authorities were notified, an appropriate investigation was conducted, and as a result Draper and his associates were arrested and put through the criminal justice system."

Patty's eyes glistened with tears. "Jason, I can't understand a person like Draper, someone who wants to seek revenge on people who were just doing their job: the police, and the federal authorities, and us? Everyone's being notified, aren't they?" She looked at me in dismay.

"Yes, honey, everyone who had anything to do with the investigation and the apprehension of Draper and his associates will be alerted to the threat that Draper allegedly made. It's going to be a wait-and-see situation. We'll just have to be careful and exercise good judgment at home and in our travels. Chief Wilson and the local troopers have already canvassed the neighborhood and surrounding area, notifying motels, hotels, bed and breakfasts, and anyplace else, even campgrounds, where an evildoer could possibly take up a temporary residence," I explained.

"I'm trying to understand, dearest," Patty said dejectedly.

"Honey, I think we should think about having dinner. What are we having? What's the big surprise?" I asked in a lighter voice, determined to change the subject.

"Homemade beef stew: it has onions, carrots, and potatoes, with really tender chunks of beef in gravy."

"You know how much I love stew!" I was beaming.

Patty reheated the stew on the stove. After loosely tying an apron around her wide middle, she quickly whipped up some dumplings and dropped them on top of the lightly bubbling stew. I prepared some cabbage salad. While she was busy with the finishing touches for dinner, I set the table. To add to the ambiance, I lit two candles.

When the stew was piping hot, and the dumplings were done, Patty removed the stew, put it on a trivet, and set it on the table. The zesty aroma quickly filled the air, teasing my taste buds. I removed my chilled cabbage salad from the refrigerator and placed it next to the pot.

When everything was ready I seated Patty at the table. I noticed with pleasure that she had added a dish of bread and butter pickles to our meal. The ice cubes cracked in our glasses as I poured water over them. After saying the blessing, I served Patty by ladling piping hot stew in her bowl. I then passed her the cabbage salad before I served myself. The flavors of the stew and the cabbage salad blended well.

"Patty, Lila's stew is wonderful. She certainly has the culinary artist's touch to preparing it. So tasty—I love it!" I exclaimed.

"She puts her heart into all the dishes she prepares at the diner. I love it, too, Jason," she agreed.

"True, Lila and John work very hard, and so do you, sweetheart."

"I love my customers, Jason. They are some of the real people of our great country. They work hard at their jobs and somehow still keep their sense of humor regardless of what problems they may be enduring at home or at work. To me they are like family."

"I know they are, honey," I remarked with pride, knowing her commitment to her employer and customers.

After we had savored our dinner I made a fresh pot of decaf for us. I asked Patty to remain seated as I cleared the table. I then reached into our colorful cookie jar on top of the refrigerator and took out three molasses cookies. I placed them on a small plate and set them on the table. I poured two cups of the decaf coffee and added cream to mine. Patty drank hers black. The candles continued flickering, casting dancing shadows on the wall. Patty went on to tell me about some of the events of her workday. Of course, I listened intently. But in the recesses of our minds, both of us were worrying about the threat that Draper had made. I remembered the day that he had passed us as we were driving on Route 28, following a slow-moving log truck into Inlet, and how Chief Todd Wilson and another officer had pulled his car over. Behind the wheel had been what any would have thought to be a blond female operator until the wig fell off Draper's head. The subsequent events caused me to rush to Todd's aid as I'd seen Draper sink his teeth into Todd's arm. I remembered, too, how I had punched the wild, uncontrollable man right in front of Patty. The evil look on his face at that moment will always remain in my memory. He was a very dangerous man, for certain.

"Jason? Jason, are you alright? You seem to be staring into space," Patty asked with a puzzled expression.

I focused again on this moment of love and trust. "I'm fine, dearest. I was just reliving the day Draper was apprehended by Chief Wilson and the small part I played in his capture. You and I both understand we've got to be watchful for any suspicious person or persons who may try to carry out Draper's threats. Lieutenant Doyle of Troop S is not going to be intimidated by the likes of Draper, and we shouldn't either. Patty, you call me immediately if you think you are in any kind of danger," I said emphatically.

"I will, honey. You can be certain of that." Her face was unable to conceal her anguish.

"It's important, Patty." I knew I was affirming it to myself as much as I was affirming it to her.

I could see my beloved wife deliberately changing the subject. "Jason, I spoke with Dale Rush this morning. He stopped by the diner for breakfast. We talked about the time that he and Evelyn took us to Maine. It was such a wonderful trip, and we had such a great time with them. Dale told me that they are planning their wedding sometime in late June, and he wants you to be his best man."

I was surprised and pleased. "Is that right? I was under the impression that Jim Jenny was going to be his best man."

"Maybe so, but he did mention that Jim and his wife are

flying to Florida for a family gathering and he will not be able to be in the wedding party."

"It seems to me I did hear that Jim was going to Florida, but I didn't know when."

Patty gave me a slow, sly smile. "Jason, I hope I'll be able to attend."

I smiled back knowingly. "Honey, hopefully we'll be able to attend—that all depends on how you're feeling at the time. There are still a few months left before the baby arrives. We'll see what happens. With all respect to Evelyn and Dale, the birth of our child has to be our major concern. After all, it probably is one of the most important events in our lives."

Patty ran her hand over her belly. "Jason, you're wonderfully right. The birth our child feels like everything."

As we continued to sit at the table, our conversation turned to the wonderful new addition to our log home. We discussed the cost of the construction and our plans to pay off any indebtedness that we had accrued as soon as we were able.

The threat that Bernard Draper had made from his prison cell was going to be steadily invasive to us all. We hoped and prayed that Lieutenant Doyle would be able to ascertain the authenticity of the threat. We were painfully aware that so often when people assist the authorities in a criminal case, their own lives become a nightmare. It was our profound wish that this matter would be resolved soon.

Patty went into the living room to knit as I did the dishes and cleaned up the kitchen. I placed the leftover stew into a small bowl and set it in the refrigerator along with the leftover cabbage salad. I'd have them for lunch in the next day or two while Patty was at work. Lila's ability to prepare beef stew was well known in this part of the Adirondacks. She would not divulge her secret recipe that gave her stew something special

Before I went into the living room to be with Patty, I took Ruben for a short walk. I then returned to the house with Ruben close behind. He went directly to his air mattress to lie comfortably until his late night walk. I joined Patty in the living room and watched her busily knitting away on the arm of a multi-colored baby's sweater. I felt the urge to comment aloud about her ability, but thought better about it, fearing I would disturb her fingers' rhythm.

I leaned over to pick up a copy of the local paper that was lying on the coffee table and made my way to my comfortable recliner to catch up on the local news. The leather covering made a squeak-like noise as I sat down. The chime on the grandfather's clock in the corner of the room rang seven times. I glanced at my wristwatch, which was two minutes slow, so I reset it. The old clock was very accurate. The room was quiet, almost too quiet. I reached over, selected a compact disc for some soft music, and placed it into the player—old time favorites began to play wonderful songs from the past. As it began, I turned my gaze toward Patty. She raised her head and looked over at me with a warm smile, showing her approval of my selection.

"You know I love that CD, honey. It's beautiful."

"Sweetheart, I do too."

Patty lay her knitting down on the end table and rose from her chair to sit on our comfortable couch. I walked over to join her. We warmly embraced. I reached down to give her a gentle kiss.

"I love you, Sherlock," she said laying her head against my shoulder.

"I love you, too, babe," I answered.

We went off to bed early, but did not fall off to sleep right away, just holding each other contentedly. Just before closing my eyes I heard the familiar sound of the neighborhood raccoons on the back roof. I was going to get up and hit the ceiling with the broom handle, but instead I gave into the overpowering need for sleep before I could force myself out of our warm cozy bed.

CHAPTER FIVE

It was May. The month of April had passed without incident. Patty, as her pregnancy filled out her body more and more, continued to work Mondays through Fridays with an occasional Saturday, depending on the need at the diner. Lila had assured Patty she should not worry when she had to take time off for doctor visits. She and John continued to treat Patty as a part of their family. Patty's doctor assured her that her pregnancy was progressing well. Each visit reassured us both.

We had received several calls from Jack Flynn and Ruby Wolkowski, our good friends in Arizona who had originally contacted us regarding Draper when Flynn's detective agency had handled Draper's wife's divorce. They expressed their concern for our safety and spoke of their own. Continually we compared notes. We thanked them for checking in and told them we were thinking of them in their jeopardy as we all exercised caution.

To my surprise and satisfaction, Jerome Huntley, father of Christine Huntley, called twice from Arizona during the month to thank me again for my help in locating his abducted daughter. He told me that the dangerous Bradley Carter had finally been sentenced to five to seven years in the Arizona prison system. The sentence should definitely have been greater, but the double standards of justice had kicked in and Carter had received special treatment because of his father's influence and money. I did not respond to Mr. Huntley concerning that bit of information because I knew the system well, realizing that sometimes a police officer or the investigator can become discouraged when preferential treatment influences the sentencing in a criminal case. It's a time to take a long walk and breathe in the fresh air, because there is not a darn thing you can do about the injustice of it. For the most part, our justice system is adequate and works well.

I had had very little contact from Lake Placid during April. Evidently, Tom and Wilt had wasted no time in the remodeling of the former logging camp. They assembled a crew of construction workers who made the necessary changes to the buildings to create the loggers museum west of Tupper Lake near Childwold.

Wilt had stockpiled items for the museum into a large shed. I donated my twenty-two two-man-saws, which included two ice-cutting saws used in days of yore long before the invention of the electric refrigerator when men would remove frozen blocks of ice from the pristine lakes to be shipped by train into cities downstate for iceboxes in restaurants and homes. Wilt was kind enough to load them into his big white pickup and take them to Tupper Lake. I learned that Charlie Perkins had gathered numerous items from the timber industry and had asked many of his logging friends to conduct a search for assorted tools including, axes, antiquated buzz saws, and old steam engines with pulleys and belts. Family members of old lumberjacks who are still alive have responded with numerous tools, preserved notes, and letters that were exchanged from the logging camps to their relatives and family members from the past.

During my several conversations with Wilt, he mentioned he was able to obtain some of the cooking ware that was used in the kitchens of the logging camps.

"Jason, I'm amazed at the response my committee members and I have received from all generations of Adirondackers that have and had connections with past generations of logging people. Some people who reside out of state heard about our efforts, while guests at the Breakshire Lodge. They are shipping me items that pertain to the timber business. I am amazed that we'd have such a response," he said, shaking his head.

"Wilt, it doesn't surprise me. Our American people are interested in causes like this. Tom's idea is brilliant. Just the movement alone has pulled families together. We are a proud people in this country. The early houses were built of wood, and where does wood come from? The forest land, naturally. Some of the people already must feel a part of the logging museum based on what you have told me."

"You're right, Jason. There seems to be a great deal of interest. Tom Huston indicated that he'd like to see the museum open just on weekends for about a month just to see if everything will run smoothly."

"During your meetings at the lodge and the museum, were there any other assignments discussed?" I inquired. I could tell that Wilt was happy to be involved with the project.

"Yep, there was. Tom asked Dale Rush if he'd be interested in flying some of the guests from the Breakshire Lodge to Tupper Lake for the purpose of visiting the museum and the Village of Tupper Lake. But you know, Jason, Dale indicated to Tom and the rest of the committee that he wouldn't be available all the time on weekends. But he decided he certainly would be willing to help out when he had free time."

"That sounds great, Wilt." I could sense Wilt's enthusiasm with this project.

I learned from Wilt that Dale Rush and Evelyn O'Brien were beginning to make plans for their wedding sometime in June. I was a little surprised that they hadn't set the exact date that they planned on being married. I passed it off that Dale and Evelyn were too busy with the reopening of the marina. They had their work cut out for them.

Dale Rush, Jim Jenny, Charlie Perkins, Jack Falsey and Wilt had done a magnificent job on our addition, creating a suitable nursery for our forthcoming child. Their dedication to the project was above and beyond the call of friendship and volunteerism. Patty and I were so very grateful for the kindness, friendship, and talent that they had displayed for us. Others also volunteered, but Wilt, thanking them, told them that he already had plenty of help.

It was that time of the year between snowmobile season and the arrival of the tourists to our mountain town.

Patty had left for work. I had just finished cleaning the kitchen when the phone rang. It was Jack Doyle.

"Jason, I've talked with Chief Wilson and told him that the threat from Draper was indeed a valid one and there is a possibility that he'll have it carried out, even though he is behind bars. I have contacted the troopers in your town; alerting them to be on the lookout for a maroon Pontiac possibly bearing an Illinois plate that may belong to hired hit men. I don't have the license number, but if it shows up in your region they'll check it out. During my conversation with Chief Wilson I gave him the same information."

"Lieutenant, I appreciate your calling me. If I should observe any such vehicle, I'll contact the troopers and the chief immediately," I advised him.

"Good. Just be careful. Keep me posted, Jason."

"I will, Jack," I said. I knew that Jack wouldn't let Patty and me down.

It was the beginning of the week—Monday, to be exact. Patty had just arrived home from the diner after a long tiresome day. I had just removed her coat and hung it in the closet when the telephone rang. I picked it up.

"Hello. Hello?"

Someone was on the other end of the phone, but didn't answer.

"Hello?" I repeated, but they hung up.

"Who was that, Jason?" Patty asked.

"Don't know, babe. Whoever it was just hung up in my ear." My voice showed my displeasure.

I didn't say anything more about the hang-up call, but it

had created a sense of uneasiness in me. I could only hope it was just a wrong number. I would be foolish to let my imagination run wild.

"Honey, I had a busy day at the diner," my beloved wife confided. "Would you mind cooking tonight?" she asked.

"Sweetheart, not at all! I'll be glad to cook. What would you like for dinner?" I looked over at her with concern. She appeared exhausted.

"How about your favorite pancakes?" She teased, knowing what my favorite quick and easy dinnertime meal was.

"Buckwheat pancakes or regular, Patty?" I asked with a chuckle.

"Buckwheat, dearest one," she responded.

"Canadian bacon or ham?"

"I think the Canadian bacon would be just fine, darling," she responded.

"I'd like you to go into the living room, sit in the recliner, and just relax for about half an hour while I do my thing. I'll call you when dinner is ready. Would you do that for me, honey?" I asked lovingly.

I placed my arm around her right shoulder noticing her body was really beginning to fill out. I walked her slowly toward the living room. When we reached the recliner I assisted her as she sat back and stretched her legs out in a comfortable position. I then reached over for the afghan to place over her to keep her warm.

I leaned down and kissed her on the forehead, then returned to the kitchen for my kitchen duties. The cupboard door stuck a little as I pulled it open to get the pancake mix out. I removed a bowl from the shelf and measured the required amount of mix into the bowl, adding two whipped eggs, along with a spoonful of sugar into the batter as I added the appropriate amount of milk that I had soured. I mixed the ingredients together to the desired consistency, taking care not to stir too much.

While the grill was heating, I sliced five thin slabs of Canadian bacon and placed them on a small plate. I then prepared a pot of decaf and removed the syrup from the refrigerator. After I poured it into a small pitcher I set it in a pan of hot water.

"Are you okay, Jason?" Patty called from the living room.

"I'm okay, sweetheart. It won't be too long before supper will be ready," I replied contentedly.

"Can I help you?" she asked. Her weary tone belied her offer.

"Just relax. You and the baby need the rest," I said.

"Okay! I'll be patient, honey."

The heated grill was ready to receive the buckwheat mixture. I hurriedly set the table with napkins and silverware.

The Canadian bacon slices fit into the smaller frying pan, which I had heated. They gave off an inviting aroma. When I turned them over I added a sprinkle of brown sugar. With the bacon in its final stages, I poured the batter onto the hot grill into four individual good-sized pancakes. Bubbles began to appear in a minute or two. At the proper time I turned the four pancakes. All were golden brown.

"Patty, a breakfast supper is about to be served," I called out.

Patty joined me in the kitchen and seated herself at the table. I had heated both of our plates. I placed two of the pancakes on her plate with two slices of Canadian bacon.

I watched Patty pour the maple syrup over her buckwheat pancakes.

"Jason, they look wonderful," she said in appreciation.

"They came out pretty good, darling. I believe the griddle should always be kept pretty hot," I responded.

She tasted a bite. "Yum, they're delicious," she said approvingly.

We each had two more. The Canadian bacon, augmented with the brown sugar, was very tasty. Instead of tea, we had decaf, which went better with our pancakes. I refilled our cups as needed. This kind of supper, quickly and easily prepared, was always a treat for me.

While I cleared the table and did the dishes, Patty took Ruben for a walk to the edge of the woods. When she returned,

Ruben went into his dog run and Patty retired to the living room with her knitting needles. I went into the office and composed a couple of letters to check passers. Many times people write checks and fail to have sufficient funds in their account to cover the instrument, sometimes deliberately but often by a simple error in addition or subtraction. The letters I send to the check maker are answered either by letter or telephone call, or the Mountain Bank notifies me that the check has been satisfied. When the procedure has been completed, all the parties involved are relieved that no criminal action had to be taken. After my office work I took care of Ruben, then joined Patty in the living room. She put her knitting down as I joined her there.

"Patty, would you like to watch television?" I asked.

"Sounds like a good idea to me," she agreed.

I walked over to switch on the television. It felt like a night to sit and relax and watch some TV, with the hope that there would be a decent sitcom or movie we would both enjoy. We finally found a movie Patty thought we would both enjoy, which we did. It was a rather nonsensical movie, but we both appreciated the comedy at this time. It gave us something to laugh about, a welcome relief. At the end of the movie we decided to go to bed and read till we got sleepy. Very soon Patty turned off her lamp.

"Morning comes early, honey. I'm so tired. I'm falling off to sleep already," she said as she turned over to sleep on her side.

Patty fell off to sleep as soon as her head hit the pillow. I continued to read until my eyelids became heavy, then I joined her in deep slumber. Evidently I was in much need of the sleep, as I never stirred again until the alarm went off at 5:15 a.m.

CHAPTER SIX

Patty arose and went into the bathroom. I pushed the covers back and crawled out of bed. I reached down for my bedroom slippers. Ruben was at the door waiting for someone to let him out. I went to the door to unlock it. As soon as I opened the door, he rushed past me at a fast pace. I watched him as he abruptly stopped before he reached the edge of the forest. He returned to me as I waited at the door.

Patty soon came out of the bedroom. Her long blond hair was done up in a bun ready for work at the diner. I gently gave her a hug and kissed her forehead. While she had been dressing I had started her Jeep so it would be warmed up for her. Patty went outside and walked to the Jeep. Before she climbed in she turned and waved as I waved back. Here she was, expecting our first child, and maintaining her positive attitude as she went off to work at John's Diner despite the possible threats against our lives. I would rather have her be able stay at home, but Patty made it clear to me that as long as she felt good she wanted to work. She trusted our law enforcement officials. I watched her Jeep pull out onto Route 28 and head toward Old Forge. After feeding Ruben I put him in the dog run, where he stood guard at full attention with his ears pointed straight up toward the heavens. For Ruben, Patty's leaving for work in the early morning hours had become somewhat of a ritual. He shared his K-9 love equally between Patty and me.

I went back into the house and put the teakettle on over the lit burner. It had been several days since I had had a cup of green tea. I placed a small skillet on the front burner and put a very small amount of butter in it. I removed one of the fresh brown eggs from the refrigerator tray, cracked it against the pan, and slid it gently into the preheated skillet. I placed one slice of whole wheat bread in the pop-up, then flipped the egg to ensure that it was cooked the way I enjoyed eating it. When the toast was done, I light-buttered it, then placed the egg on top. With the green tea and my fried egg on toast, my breakfast was complete. After completing my meal, I sat down at the table with a copy of one of the local weekly newspapers as I sipped a second cup of tea.

I read an article concerning the taxpayers' complaint about the increase in both the property and school taxes. They felt the township and the county were doing very well at the expense of many of the lakefront property owners, who felt they were filling more than their share of the coffers. Many felt they were being driven from the homes that they had purchased years before at very moderate prices. The bureaucrats at work, I thought. Oh, the games they play. Interesting stuff—I had observed it so many times in many of the towns and places that I had worked and lived in before. Oh, well! So it goes.

After my light breakfast I quickly cleaned the log home, dusting, mopping, and running the trusty cleaner over the living room rug. It was going on ten o'clock when I had completed the job. I had just finished dusting off my desk in the office when the telephone rang. I picked up the receiver.

"Hello, may I help you?" I inquired.

"Good morning, Jason." I recognized the voice.

"Lieutenant Doyle. What's up?" I asked quizzically.

"Jason, I've got some additional information regarding the Draper threat. It seems that the warden at Draper's institution has another informant. He shares a common area with Draper. Jason, believe me, Mr. Draper is a revengeful person. Apparently, when you assisted Chief Wilson near Inlet, you punched him, which aided the chief in the capture. So Draper is telling this informant that he is going to get even with you. Yesterday, I received some intelligence to the fact that Draper had a couple of his contacts on the outside travel to the Adirondacks to obtain any information they could about you."

"What?" I became infuriated.

"Now, settle down, Jason. Watch your blood pressure." He sounded truly concerned by my reaction.

I tried to calm myself. "I'm cool, Lieutenant. Don't worry about me."

"You know how those tough guys react, especially when they have an audience. I just wanted to let you know. The Phoenix PD detective division knows who they are, and their telephones are being monitored as I speak. I wanted you to know that they are on top of this situation."

"Are you going to tell me who these two people are?"

"Jason, I'd like to, but it's an ongoing investigation and I think it is best that I don't. Depending on what transpires, I may share it with you. Right now it is a wait-and-see situation. My advice to you, Jason, is to be alert for anything that seems suspicious and notify us right away if anything further develops. I know that you are always in the alert mode, but it's my duty to pass on to you what information I deem important for your security and safety. You and Patty are like family to me. Do you understand, Jason?" he tried to assure me.

"Jack, you and I have been through a great deal together. But I'm not on the job anymore. I've always done it my way and you know how I am. It is a darn good thing that I haven't run into Draper's henchmen yet, especially for them."

"I believe that, Jason, I believe it."

"Jack, I appreciate your call. Please keep me posted! You know how much I'd like to fly to Michigan and face that bastard."

"I wish we could, but I have one of our investigators out in Michigan who will let me know what develops."

"Oh, I hope he's a good one."

"Jason, all my people are good. Don't forget: I trained them," he said confidently.

"I know they are, Lieutenant. I was just busting your chops. Remember how we used to kid each other all the time, Irish?" I chided.

"That we did, lad. I never forget. Well, I've got to go now, Jason. Be good, be careful, and be sure to say hello to your beautiful wife."

"That I will, lad. Goodbye." I wasn't happy with his call.

As soon as I hung up the telephone I called my buddy Jack Flynn in Phoenix, Arizona.

"Good morning. Flynn Investigations," Ruby Wolkowski answered in her most efficient voice.

"Ruby, Jason Black speaking. How are you, babe?" I asked.

"Somehow I had a feeling it was you, Jason! How's Patty doing?" Ruby asked.

"My angel is doing fine. The pregnancy has been wonderful so far and she is still working at the diner."

"Jason, I wish you and Patty the very best. I bet you both are looking forward to the blessed event."

"Yes, we are, Ruby. My friends have pitched in to build an addition to our home for a nursery for the newborn baby when he or she arrives. What a gift! I purchased the material and they did all the work. I wish you could see it."

"I think that is wonderful. Would you like to speak with Jack? He's in. We have been busy here since you and Patty returned to New York. I'll buzz him for you. Talk with you later, Jason, and give Patty my love," Ruby said, before she connected me to Jack.

"Flynn here," he answered.

"Jack, it's Jason speaking," I said.

"How's my buddy doing? When's the baby due and how is that beautiful wife of yours?"

"Still a couple of months to go, around the middle of July and Patty is doing well, still working. That was her decision. The doctor told her that if she feels good and wants to work, that will be fine."

"Tell Patty that Ruby and I are rooting for her. Listen,

Jason, I want you to know that I sincerely appreciate everything you did for me on the Jerome Huntley case. I see Huntley about twice a month. Ruby and I have been invited to the ranch for dinner several times. Jerome mentions you and Patty often to us. Yes, Jason, my boy, you made friends for life on that caper. In fact, Jerome asked me if you'd consider taking over as a security director for his complete organization. As you know, he has several companies and holdings."

"That would be impossible, Jack. My life is with Patty right where we are in the six-million-acre park of Northern New York State. I had a feeling that Huntley was thinking along those lines from our past conversations, but you can put that idea to rest right now. He's a fine gentleman, but no matter what the financial package might contain for a proposed salary, it would mean an unacceptable difference with the lifestyle that we enjoy and are accustomed to. It's a polite 'no, thank you'."

I knew by the tone of Jack's voice that he was disappointed.

"Jason, it's an opportunity of a lifetime. If I wasn't so involved with Flynn Investigations I'd consider it myself, but I can't. Too much invested here."

"I understand. But listen, Jack, old buddy: I'm calling today with a dilemma. Bernard Draper is sending out threats from his Michigan prison cell. I assume you've already heard."

"Hold it, Jason. I was going to call you today. I received that information late last night. Seems he wants a contract on everybody that had something to do with his incarceration. I heard he sent two of his bad boys to the Adirondacks to check out you and a Lieutenant Doyle and also the police chief. Is his name Todd Wilson?"

"Yes, it is Chief Todd Wilson. I'm amazed you already know. You must have stellar sources."

"Jason, you know I have hundreds of informants here in the Phoenix area and I've done many of them a few favors. Being a former law enforcement officer yourself you know very well the definition of the networking of informants."

"Yes, you're right. I do have a few, myself. For your information, Jack, there are certain steps being taken to keep the intelligence flowing to Troop S in the Adirondacks. Lieutenant Doyle of the Bureau of Criminal Investigation is one of the sharpest in his profession. By the time he's done with Draper, that con will be mopping the prison kitchen floors on his hands and knees. Doyle has a smile and a soft approach to people, but, he's tough as 10-inch nails and knows the drill very well."

"That's all well and good, Jason, but Draper is a strange one with a dual personality. Your friend Lieutenant Doyle will have his hands full. Believe me. I even heard that you socked Draper pretty good when he was apprehended in New York."

"All I can say, Jack, that Draper had a good portion of the chief's bicep in his mouth, which did some damage to nerves in his arm. All I did was come to the chief's rescue by relaxing Draper's jaw a little."

"Yeah! I know you, Jason Black; you're always coming to somebody's rescue. You were in the U.S. Marine Corps! Remember the time we had that two-day pass in San Diego and I stopped at a grocery store for some gum and you were outside waiting for me, a big fellow chasing his wife came out of the tavern across the street? He knocked her down, and you jumped on the guy's back. Remember that? You finally won, but it took a while as a large crowd gathered around. And then the police arrived only to find the big brute lying on the street with a couple of black eyes. You remember!"

The memories came flashing back. "Yes, I remember. That fellow had no right to beat his wife," I replied darkly.

"Well said. Oh, I've got to get going Jason. I've got an appointment with a client regarding a pending divorce action. Have you been tapped to work on any recent domestic cases in the Adirondacks?"

"No, Jack. I usually tell them to go home and try to settle their differences themselves. Sometimes they do and other times they consult with an attorney. I try to avoid these types of cases."

"I agree with you, but we have so many here in Arizona. Well, if I hear any more about the Draper threats I'll give you a call. Just be careful, Jason. Remember, you have to protect your lovely wife and, soon, your child."

"Thanks. Take care, Jack. Say hello to Mr. Huntley next time you talk with him."

"So long, Jason."

I could have talked for hours with my old friend, Jack Flynn. I was amazed that he already knew of the Draper threats, but on the other hand, why wouldn't he? Twenty years on the streets of Phoenix had been the training ground for my buddy Jack. He was a dedicated police officer, and during his twenty-year career he had seen it all. But it was his years as a detective that had brought out his full potential. He had solved many of the major cases that had hit the news media on the Phoenix scene, earning him respect in all sectors of this continuously growing community. From the beginning of his exciting career he had known in his mind and heart that you don't browbeat the public. He didn't. Jack won their hearts with kindness and still made his arrests, and when he had to be officially stern, he was so with dignity.

I glanced at my watch, then turned on the radio for the noon news. After it ended I turned the radio off and went outside for some fresh air. Ruben came over to the gate of the dog run and waited for me to open it. I swung it open and the big K-9 rushed out and headed to the woods. He suddenly turned and made a beeline toward me. I could tell he wanted to play. When he reached me I rubbed the back of his neck and we wrestled for a few minutes. He was full of spirit and still strong. We continued on toward the woods.

I noticed that several old trees had succumbed to a recent strong wind. They lay on the ground. Like the elderly they had tired and passed away. Three other trees still had strong limbs that supported their trunks just off the floor of the forest.

The May air was refreshing. In our mountains there always seems to be a breeze that cools your face. It's fresh and clear, without the industrial pollution that has soiled so many of our urban areas. Mother Nature cleanses the great Adirondack Park with adequate rainfall for the survival and growth of the trees and wildflowers. Soon the region would be welcoming the seasonal residents returning to their summer homes while thousands of others would travel to the mountains for vacations. I wondered if our child would share our love and reverence for these Adirondack Mountains?

My attention was brought back to Ruben, who was trying to sniff around an old brush pile in an attempt to seek out a chippie. I stood in the forest looking up, straining my neck to view the tops of the tallest of the trees. I heard a giant woodpecker pecking at a tree in the distance with a staccato beat. It stopped, then started again. There is nothing like such a moment of solitude, beneficial for everyone on occasion, to reflect back on one's life. Both Patty and I loved this place. We knew so many others did, too. Ruben moved on to another pile of brush while I continued my meditation. The woods suddenly went silent until the woodpecker again began his drum beat against the trunk of the tree. The staccato beat repeated—then silence—only to repeat again.

It was about 1:30 when we returned to the log home. Ruben went to his dog run and I closed the gate. I heard the telephone ringing and rushed into the house to answer it.

"Hello, Jason Black here," I said.

"Jason, Tom Huston. Are you free to talk for a few minutes?" he asked.

"Yes, Tom, of course. How are you?" I inquired. Tom's voice sounded a bit unusual, I thought with concern.

"Jason, the Loggers Museum is going to open in two weeks. Two or three minor details have to be taken care of first. Wilt and his committee have certainly done a most efficient job in getting the place organized. You've got a good friend in Wilt, Jason. I know you realize that. He certainly thinks a great deal of Patty and you," Tom said. His voice seemed to sound more normal now.

"He always speaks well of you and your staff at the lodge. Tom, Wilt is a generous man. He devotes his energies one hundred percent on any project he undertakes. That is just the way he is."

"I know. I know. Jason you're right."

"You can't go wrong with Wilt, or Charlie Perkins either. They are good friends, and they truly represent themselves as professional timber men. Lumberjacks and loggers have a proud history here inside the Blue Line."

"Yes, I'm well aware of their historical past, and also that of the present day timber men. The main purpose for this call is to see if you and Patty will be able to come to the official opening of the museum. I would like you to say a few words. You and Patty, of course, would be at the head table."

"Are you certain you would want me to speak?" I asked, somewhat surprised. I was actually pleased and honored to be asked, though my personal feelings about public speaking were mixed. "Yes, I will."

"Good! That's what I wanted to know. I have to rush off; my secretary just informed me that as usual I have another call. Talk with you later, Jason!" he said hastily.

I hadn't intended to spend half the day on the telephone; however, it had been informative, and I realized I had actually missed talking with Jack Flynn. Our relationship was more like brothers 'than good friends'. During our military days and especially in San Diego, Jack had come to my rescue more than once, and in particular I had come to his aid when he had innocently become involved in an unpleasant barroom scene. We were always there for each other. Undoubtedly this was the true reason that we had become police officers: the concept of helping or coming to the aid of humankind was important to us both.

It was long past lunchtime, so I decided to make myself a cup of coffee, toast two slices of whole wheat bread, spread peanut butter and jelly over the toast, and sit down at the table to enjoy one of my favorite treats.

After my late lunch I went into the hamlet of Old Forge to stop by the post office for the daily mail. What a disappointment! The postal box was empty except for an advertisement, which I deposited in the recyclable-paper basket conveniently placed by the door. My next stop was to check in with Dr. Don at the garage.

"Jason Black, where have you been hiding? I haven't seen you around lately."

"Doc, I've been around. You are under these cars and trucks all day long, so how do you expect to see folks around town, except when you run down to the diner for soup and a sandwich?"

"Hey! Jason, how do you know I have soup and a sandwich?" Don said with curiosity.

"I have the all-seeing-eye, Doc. People keep a lookout on one of their favorite mechanics around here, and naturally the information leaks out."

"I just wondered. You know I'm kidding you a little bit, Jason. I know who you're married to. Well, what can I do for you?"

"Doc, this old Bronco has many, many miles on it. I don't want to part with it, but I can't afford another vehicle right now, especially with the birth of our baby due in July. So I'm trying to preserve it the best I can. The timing needs to be adjusted and I'd like you to check the brakes and fix the emergency brake, which may need to be replaced. If you have a good used battery I'd like to replace the one in the vehicle when you do the work. Also, the right rear tire needs a good used replacement." I made a list as we talked.

"Is that all, Sherlock?" Don chuckled, as I appeared puzzled. "Don't get shook up, Jason, Patty stopped in with her Jeep the other day and called you that. She then explained that was her pet name for you."

"Huh! I wondered how you knew about that. It'll take more than that to rile me up. When can you do the work?"

"Well, let's see. Maybe next week, if that's alright with you."

"Fine. Just call the house with the date and time, and I'll bring the Bronco down," I said.

"Listen, Sherlock, I can't be gabbing here all day. I've got a muffler to change on Jack Falsey's pickup. Jack is expecting it to be done by four. He believes in being prompt."

"Have you seen Dale Rush lately?"

"No, Jason, I haven't, but I did hear through the grapevine that he and Evelyn are planning a summer wedding."

"I heard that, too. I'm not certain of the date, though." I wondered why I hadn't heard from Dale lately. I figured he must be busy at the marina.

"Gotta go, Jason. Talk with you later," he said, returning to his vehicle.

"Take care, Doc," I said, knowing that I had been keeping him from his other work.

Doctor Don was sliding beneath the front of Jack Falsey's pickup as I went to the Bronco and climbed in. When I engaged the ignition the Bronco coughed a little, but the engine straightened out and sounded good. As I drove past John's Diner I caught a glimpse of Patty's red Jeep at the far end of the parking lot. My watch showed me it was 2:45; Patty would be headed home in a couple of hours. I hoped she wouldn't be too tired. There were still some of the vehicles in the parking lot, probably customers enjoying that mid-afternoon green tea or coffee with a piece of Lila's great pie.

As I pulled into our driveway, I was surprised to see the big white Dodge pickup backed up near the dog run, with large, burly Wilt next to Ruben, who was enjoying all the attention. I swung in next to the Dodge and turned the ignition off. The Bronco reacted with its usual cough before it stopped, which confirmed my suspicion that my faithful vehicle was due for some TLC. I was pleased I had decided to make that visit to Doctor Don's garage.

Ruben barked happily when he saw me. I lovingly told him to settle down as I petted his back.

"Jason, I was right in the neighborhood checking out a couple of white oaks, so I thought I'd stop by for a few minutes just to see you if you were here," Wilt said, reaching out to shake my hand.

"Wilt, I'm happy that you did." I said sincerely. Then I joked, "I know you just wanted to admire that wonderful work you and the fellows did on the addition." I smiled widely at him. "Seriously, all of you did a splendid job and Patty and I appreciate it with all our hearts."

"Actually I didn't come about that. Nope, I wanted to update you on the loggers' museum we've been working on. We're moving right along with that project," he said with satisfaction.

I nodded. "I was talking with Tom Huston earlier today and he told me about how the museum is progressing."

"Yes sir, we've had many families, as well as retired logging people make donations of all kinds of tools from the past and present. You wouldn't believe it. It's like a story coming together from all different directions. They are pouring out their hearts with true Adirondack spirit." He was visibly excited about the project.

"I wouldn't expect anything less. Sometimes we all have differences of opinions and strong words can be passed back and forth, but the Adirondackers are a special group of people. When there is a special project or purpose, we tend to be very generous when it comes to lending a hand or money for a worthy cause."

"Don't I know it! That's for sure," he confirmed, nodding.

I wanted to keep our conversation going. "Wilt, let's go inside and I'll put some coffee on."

Wilt followed me to the door and I unlocked it. I encouraged him to remove his jacket and have a seat. He went into the bathroom to wash his hands while I washed mine in the kitchen. I filled the teakettle with water and set it on the stove to boil, then reached into the cupboard for the coffee. First I checked the pantry for a couple of goodies, but then remembered our cookie jar contained molasses cookies. I reached in for some and placed them neatly on a plate. I poured the water through our small Melita drip coffee-maker, waited for it to go through, and filled both our cups with steaming coffee. I placed the pot back on the stove and sat down across from Wilt. He looked tired. It showed that he was working hard with his own timber business, several organizations to which he belonged, and now the loggers' museum project for

Tom Huston. And I didn't forget the long hours he had put in working on the addition to our home!

"Wilt, how many hours do you sleep at night?" I asked with concern.

"I try to get at least six hours a night. Why do you ask, Jason?"

"I'm worried you're overdoing it, Wilt. You should probably try to get a little more sleep," I advised him.

"I know you're right, Jason, but I've been a pretty busy man lately," he explained with satisfaction.

I didn't want to press the matter, so I changed the subject and asked Wilt about what was transpiring at the new museum.

He replied eagerly, "Jason, we have already set up a replica of an old logging camp on the grounds so that the visitors can look back in history to see what the logging camps consisted of, a well-stocked gift shop of miniature replicas of tools of that era, and a small restaurant. I hope I'm not boring you with all this, am I?" he asked thoughtfully.

"No, Wilt, of course not. Go ahead and tell me about it." I was genuinely interested in hearing of the loggers and the ongoing project. I could see by his eagerness in relating all the details to me how very much it all meant to him. He was very proud of his association with the project.

"Here is how it has been set up. First we have recreated a room called the dog room. It has shelf-like bunks where the lumberjacks slept and a wood stove in the center of the room heats it. The bunks have been straw-filled the way they were years ago. Before the 1930's, men used to wash their clothes in an iron kettle outside in the snow. Later on they were furnished a shed called a dingle located between their sleeping area and the mess hall where they were able to wash themselves. As you know, Jason, the lumberjacks of yore were required to leave their homes and families for many months of the year in order to make a living in those early days. They didn't have it too easy back then."

"I'm familiar with many of those terms because my father was involved with logging and pulping in the twenties and thirties. Go ahead, Wilt. Tell me more," I said. I delighted in the fact that Wilt possessed a vast knowledge of the timber industry and was a true historian of life in a lumberjacks' camp.

"Jason, if you and I had been alive and visited a logging camp back then around dinner time the meal would have consisted of fried salt pork, beans, and baked bread. They were heavy eaters. Remember, these men worked close to fourteen hours each day in the woods. And after dinner—remember, it was before modern technology began to change things, they would light their pipes and play cards while some of them told stories until bedtime. Sometimes if they were so blessed, a few of the loggers would play their fiddles, guitars, banjos or harmonicas, and maybe even engage in a clog dance for entertainment," he went on. Then he added with feeling, "But I still bet it was hard on them to have to leave their wives and kids for all that time."

"That's all so interesting Wilt, very interesting. And all without trucks, right? Didn't they use horses in those days? Where were they kept?" I asked.

"Along with the cookhouse and bunkhouse, they usually had a long barn structure for the horses and a blacksmith shop for shoeing them. There was also an office for their boss or supervisor. And they had a store that was called the Van, where the lumberjacks could purchase mittens and long stockings along with shoes and boots," Wilt announced, sounding more like an historian than the daily woodsman he was.

"Wilt, can I get you a refill on your coffee?" I asked, noticing his empty cup.

"Yeah, sure, I could use one. Thanks." He handed me the cup. "Good coffee, Jason."

"Yes, we buy it at DiOrio's. We really like it."

"Yes, we have a couple of good stores in Boonville where I do my shopping," he answered. Then he returned to describing the museum project. "As you know, Jason, the committee and I have met with Tom Huston several times. He suggested that it would really show the true spirit of the Adirondack region by having old-time lumberjack meals served in the cookhouse. It wouldn't be every day, but possibly twice each week, during all four seasons."

"Fantastic! I'm certain people would turn out for that. It sounds as though you and Tom and the committee are traveling down the right path. I'll bet the tourists will love it."

Wilt looked down at his watch. "Jason, old buddy, I'd better be moving on. I have a meeting with some of my men in Boonville up at Charlie's Bistro. We'd originally thought we'd go to Slim's, but he closes early in the afternoon, so the decision was made by my tree foreman to have the fellows meet at Charlie's."

"That sounds good, Wilt. By the way, your dissertation of lumberjack lore was excellent."

"Glad you enjoyed it, Jason. The next time we get together I'll have more, but for now I'd best be going."

"I know it, Wilt. I'll see you later."

"Be sure to say hello to Patty for me," Wilt said with a warm smile.

"I certainly will. She'll be sorry she missed you."

I watched Wilt as he walked out to his truck. He slipped a dog biscuit to Ruben before opening the door of his Dodge. The big man climbed in and started the engine. I watched him throw another dog biscuit to Ruben over the fence, and then the truck roared out of the driveway towards Boonville and his meeting with his men.

I felt the urge to call John's Diner then, since I hadn't heard from Patty.

"Good afternoon. John's Diner." My lovely wife's voice filled the line.

"Honey, do you mind if we just have franks and beans for dinner tonight, as Wilt just left and I hadn't pulled anything big out of the freezer before his unexpected visit?"

"Jason, that'll be fine. I'm very tired and not that hungry anyway. That will be fast and easy to prepare. By the way, I've been thinking about you all afternoon, even more than usual.

I'll be home in about an hour, sweetheart."

"Okay, Patty, I'll see you shortly." I could tell from her voice that she was rushed, but also that she was very happy I had called.

I hung up the telephone, went to the freezer, pulled out the franks and hot dog rolls, and set them on the counter.

I grabbed a can of beans from the cupboard, opened it, and poured the contents into an ovenproof dish. After quickly adding some brown sugar, I set them into our countertop oven to bake. I decided I had better boil the franks to defrost them a few minutes before grilling them, so I filled the pan, brought the water to a boil, and added the franks to it. While they were boiling, I set the table. I remembered we had some leftover coleslaw, which would go well with the dogs. When they were completely heated through, I put them on a plate, poured out the water, dried the pan with a paper towel, added butter to the pan, and placed the franks back in to brown. I decided I had better check on Ruben, so I lowered the heat on the stove and oven to ensure nothing would burn. Out at the dog run I filled Ruben's food and water dishes, then quickly swept the run and let Ruben out for some exercise. He returned in a few minutes and went directly for his food and water.

I was just about to enter the house when I looked over and saw the Jeep pull into the driveway. Patty pulled up close to the dog run. I hurried over to her to open her driver's side-door to help her out of the car because her added weight was making it difficult.

"Dearest, I'm so glad you're home," I said, happy to see my wife.

"Sherlock, I am, too. Today was a difficult one. We had a mishap at the diner today. I was carrying a tray containing a plate of hash with an egg on top when another customer backed his chair into me causing my tray to slip and the plate fell off the tray and landed on a customer's head. I was so embarrassed, Jason. Several regulars rushed over to help. One of the men grabbed a towel and helped me clean it all up, but to tell you the truth, it ruined my whole day." She blushed as she related her tale of woe to me. I felt so bad for Patty I couldn't tell her the humor I saw in the incident.

"Was it a local man?"

"No, he was just a stranger passing through Old Forge. To my surprise he didn't get angry. In fact, he told me not to worry, and simply went into the men's room to clean up. Lila came running around from behind the counter when she saw my dilemma. One of the kitchen help came with a broom and mop."

"I imagine there was plenty of excitement for a few minutes," I said, showing concern for her.

"Believe me, honey, there was, but surprisingly, everyone remained calm, except me. I went into the ladies room to cry," she said, with tears forming in her eyes as she relived the incident.

I pulled her to me to hold her close in my arms. I felt her body quiver as she started to sob. In my heart I felt that some of her emotional state was due to her being pregnant. I understood and felt compassion for my wife.

"Nothing like that has ever happened before, Jason. The man was such a gentleman. Before he left the diner he came over to me and asked if I was alright he told me not to worry, that he understood it was an accident."

"That was decent of him. Did you get his name?"

"Yes, I did. It's Clayton Miller. He works for a New York City real estate firm. He told me he had invested in property in the Lake Placid region, and that's where he was going. He was a kind person, Jason."

"Yes, that was nice of him. It tells me that this man has good character."

I could feel Patty's frustration as she unwound from this incident at the diner. I looked at her tenderly. "Just try to forget it, hon. No one was hurt and no one blames you. Now, are you hungry, dear?"

"I'm sure I can eat a little bit," she answered.

"That's good," I responded. "I've got everything about ready."

I turned up the burner, rolled the dogs to cook their other side, and checked the beans in the oven. While Patty went in to freshen up, I went to the refrigerator for the mustard, ketchup, pickle relish, and coleslaw. I placed them all on the table, then poured us each a glass of water. I called to Patty to let her know everything was just about ready. After fixing our plates at the counter, I put them on the table as my wife came out to seat herself. I joined her at the table to enjoy our meal. Though hastily prepared, the hot dogs tasted delicious, as usual, such an easy meal to prepare! During our dinner we discussed Wilt's visit and the enthusiasm he had displayed about the museum project.

With dinner over, Patty retired to the living room to put her feet up and knit. I cleared the table, did the dishes, and cleaned the kitchen. During the clean up I peeked into the living room and observed her working away.

I went outside to let Ruben run to the woods. He soon returned and followed me into the house, taking up his place on the air mattress. I settled on my recliner with a book that I had wanted to read. And Patty worked diligently on her pastel variegated-colored Afghan.

We decided to retire early, as we both needed our sleep. After we hugged and kissed, Patty turned over on her side and fell off to sleep. It had been a busy day for her, and stressful, too, with the unpleasant incident that she had experienced. I was glad she was able to fall asleep right away. My own eyelids grew heavy as I read, and soon I followed her into slumber land.

CHAPTER SEVEN

Over the next two weeks, Patty visited her doctor, again receiving another good report on her pregnancy. She was especially happy because the doctor had told her that he was pleased with the fact that she was keeping her weight gain within an acceptable level even though she was beginning to feel like a blimp.

There had been no further incidents of sliding plates at the diner to upset her. Clayton Miller even stopped by the diner again on his return trip to New York City, and Patty once again waited on him. Mr. Miller assured Patty that he had forgiven her, and quietly affirmed it: Patty was pleasantly surprised by the size of the gratuity by his plate after he left. Events in her life seemed to be moving along smoothly.

One May morning while Patty was working at the diner and I was home, the phone rang.

"Hello," I said calmly.

"Jason, Jack Doyle here!" His voice showed he was upset.

I was immediately alert. "Good morning, Lieutenant. What's the matter? You sound alarmed."

"Jason, no joke. I am alarmed. I received a telephone call from the Michigan State Police this morning. Bernard Draper somehow escaped from prison yesterday."

"What? He... he escaped!" I was shocked. For weeks I'd been living on the lookout, but I'd never expected this development.

"You heard me right. He escaped! There's an extensive manhunt going on as we speak, but so far there's no sign of him."

"Jack, what bad news! After what we went through to put that criminal away...."

"Believe it. He injured two correction officers and they're now in the hospital."

"How badly are they injured?" I asked grimly.

"One is critical. He might die. So far it appears that the other will be alright."

"I can understand why you are so upset."

"You're damned right I am. Apparently he worked in the laundry. When a truck delivered some freight of some kind, it is believed that he hid in an empty container in the trailer. The Illinois State Police checked the truck in Effingham, and all they found was a discarded prison shirt that he had been wearing. They have road blocks in several states, but so far, as I said, no sightings."

"Do you believe he's coming this way?" I asked. I could not help but focus on Patty's and my safety.

"Indeed, I do. Draper has a big mouth. We now know he told several inmates that he's going to be vindicated one way or another. I haven't spoken to Chief Wilson yet. I have a call in to him, but he's tied up on an investigation. His dispatcher is going to have him call me when he returns to his station."

"Lieutenant, you and I both know this means we will all have to go through stress and strain again. I can't believe it. I'm so very upset about it. There are so many injustices, Jack."

"You're right, you're right, there are. But Jason, we have to roll with the punches. You know from your military service days and the days you served in the troopers how things can happen."

"Yep, sure do." I knew I had to try to be philosophical.

"Now, keep in mind, that, even though he's a criminal, Draper's clever and still has many contacts across the country, made possible by his many payoffs to people for favors. He knows who you are, Jason, and he remembers that day he was apprehended south of Inlet. You and the chief have to keep your eyes open. The authorities surmised that he was able to get out of the trailer somewhere between the prison and Effingham. I'll personally keep you and the chief informed of any additional intelligence we should receive at Troop S," he said.

"Jack, I sure would appreciate any advance notice in the event Draper should be spotted here or any other region. What about the vehicle that is supposedly involved?" I asked.

"That may have been false information. We don't know yet. The investigator we sent to Michigan has mixed opinions about the vehicle. The escape from the prison was a complete surprise to the warden, according to the investigator. It was cleverly planned and Draper has disappeared. The investigator learned that Draper had several visitors during the past month. The authorities are checking all of them out."

"It's a damned good idea, Lieutenant. As you know Patty is expecting our child in about two months, and we really do not need this added pressure on us. If Draper comes around looking for trouble, believe me, he'll have his hands full. For the safety of my wife and child, I have to take precautions."

"Jason, I have confidence in your judgment. But don't take any chances. For your information, Mr. Draper still believes he is immune from the authorities in prison or outside prison. In other words, take his threats seriously," Jack said.

"Don't worry, Lieutenant. Patty and the baby always remain my top priority. I'll do anything to keep them safe and secure."

"I'll keep you posted. Don't hesitate to call the troopers and Chief Wilson if Draper shows up here in the Adirondacks. I'm certain that he is still enraged that we closed down his operation outside of Tupper Lake. He thought he was going to fool the public into thinking that his jewelry business was his only activity. We know, and so does the public now, that his intentions were to make money through his illicit activities of smuggling drugs into that area. Just be careful."

"Thanks for calling. I'll stay in touch. Say hello to your family. Oh, and congratulate Roy Garrison on his promotion to major."

"I certainly will. Roy was thinking about retirement, but when the promotion came through, he decided to stay."

"I heard that he had been planning to go to Alaska to invest in a fishing trawler. It's been a longtime dream of his."

"He already has, and will undoubtedly use it on vacation until he retires. Then the salmon had better watch out. He loves to fish and is desirous of becoming involved in a commercial venture with it."

"That's great! Take care, Jack."

"Be safe, Jason."

As I placed the receiver on the holder, memories returned to my mind of past days with the troopers on the shooting range to qualify alongside Jack and many of the now-retired men currently in pursuit of other activities to occupy the hours available. In the many complex cases we investigated together, developing leads was always a challenge; all we did was a continual learning experience.

Now, in my own retirement pursuing the private investigation business, I continually found that the training I had experienced was indeed beneficial to me. Society really didn't need the likes of Draper, allegedly bent on revenge toward those of us who were involved in his apprehension. I was determined to protect Patty, our expected child, and myself from his reckless behavior.

The telephone call from Doyle had upset me. My mind raced, trying to put the details in the proper perspective. If Draper or any of his cohorts came to our area, it wouldn't take long before the local troopers or town police would become aware of their arrival. They knew their territory well. If suspicious strangers registered at a local motel, bed and breakfast, or campground, word would soon be out regarding their arrival; all owners and managers had been advised to let the police know of any unusual tourists. Or if they decided to camp out in the forest, the rangers had also been alerted. Forest

Ranger Gary Leach would be on them like an eagle on his prey and would be able to pinpoint an exact location. Gary, a seasoned ranger with plenty of smarts and a thorough knowledge of his assigned district, was an expert in locating people, as evidenced by many a lost hunter or tourist who strayed from a trail in the deep woods.

Draper could possibly come into the region alone without any accomplices. Of course, there was always the distinct possibility of another disguise, like the blond wig he wore at the time of his previous apprehension. Draper apparently possessed a flair for theatrics. The blond wig was a good example, and who knew what else he could come up with? After reviewing these memories I dialed Chief Wilson's office. He answered promptly.

"Chief, Jason Black speaking," I began. "Did Lieutenant Doyle get in touch with you?"

"I just got off the phone with him, Jason. He filled me in on all the details regarding Draper. Apparently we're going to be blessed with him again. As you know, I have one permanent scar from that individual, and I do not intend to acquire another."

"I can't believe we have to deal with him again. He's trouble. We both know that he is slippery and has many contacts all over the country," I said.

"Jason, I don't want you to worry. I've already alerted all my people, and the lieutenant advised me that the local troopers have been advised of the news. From what I gather, Draper made his threats known to other inmates in prison. We cannot and will not disregard these threats. From what I gather, there haven't been any sightings of him as yet. We have been alerted to watch out for an Illinois-registered vehicle, but that may be incorrect. Nevertheless we'll be observing Route 28 very closely. We'll have to wait and see."

"I'll notify you and the troopers right away in the event that I should spot him."

"I'd appreciate it. Try not to worry Patty too much. She's a wonderful young lady, and we don't want to frighten her at this time."

"I appreciate your concern, Todd."

"The dispatcher just gave me an assignment, so I have to rush off. Talk with you later, Jason. Take care!"

"See you, Todd. You watch yourself," I cautioned him.

I let Ruben out for a run into the woods. He returned in a few minutes to dart into the dog run. I went through the house with the dust mop and then into my office to file some of the bad check cases that I had left on my desk. After completing the task I locked the house and went down to the post office. There were a few letters from Mountain Bank, some with bad checks and another with legal papers to be served.

I then stopped by Dr. Don's to determine when he'd be able to work on the Bronco. On my return home, I decided not to stop at the diner to see Patty. The parking lot was full with cars and pickups, so I concluded she might be rather busy. I continued past the diner and stopped by O'Brien's Marina to see if I could talk with Dale. I pulled into a parking space next to Jim Jenny's black Jeep Station Wagon. I got out of the Bronco and went inside. Evelyn came out of the office when she heard the door.

"Jason, it's been sometime since I've seen you. How's Patty doing?" she asked.

"She's doing great, Evelyn. How have you and Dale been?" I asked.

"We have been busy—ordering parts, preparing to take boats out of storage, and a multitude of other things," she replied. "There's a lot to do to get ready for the season."

I nodded sympathetically "I know. Would Dale be around?" I asked.

"Jason, Dale and Jim are out in the shop working on an inboard. Dale will be glad to see you."

"Thanks, Evelyn. We'll have to get together soon. We sure enjoyed our trip to Maine. It will always be in our memories."

"Yes, didn't we have a great time? Dale and I talk about it many times. You go ahead into the shop. I've got to return to the office. Lots of book work to catch up on," she said.

I could sense Evelyn was feeling a bit rushed. "Hope we'll be seeing you soon," I said understandingly, as I walked toward the shop door.

When I entered, I saw Dale and Jim Jenny bent over a large inboard engine. They looked up, surprised to see me.

"Jason Black, good grief, where in the heck have you been hiding? Are you trailing a suspect?" Dale asked jokingly.

"No, I'm not trailing any suspect at the moment, but I do have some important information to share with you both."

Dale caught the tone in my voice that showed I was serious. Concerned, he said, "It's good to see you, Jason. What's up?"

"You both remember the drug case I worked on with the troopers in the Tupper Lake area?"

"I certainly do. That was when the smuggler who was wearing a blond wig bit Chief Wilson," Jim responded. "I remember you assisted the chief in the apprehension near Inlet. Right?" He looked perplexed.

"That's correct. He was Bernard Draper, the target of the investigation. Well, sorry to say, he's escaped from the prison in Michigan where he was serving his sentence."

"No way!" Dale responded in disbelief.

I nodded solemnly. "I received a telephone call from Jack Doyle, my former associate at Troop S, this morning. Not only has Draper escaped, but he has made known to a couple of informants there that he's seeking revenge against anyone who had anything to do with his capture and arrest. I'm sharing this information with you to let you know to keep your eyes peeled for any suspicious strangers. I'll try to contact Wilt, Jack, Charlie, and Penny. They're pretty well connected to the community here in Old Forge as well as the Boonville area. I can count on them to be aware of any suspicious characters or happenings in the region," I said, stressing the importance of the situation.

"Have all the police in our community been given all this information?" Dale asked with concern.

"Yes, they've all been notified. Who knows what kind of

trick Draper may be capable of? He may have arranged for a hit man from anywhere. I'm truly concerned for Patty and our expected child. And who knows where I stand on his list?" I shook my head dejectedly.

"Listen, Jason: you have to know Jim and I will be on the watch for anything unusual. Try not to worry too much. You and Patty are a part of our lives—in fact, almost like family," Dale added.

Jim nodded his head in agreement.

"Jason, I'll call you if I observe or hear anything of importance."

"I'll appreciate that, Jim, and I know that Patty will, too." To shake loose the darkness of the moment, I asked, "Dale, I just have to ask you this: have you set the wedding day yet?"

"Well, we are still looking at June. And I'm still undecided over who is going to be best man because Jim's plans are still up in the air, and of course you've got the new baby on the way. Rest assured that you'll be receiving an invitation as soon as we set the date or I'll stop by and tell Patty at the diner."

"Okay, buddy. It's just that I've heard all different rumors about the date," I said, understanding that he and Jim had gotten very close due to working together so well.

Dale smiled and shrugged his shoulders. I knew how stories spread so quickly at the local diner.

I advised Dale and Jim to keep the information about Draper confidential, but again urged them to keep their eyes open for any suspicious activity or persons in the area. I thanked them both and left the shop. As I turned to close the door, they waved as they returned to continue their work on the inboard motor.

I was just about to pass the office door of the marina when Evelyn O'Brien came rushing out of the office and bumped into me.

"Oh, Jason! I'm sorry. I didn't see you coming," Evelyn apologized.

"No problem. It could have been worse, especially if you were carrying a hot pot of coffee for the men in the shop." I laughed to show her I understood.

"Good thing for both of us I wasn't," she quipped.

"No damage! We're both lucky!"

"I imagine you and Patty are becoming eager with the baby due soon. I understand that your nursery is beautiful."

"Yes, Wilt, Dale, and the other fellows did an outstanding job with the addition. We'll be forever in their debt," I acknowledged.

"That is what neighbors and friends are supposed to do. Help one another when it's necessary. Dale has always told me about the many people you have helped over the years."

"Oh, he has! Well, all I can say is that when I was a small child I can remember how my parents helped their neighbors and in turn they helped my parents."

"Yes, Jason, my parents lived that ideology themselves. I guess we were both fortunate to have the parents we did." She smiled. "Have a good afternoon now. Say hello to Patty for me." She continued to walk toward the shop.

"I will, Evelyn." It was good seeing her again.

I left the building to walk down the path to the Bronco. Glancing at my watch I noticed that it was well past lunch time. I decided I had better stop at the store to pick up some groceries. I made a quick trip and selected a few items that I remembered were getting low.

After leaving the store, I drove by the Town of Webb offices and observed Old Glory furling in the breeze. A lump caught in my throat as my memory raced back to Camp Pendleton where we, as proud marines, marched in step on the parade grounds. Patriotism flowed through my veins as I reflected back to my dad, who at seventeen boarded a troop ship in New York harbor in 1917 en route to fight the war to end all wars. It had proved to be a difficult time, although he survived, he unfortunately had been one of the many who had suffered exposure to the mustard gas the enemy used. The damage he had suffered to his lungs plagued him until the end of his life. As his son I watched him slowly die at an early age, his health diminishing every day of my young life.

Ruben was sitting by the entrance to his doghouse when I drove in next to the log home. His ears were pointed straight to the heavens and his tail was wagging non-stop as he eagerly welcomed my return. As soon as I exited the vehicle I strode over to the dog run and opened the gate. My faithful K-9 came to me to nudge against my pant leg, a sign of his devotion. I felt that he wanted to roughhouse, so I decided to let him out of the enclosure for a playful confrontation after I put the groceries away. Since his retirement from the troopers, Ruben had put on a few pounds. But he was still strong and definitely eager to win the match between the two of us. I also remembered that Russ, his dog handler from Saranac Lake, had told me that as he had trained him he had sensed that Ruben had a strong sense of competitiveness. He had certainly maintained his strength. After our skirmish I returned him to his dog run, making sure to fill his water and food dishes. I could hear the telephone ringing inside. I rushed in to answer it.

"Hello, Jason here."

"Sherlock, where have you been? Are you okay?" Patty asked, sounding a little upset. Evidently she hadn't been able to contact me at home.

"Fine, darling. After I picked up the mail I stopped at the marina to talk with Dale and Jim Jenny."

"How are they? I haven't seen them lately."

"They're busy getting the boats ready for the oncoming season. By the way, Evelyn sent her regards to you. What time will you be home? I thought I would make some salmon patties for supper. Is that alright?" I asked.

"That's super, sweetheart. I'll see you about five-thirty. I have to rush now, a customer."

"See you later, Patty."

I heard the click as she hung up the telephone. I walked into the bathroom and washed my hands. For some unknown reason I was tired this afternoon—*must be the workout with the dog,* I thought. Turning on the faucet in the bathroom, I cupped my hands, filled them with ice cold water, and splashed it in my face till I felt refreshed. It gave me a lift. Now I felt fully alert. How was Patty going to take the news when I told her of that call about Draper? Before I started to prepare our evening meal, I took a minute to check my .44 caliber revolver. It looked a little dusty, so I took a soft cloth to wipe it off. I put the gun away and returned to the bathroom to wash my hands again before I started to cook. I turned on the radio to listen to the news and music.

I opened the refrigerator door and took out a head of cabbage. I removed the outer leaves and cut the cabbage in quarters. It was nice and fresh as I finely shredded it with carrots into a large glass bowl. After mixing these ingredients in the bowl, I added mayonnaise, vinegar, sugar, and pepper, along with a little milk. When I finished the process, I took a forkful to check the taste. Delicious! I covered the coleslaw with a piece of plastic wrap and placed it in the refrigerator to cool.

I opened a can of salmon and carefully removed the skin and bones, then placed the contents into a glass bowl for mixing. I added two eggs, some chopped onion, dry mustard, pepper, dried bread crumbs, and the liquid from the can. After mixing all the ingredients thoroughly, I then shaped them into patties. I shook some bread crumbs onto a piece of plastic wrap, breaded the patties, placed them on a plate, covered them, and set them in the refrigerator until I was ready to fry them.

I washed three medium-sized potatoes, stabbed them with a fork, and placed them in the preheated oven. After cleaning up the kitchen and work area, I set the table.

Soon I heard Patty pull into the driveway. I went outside to meet her. Ruben was out of his doghouse waiting for Patty's hug. She went over to him inside the run and petted the big guy. Then she came out of the run to walk over to me, and fell into my arms. I gave her a welcoming hug, then I kissed her warmly.

"How was your day, sweetheart?" I asked tenderly.

"It went well, except I'm especially tired tonight, my love.

The baby did a lot of moving around today."

"Oh, honey. Maybe you should think of quitting to stay home. We'll make out somehow. I can always find some kind of work to supplement my investigative work and my pension."

"Jason, of course not. The doctor told me that I can work if I want to. I'm just tired tonight, that's all. I'll be alright after I rest a little. Honey, I want to work. I have about three months to go. It helps pass the time for me, and I can't let my customers down. Sherlock, don't worry so much, I'll be fine. What can I do to assist you with supper? Yum, I smell the baked potatoes."

"Patty, you just relax for a while. Go into the living room and sit in my lounge chair and close those beautiful eyes. I'll let you know when everything is ready." I went over to Patty and we embraced. She then disappeared into the living room.

The salmon patties looked great as I placed them on the large iron skillet that I had preheated and added a small amount of olive oil to cook them in. I prepared some tartar sauce and mixed the coleslaw, sprinkling some paprika on top for garnish. I then placed a small pitcher of warmed barbecue sauce on the table with a bowl of chunky applesauce. With everything ready, I lit our two beige candles and went into the living room to let Patty know that dinner was a minute or two from being served.

In her few minutes of rest she had almost fallen off to sleep.

"Is everything ready, darling?" she inquired groggily.

"All set, dearest," I answered with the greatest tenderness.

Patty roused herself and followed me into the kitchen. I seated her at the table. The shadows from the candles were doing their dance on the walls. I went over to the stove and fixed the plates, preparing Patty's first. I placed the patty on the plate next to the baked potato and served the coleslaw in a separate dish.

I prepared my own plate and said the blessing.

Patty smiled gratefully. "Jason, honey, the salmon patties

are so tasty. Did you add some special seasoning to them?"

"That's my secret, darling. All I can tell you is that I combined three seasonings," I teased. But I will share one bit of information with you: I added some dry mustard."

"You have me curious, sweetheart," she replied, one eyebrow raised.

"Someday I will share all my culinary secrets with you. I love you, Patty."

"I love you, too, Jason." Her face said it all.

We quietly finished our meal with a cup of decaf and my favorite oatmeal cookies. I knew that I still had to share the bad news I had received from Jack Doyle concerning Draper's escape and the escalation of the threats he had made from his prison cell. I decided to hold off until I cleaned up the kitchen and did the dishes.

"Patty," I offered, "if you'd like to take Ruben for a walk, I'll finish up here in the kitchen. Some fresh air will be good for you. Working in a diner all day doesn't give you a chance to breathe in the good Adirondack air."

"I'd love to take the big fellow for a walk to the woods. What a great idea, Jason."

"Better put on a jacket. It's supposed to cool down this evening. And be careful walking, sweetheart."

I helped her on with her denim jacket. We hugged and she went outside to the dog run. I watched through the window. It was obvious to me that Ruben was exultant to be walking with Patty. The K-9 heeled close to her as they headed toward the woods.

I snuffed out the flickering candles and quickly cleared the table then went over to the sink and prepared the dishwater. Our plates glistened after I rinsed them and placed them in the drainer. The heavy iron skillet almost slipped out of my hands when I went to hang it from the wooden peg next to the refrigerator.

I finished my chores just as Patty appeared at the door. She had placed Ruben back into his dog run and was just about to open the door when I held it open for her. I helped her remove her denim jacket. How was I going to tell her about Draper's escape?

We retired to the living room and sat down close to each other on the couch. It was time to share the grim news with her.

"Jason, please put some music on?" she asked.

I felt silenced. "Honey, I will. But first, can I tell you something? It's important."

"What is it, dear?" she inquired intently.

I had to tell her as gently as possible. I did not want to upset her. "This morning Jack Doyle called from headquarters. He told me Michigan authorities have reported that Bernard Draper has made an escape."

"Wha-what? He escaped from prison? Oh, no! No, I can't believe it!" she said, as tears began to appear in her eyes. "After all you did!"

"Don't cry, honey. I didn't want to frighten you." I offered.

"I can't help it, Jason. He's so dangerous. What's going to happen?" She visibly tried to control herself.

"Jack called everyone who had something to do with Draper's apprehension. He knew we should be aware of it. Draper's threats involve all of us. Sweetheart, now we have to be alert, extra careful in our day-to-day activities—at least, until he's captured."

I looked at my wonderful wife. Tears rolled down her cheeks and then she began to sob. I put my arms around her shoulders and brought her close to me, comforting her as best as I could. I'd known she would react this way.

"Jason, what should we do? He knows who we both are, and it won't take him long to find out where we live and where I work. What if he finds us?"

I held her even more tightly. "I know, honey. Chief Wilson and his men are aware of the threat, and the local troopers are already keeping a watchful eye out for him. Doyle has pressed his people into service and the uniformed force of the entire Troop S territory has been alerted. Doyle will have undercover officers peering into all the beer joints and restaurants for signs of Draper or his cohorts." I hesitated, then added, "My own fear is that Draper might disguise himself again in some fashion and sneak unnoticed into the Tupper Lake area."

Patty pulled back in surprise. "Why do you think that, Jason?"

"Oh, it's just a hunch I have. That's where he invested his money, started a business, and even purchased a home. Yeah, all his properties were seized and have been auctioned off, but I think I know this character. He's sweet on revenge, and I feel that Tupper Lake is where he'll eventually make an appearance. Like I say, it's just a hunch. We can't let our guard down here for a minute. Keep in mind, Patty, Draper made some friends, seemingly buying loyalty with his southwestern jewelry. But the Adirondackers are smart and shrewd people; any who get wind of his presence in their area will notify the troopers. Yet a few people whom Draper influenced would hide him for money if he asked them."

"You really think they would, Jason?" Patty asked in trepidation.

"Sweetheart, I hate to say it, but I think they would. But remember, Patty, we can't let Draper take over all our thoughts. Just be careful around town and be vigilant at the diner. I shared the information with Dale and Jim. Not only will they be watching here in the Old Forge area, but Wilt, Jack, and Charlie will be on alert as soon as I let them know about it."

"I'm so glad that you've told Dale and Jim. They know everything that's going on in town. I'll try not to worry, Jason." Patty smiled with determination.

"My darling, I want so much to protect you from stress. Be assured that if Draper shows up in Tupper Lake, I'll be going there to do some snooping myself."

"Why not let the troopers handle that?" Patty's face showed concern.

"Oh, they'll take care of Draper. My purpose in going there is personal. Jack Doyle told me confidentially that Draper wants to get even with me for punching him when he was biting the chief's arm during their altercation at Eagle Bay. Patty, for myself, I want to see him eyeball to eyeball."

I saw my beloved's eyes begin to tear. "Oh, please be careful, Jason. Remember, Sherlock, you're dealing with a very dangerous man."

"I know sweetheart," I responded, understanding her concern. "But you know me. I won't accept threats."

It was important to me that I had shared Jack's phone call with her. We both knew we needed to change the subject, so we listened to some relaxing music. Patty knitted until we went to bed. I rechecked the doors and petted Ruben before I went into the bedroom. The loaded .44 Caliber revolver was close by. Somehow we finally fell off to sleep.

CHAPTER EIGHT

The bulldozer was sending puffs of black smoke out of its exhaust pipe as it headed toward the lake. No one was at the controls. I heard a bell off in the distance. As I gathered my senses I realized the alarm clock was going off. I reached over Patty to push the alarm button down and stopped the ringing.

Patty turned to me and we hugged for a few minutes. I felt our child between us. She pushed the covers back and carefully got out of bed. As she went into the bathroom for her shower, I walked to the kitchen and let Ruben outside. He took off for the woods. A chippie on the porch froze in place as the big K-9 passed without seeing him. The chippie then darted up the tree next to the log home. That was one good chase Ruben missed. I went to the stove, turned the burner on, filled the teakettle, and placed it over the burner.

When Patty came out of the bathroom I said, "Honey, I had the strangest dream: a bulldozer was headed to the lake with no one at the controls. What does that signify?"

My wife look perplexed. "Jason, I don't know. But I'd better get dressed. It's getting late and I have to open the diner this morning." She untied her bathrobe. I could see her still shaking her head over my description of the dream of the runaway bulldozer.

While Patty was dressing I went into the bathroom to take a fast shower. I turned the lever on the shower to cold, and the water felt refreshing. Quickly drying off, I donned my robe and went into the bedroom to dress. Patty returned to the bathroom to pull her long flowing blond hair back neatly into a bun. I dressed hurriedly and put on a green jacket.

Outside, a breeze had come up and the tree tops were swaying back and forth. Ruben had gone into his dog run and was sitting by the entrance to his house. I proceeded to unlock the Jeep and climb in. After I placed the key in the ignition and started it, I got back out as it idled. Patty came out of the log home with a couple of letters for me to mail. I walked over to the driver's side door and we embraced. I didn't want to smear her lipstick, so I leaned down and kissed her on the forehead.

"Honey, have a great day," I told her from my heart, "Be very careful and keep your eye open for any strangers or anything suspicious at the diner. Do not mention Draper to anyone. Our friends already know about the escape and are keeping a watchful lookout for any activity out of the ordinary. I'll drive to Tupper Lake and look around the area. Before I go I'll call the chief. Be careful, my darling."

"I will. Don't worry, Jason. I'll be cautious. You be careful driving to Tupper Lake." She looked back at me as she climbed into the Jeep.

"Yes, dear, I'll be careful. Understand, I may be late getting back," I said to my beloved wife as she closed the door.

I watched Patty back the Jeep up and turn toward Route 28. I couldn't help but remember that fateful night when she left my house after we enjoyed a romantic dinner and never made it to her home. Memory of her kidnapping haunted me. Patty had been lucky to survive the harrowing experience, and her survival had changed my life.

Inside the log home I hurriedly made our bed and placed fresh towels and washcloths on the bathroom towel racks. I decided to postpone breakfast until I could stop at Gertie's Diner in Long Lake. I finished straightening up the kitchen, then hastily ran the vacuum cleaner before I went in to the office to call the chief.

"Town of Webb Police Department, Chief Wilson

speaking." The voice was that of authority.

"Good morning, Chief. Jason Black here. Can you talk for a minute, Todd?"

"Certainly, Jason, you are just the person I wanted to speak to. I'm certain you've heard about Draper's flight from the prison in Michigan." His voice sounded concerned.

"Yes, Chief, Lieutenant Doyle notified me. He told me that Draper has made certain threats against anyone who was involved in his arrest and the downfall of his jewelry business west of Childwold, just off Route 3 on Route 56."

"That is my concern, Jason. We should remain vigilant in our travels and everyday routine. I know from personal experience just how desperate he can be. My arm is scarred for life because of his fierce temperament. It is a damned good thing that you were there that day, Jason. I could have been hurt even more seriously."

"I realize that, and I agree with you, Todd. All of us have to be on constant alert. Have you any further information or sightings concerning a reddish colored car bearing Illinois plates?" I asked.

"That could be just a rumor. We'll be keeping a lookout for that Illinois plate or any other vehicle that could be coming into the area. We don't see too many of those plates here in the North Country at this time of the year. But if my memory serves me correctly, I believe Lieutenant Doyle indicated to me that the car with Illinois plates could have been false information." He sighed, then added, "It boils down to this, Jason: Draper is very creative, and if his resolve is to avenge his apprehension and arrest near Eagle Bay, he'll do something or at least try something to fulfill his agenda."

"Todd, before we hang up, I'd like to ask you a question about the confidentiality of the Draper matter. Doyle had advised me not to say anything about it to anyone. But now that he has escaped, there are many contacts I know of who are very much aware of strangers who come into town for no apparent reason, not for hunting or fishing, for example. I'd like to mention it to a few people if you'd feel that it would be all right."

He paused for a moment before he replied. "I can't see why that wouldn't be a good idea now that he's actually escaped."

"That's a relief to hear, because I've already mentioned it to a few close friends." I was glad to know that he sanctioned it. "Thanks for calling. I'd better be going now, Todd. I'm driving to Tupper Lake area this morning just to look around and check out the new loggers' museum that is being built there. I'm kind of eager to see how it's progressing. It was a dream of my friend, Tom Huston, and Wilt is quite involved in this project," I explained.

"Yes, Jason, Wilt mentioned something to me about that a few days ago. Guess he heads up a committee regarding the project. That man certainly keeps busy. He's a very ambitious guy."

"That he is, Todd. Well, Chief, I'll talk with you later."

"Be careful, Jason. Remember, you're going to be a daddy in a few months."

"I'll be careful."

After my conversation with Todd, I secured the log house and checked on Ruben. He had sufficient food and water. I let him out for a fast run into the woods. He returned and I put him in the run after petting him and rubbing his strong back.

When I pulled onto Route 28 heading north toward Eagle Bay, I saw a large log truck bearing down on me from the north. When it neared I heard the loud air horns. The sound penetrated the crisp air of this May morning. The logger blinked his lights and I waved at him. Charlie Perkins must have driven most of the night down from northern Vermont. He was pushing his log truck right along, probably eager to return home to his lovely wife and kids. Charlie and his family were very close and depicted a wholesome example of what North Country living was all about. Not only did Charlie and his wife set the example for their growing children, but the kids themselves were properly trained and each of them had independent chores to perform. When Sunday came around they would all be seen in church. After the services they'd go to Charlie's Bistro for brunch. I was proud to call Charlie Perkins one of my friends. I knew I was fortunate to have developed a group of friends who were always there to offer assistance in a time of a fellow neighbor's need. It was these friends who had worked tirelessly on the new addition to our log home. Patty and I continued to appreciate their efforts so very much.

It was about ten when I pulled into Long Lake. The breakfast crowd at Gertie's had already dispersed. The diner was empty, except for Gertie and the waitress, whom I didn't recognize.

"Good morning, Gertie. Where's everybody?" I asked, looking around for Bob, her husband.

"Jason, it's good to see you. We were really busy earlier, but you know they're early risers around here. How is Patty, Jason?" she inquired as she wiped off the counter.

"Patty is doing fine. She's still working. Her doctor's visits have been very good. The pregnancy is normal, with no problems, so far. By the way, Gertie, where's Bob?" To my disappointment I seldom found Bob at the diner.

"He drove to Saranac Lake this morning on business. He left just about an hour ago. Have you had your breakfast this morning?" she asked, smiling.

"No, that's why I stopped, Gertie."

"What would you like today?"

I could see that the waitress was busy cleaning some of the front windows, so I decided to sit at the counter, which also better enabled me to converse with Gertie.

"A cup of coffee, scramble me two eggs with sausage, and Texas toast. You might start me off with a medium-sized glass of orange juice."

"It's coming right up. I know just exactly how you like your eggs."

While Gertie was preparing my breakfast I went to the rest room to wash my hands. When I returned to the counter I noticed that a couple had come in and taken a table near the window. The waitress was already taking their order.

Gertie brought over one of her special platters. I could tell that she must have scrambled three eggs by the portion. There were two large sausage patties and two slices of Texas toast on the side.

"Boy, that sure looks great, Gertie!" I placed my napkin on my lap.

"I hope you enjoy your breakfast, Jason. You look as though you've lost some weight."

The petite waitress gave me a pleasant smile as she delivered the couple's order to their table.

Gertie called over to me, "Good thing you ordered coffee today, as I'm out of green tea,"

"No problem. I drink green tea at home, but I'm beginning to drink coffee when I'm on the road. Guess it's good for you, too."

"That's what some of the medical journals seem to be saying, according to my doctor. I guess it's a matter of quantity."

"Gertie, I believe some of the things in the environment such as chemicals in the water, additives and preservatives in some of our foods, and pesticides on the crops all add to the medical problems we face today. I observe shoppers checking the ingredients in the products they purchase to see what they contain. When I'm grocery shopping I notice it more and more. I don't do it myself, as Patty does most of the grocery shopping. And I'm certain there are other factors, too. Old in-ground gas tanks that leak into the ground and eventually into wells and other water sources all play a part as well."

"I think you're right, Jason," she said, nodding her head.

"I've smelled the raw gas go into our precious lakes right here in the mountains from many of the older boats—sometimes from some of the newer ones, too—as they go by. I fully understand why the residents on some lakes ban the use of motorized watercraft on them in order to keep their water clean. I've heard other people complain about fuel smells. I can't swear to any of these facts as being gospel, but *something* causes cancer clusters in so many areas."

"Yes, perhaps there is some truth to possible fuel leakages into lakes."

I decided to change the subject. "Gertie, my breakfast is wonderful. The sausage is just the way I like it. It'll help me make my trip. I'm headed to Tupper Lake. Confidentially, Gertie, I've some frightening news."

"What kind of news, Jason?" Gertie's eyebrows lifted as she looked directly into my eyes.

"You remember the jewelry store case involving Bernard Draper."

"Indeed I do! It was the talk of the Adirondacks, especially in this area. What's up, Jason? It happened right around here."

"Gertie, he's escaped from prison in Michigan. He's a very dangerous person and is bent on revenge to anyone who had anything to do with his apprehension and arrest. I'd like you and Bob to keep your eyes open for any strange characters who may come in here. And, Gertie, I want you and Bob to always be careful, especially closing up at night."

"We are always very cautious anyway, Jason, especially in this day and age. You can't be too trusting, you know."

"Our Adirondackers are smart and shrewd, but this Draper plays all the angles. He can really assert his charm, but underneath that façade is a calculating crook." I paused. "Well, I must be going before it gets any later. You undoubtedly have heard of the museum that Tom Huston from Lake Placid is creating?"

"Yes, your friend Wilt Chambers stopped by about a week ago and was telling a group of us about it. I'm glad to see it happen. It will give our loggers a true place in the history of our region. Wilt's certainly a wonderful person. He was here for an hour."

"Yes, Gertie, Wilt is one of a kind. He's in charge of the museum committee for Tom Huston." I stood up to pay my bill. "Well, that's it. Have to go, Gertie."

"Take care, Jason."

"Say hello to Bob."

"I will. Tell Patty I'm thinking of her."

I nodded to Gertie and the new waitress and left the diner.

I climbed into the Bronco and headed for Tupper Lake. When I turned the radio station to Boonville I was surprised to pick up George Capron's show. As I proceeded north, the radio cut out on me. The mountains evidently interfered. I drove into Tupper Lake, once a thriving lumbering community, and onto Route 3, then headed west past Raquette Pond and Piercefield, where the road cuts off toward Conifer.

I wasn't surprised when I observed Wilt Chambers' big Dodge pickup parked in front of the loggers' museum. I pulled into the parking area and stopped next to Wilt's truck. I got out and made my way to the museum's main door. The rustic buildings made me feel that I had just caught a ride on a time machine back to the period when logging in the area was a flourishing industry. Wilt's formidable knowledge of the historical logging era had been passed down to him from his father and his grandfather and then augmented by his own hours of research in libraries. It was wonderful that Tom Huston, as creator of this museum, could provide Wilt with the financial support needed to bring the project to fruition.

As I drove through the area, memories returned of how these quiet communities were once busily filled with hotels and restaurants that catered to the many people who earned a living at the local mills and lumber yards. With them now closed, the region had taken on an aura of a ghost town, compared to the once thriving bustle of people.

When I entered the low one-story structure I found Wilt busying himself in putting up pipe to a potbelly stove at one end of the building. On the way to meet him I observed many antiquated saws, axes, and numerous tools used in the harvesting of timber. I also saw a display of clothes that the loggers probably wore years ago, along with tables, chairs, pots and pans, bedding, and other articles that depicted the life of the lumberjack.

"Wilt, you've certainly put together a very interesting assortment of things for the museum. I'm truly impressed," I congratulated him.

"Jason! Good to see you. Glad you like them. You would have made a good lumberjack if you'd been born in those years before industrialization got such a foothold in our country."

"Oh, you really think so, do you?" I said with a smile.

"Yeah, I do. You'd like to work ten or twelve hours a day in the woods to get plenty of exercise," he replied, flexing his arm.

"That's why you're in such good shape, Wilt." I reached over to feel his bicep.

"With the machinery they have today, the men and women in the industry of lumbering do not get the exercise the old-time loggers did. However, you and I both know that the folks who participate in exhibitions today are in good physical condition. They have to be in order to compete. The annual Woodsman Field Days held at Boonville is a fine example of their stamina and ability."

"That's true." I changed my tone to a more serious one. "Wilt, by the way, did Dale get in touch with you?"

Wilt's face darkened. "Yes, he did. Why do you think I've got my semi-automatic 12-gauge in the Dodge? If I catch that Arizona polecat around here, he'll be in for a real challenge." Wilt's mouth turned downward. "Jason, I'm serious. You and Patty are family to me, and with the new baby on the way, the two of you need to be free from this added stress."

"I know, I know, Wilt. But, remember, if you should catch a glimpse of Draper, contact the authorities immediately. I personally believe that in some way he'll try to disguise himself again. You can expect anything from him. He's a clever person with a truly dark side. I'm glad that Dale contacted you. As a precaution I'm still going to carry a weapon with me until Draper is apprehended."

"I think that's a good idea under the circumstances."

I turned to a more positive subject. "Wilt, I certainly want to commend you for helping Tom Huston get this loggers' museum off the ground. I know that Tom thinks a great deal of you and has a lot of confidence in your knowledge of the timber industry. From what I have observed in the few minutes

I've been here, I'm thoroughly impressed. I even like the idea of the gift shop with all the products associated with logging. The t-shirts depicting logger events, and all the stuffed animals of black bears and moose should go well with the children who will be visiting here with their parents. I particularly like the toy trucks and lumber trucks. They'll be a real popular item—and probably not just for kids!"

"You know, Jason, we've worked really hard on trying to recreate the setting of an old logging camp with the kitchen, sleeping quarters, and the building to store the tools. If some of the old-time loggers could come here and visit, they would, I assure you, feel right at home."

"Has Charlie Perkins been in to see what you have accomplished?"

"Sure has. Charlie has helped out on the committee and he has furnished samples of some of the equipment still used in the woods today. We want it to be as authentic as possible. Present generations know what the bulldozers, skidders, and chain saws are. We want the old story to be told through viewing of the antiques."

"I will say one thing: I'm convinced. It was like traveling back in time when I came through the front door."

"That's it, Jason. That's what we want."

I could see he was pleased with my reaction. "Say, how about a cup of coffee?" he offered.

"Sounds good to me, Wilt"

We sat down at one of the tables located near the gift shop. Wilt had made a pot of coffee and had some pastries on hand in the event some of his committee members stopped by. His enthusiasm seemed to grow as we continued to discuss the museum. He produced a large journal that contained a guide schedule to be used by the staff in greeting the public when the museum was officially opened. It was well thought out. Wilt told me that the majority of the workers would consist of volunteers until the establishment could support paid help.

Several administrative positions would be salaried from the funds generated by the admittance fee. It was almost amusing to hear Wilt as he explained the workings of the organization. He explained that the gift shop had been organized by Irene, Jack Falsey's wife, who had so generously volunteered to help them until they were able to hire someone with sufficient knowledge to manage it. Because of her past experience in the business, Wilt had requested her assistance, but because of the distance from Old Forge, she definitely could not continue on a permanent basis, as much as she would like to. He informed me that it was going to be open on a weekend schedule for a while until interest in it was determined. Wilt was certain the new museum would be an important part of the historical and the economic origin of this part of the country.

I shared with him some of the observations I had made a few years before at Newport, Oregon, where thousands of logs were placed in the waters. I was told by a native of the area that the logs were being sold to the Japanese, who after a period of time would process the logs into lumber on their ships sitting off the coast and resell the lumber back to the United States. I had no idea as to the validity of the statement because it sounded so incredulous. Wilt winced as I related the story to him.

"Thank you, Wilt. You certainly have an excellent grasp of the project," I complimented him.

"Has Tom Huston decided on an official name for the museum yet?" I asked out of curiosity.

"Yes, Jason, he has. It will simply be called pretty much what we've all been calling it already—the Loggers' Museum. How do you like that?" He looked over to see my reaction.

"Great! It will get a lot of attention when the tourists come. Is it going to be seasonal?" I asked.

"We're hoping to have it open from April 15th till October 15th each year—but, of course, that plan could change. Eventually we'd like to have a log drive and some log rolling contests and other exhibitions, like the climbing of the greased poles—they're always a crowd-pleaser."

"That's a fantastic idea, Wilt. I'm certain that the museum will draw a lot of tourists. They're always looking for something new to do." I nodded. "Well, I'd better think about moving on. Please be sure to keep your eyes open regarding Draper. As I mentioned, he's bent on some kind of revenge. Remember: he's dangerous."

"I will, Jason. You can be certain of that. And I'll bet you didn't drive up just to see the museum, did you?" he inquired.

"No, I'm going to Star Lake to see a former marine buddy, Luther Johnson, who knows this Adirondack Park better than anyone except maybe retired forest ranger Gary Leach. I trust Luther like I trust you, Wilt. I want to share some information with him."

"I didn't mean to pry, Jason."

"That's alright, Wilt. I was going to tell you anyways. Talk with you later."

"Tell Patty to take care."

"I will, buddy. You take care of yourself."

I left the museum and walked to the Bronco. Traffic on Route 3 was light. When I reached Childwold I stopped by the leather shop to look at some purses thinking of a gift for my wife. The owner manufactures them from scratch, cutting the leather to patterns and then sewing them on his machine to arrive at his finished product. There were all shapes and sizes on display. I eyed one or two in particular that I liked. Not sure of the size or color Patty might want, I told him I would contact him at a later date. I thanked him as I departed.

It was approximately 2:15 p.m. when I pulled up near Luther Johnson's modest one-story home. It was situated just outside of Star Lake. It was always neat as a pin: Luther's marine corps training was still intact. He was sitting on the porch in his oak rocking chair on this mild May afternoon.

I turned off the ignition, then climbed out of the Bronco.

"Hello, Jason Black. Where have you been?" he inquired with a wide grin. The big man appeared to be in good condition, but he seemed to be moving a little more slowly. He rose from his rocker to come over and greet me.

"I've been busy, Luther," I answered.

"Come on up here and sit a while," Luther said as he pulled

out another chair.

"Sure, why not! How have you been?"

"Good. Could use a little more detective work. It's been a little slow in that department. But it's been slow all over. Jason, this used to be a busy place, but not anymore. All the jobs seem to be disappearing. It's slim pickings around here."

"I know, I know. It truly looks that way." I decided to bring up the reason I had come. "How's your memory, Luther?"

"Like a sprung bear trap, detective! Why do you ask?"

"You remember the name Draper?"

"How could I forget that name? It was plastered all over the papers a couple of years ago! He's in prison, isn't he?"

"He was, but now he's escaped and on the run," I explained.

"That son-of-dead crow! How'd that happen?" Luther expressed his shock at the news.

"I don't know all the facts yet, but he's a clever one."

"I know he is. I met him once or twice when he was over here in Star Lake trying to push that southwest jewelry junk. He had his man with him, the one I told you about at the time. Remember?"

"I sure do. Well, according to the lieutenant at Troop S, Draper has made some powerful threats against anyone who may have had something to do with his apprehension and arrest."

Luther frowned deeply. "You don't say, Jason. Yes, he could be dangerous. I didn't like his face when I saw him down in Star Lake. He acted like a real big shot. You know the type—the kind that push their weight around without any feeling for anyone who may stand in their way."

"Yes, sir, I know the type. That's why I'm here to see you: I know that you know what happens in this region, even sometimes before it happens."

My comment made Luther smile a bit. "I don't know about that, Jason, but the news seems to find my ears sometimes."

"Keep those ears open. My wife is expecting, and I'm concerned for her safety as well as my own—and all concerned, for that matter."

"I will, I will Jason. You can count on it. Don't worry so much. If that bird shows up here, I'll hear about it."

"Keep in mind he may be in a disguise of some fashion. Right now, I have no idea what he may be up to. He may be traveling with someone, or alone. I personally believe he will come to the Tupper Lake area. It's just a hunch. Sometimes my sixth sense kicks in. Not certain, though. There's no telling what scheme he might attempt to use."

"Listen, Jason, if he shows up in these parts we'll know, even if he is in disguise."

"Everyone involved in this case will be appreciative to you if you can possibly come up with any information," I assured Luther.

"Well to change the subject, Jason, how is your wife doing? You know we have folks here in Star Lake who have eaten at John's Diner and they all speak highly of your Patty."

"That's wonderful to hear, Luther. Believe me, I am a lucky fellow."

"When is she expecting?"

"In about three months if everything goes as predicted."

"I'm happy for you folks."

"Yes, we've been most fortunate. Not only have we been able to survive here in the Adirondacks, but we've been blessed with great friends. Time and time again they have shown their support in many different ways."

"Jason, I remember only too well what your dear wife went through when she was abducted in Old Forge. You've both been through a time of uncertainty, but it seems that you're on a good path for happiness, especially with Patty expecting a child."

"Luther, I agree. And now I'd better be on my way, as it's getting to be late and it is a ways back to Old Forge."

"Have a safe trip and try not to worry. If this Draper shows his face around these parts, I'll contact you immediately," he assured me.

"Appreciate it very much. Take care, Luther, and my best

to your family."

"So long, Jason." Luther stood up from his porch rocker to shake hands. The old marine still had a firm grip.

He waved as I backed out of his driveway. I turned east on Route 3 towards Cranberry Lake. Driving past the motel there flooded my mind with memories of days gone by when I did some relief duty at the Star Lake patrol station. There had been one unforgettable weekend when six of my Syracuse buddies and I had hunted in the region. We had stayed at the Newton Falls Hotel, a popular retreat. On the Saturday night as the sun sank over the mountains in the west, one member of our hunting party failed to come out of the woods. Charlie was a rugged individual, in his mid-twenties at the time. He wasn't the type of person who would panic if he found himself turned around in the woods. So we were concerned, but not overly worried. Darkness set in as we six continued to wait in the area where Charlie had last been seen. Suddenly we heard three shots evenly spaced. We realized that it must be Charlie firing his 30.06 rifle. One of our group responded with one shot to acknowledge his retort. All was quiet until we heard a voice off in the distance: "Hey, fellas, where are ya?" We all shouted mixed responses to acknowledge Charlie's call for help. "Over here, over here, Charlie!" we called, hoping he would be able to make his way back. We kept yelling and Charlie continued to respond. His voice kept getting louder, and in about fifteen minutes he finally stumbled out of the woods to where we were all waiting. One of our party turned on his flashlight to find our friend pale and exhausted, but unhurt.

Charlie thanked us all for being there for him. Then he said something like "I'm hungry, guys. Let's go eat." It was only one of many fine memories of a time long ago.

I stopped in Tupper Lake to gas up. Traffic on the drive into Long Lake was light, as was usual for this time of the year. I pulled into Hoss's for some of their strong cheese. The clerk sliced off almost two pounds and wrapped it up. Patty and I loved the macaroni and cheese she made from this flavorful treat. It really enhanced the flavor.

Ruben was not in his run when I pulled into the yard. As I looked around I spied Patty and him coming up the slight hill toward our log home. I pulled in next to her Jeep, turned off the ignition, and sat in the vehicle to observe them. Ruben was heeling just to the rear of Patty's side. She had a way with the big K-9. When she gave a command, either by voice or hand signal, Ruben obeyed without hesitation. I could visualize what action he would take if anyone tried to hurt or harm her in any way. Ruben's sense of responsibility was uncanny. He would always be there for us. I was sure of that.

Patty walked slowly as she came toward the vehicle. I got out to greet her. We hugged as we warmly gave each other a kiss. After putting Ruben in his run, we headed into the house.

"How was your day, my darling?" she asked.

"It was rather productive. I stopped at the new loggers' museum and spoke with Wilt for a while, then drove over to Star Lake to see Luther. You remember him. He was one of my informants during my trooper days."

"Yes, I do. And how is Wilt anyway?" she inquired. "It feels like I haven't seen him in quite a while."

"He's good, but very busy putting the finishing touches on the museum. You know how Wilt is. Things have to be right. By the way, I stopped at Hoss's on the way home."

"Did you pick up some of their delicious cheese, honey?" she asked.

"Yes, I did, sweetheart. I know how much we enjoy it. It's a popular cheese, just the right flavor."

"You're a dear. What would you like for dinner?"

"I'm sorry, but I never thought of pulling anything out of the freezer before I left this morning," I said apologetically. "What do you think? Any ideas?"

"Well, since you were so farsighted and stopped at Hoss's, I'll make macaroni and cheese. How does that sound to you? It won't take long if I just don't bake it."

"Great idea!"

"I'll take care of the cheese sauce and the noodles, and you can cut up a salad and set the table." So saying, she opened the cupboard, filled a pan of water, set it on the stove to boil the macaroni, then took out another for the cream sauce. She removed the butter and milk from the refrigerator and set them on the counter.

I went into the bathroom to wash my hands before I started my KP detail. When I returned to the kitchen, I took the ingredients for the salad to the other end of the counter to cut up for individual plates. After slicing the tomatoes, cucumbers, and green pepper for the top, I returned everything to the refrigerator, then went on to set the table. I looked over as Patty poured the elbows into boiling water.

She measured flour into the melted butter in the large pan and stirred it until it was smooth enough for the milk to be added. After stirring it frequently until it had thickened into the desired consistency, she added the cheese she had already chunked up so it would melt thoroughly. She also quickly made a batch of biscuits from the mix in the cupboard, dropping them onto the baking pan and setting them into our preheated countertop oven to bake. After the noodles had melded with the flavor of the sauce and the biscuits had baked, we sat down to enjoy our quickly prepared meal.

After the main course, we each sipped on a cup of decaf and talked as we usually enjoyed doing. This time our conversation had a dark note. We discussed the possibility of Draper trying to carry out the threats he had made in prison and our concern about his recent escape. I tried to soothe Patty's anxiety and assured her that Jack Doyle was monitoring the situation closely, taking all kinds of precautions to ensure our safety.

CHAPTER NINE

Unbeknown to Patty and Jason, the escapee, Bernard Draper, accompanied by a freckled woman, who was in her late forties, with flaming red hair, was checking into a small motel located in northern Ohio near the Pennsylvania state line. Draper, who had disguised himself as a bent-over elderly man, gave the impression that it was hard for him to walk. He was clothed in a brown leather jacket, tan trousers, and a light beige-colored shirt, and he wore horn-rimmed eyeglasses with tinted lenses, and a green wool cap on his head. Draper carried a bone-handled cane in his right hand. He accompanied the woman into the motel reception area.

The woman, wearing a dark brown pant suit under a three-quarter-length oyster-colored leather coat, clutched Draper's left arm as they made their way to the counter. To an outside observer the two appeared to be a father and daughter just stopping for the night. They stood at the counter. The redhead hit the plunger on the bell to summon a hotel clerk. It was a minute or two before a bespectacled female clerk appeared.

"Good afternoon, folks. May I be of assistance?" she asked, looking over the top of her glasses.

"My father and I would like a room with two beds for the evening, ma'am. We have been traveling all day and my dad is tired," she said, glancing over at Draper, who had his head down and was staring at the floor.

"Here is a registration card. Please fill it out. Will it be

126

cash or charge?" the clerk asked cordially.

The redhead took the pen in her left hand and printed her name as Mildred Nichols. She put down an address of 3231 67th Avenue, Bradenton, Florida.

"I'll be paying with cash. Do you want my father's name?"

"No, that's not necessary. Here's your room key, 106. You can park right in front. Just turn left when you leave the office," instructed the clerk. "The rate is sixty dollars plus tax."

Draper's companion paid with a hundred-dollar bill. "Thanks," she said as the clerk handed her the change.

"Father, we must go to our room now," she said to the man holding the cane. She walked over and took his arm as if to assist him. With his gaze still down he took short steps toward the door. Hilda—the woman's actual name—was grasping onto his right arm as they quietly left the office. The clerk watched them leave, then placed the hundred-dollar bill in the cash drawer.

Unknown to the desk clerk, the redheaded "Mildred" had given a phony name and address on the registration card. How could the clerk imagine that the man posing as her father was Draper, escaped from a Michigan prison? Or that prior to his divorce, he had once had it all: a lovely wife, a beautiful home, and a prominent position in the Phoenix community? His greed had overcome him, and it had led to murder, smuggling, and a slew of other crimes against both federal and state laws. As the owner of the Over-The-Road-Freightways he had formerly been on the road to success, but his uncontrolled appetite for money became an obsession. Now on the run with the help of his lover, he was embittered by the loss of all his worldly possessions. Now his obsession was revenge.

Bernard Draper followed Hilda into the motel room. He immediately threw his cap onto the bed and placed the cane in the corner near the antiquated television set. He took off his coat and straightened up. He appeared fifteen years younger than the elderly man he had portrayed when he had entered the office. Hilda went back outside to her Mustang to bring in a small suitcase and a leather bag. When she re-entered she set both in a corner of the room.

Draper and Hilda embraced. He kissed her neck and then their lips met. She tore at his shirt and unbuttoned it. The rages of delayed passion took over. An escaped convict and his redhead in a small hotel off the beaten path of the Ohio highway system found solace in each others' arms. As they lay together afterward on the bed, Draper spoke. "Hilda, we've got to be careful. By now every police agency in the United States has been alerted about my escape and will be on the lookout for me."

"Bernie, don't worry. We'll be careful. We've got to be!" she responded.

"Do you still have that cold fried chicken in the Mustang? I'm hungry."

"I'll go out and get it for you, Bernie. Oh, I love you, Bernie!"

"Ditto, babe!"

Hilda remembered the night at the Cactus Café when she and Bernie had been at the bar. She had recognized the former homicide detective from the Phoenix PD who was sitting at the table near them. What she hadn't known was that Jack Flynn, now retired, was a private detective working on a domestic case—gathering evidence, in fact, on the impending divorce of Bernard Draper. Had she known, she would have grabbed Bernie and left the bar immediately. But she'd figured the homicide detective was just out enjoying an evening on the town with a drink or two. She and Draper had been completely unaware of the tiny eye of his camera clicking away, recording pictures of their outrageous behavior.

"I'll be right back, Bernie," Hilda said, taking her car keys. She went outside to bring in the cold fried chicken along with some leftover baked beans.

Hilda took a paper towel from the small suitcase and laid it on the table. Then she removed several pieces of the cold chicken and spooned out the beans into two plastic cups from the motel bathroom.

"Hard to believe it, Hilda," he said, "but at one time my former wife and I used to dine at some of the best restaurants and be waited on hand and foot. I commanded respect at one time. Now look at me: an escapee on the run. If it wasn't for that state police lieutenant and that rotten private detective, I'd still be having the very best that this society has to offer. Hilda, I'm going to get even with those two bastards."

Hilda wanted to tell Bernie that he had brought many of his problems upon himself. She was sure it wasn't the fault of the police or the private eye. But she didn't dare tell him so, as she knew that he would go into a rage. She wanted to tell him her dream: that since he had escaped, they should go away and pursue a life together. But she didn't. She kept quiet. She truly was in love with him.

Hilda removed a bottle of whiskey from the suitcase and poured them each a drink. She thought perhaps some alcohol would relax him. Hilda's life had been in constant turmoil since her father's death, bouncing from one foster home to another. Circumstances brought her into prostitution as a teenager, her occupation at the time Bernie had come into her life four years ago. Bernie had convinced her to change her lifestyle. He had been good to her buying her clothes and expensive gifts, and she had remained loyal to him.

Through cleverly manipulated and manipulative telephone calls from prison, Bernie had been able to persuade Hilda to come to Michigan to help him execute his escape plans. She had aided him with street clothes, money, and the use of her blue Mustang. He knew that although she had been a prostitute, she had kept clear of any serious crimes that would mean a prison sentence. But Bernie had been convincing. And now he was pulling Hilda down the wrong path.

One drink led to another, and another. The more he drank, the more Bernie loosened up about his plans for revenge. He described them to Hilda in gloating detail well into the early morning hours before sleep finally overtook him. But it was not so for Hilda. She lay there silently biting her lips to hold back the tears.

CHAPTER TEN

Our evening passed quickly. We began to fall asleep in each other's arms around eleven, after talking even more about Draper's escape and his vow to vindicate the perceived wrongdoing toward him. Just as we drifted off, Ruben appeared at the bedroom door, waking us with a low growl.

"What's the matter, Ruben?" I asked, disturbed by his behavior.

His growl persisted steadily enough for me to slip out of bed and reach for my .44 Caliber fully loaded revolver.

"Quiet down, Ruben," I said firmly, stepping into my trousers.

I cautiously moved out of our room after advising Patty to stay in bed. I didn't turn any lights on. Making my way to the window I carefully pulled the curtain to the side to peer outdoors.

"Wow!" I was so surprised I almost choked on my exclamation.

Throughout my many years in the Adirondacks I had seen only one cow moose and plenty of moose tracks, but here, about seventy feet from our door, stood a large bull-moose that had sauntered onto our property. I looked around behind me. Patty, hearing me cry out, was up and making her way to the window to join me.

"Honey, what is it?" she asked in a hushed voice.

"Come here, dear. Look out the window!" I replied eagerly.

We both peered out.

"He's huge, Jason," Patty said, astounded.

I carefully placed my revolver on the top shelf of the cabinet. My camera in the office was on the top of the filing cabinet—ready to take pictures. I picked it up and quietly opened a window. The bull-moose remained where he had been standing; evidently he had not heard the raising of the window. I aimed the camera in his direction and extended the telescopic lens. But the camera flash evidently startled him, and I was able to take only three pictures before he moved out of sight.

I returned to Patty. "I've seen moose in other areas of the country, but this was the largest, honey."

"I'm amazed, Jason. Wonder where he's headed!"

"He may move down along the lake and go north. Patty, this may sound strange after we saw such a magnificent beast, but did you ever taste moose steaks fried in butter with a touch of garlic?" I asked.

"No, not moose, but I've had plenty of venison tenderloin fried in butter when I lived in Kentucky. It was tasty!"

"I love it myself prepared that way, Patty."

Now we were both fully awake. I glanced at the wall clock in the kitchen, 1:00 a.m.

"Let's try to get some sleep, Jason. I'll have to get up in about four hours," she said, rubbing her eyes.

"Okay, sweetheart, we've had enough excitement," I agreed. "And you really need your rest."

Ruben had already returned to his air mattress. His head lay between his paws and his gaze moved from left to right. It was cool in the house as I climbed in between the sheets and pulled the blankets up over our shoulders. Patty had already fallen off to sleep. I held her close to me. I closed my eyes and quietly thanked God for my angel as sleep took over.

An antique fire truck rushing down a narrow road with a bell clanging seemed to get louder and louder as I finally became aware that the alarm clock was ringing. Only another vivid dream! I looked toward Patty as her slender arm reached out from beneath the covers to push the plunger down to the off position. She sprang out of bed to get ready for work, as she had to be at the diner by six to open up for the early customers.

"Jason, will you have time this morning to do the laundry?" Patty asked sleepily.

"Certainly, darling. I was planning on doing that, and I'll go through the house today with a dust cloth and run the cleaner."

"You're a sweetie, Jason."

"I don't know about that, but we always work together, honey."

"Yes, Jason, we're most fortunate to have each other."

Patty went to the bathroom for a quick shower and to prepare herself for work. I pushed the covers back and reluctantly got out of our warm bed. After putting on my bathrobe I proceeded to let Ruben out for his run into the woods. While he was gone I turned the burner on under the filled teakettle and placed the cone filter in the coffee maker, adding scoops of fresh coffee.

It wasn't long before Patty came into the kitchen. She looked beautiful. Her blond hair was pulled back into a bun. She wore her blue maternity blouse over smooth slacks.

"Jason, would you drop a couple of slices of whole wheat bread into the toaster?"

"I have the bread in the toaster already, dear."

When the toast popped up I buttered it and poured Patty a fresh cup of decaf. She had opened the refrigerator and taken out the jar of grape jelly. I loved grape jelly and peanut butter, obviously a carryover from my childhood. During the few minutes we had together before she had to leave for work, I again asked her to exert caution because of the threats Draper had made. Living in fear is not conducive to a happy existence but we had to take his threats seriously. From the conversations I had had with my good friend, private investigator Jack Flynn in Phoenix, and from my own experience with Draper during his apprehension in New York, I had a good idea of what we had to contend with. I was more and more certain he was headed east to avenge his wounded ego. I could only hope that somehow he would be apprehended before he could mete out any of his wrongful deeds—and before he got anywhere near Patty and me and our unborn child.

As I looked across the table at my pregnant wife, I vowed to myself that if Draper were to harm *anyone* he would be dealt with harshly if I had anything to say about it. And I know that no matter what the law dictated, the safety of Patty, our baby, and me was foremost on my mind: so be it.

"Patty, aside from this Draper situation, we should at least consider Tom's invitation to move to Lake Placid. I know our love for Old Forge will forever be lasting, but we have to consider that the financial terms of his offer of employment would make it possible for us to keep our log home as well. I know Tom has great things in mind for us. I just have a feeling."

"Why, Jason, I didn't hear him repeat any offer when we were there," she pointed out.

"He didn't, that day, but he has always assured me a position will be there for me any time I change my mind. And with our child on the way, we need to consider that such a move would solve any financial problems."

"Jason, wherever you go or whatever decision you make, I will be with you. I know you are worried about our safety and our future. Tom's offer is a splendid opportunity for both of us. I know that our friends would understand if we decided to move to another area."

"Well, it's something to mull over seriously. But let's not say anything about it to anyone until we make a final decision. You know how talk gets around in any small town."

"Yes, I'm aware of that," she agreed, with a knowing smile. Then she glanced over at the clock. "I had better get going, dearest. I will just about make it on time. I love you, honey," she said, giving me a kiss on the forehead as she rushed by.

"I love you, too, my dear, with all my heart."

CHAPTER ELEVEN

It was early morning in the motel room where Bernard Draper and Hilda Furman were staying. They had discussed whether or not they should stay at the motel for another day to give him a day of rest before their drive to New York. Draper decided they should pack up and continue east to the northern part of New York State. He continued to seethe with rage over his imprisonment and is vowing to avenge the action taken against him by the New York authorities.

"Hilda, here are a couple of fresh towels. Put them in the suitcase."

"Bernie, you know that's stealing. We shouldn't alert anyone, especially the motel people. They might call the police!"

"I don't give a damn if they do. We'll be a hundred miles down the road before they discover the missing towels," he replied with a wild look in his eyes and added, "And, anyways, we didn't use our own name when we signed in, and we used cash to pay for the room, and the plate number on the registration card is two numbers off the right plate number. Hilda, do you think I'm stupid?"

"No, honey, but we've got to be careful not to bring any undue attention to us. If we ever get stopped, it'll be over for the both of us," Hilda said with a worried expression on her freckled face. Yet helplessly she stuffed the fresh towels under

134

her slacks in the suitcase.

"Don't worry about it," he retorted.

It was 6:45 a.m. when Hilda wheeled her Mustang out of the motel driveway and headed east. The athletic Draper was again the bent over old man wearing glasses with his hat pulled low over his forehead. The bone-handled cane was slid down between the passenger side door and the seat. An observer would never guess that the bent old man sitting next to the sexy former hooker was in tip-top physical condition. Prior to his escape he had been lifting weights in prison and had tussled with two other inmates, putting them both in the prison hospital. Since his incarceration, Draper had focused on shaping up his physical strength.

Hilda carefully kept the speedometer of the Mustang just under the speed limit, not wanting to attract the attention of any roving police cruisers.

Draper discussed with Hilda his rental of a cottage just outside of Star Lake. He had paid a large sum of money through a third party to the owner of the cabin. The arrangements were already in place long before he escaped. Not only was the cabin rented, but it was well stocked with food, beer, whiskey, and wine. In his calculating mind Draper believed that no one would think that he would return to the scene of the crime.

The Mustang continued eastbound. There was a slight smile on Draper's face.

"Where are we going to stay tonight, Bernie?" Hilda asked, glancing over at her lover.

"Don't worry, Hilda. We'll make it to the Adirondacks. The cabin's stocked with plenty of food, as I said, and it has a television, a radio, and some firearms," Bernie said. He glanced at his watch and continued, "It'll be late when we arrive."

"Do you think it's safe?"

"I told you once, Hilda, and I'm not going to tell you again: it's a safe place. We'll lay low and stay out of town," he said, raising his voice.

"I've gotcha. You don't have to holler, Bernie. I'm not deaf!" she retorted, her freckles reddening. She stepped down on the accelerator and the Mustang lurched forward. Hilda thought, **What am I getting into, speeding toward the Adirondacks with an escaped killer?** *Her knuckles turned white as she tightly gripped the steering wheel. She worried about the dangers ahead. Was the man she loved going to carry out his threats of getting even? She didn't know. Only time would tell.*

CHAPTER TWELVE

After Patty left I took Ruben for a short walk on his leash. I decided to release him for a run into the woods. When he returned he tried to nudge me into a wrestling match.

"Settle down, Ruben. Not now—maybe later," I said, petting him.

I secured him in his dog run and returned to the house. I made myself a cup of coffee and two slices of toast smothered with grape jelly and peanut butter, and then started to clean. Beginning in our room, I made up the bed, picked up all scattered clothes, dusted, and ran the cleaner. I went from room to room of our log home. The last of the cleaning took place in my office. The dust was no match for the cleaner as I pushed it over the floor. The whole task took me an hour and a half. After drinking a glass of cold water, I reentered my office. Sitting at the desk and going through my bad check files, I discovered four check cases that had not responded to my letters notifying them. I placed them in an envelope with an informative memo to Chief Wilson; these particular checks appeared to be headed into the criminal-justice process.

I decided to call Lieutenant Doyle at Troop S. The thought of Draper's escape weighed upon me. I dialed the telephone.

"Troop S Headquarters, Trooper Johnson speaking. May I be of service?" the voice asked.

"This is Jason Black from Old Forge. I would like to speak

with Lieutenant Doyle, please."

"Just a moment, sir." I could hear the connection being made.

"Jason, this is a surprise! I was just going to call you. I have received a bit of information that should interest you."

"Good morning, Jack. What type of information?"

"We have learned that Draper is definitely with a woman whose name is Hilda Furman. I called your friend, Jack Flynn, and through his contacts at the Phoenix PD and through some of his informants, he learned that she had left her waitress position at a Phoenix restaurant and supposedly moved to Michigan. We believe she helped with Draper's escape. You probably already theorized this, she's very close to Draper."

"Oh, yes! Hilda Furman, I'm not surprised. She's the reason that Draper's wife divorced him."

"But there's even more to this. Evidently, before she left Arizona, she made a purchase of firearms—a rifle, a 300 Ruger with a scope, and a 12-gauge semi-automatic shotgun, along with a healthy supply of ammunition for each. I don't have the make of the shotgun. Draper somehow got word to her. The Phoenix detectives are looking for her as we speak."

I felt as if my blood were turning cold and hot at the same time. "It's quite apparent to me, Jack, that Draper is trying to carry out the threats he made in Michigan."

"That's why we have to be on constant alert. Draper is no one anyone can take lightly. Did I mention that her car, a Mustang, is blue? Probably they had stolen license plates put on it. Our patrols statewide have been alerted as well as other police departments throughout the area. All the patrols are cautioned not to try an apprehension until backup personnel have been put in place."

"Good idea! And I hope the patrols have been alerted to the fact that Draper may attempt a disguise of some kind."

"Yes, that information went out with the notice to all patrols. He may be planning to lay low for a while when and if he comes to the Adirondacks. Jason, I'm certain he made some helpful contacts here when he was in business."

"I don't doubt it."

"Jason, I'll talk to you again. You know this office is busy and there are other matters I have to attend to. If anything develops regarding Draper and his mistress, I'll be in touch. Talk with you later. I'm thinking of you, friend. Say hello to Patty for me."

"I will, Jack. Take care."

After my telephone conversation with the lieutenant, I made myself another cup of coffee. Sitting at the table in our kitchen I tried to visualize what action I would have to take in the event Draper made an appearance in our town. Taking into consideration Patty's pregnancy and with the birth of our child in a few months, I anguished over the fears that were now challenging us.

Looking around our kitchen I saw the presence of my wife and her special touches throughout our mountain home. Wicker baskets were lined in a row so decoratively with some of our most treasured belongings. Woodcarvings, purchased from the former Chimney Mountain furniture store in Indian Lake before they closed their doors, added a distinctive element. Paintings and prints neatly hung on the walls. All were a reminder of the life and home we had worked on so hard to build together. We both understood the ability and painstaking hours expended by the elderly woodcarver to create such works of art sold for such low prices. Like the work Patty and I offered the world, they were truly a work of love on his part. The patience it had taken to create these carvings had to be immense, along with his extraordinary skill. To this day they still adorn the top of our cabinets.

Patty's talent for decorating continued to show itself to me throughout our log home—kitchen to living room to bedrooms, and even my combination office and den. She truly enjoyed the challenge decorating posed. I was blessed and fortunate to have Patty as my wife and friend.

I was distracted from my thoughts by a loud bark from Ruben. Looking out the window toward the dog run, I saw a large black bear crossing our property about fifty yards from him. Ruben's growl increased ominously. The bear glanced over at Ruben, stopped momentarily—apparently sizing up the situation—and soon meandered on his way. Apparently annoyed by such a lack of attention, Ruben's barking continued. I was relieved that the large animal had sauntered off into the deep woods adjacent to our property. This bear was no stranger to us and had crossed in front of our log home several times before. We had learned to never leave any refuse outside our home and had given up our bird feeder long ago. Living alongside forest animals, one learns quickly the proper rules to follow, which are important factors but not necessarily foolproof when it comes to the Adirondack Black Bear. Over the years bears have even entered homes, usually because they smell the aroma emanating from the food being cooked indoors.

With the temporary excitement subsided I went to the refrigerator and took out our pitcher of ice-cold water. I poured a large glass full and drank it. It quenched my thirst. Patty and I were fortunate to have a good well. I refilled the pitcher and returned it to the refrigerator. I then went outside to let Ruben out of his dog run. The big K-9 took off at a rapid run into the woods before returning to me. I snapped on his leash and we walked toward the woods together, taking a trail in the opposite direction from where the bear had entered.

The path, in good shape, was rarely used by the public except for an occasional E-Con person checking out the area. Gary Leach, our local forest ranger, who knew the entire region very well, visited this section of the forest several times each year. It was an educational treat when we met along the trail. I had often posed questions to him relative to the Adirondack Park, and without hesitation Gary always responded with answers, whether the topic dealt with animals, trees, plants, or wildflowers. Over the years I had attended many of his presentations to the interested public on their visits to the park. Through the years Gary had also been involved in rescue teams searching for hikers or hunters who got confused and lost their way in the back country of the mountain trails.

Ruben heeled close to my right side. With the leash applied he knew better than to dart out into brush piles seeking out the scampering chippies. In the shadows of the forest trees the air was cool, but comfortable. Luckily I had decided to wear my favorite jacket—an old brown leather three-quarter-length jacket with a rip in the right-side pocket. I knew that on one of my trips to Utica I needed to stop by a repair shop to have it stitched.

As we neared the end of the trail where we usually turned to return to the house, we were surprised to see a partridge take off in flight from the base of a downed pine tree. Ruben's ears shot to attention for the hunt. I felt the leash tighten so I immediately gripped it firmly, knowing that he would try to pursue the swift-moving bird.

"Settle down, boy," I commanded. He promptly obeyed. A crow cawed overhead.

Just as we ended our walk I luckily remembered that Patty had asked me to do the laundry. Not wanting to disappoint her, I quickly returned Ruben to his dog run and secured it, then rushed into the house to pick up the wash that she had presorted into three piles; a load of whites, another of linens, and the third a mixed one. I placed them all into the Bronco, checked my change, and headed to the laundromat. Once again I realized how much I wanted us to have our own washer and dryer. I knew we would really need one after the baby was born.

It was a slow time of the year, so I was able to find three available washers. I loaded them, added the soap (and a cup of bleach for the whites), inserted the coins, and turned the machines on. I selected a magazine from the rack, sat down, and found an interesting article to read. It held my attention until the washers completed their cycle. I removed each load and placed them in three separate dryers. I set the dials, added the coins, started the machines, and decided I had time to drive to the post office.

The parking area was busy as usual, but I managed to find a space at the end of the line. I walked in and opened my box, only to be disappointed at finding it empty. As I returned to the Bronco I decided to take a short drive through town, since I knew it would be at least a quarter of an hour before the wash would be dry. The streets were somewhat deserted because the summer residents had not returned yet. Back at the laundromat I was pleased to discover one dryer was ready to be emptied. I quickly folded that batch, placing the items into the laundry basket, then did the same as the others finished.

I returned home, greeted Ruben, unlocked the door, and carried the laundry into the house. I put away clothes, placed sheets and pillowcases in the linen closet, tucked undergarments into their respective dresser drawers, and left the items to be ironed folded neatly in the laundry basket for Patty. With that big chore out of the way, I was ready to relax for a moment, but then I heard the phone ringing. I ran to answer it.

"Hi, honey. It's your wife. You needn't start supper, dearest. I'm going to stop and pick up a pizza tonight. If that's alright with you, I'll call ahead and order it. Could you please just cut up a salad and set the table? You cleaned the house and did the laundry, so I thought getting a pizza would be a good idea for a change," she said.

"That's a great idea!" I agreed. Then we won't have much to clean up."

"Oh, by the way, I almost forgot: I love you, Sherlock!"

I chuckled. "I love you, too, baby."

I went into the bathroom to wash my hands, then splashed cold water on my face. I enjoyed the feeling; it always made me feel refreshed and invigorated.

Following Patty's suggestion I removed ingredients from the refrigerator, cut up everything into separate plates, and returned the salads to the refrigerator to keep them cold. Nothing I enjoyed more than a cold, crispy salad! Next I set the table, deciding not to light any candles to accompany pizza. I looked around to check the table, went back to remove salad dressings and grated cheese from the fridge.

At about five-forty I heard Patty's Jeep pull up next to the dog run. I went outside to assist her. She was already out of the vehicle and at the fence patting Ruben.

"Hi, sweetheart," I said, happy to see her.

Patty turned to give me a quick hug. I held her gently and gave her a warm kiss of welcome.

"I'm sure glad to be home, honey. We had a busy day today. As I was taking a tray of food to a table of five, it tipped slightly, but luckily I was able to steady it before I spilled anything on my customer. Remember how upset I was over that incident where I dropped a breakfast on a customer's head! I was so embarrassed, Jason. I felt like such a klutz. It rattled me so much that I'm starting to shake again just thinking about it." Tears formed in her eyes as she relived the bad experience.

"Oh, Patty, I'm so sorry. That would have shaken me up, too. Are you alright now, baby?" I asked, trying to comfort her. Things were certainly not rolling over her very easily now. Probably it was hormonal imbalance.

"Yes, honey, I'm alright. It was my own fault I overloaded the tray. It did stir up some emotion for a few minutes."

"I bet it did. Say, where's the pizza? I'll get it out of the car. I'm famished."

"It's in the rear seat. It was very hot when I picked it up," she added. "If it's cooled, we can always heat our slices in the toaster oven."

"Sounds good to me," I replied.

I went to the rear door of the Jeep and opened it. The large pizza box still felt hot: nothing like the aroma of hot pizza to make my mouth water. I carefully picked it up and carried it into the house as Patty held the door open for me. Placing it on the counter, I asked Patty to make the decision about whether or not we should heat it in the toaster oven for a few minutes.

"Give me a minute, hon. I'd like to go in and freshen up."

After just a few minutes, Patty reappeared in the kitchen, her soft blond hair released from her bun. She checked the pizza.

"It wouldn't hurt to heat it for five minutes. I know how you like your food nice and hot," she chided me.

I laughed. "That's a good idea."

I turned to the refrigerator to reach in for the salads and set them on the table.

"Everything looks wonderful, Sherlock. You are such a kind husband. How come I'm so lucky?"

"I'm the one that's fortunate, Patty. You have brought me contentment, and I'm so proud of you."

"Let's start on our salads, darling. I'm famished! I do appreciate your love, and I feel the same, Jason."

We said very little while we ate our salads. In a few minutes she served us each a slice of the piping hot pizza, then added two more pieces to heat. I could tell that her appetite was intact.

"Patty, the pizza was delicious. What a treat for a change!"

"I'm glad you're enjoying it," she said with a big grin. "I like it, too. Let's do it occasionally."

"I agree. But not too often. We must remember our waistlines."

We continued to munch on our delicious slices in silence. Then I offered, "Okay, Patty, you said you were tired, so take Ruben for a short walk while I do the few dishes and clean up.

"That's a deal, Jason," she said in relief.

She went to the closet for a wrap and went out. While she was gone I hastily did the chores. As I finished I heard the door open. She returned, with Ruben not far behind.

We went into the living room, Patty to her knitting and me to my recliner with my book in hand.

"By the way, Jason, remember this morning when I had to open up early and I was almost late. Well, guess who was there waiting: Wilt and Dale. Evidently they'd been there before six, and as they entered, a group of four men—none of whom I knew—followed close behind. Fortunately, just as I was putting on the coffee, the door burst open and Lila rushed in."

"Is that right?" I asked. "Wonder what they were doing there so early. Did they tell you?"

"They were on their way to Cranberry Lake. Dale was flying Wilt in to look at a wood lot he was thinking about buying. It was good to see Wilt. I hadn't seen him in quite a while," she added.

"Hmmm, that's interesting. He didn't say anything about such a plan when I saw him. Who were the four men? That's rather early for strangers to be there at that time," I asked with curiosity.

"I have no idea. But you must have mentioned Draper to Wilt, because he sure lectured me on being extremely cautious. He's very concerned for our welfare."

"I did, dear. You know that. I told the guys because they get around the territory and are very aware of any strangers in town."

"I know they are. And they're all good friends to us."

"If we ever do decide to leave the area, how would we ever find friends as loyal as they have been through the years?" I asked Patty, almost rhetorically.

The rest of the evening passed rather quietly, she with her knitting and I with my book. When darkness arrived I noticed only one security light had come on. I decided to go out and change the blown lamp. After I replaced it with a new one I turned it on, only to observe two sets of eyes peering from the darkness. I knew I had glimpsed our nightly culprits. Almost every evening two deer would approach the log home and leave evidence of their visit: missing leaves and flowers from our beautiful hydrangea plants. We loved the deer, but they did cause a great amount of damage to some of our floral life.

At about ten we retired to the bedroom. Patty read for a while but it wasn't long before she leaned over to kiss me on the cheek, turned over, and fell off to sleep. I read for approximately another hour before my eyelids got heavy. After laying the book on the table next to our bed, I turned off the light and drifted off to sleep.

CHAPTER THIRTEEN

It wasn't sleep for Bernard Draper and his girlfriend, Hilda Furman. Near Star Lake, approximately seven miles away, the small mountain cabin was filled with cigarette smoke. Hilda, wearing a scant looking nightgown, was sitting on the edge of the queen-sized bed. She was shaping her fingernails with an emery board. A cigarette hung from the side of her mouth. Her scraggly bright red hair was cut short. The lamplight brought out the prominence of her dotted freckles as she inhaled deeply, taking the nicotine into her lungs. This inhalation was followed by a hacking cough. Bernard Draper sat close to the bed in a leather-backed rocking chair. His lined face emanated his evilness.

Draper had made several contacts while operating his southwestern jewelry store in this area. With his ability to cleverly manipulate people he had made a pact with a man from Payson, Arizona. Sheldon Blake, approximately sixty years of age, had been born in Bumble Bee, Arizona, and been left a large sum of money from an uncle who had had ties with copper mining in Jerome, Arizona. Blake had become involved with other people of means in Maricopa County—one of those being Bernard Draper, with whom he had become close friends. Blake had invested money in the Draper organization along with other investments he had made throughout the United States. It wasn't proven at the time of Draper's

146

apprehension, but strong rumors were uttered around the Adirondacks that a man by the name of Blake could have been a co-owner of the successful jewelry store that Draper had operated.

"Hilda, make some coffee!" Draper bellowed from his rocker.

"Would you like a sandwich, too, sweetheart?" she asked as she buttoned her scanty housecoat.

"Why not! There's plenty of cold cuts in the refrigerator. Make it plenty large with mustard on both slices of bread," he replied coldly, looking up from the New York State road map he had been studying.

"Okay, baby, nice and thick it will be. I think I'll make one for myself, too."

"There's plenty of food, Hilda. I'll come to the table as soon as I finish looking this map over."

"Okay, Bernie! And we've got donuts for dessert. What are you looking for on the map?" she asked timidly.

"I'm just checking the highway system. I want to go to Utica tomorrow."

"Do you think that's smart, Bernie? You know the police are looking for us."

"I know, I know, but we have to. Just before I left the joint I made contact with Shelly. He arranged to have a car placed in a parking lot just off Turner Street in Utica. It's very close to an old shopping center."

"How did you manage this Bernie? You have never mentioned it before." She looked over at him in surprise.

"Baby, you know how much I love you. I just can't tell you everything," he said trying to cajole her. "I've had a long time to plan this. I've got my mind made up. That state police guy and that private detective have ruined my life. Somehow, I've got to get even with them. I've just got to," he emphasized. "We've got to pick up the car. I know how much you love your Mustang, but we're ditching it in Utica. So, clean out everything in it."

"Bernie... Bernie, I worked so hard to save money to buy

my car," she said with tears welling in her eyes.

"Don't cry, sweetheart. After I get even with this Doyle and Black, we're leaving the country. I've got plenty of money hidden overseas. I'll buy you any type of car you want, but the Mustang goes. Do you hear me?" he said raising his voice angrily. He was full of rage. His dilated red eyes held a look so frightening that it made her tremble.

"How can we get out of the country?" she asked, her voice shaking.

"I've arranged everything. Don't even think about it. We'll get some sleep tonight and then we'll get up around one in the morning to leave for Utica."

Hilda finished making the sandwiches and placed them on the small table. Draper got out of the rocker and went to the sink to wash his hands.

In contrast to his appearance of a bent-over old man while out in public, in reality he was in good physical shape because of lifting weights and exercising regularly while incarcerated in prison. His gray wig lay on the small dresser of the cabin's bedroom.

Draper joined Hilda at the small table. They drank their coffee and ate their sandwiches, no longer saying a word.

CHAPTER FOURTEEN

It was an evening on Patty's day off, so we decided we had best work on our budget to help us determine how we could manage our expenses once she left her job. Patty's tips at the diner were always generous and augmented her paycheck, combined with my pension from the State of New York and my fees from my investigation business, they meant we had been able to make ends meet. However, with the baby arriving in a few months, hard decisions would undoubtedly have to be made, as her income and tips would come to an end. Tom Huston's generous offer of a position at the Breakshire Lodge at Lake Placid weighed heavily on my mind at this time. It would certainly stabilize our income, and Patty would not be required to return to work right away.

"Patty, those are the hard, cold facts. We've got to make a decision. We have to discuss this. First of all, you know there is no place I'd rather live than here in Old Forge. We're fairly close to Utica, which has all the necessary services we don't have here. Our area is unique, with a good medical facility and excellent physicians, a great school for the children, wonderful restaurants and, most important of all, our great friends. But I'm certain Lake Placid, once we become acclimated, will have just as many favorable services as we have here. You know just as well as I do that people are pretty much the same wherever you go, both the good and the bad."

"I agree with you, Jason. I know what you're saying." Yet tears began to well up in her eyes at the mere thought of leaving her beloved home and friends.

"What I am trying to convey is that private investigation work here in the Adirondacks isn't that plentiful. It sufficed when I was alone, but now with you and our child, I have to seriously think about the offer that Tom has made us. If I did take a security or managerial position with the lodge, I'd be making a respectable wage, perhaps even enough for us to be able to maintain our log home here in Old Forge," I said, trying to cheer her up.

"I can understand that. It's been on my mind, too. But what do you think our friends will say? Look how they worked so very hard to finish the baby's room and the addition."

"I've thought about that, too." I sat back to wait for her reaction.

"I know Wilt would understand, and the other guys, too. I'll leave it up to you. Whatever decision you have to make, I'll go along with you, Jason. You know that." She tried her best to give me a full smile.

"I know I can depend on you, precious one. We have to look ahead, especially with our child coming. I want to give you the best, my dear. I love you, Patty." I looked over at her tenderly. We rose from the table, hugged, and kissed as tears began to stream down our cheeks. We had made a painful but necessary decision. I glanced at the clock. It was almost ten-thirty—time to put our budget material away before we went to bed.

Patty went off to sleep as soon as her head hit the pillow. I rolled and tossed, but couldn't fall to sleep. I kept mulling over Tom's job offer and the responsibilities that I would have if I accepted the job. Not only would I be overseeing his many properties, but the Loggers' Museum would require a great deal of attention as it entered its first tourist season.

And, of course, there was the matter of Morey Harris, now his head groundskeeper. I wondered if he would be carrying any animosity towards me for having him apprehended. Tom

Huston had given him a second chance in life by hiring him. I was pleased to know that Morey had turned his life around. Finally, my eyelids felt heavy and I succumbed to sleep.

CHAPTER FIFTEEN

Outside of Star Lake a light appeared in the small window of the cabin that contained Bernard Draper, the escapee, and his girlfriend, Hilda Furman. The sturdy Draper once again appeared as the bent-over old man wearing a gray wig. He wore brown trousers, a gold-colored shirt, and checkered suspenders. Dark horn-rimmed glasses hid his eyes. Hilda was wearing a beige pantsuit. No one observing this couple would believe that they were on the run from the law. They appeared to be a father traveling with his daughter.

Before they left, Hilda had tidied up the cabin. The bed was made and the kitchen was neatly in order. She had helped Draper on with his jacket, then donned her coat. The night air was cool in the area.

It was pitch black outside the cabin. Hilda locked the front door and then they made their way to the Mustang. Draper opened the passenger side door and got in. Hilda went around to the driver's door, opened it, and slid behind the steering wheel. She started the car and slowly drove out of the long winding lane to the macadam highway, which led to Route 3. Draper told her to drive west toward Watertown.

"Bernie, when did you arrange for this car we're going to pick up?" she asked plaintively.

"Never mind. I can't tell you that. But the car will be parked in the lot. Maybe I'll tell you later, Hilda."

152

They spoke very little on the way to Utica. They drove Route 81 south from Watertown to Adams and turned onto Route 177 toward Barnes Corners and Lowville. Draper had studied the maps he had while at the cabin and knew exactly which roads to take.

It was still dark out when Hilda pulled into the deserted parking lot near the old Charlestown Shopping Center just off Turner Street, which was now occupied by several business offices. The headlights revealed a maroon colored Ford sedan bearing New York registration plates.

"Turn the lights off. This is the car, Hilda," he said as though bragging.

"Do you have the keys for it?" Hilda asked.

"They should be taped on the inside of the front left fender. You take the plates off your car. We'll take them with us. Are you certain you cleaned everything out of your car?" he asked impatiently.

"I did, I did, Bernie. Everything has been removed," she replied somewhat angrily as she opened the driver's side door and got out. Tears rolled down her cheeks as she removed the license plates from her beloved Mustang. She hurriedly brushed them away, as she did not want Draper to see her crying. He went around to the left front fender and ran his hand under it to look for the taped key.

"I've got the key," he said excitedly.

"Here, give it to me," she said. "We'd better get out of here."

Draper handed the key to her and took the plates. They both entered the maroon Ford.

At the end of the parking lot was a large refuse container. Draper told Hilda to pull over next to it. He got out and threw the plates in. As they fell they clanged noisily against the metal sides. He climbed back into the car.

"Let's get out of here!" he instructed her loudly.

Hilda pushed her foot down on the accelerator pedal and the Ford lurched ahead leaving a trace of rubber on the street pavement.

"Where to now, Bernie?"

"Let's get on Route 12 and head north," he added.

Hilda followed Bernie Draper's directions, and after a few turns the signs for Routes 8 and 12 loomed before them. She wheeled to the right and up the ramp that brought them onto the service road to Routes 8 and 12. Once on the road, she immediately lowered her speed to fifty-five miles per hour, as she didn't want to alert any roving police patrols. The couple felt somewhat confident that the pressure was alleviated as they continued on their way.

It was beginning to get light outdoors as they approached Route 365 and continued to climb the hill just before Tam's Diner, located on the east side of Route 12.

"Are you hungry, Hilda?" Draper asked, looking over toward her.

"I'm famished," she replied.

"Pull in here. It's early and there aren't too many cars in the parking lot."

Hilda pulled behind the diner to park. They got out of the Ford. Draper assumed the role of an elderly man as he walked, leaning on Hilda and using the cane toward the entrance. To the casual observer, he would appear to be a frail, gray-haired gentleman making his entrance into the restaurant with the help of his daughter.

She held the door open for him as they went inside and took a seat in a booth. Draper kept his head down. Hilda took one of the two menus and handed it to him.

Tammy, the owner, was in the kitchen and noticed the couple sitting in the booth. Two waitresses on duty were busy at the counter waiting on customers. Shortly one of them approached their booth, identifying herself as Gerrie.

"Good morning. May I help you?" she asked with a warm, friendly smile.

"We would like your daily special, the two orders of French toast with two glasses of orange juice and two cups of coffee, please. We'd like the coffee now."

She repeated the order as she wrote it down on her pad.

"Oh, waitress! Could we have two glasses of water?" Hilda asked.

"You certainly can. Just a moment," Gerrie added.

Soon she returned to the booth with a tray carrying two juices, two waters, and two steaming hot mugs of coffee.

Hilda and Draper spoke quietly as they waited for Tammy to prepare their French toast, not wanting to attract attention. In a few minutes, the waitress returned with two plates of French toast. Each had a side of crisp bacon accompanied by a pitcher of syrup. They quickly cleaned their plates, particularly hungry because of their early rising and their drive into Utica.

When Gerrie returned with coffee refills, Hilda commended her on the quality of the French toast. Gerrie told her that Tammy was noted for her French toast made with thick slices of her homemade bread.

Gerrie returned to the kitchen to convey to Tammy and the other waitress, Bea, the compliment she had received from the strangers in the booth. Little did they realize who the couple was; if they had, the local troopers who often frequented this establishment would have been alerted.

CHAPTER SIXTEEN

The rapids came up fast. The raft rose into the air and came down hard on the water with a splat. Then I heard the ringing sound. It was somewhere off in the distance. It took me a minute to realize that our trusty alarm clock was sounding the call of 5:15 a.m., time to get out of our warm bed.

Patty turned over toward me and my lips met hers. There was a gentle tug of the bedspread at the foot of the bed: Ruben was reminding me it was also time for his early morning walk.

I rose a bit grudgingly to don my robe as he headed to the rear door to wait for me to open it. I gave him a pat on the head and he ran off the porch and toward the woods. I watched him as he disappeared into the forest.

Going back inside, I went over to the sink to fill the teakettle with water and placed it over the flames of the burner. I readied the coffeepot and waited till the water boiled.

I could hear the shower running. When it stopped I heard a strange grating sound from the water pipes. I'd have to ask Falsey to take a look at the plumbing system.

Patty came out of the bathroom. "Did you hear that noise, Jason?" she asked, somewhat perplexed, still drying her long blond hair with the fluffy towel as she moved hurriedly to the bedroom.

"Yes, honey, I did. I'll have Jack look at it soon," I replied.

"I don't think it's serious, do you?"

"I hope not. It's probably something to do with the pump. Patty, stop worrying about it. Jack will find out what's the matter with it. You wait and see. Everything will work out okay."

"Okay, Jason. I understand. You know I have a lot of things on my mind with the baby coming. My extra weight has really been getting to me lately and the baby is more active, too!" she exclaimed.

I went into the bedroom, gave her a hug, and held her close to me.

"I know, dearest. I understand. We'll work out everything together, sweetheart." I tried to comfort her.

We held each other for a couple of minutes before returning to getting dressed. I went into the kitchen and to pour our wake-up cups of hot coffee. I popped two slices of whole wheat into the toaster and removed the grape jelly from the refrigerator. Patty soon joined me at the table, looking her radiant self. She had pulled her hair back into a tight bun as she did every morning when she had to work. Her soft cotton maternity outfit looked stunning on her. I studied her face. She looked at me with her wonderful smile. The toast finally popped up to bring me back to my task.

"Would you like a slice of toast, Patty?"

"No, hon, I'll probably have something with Lila when I get to work. She's giving me some advice on the do's and don'ts of child rearing," she said with another smile.

"Oh, I see. Great! We can use some advice." I chuckled.

Before Patty left she came over to me to say goodbye. I gave her a gentle hug and a warm kiss. I walked outside with her to start her Jeep. After it warmed up for a few minutes she climbed in and rolled down the window to talk.

"Jason, I've been thinking pretty steadily about the offer Tom Huston presented to us. I think it's a really good opportunity. With the baby coming and our additional expenses, it probably would be a good idea to talk with Tom about it."

"I have to agree, Patty. I'll talk with him further about the subject soon."

"See you later, Jason," she said as she waved goodbye.

I watched as she left the yard and headed toward Route 28.

"Yes, Patty, I believe you are right!" I said to myself.

I went back inside and waited till seven before placing a call to Jack Falsey about our strange plumbing problem. I explained the dilemma as best I could. He indicated that he didn't think it was serious but would stop by the next day to check it out. I thanked him, said goodbye, and hung up the telephone.

I checked the interior of our house and found it looked pretty good. I made the bed and ran the cleaner throughout the log home. After I placed the cleaner in the utility closet, I heard the telephone ringing.

"Hello," I answered.

"Is this the Jason Black residence?" the man on the other end asked.

I immediately recognized the deep voice on the other end of the phone even though it had been a long time since I had heard it. "Well, good morning!" I offered warmly.

"Jason Black, how have you been?"

"Charlie Koran, it's so good to hear from you. It's been years. How are you and the wife?"

"Good, Jason. Like anyone else we've had some health issues, but we're doing fine. I don't know if you knew this or not, but I'm doing some private investigation work and have been for a couple years. The wife and I talk about you every so often and think about some of those good days, especially investigators' school."

"Yes, Charlie, we have some fond memories of those days. I've often wondered how and what you were doing. I knew you had retired from the division."

"Yeah, I gave it a good run—thirty-seven years on the street working with others trying to keep the fiber of society intact."

"Well said, Charlie. I'm sure you gave it your all."

"How about you, Jason? What have you been up to?"

"Did you hear I'm married to a wonderful gal named Patty, who is expecting our baby shortly? She is a waitress at one of our local restaurants. I'm working on a few check cases, and occasionally we do have some excitement going on. We sure do right now. I once assisted the troopers on a case where the defendant violated state and federal laws. With my help he was apprehended and sentenced to a prison in Michigan. Well, unfortunately he recently escaped, and we know that while he was in prison he made some serious threats against the people who were involved in his original apprehension."

"And you're one of them, Jason?" Charlie asked grimly.

"Yeah, Charlie, I am, and also Lieutenant Jack Doyle at Troop S."

"Is this the guy from Arizona? I think I heard about that caper through the grapevine."

"You heard correctly. Supposedly he's with a girlfriend. His name is Bernard Draper and hers is Hilda Furman."

"Watch your step, Jason! These people don't sound like the friendly type you meet in the supermarket."

"I do think he'll show up here in the mountains, if he isn't here already. He uses disguises, such as wigs and hats and horn-rimmed glasses. He owned a large trucking concern and was a smooth operator with lots of connections. He belonged to the Arizona social sets, polished the hands of politicians, and traveled in the right crowd. Then he came to our mountains and started his smuggling operation, which proved to be his downfall. Yes, Charlie, that was his number one mistake. You don't con the Adirondackers. Oh, a few may have purchased some of his southwestern jewelry, but he mostly attracted the Canadian tourists. It appeared he was headed to a pot of gold until he was arrested."

"I believe they call it greed, Jason."

"That's what it is, Charlie, greed."

"Jason, I'm currently working on a missing-person case in the Newburgh area. The family of Lawrence Gleason has contacted my office. They feel that he may be having some dementia problems. He's seventy-five and apparently has begun to exhibit notable absent-mindedness. Supposedly he was going on a two-day trip to the Adirondacks, but he has not returned home as yet or called anyone. He's driving a 1989 Cadillac De Ville, color gold, plate number LGS-385. I alerted the troopers even though the family didn't want me to— apparently they are a very private family. Maybe he decided to stay at a motel or hotel longer than he anticipated."

"Charlie, what was his destination? Did they know?" I asked.

"According to his sister he mentioned Blue Mountain Lake. He's always been a museum buff and has visited the Adirondack Museum on previous occasions. I contacted the museum by telephone. They are acquainted with him, but claimed he hasn't been seen."

"I've written down the plate number and information. I'll check it out further for you, Charlie, and will get back to you if I can come up with anything."

"I'd appreciate that, Jason. Well, it's been great talking with you—been a long time. Let me know if you come up with anything. You, Dave Wachtel, and me have some great memories together from back in those days of our BCI classes in the Albany area," he said, recalling our long-time association.

"That's right, Charlie. No one can take those memories away from us. We had some fine gentlemen in that class."

"Yes, we did. How the time has flown by. Life is too short, Jason. You want to enjoy every bit of it while you can."

"I agree with you, Charlie. And don't worry, I'll check out the Blue Mountain area for you. If he should return to his family or call them, kindly let me know."

"I will, Jason. Keep track of any time that you spend on the case and I'll take care of it."

"I will, Charlie. Good hearing from you. By the way, give your wife my regards."

"I certainly will. Say, you know your voice hasn't changed a bit."

"Neither has yours."

After saying goodbye and promising to stay in touch, we concluded our conversation. It was good to hear from private detective Koran. Charlie was a great guy. He loved his family and the troopers, and enjoyed hunting in the Catskills and the Adirondacks as well as the Southern Tier of our state. I often compared Wilt and Charlie. Both were big men, with hearts larger than themselves. Good guys. What a night patrol those two fellows would have made together! Crime would have come to a standstill in any area they were assigned to. Ah! Charlie's call had stirred up sweet memories of many days and nights spent patrolling the rural districts of my beloved New York State.

CHAPTER SEVENTEEN

After their good breakfast, Bernie and Hilda left Tam's Diner and reentered the Ford. Before leaving the parking area they sat in the car to discuss their next move. Suddenly they turned ashen white when they spotted a trooper's car pull in on the far side of the diner. Draper immediately reached up to pull his hat further down over his eyes as Hilda began to check both rear and side-view mirrors. Not only one, but two troopers entered the diner. Immediately she started the engine, put it in gear, and slowly left the parking lot for Route 12 to head north, definitely not wanting to attract attention. When the Ford reached the turn to Old Forge, she pulled off onto the shoulder, not knowing what Bernie wanted to do. Should they continue on the road to Watertown on their way back to their cabin at Star Lake, or head on toward Old Forge? Draper again expressed to her his strong desire for revenge against the private detective who had slugged him and thus caused his arrest. He told her to drive on toward Old Forge via Route 28.

"Hilda, we've just got to be extremely careful when we go into Old Forge. I happen to know from personal experience how effective their police department is. They're the pigs that arrested me. I want you to slow down when we enter that place. Somehow we've got to figure out exactly where this Black lives." His voice began to shake with the anger he could no longer suppress.

"Bernie, I don't think you should even take a chance on that," Hilda begged. "From what you've told me, this Black is a pretty tough guy. You'd better watch your step." She was anxious to calm him down.

"I have to admit, he sure packs a wallop that I'll never forget. Nevertheless, I'm going to find him. I've got my gun with me. I'll do what I came to do, and then we'll go back to the cabin. I've got my mind made up. Do you understand?" he demanded emphatically.

"Yes, I understand, Bernie, but I'm telling you, we've got to be cautious. We are being sought all across the country, or have you forgotten? I can't believe that I've gotten myself into this mess by helping you after your escape. If we get caught I'll end up in prison. I'm really having second thoughts, Bernie! I don't want to go to jail."

"You what?" Bernie shouted angrily.

"Bernie, I love you, but this is too much pressure. We could be shot, understand?"

"Do I understand? Of course I do. Hilda, I've always lived on the edge. I've worked hard and I've played hard, but I'm getting even. Either you're with me or against me."

Hilda fought back tears. "I'm with you, but you know what I mean. I'm scared."

"Yeah, I know, but let's cool it. We'll be extra careful not to make waves in Old Forge. I love you, Hilda, and my dream is to take you to a faraway place to spend the rest of my life with you," he said, trying to calm her fears.

"Oh! Bernie, you're so sweet!"

The maroon Ford containing the two wanted people continued northward. With the disposal of the Mustang and the license plates they felt confident that they wouldn't be checked out and would be able to move around the area without arousing suspicion.

CHAPTER EIGHTEEN

After receiving the telephone call from my former associate Charles Koran, I called one of my contacts at Blue Mountain Lake: Paul Provost, the owner of Hemlock Hall. I asked him if a Lawrence Gleason had ever been registered as a guest there. He quickly checked his computer records and advised me that Mr. Gleason had been a guest at Hemlock Hall about five years before. I informed him of the reason for my call, and he said he would notify me if the man should show up there.

We conversed for a few minutes and he told me that they were serving roast pork with all the trimmings that night and if I cared to come to the Hall, I certainly would be welcome. He remembered it was one of my favorites. I told him that, regretfully, I wouldn't be able to make it for dinner, but that I would look forward to our next meeting. Patty and I had dined at Hemlock Hall in the past and we agreed both the cuisine and the hospitality were outstanding. I thanked Paul and we said our goodbyes.

After working on a few bad check files I went outside to join Ruben, who was sitting near his doghouse. When he saw me approach he jumped up and his ears rose to attention. I entered the dog run and snapped his leash onto his leather collar. He immediately rubbed his big head against my pant leg with great affection. Ruben knew he was going for a walk with his master. I led him out of the run and we headed toward the woods.

Since we had become aware of Draper's threats, I had never left our home without my fully loaded 9mm semi-automatic pistol. Patty and our expected child meant everything to me, and I was determined to take all necessary precautions.

Ruben heeled close to my right leg. He evidently sensed my uneasiness, as he seemed to be on guard. It was uncanny. I felt that he was ready to go into an attack mode if we were threatened in any way. I glanced at my watch: one-thirty. The lunch rush hour was probably over at the diner and would find Patty and Lila most likely having their lunch at the back table—Patty probably having a green salad with sliced grilled chicken, as she was trying to be careful with her diet during her pregnancy so as to eat healthfully and not gain too much weight.

My mind kept racing in all directions: my concern about Patty and our child, the threats from Draper that kept me on edge, the big decision of whether or not to accept Tom Huston's offer. Might he become discouraged and hire someone else to fill the personnel-security position he had so generously offered me? I felt deep in my heart that Tom's decision to create the loggers' museum was based in part on his hope that I would accept the position at the Breakshire Lodge. Well, Patty had said whatever decision I made, she would certainly go along with. I decided that I would have to take a few more days before I could make this important decision—the chance of a lifetime.

CHAPTER NINETEEN

The car proceeded ever closer to their Old Forge destination. They had no idea once they arrived how they would locate their target, Jason Black. When they stopped at the local convenience store to fill the gas tank, Hilda went into the building to pay with cash. She asked the clerk if she could borrow the local phone book, only to find there was no listing for Jason Black, evidently he had an unlisted number. As she handed the book back, she rolled her eyes at the young attendant.

"Hey, handsome, I'm looking for an old school chum," she said flirtatiously.

"Who's that, ma'am?" he asked, while ogling her low cut blouse.

"I do so want to surprise him. His name is Jason Black. A big guy," she added, continuing to flirt with the clerk.

"Oh." He thought for a moment. "Jason lives just out of town. Stay on Route 28 just past the campgrounds on the left. It's easy to find."

"Thank you so much, honey," she said as she hurriedly left the store to share the good news with Bernie.

The face of the clerk reddened and he retreated to finish stocking the shelves.

Hilda walked to the maroon Ford with a smug smile and slid behind the steering wheel.

"*Well, Hilda, how did you make out?*" *Bernie asked, while peering over his glasses.*

"*I know where he lives, Bernie,*" *she answered. She was proud but rather surprised that it had been so easy.*

"*Good girl,*" *he responded with dark satisfaction.*

CHAPTER TWENTY

"Stay, Ruben," I commanded as he began to tug on his leash.

The large black bear that had been pestering us had stopped in the middle of the well-worn trail where we had walked so many times, but evidently we now had competition in the form of this huge animal that was approaching and was only about a hundred feet from us. Shivers ran up and down my spine when a low, threatening growl emanated from the depths of his throat. I did not move a muscle. Ruben also stood at attention, his eyes fixed on the bear. I decided I had better just wait him out. For an unknown reason, after staring us down for what seemed an eternity, but in reality was only a few minutes, the big bear ambled off on his own. With the trail now free, we made our way out of the woods. I now knew that it would not be wise to allow Patty to walk Ruben into the woods any longer.

General belief was that such a black bear would not be a danger to anyone; however, of late I had heard of bears threatening humans while in pursuit of food. I certainly did not want any one of us to be a test case to see if they could be harmful. No, we humans needed to adopt habits of good common sense as we dwelt in shared habitat.

Ruben and I exited the forest trail just in time to see a maroon car backing out of the driveway. I waved at the car to let the driver know that I was at home. Whether the occupant saw us or not, I do not know, but to my surprise he or she seemed to speed out of the driveway. I wondered who had come into the yard and not found anyone at home. We seldom had visitors that turned around and left. The maroon-colored Ford was not familiar to me. Could this possibly have been Draper? Or was I becoming paranoid? I shrugged it off as I secured Ruben into his dog run, where he slurped some water and lay down near the entrance to his doghouse. I went into the house, picked up some letters for mailing from my desk, placed them in my briefcase, and then checked through the log home to ensure all was well. I grabbed my case, locked the door behind me, and walked to the car as I called over to Ruben to let him know that I would return soon. I unlocked the door, slid behind the steering wheel, and started the car. After warming the engine for a few minutes, I left the yard and headed to the post office.

I passed the fire department, where two firefighters were busy polishing one of their trucks. The well-known volunteers at the fire department took pride in their organization and were meticulous when it came to maintaining their equipment.

I pulled into the parking area of the post office and turned the engine off. I proceeded inside with my letters and placed them in the mail slot.

I went to my box and with gratitude found several letters from banking institutions, which added financially to my existence as a private detective. The spring of the year was a slow time for the businesses in the area, thus diminishing my income.

Back home again I went into the office to open my mail. I had received a few bad checks, and now entered them into my bad check files, each with its own individual report. I made out file cards and placed them in my alphabetized metal file drawer.

When I called the diner at three-thirty, my wife answered the telephone.

"John's Diner, Patty speaking. May I help you?" she asked

politely.

"Honey, it's me, your hubby," I said.

"I knew it had to be you, darling. Boy! Have we been busy! Besides the regular crowd, we were really swamped when a bus pulled in. John had to call two extra waitresses in. Somehow, we served them all. I made some good tip money, Jason."

"Honey, are you terribly tired?" I asked with concern. "You must be after all of that activity."

"I have to admit, I am a bit worn out," she said, sounding bushed.

"Don't worry, honey. I'll have dinner ready for you when you get here. Then you can go in and have a good rest."

"Thanks. I'm looking forward to that," she answered. "By the way, I've been thinking more and more about Tom's offer. It sounds better every day."

"I'm kind of seeing it that way, too. We'll continue to talk about it."

"Well, I'd better get going. Someone just came in. Bye for now," she said.

"See you soon," I answered as we hung up. How I wished she could be working fewer hours.

CHAPTER TWENTY-ONE

It was late in the afternoon when Hilda Furman pulled the maroon Ford next to their rented cabin. Draper was sound asleep. His wig had slipped off and had caught between the back of his head and the top of the passenger side seat.

"Come on, Bernie, wake up! We're back at the cabin. Come on, wake up!" she said forcefully as she shook him, trying to arouse him. Draper's eyes opened slightly, both watering and fluttering. Without further coaxing, he straightened up, pushed his wig back into place, and took a deep breath. He reached into his left-hand shirt pocket and removed a pack of long filtered cigarettes. His hand shook as he pulled a cigarette from the pack. He jammed it into his mouth while pulling out a lighter, which with his other thumb he began to try to light. It took six tries before the weak flame ignited. He moved the lighter to the end of the cigarette. His hand kept shaking badly, missing the end of the cigarette. Finally he was successful. The cigarette sent curling smoke spiraling toward the car's roof.

Hilda realized that he had consumed too much to drink from his flask, but neglected to say anything fearful of his rage. She opened the driver's side door to rush over to the passenger side to assist her lover from the car. As soon as they entered the cabin, Draper started ranting and raving about Jason Black. More wildly than ever he swore to Hilda that he was

171

going to settle the score with that son-of-a-b....!

"Bernie, he's no fool," Hilda repeated for the hundredth time. "He could cause us a lot of trouble," she emphasized.

"Listen, Hilda, whose side are you on, anyways?" Draper snarled.

"On your side, Bernie, you know that. But Black is apparently a clever, crafty, former cop with a great deal of moxie. Listen, I come from the streets of Phoenix. Before I met you I was in constant contact with cops, especially the vice cops. They know the street, too. Don't fool yourself, Bernie. Black is one of those ex-coppers that you don't want on your case. I don't know him personally, but believe me, I know the type and they can be your worst nightmare."

"I don't think you know what you're talking about Hilda," he replied cuttingly.

"You wait and see, know-it-all, you just wait and see." Even in her pain and bitterness, little did she know how much truth was in that warning.

CHAPTER TWENTY-TWO

I was looking out of the back window around five-thirty just as Patty's red Jeep pulled into the yard. Dinner was ready and waiting. Golden brown salmon patties were warming in the oven, and firm broccoli was in the steamer along with two yams all set for the dinner plate. The assorted pickles adorned the table in Patty's favorite cut glass-serving dish. Fresh rolls, wrapped in a clean towel and accompanied by sweet butter, were already on the table.

I went to the kitchen door to greet her.

"Something sure smells good, Jason," she said enthusiastically.

I wrapped my arms around her, careful not to squeeze her too tightly.

"Yes, darling, everything is about ready. You go wash and freshen up a bit. While you're doing that I'll get things set for serving. It'll be ready in about two minutes."

"Okay, honey, it won't take me long. I'm really hungry. I had very little for lunch—just a bowl of chicken noodle soup with some salad."

"That sounds like a good choice for both you and the baby, sweetheart!"

Patty left the kitchen for the bathroom.

I went to the oven and opened the door. The salmon patties were done perfectly. I removed them from the oven and placed them on a small platter. Steam rose from each of the yams as I peeled them. I had sweetened the coleslaw with some sugar while stirring in the mayonnaise, vinegar, and a small amount of lemon juice. I had also prepared some tartar sauce for the salmon patties.

Patty arrived at the table and seated herself just as I finished placing everything out on the table. I began serving the meal to each of the warmed plates.

"Jason, everything looks wonderful!" she said in gratitude, looking down at her tastefully prepared dinner.

"I try," I replied, pleased with her words.

I said the blessing before we began our dinner. I was happy to see Patty enjoy her meal.

"Jason, those yams are especially tasty. I see that you were into the brown sugar and maple syrup again."

"I thought I'd sweeten them up for you. The taste seems just right. I have to agree. Glad you're enjoying them."

"Jason, 'enjoying' is not the word. I love this meal. I really appreciate your preparing dinner tonight, and every night. I'm just beat. I think the bus that stopped today put a strain on everyone. Normally, I take it in stride, but it was a hectic day."

"I know. I know exactly what you're saying, Patty."

"Oh! By the way, Irene Falsey stopped in this afternoon for a cup of tea. She loves helping out at the Loggers' Museum. She said she worked very hard last weekend in the gift shop. People are already starting to come in. In fact, it looks like Tom has found someone to take over as manager, but Irene will stay on until it looks like she'll work out."

"Wonderful! I'm glad to hear that Tom's vision is being accepted very well. I believe all the loggers will enjoy having their own museum as a testimonial to their contribution to the development of this great land of ours. The early lumber industry was an important part of the past, so long before the invention of today's chain-saw, skidders, heavy-duty log-trucks, and the many more things that have helped to make the logging industry much easier."

After the completion of our meal I told Patty I wanted her

to relax while I took care of the dishes and the clean-up of the kitchen. I told her about Ruben's and my incident with the bear and warned her not to take our beloved K-9 for a walk that night.

"It must have frightened you, Jason!"

"Believe me, I was wary. He's about the largest bear I have ever laid my eyes on, maybe with the exception of the large Polar bear at the San Diego zoo. Ruben and I just stood there not moving a bit. That bear was probably just as surprised as we were. Thank God he finally sauntered off. You never know: usually they don't bother humans, but lately there have been a few incidents of bear attacks. Ruben and I were very lucky."

"That's why it's so important not to feed the wild animals, Jason. I wish folks wouldn't do it," Patty asserted.

"You and I both know that, sweetheart, but we can't control other people," I commented.

Patty went into the living room and sat on the couch and sat with her feet up while I finished cleaning the kitchen before joining her in the living room.

We decided to play some soft music so we could sit relaxing and listening to some of our old favorites. I realized it was a good time to bring up the decision that weighed so heavily on our minds.

"Patty, would you really be okay if I decide to accept Tom Huston's offer and move to Lake Placid?" I asked, looking over to watch her expression.

There was a moment of silence.

"Dearest, wherever you go, I will go. I told you that before. I have been very seriously thinking about it. For myself, after the baby arrives, if I still want to work, it would be easier holding a hostess position than working at John's Diner. I do feel some sadness about it, because the folks in this area have been so wonderful to us. But, Jason, we have to think about our own well-being and our child's future and our financial stability." Patty looked at me solemnly.

"I know that Tom *would* like you to be his hostess someday. And besides being better off financially, I think I'd truly enjoy working as Tom's security director and personnel relations person."

"It'll be alright with me, darling. The one thing I really feel badly about is the work the guys did on the addition and the baby's nursery. Wilt and the fellows worked so hard on it to have it ready before the baby's birth. Yes, this really bothers me, but other than that I believe it's the right thing to do. I do know that Tom will be overjoyed if you accept."

I realized we had just committed to a big change in our lives. "I'll inform him, but not over the telephone. It'll be better for us to go see him together. This is a major decision. And we can't let it make us forget the Draper situation, which has me really worried. I've got to check with Lieutenant Doyle again very soon."

"I understand, Jason, I know how worried you are and so am I. But keep in mind that Chief Wilson or the local troopers stop in and out of the diner all day long. And if they are not in the diner, one of the officers is someplace close by. I know why they're there. Also, the guys are always around the diner. Charlie Perkins has even sent a couple of his loggers to the diner to check on my well-being. Believe me, I know what's going on."

"I'm glad they are. Wilt is very concerned. You're like a daughter to him."

"I know that, Jason."

"Why don't you call Lila this evening and ask her if you can take the day off tomorrow? I do think that we should see Tom without further hesitation. In no way, honey, do I want to rush you into any fast decisions, but I feel that this is important enough to move on it as soon as possible."

"Jason, I agree. I've told you before: where you go, so do I. I'll call Lila in a few minutes. Let me gather my thoughts."

A short time later, she rose to use the phone. First she placed a call to Sally, one of the waitresses whom Lila had called in that day when the unexpected bus had arrived. Then she called Lila and explained that she'd like the next day off and had already called Sally to see if she were available to sub for her, which she was.

Lila told her that there was no problem as long as she had found someone to fill in for her and that she deserved a day off. Lila and Patty talked for a few minutes longer, and then my lovely wife returned to the living room to join me on the couch. We sat in contemplative good silence, just holding hands for awhile.

Before long we retired to the bedroom. We discussed a few details of our imminent move to Lake Placid. Increasingly we were sure this change was the right decision. Even so, Patty fell off to sleep rather fitfully while I continued to toss and turn before finally settling into sleep.

The aroma of fresh coffee wafting through my nostrils brought me awake the next morning.

"Patty...? Oh, Patty! That coffee smells terrific!" I called out to her groggily from the bed.

"When I woke up you were in a deep sleep, Jason, so I decided to get up and make us some coffee."

"I'll be right out, dearest," I said as I threw the covers back. I went into the bathroom to splash some cold water on my face. It felt good and woke me fully. I combed my hair and went into the kitchen to join her.

I gave her a warm embrace and a kiss. "Good morning, my love," I greeted her.

"Jason, let's have our coffee, and then I have an idea."

"What's that, babe?" I asked.

"As long as it's on the way to Lake Placid, wouldn't it be nice if we stopped at Gertie's for breakfast? I'd love to see her."

"Good thinking! You take your shower first and then I'll quickly shave and shower. In the meantime, I'll call Lynn at the Kliffside Kennel and see if she can take Ruben today for a bath and some grooming."

"Great plan." She stood up. "How was your coffee?"

"Great, Patty," I said. I swallowed the last drop.

While Patty slipped into the shower, I called Lynn.

"Kliffside Kennel. Can I help you?" she answered.

"Good morning, Lynn. Sorry to be calling so early. Would you able to take Ruben in today for bathing and grooming this morning?"

"Jason, I certainly can. I'll see you when you get here."

"Probably within the hour. See you then."

Patty came out of the bathroom. Her long blond hair flowed around her shoulders in her lavender bathrobe. She made a bee-line for the bedroom to dress.

The hot shower relaxed my tense muscles, and the cold one swept away the sleepiness that lingered in me. I was now fully awake and shivering. I donned my thick robe and joined Patty in the bedroom.

"Honey, come here!" she said excitedly.

"What's the matter?" I asked in concern.

She smiled. "Just come here for a moment."

I went to her and she took my hand and placed it on her tummy to feel the movement of our baby. She looked up at me tenderly. With deep joy I embraced her and kissed her gently.

Patty finally broke the spell. "Well, if we're going to Lake Placid, Sherlock, we'd better get a move on."

It wasn't long before I was opening the rear gate of the Bronco for Ruben to leap in. I opened the passenger side door for Patty, then returned to the house to give everything a quick check before locking it.

The Bronco started right away: evidently the tune-up had helped. Ruben began anxiously pacing back and forth; perhaps realizing his destination would be the kennel at Eagle Bay. It was only a few minutes before we pulled up in front. I set the brake and left the Bronco running while I took Ruben inside. Patty had brought along her knitting, and her needles were already in motion.

Lynn, happy to see Ruben, gave the big dog a hug.

"Just a bath and some grooming. You might have to clip his nails, too."

"I'll check him all over, Jason. As you know, Ruben is the king when he visits us."

"Yes, I know, and it's most appreciated, too."

Ruben followed Lynn into the bathing room.

I left the kennel to rejoin Patty in the Bronco. The arm of a pastel-colored baby's sweater was beginning to take form beneath her needles.

As we drove through Inlet I looked over toward the public parking lot. Two large motor homes were parked side by side at the far end of the area. Their owners were standing in front of the units, probably exchanging their motor-home experiences. Route 28 was clear ahead. Several vehicles were already driving into the golf club parking lot.

The diner was busy. I was able to slip between two cars to park. We got out of the vehicle and walked up the steps to go inside. Just then a seaplane came in for a landing. Its floats cut the water of Long Lake, throwing sparkling-diamond spray into the air. We both agreed it was a perfect landing and a wonderful sight to see. Patty and I had some idea of what a perfect landing was like because of our flights with Dale Rush in the past. Those were memories that we'd never forget.

"Good morning, Gertie," Patty said happily as she walked into the diner.

"Patty and Jason, how are you two?" Gertie asked in delight. She was flipping a golden brown flapjack onto a plate.

"We're going along twenty miles an hour, trying to keep it right side up," I said with a chuckle, my attempt at humor.

Gertie laughed with me. "Pardon me for not pausing," she said. "I'm working alone this morning as our waitress is out with a cold."

"I know how that can be," Patty replied.

We found a small table in the corner of the diner and seated ourselves. I passed a menu to my wife. It didn't take too long to determine what we wanted for breakfast. Gertie scrambled an order of eggs for a customer at the counter and after serving him she came from behind the counter to take our order.

"Gertie, would you like me to put on an apron and help you?" Patty asked.

"No, Patty, you're taking a day off! Besides, I'm used to wearing several hats here in the diner. I certainly appreciate the offer, though. How have you been, Patty? You look wonderful. Nice and round. Jason, it's so good to see you both. Bob had to leave early this morning for Syracuse. He has an appointment to have his pickup worked on. Whatever it is, they only do it in Syracuse and Albany. Well, what'll you have for breakfast?"

"I believe I would like a poached egg on some of that toasted homemade bread, and a cup of decaf, please. And I'm doing fine, Gertie. Thanks for asking."

"Jason, your turn," Gertie said, with her pad poised to take my order.

"It's so good to see you. Sorry we missed seeing Bob. I'll have a short stack of buckwheat pancakes, crisp bacon, one egg sunny-side, and a cup of green tea."

"Yes, sir, coming right up," she said, displaying a warm grin before returning to the grill.

While we waited for our breakfast, Patty and I discussed our meeting with Tom Huston. Over the years Tom had become a close friend to us. We realized we probably should have called first before starting out for Lake Placid: however, we had decided to take the chance that Tom would be at the lodge where he could usually be found and not on a trip to New York City for a business meeting. Again we reviewed the pros and cons about our choice to move to Placid, and we decided that if Tom still wanted us on his staff, we were now ready to accept his offer.

In a few minutes Gertie reappeared at our table with our steaming hot breakfasts. She set the tray on a serving table in order to remove the hot plates. She served Patty first, then delivered my golden brown buckwheat pancakes to me. The sunny-side-up egg was on a side dish along with three strips of crisp bacon. A pitcher of warmed maple syrup accompanied the cakes. I poured my green tea from a small white teapot.

Patty said the blessing and then we began to eat our breakfast. More customers had entered the diner so Gertie continued her dual roll of cook and waitress. She always worked very hard and was dedicated to her loyal customers.

"Jason, my poached egg is wonderful, nice and fresh,"

Patty commented. "And it looks as though you are enjoying your cakes and bacon."

"Hmmm!" I heard myself responding. "They're wonderful, sweetheart. Here, have a strip of my bacon."

"Thank you, Jason. You're always so generous, my darling, always."

"Patty, all my life I have strived to treat people the same way I like to be treated," I said with a smile. "You know I'm a country boy. What you see is what you get."

"And you know I'm the same way, Jason. That's why we get along so well. I'm very happy with you. And I believe we'll feel the same about our child. We have good friends in Old Forge, that's one of the reasons I will hate to leave."

"Yes, we do. And I feel the same about our child. Speaking of friends, when is Dale Rush's wedding planned? Have you heard anything?"

"Oh, Jason, I forgot to mention it! Dale stopped at the diner yesterday. They have set the date for a month from next Saturday. I'm so sorry I didn't tell you!"

"That's wonderful!" I exclaimed, somewhat surprised that she had forgotten to tell me when she knew I was interested.

"Dale told me the invitations will go out this week. The ceremony will be at the St. Olaf Chapel on South Shore Road, Pastor John O'Connor from Rome. Rolf Brynilsen will be singing a solo."

"That's wonderful, honey. He has such a great voice! Where will the reception be held?"

"Right across the road after the ceremony at Brynilsen's Viking Village. With music by Penny Younger and the Rhythm Riders. Isn't that great?" she said enthusiastically. "With all the activity at the diner, it must have slipped my mind. He said he would be calling you. I cannot believe I forgot to mention it. Forgive me."

"Did he say anything about a bachelor party before the wedding?" I asked, somewhat disappointed Dale hadn't called me.

"It'll be three weeks from Friday at the Trails End. All the plans have already been made for it," she said as she noticed my crestfallen face. "Oh, Jason, I'm sorry. I didn't mean to hurt you. Dale stopped in especially to tell me to let you know because he and Jim have been so busy."

"It's all right. I just wondered why Dale hadn't called me himself?"

"I asked him the same question. He said he had tried a couple of times but the line was busy."

"I'm happy for them," I responded, somewhat pacified with the explanation.

"So am I, honey. I know they are a great couple."

Our conversation was brought to an end as Gertie delivered our check.

"The breakfast was wonderful, Gertie. We'll certainly look forward to seeing you in the near future. Tell Bob not to be so scarce. I miss seeing him. Give him my best," I said.

"Glad you enjoyed it. I'll look forward to seeing you both again. It won't be long before we'll be seeing three of you," Gertie replied giving Patty a little hug.

"We are looking forward to it. Take care, Gertie," Patty acknowledged.

"I will. So long for now."

We left the diner and proceeded on our way.

CHAPTER TWENTY-THREE

At the small rented cabin in the Star Lake area, Bernie Draper and Hilda Furman were sitting on the davenport having a drink. The wanted couple's eyes were glued to the television news programs to see if any developments were on about his escape. They felt fairly secure in this remote cabin area without any close neighbors. Draper's gray hairpiece lay draped over one of the bedposts at the head of the bed. He had removed his disguise, and his cane was resting in the corner of the room. Draper felt safe tucked away here in the Adirondacks, he believed the authorities would never expect him to return to the area where he had committed his crimes. But he was completely unaware of the resolve that Jack Doyle possessed. Draper was consumed with the type of blind rage that renders clear thought processes completely useless. If he could comprehend the capability of Jack Doyle or Jason Black, he would voluntarily leap into his vehicle and leave the territory under his own volition. Instead he steadfastly maintained his brazen demented demeanor.

Hilda Furman, blindly in love with the former trucking company tycoon, only remembered the nights of their early romance when they had begun a casual affair that had finally led to his divorce from his wife. It had by now developed into a serious relationship and the two had bonded together. In fact, Hilda, predominantly a quiet person, whom Draper had found

183

to be a good listener, had actually fallen in love. During his pursuit of evidence for the Cynthia and Bernie Draper divorce case, private investigator Jack Flynn had found that during the surveillance it was Draper who was doing the talking to Hilda and it was Hilda who was listening intently to the braggart.

Now, Hilda, caught in the whirlpool of events, was equally as wanted by the authorities for aiding and abetting the escapee, Draper. He, with contacts across the country, had arranged for a car to be picked up in Utica, which he felt was a clever maneuver, knowing that in no way could this exchange be traced back to him. He was certain it would give him more time to carry out the revenge he so desperately sought against the two men responsible for his capture: Lieutenant Jack Doyle and Jason Black.

"Bernie, I love you and I always will, but do you think it's smart for us to go ahead with your plan?" she asked, still hoping to dissuade him. "Now that you're out, we could just go on and try to find a new life together. If we get caught, we're both going to prison for a long time," Hilda said, her bright fiery red hair glistening in the sunlight beaming through the window.

"Hilda, let me worry about that. I love you, too, Hilda, and if you remember right you told me that you'd stick by me all the way. I have some unfinished business here in the Adirondacks and you know I'm destined to see it through. My jewelry business and other activities were doing fine until those two got on my case. Well, it's my turn now," he said with vengeance in his voice.

"You told me that if I came to Michigan to pick you up that we'd go to Canada to live. Are you going back on your word, Bernie?" Hilda asked, trying to disguise her ever growing anger.

CHAPTER TWENTY-FOUR

We arrived at the Breakshire Lodge shortly after eleven. I had been there so often, the Bronco seemed to know its way into the parking area of the stately looking lodge. The structures themselves blended well into this mountain environment. The adjacent lawns, bordered with shrubs and scattered trellises that supported the flowering plants, added to the ambience. I spotted Morey Harris, along with another groundskeeper, clipping hedges on the west side of the lodge. Clearly they were engrossed in their mission. I was so pleased to see Morey obviously not a disappointment to Tom, who had put so much faith in him. I exited the Bronco and went around to the passenger side to open the door for Patty.

"Jason, the flowers are lovely," she remarked as she stepped out of the car.

"Honey, yes, they are," I agreed, enjoying the genuine smile that lit up her face. Soon, I knew, this might be her home.

We walked to the front entrance, climbed the six stone steps, and entered. The carved bears that Wilt had presented to Tom Huston stood in the lobby like sentries on guard. The desk clerk—evidently new, because I did not recognize him—looked up with a pleasant smile to greet us.

"May I be of assistance?" he asked.

"Would Mr. Huston be in this morning?" I inquired,

185

choosing a formal approach.

"Yes. Who shall I say is calling, sir?"

"Patty and Jason Black from Old Forge," I responded.

"Are you the private detective I have heard so much about?" he asked excitedly, peering over his steel-rimmed glasses while picking up the in-house telephone.

"That's correct. I'm Jason Black, and this is my wife, Patty," I said, introducing ourselves.

"It's a pleasure to meet you both," he said, appearing a little nervous. "Just a moment—I'll ring Mr. Huston's office."

I looked at Patty and caught the expression on her face. She whispered apprehensively to me, "He's very formal, Jason."

I didn't respond, but I smiled reassuringly and patted her on the shoulder.

"Mr. Black, Mr. Huston will be with you in a moment, sir," the clerk said. His respect for us was evident.

I thanked him, and we strolled over to the chairs in the lobby to await Tom. It wasn't long before we heard a familiar voice behind us.

"Patty and Jason, what a wonderful surprise!" Tom said warmly as he approached.

We turned, hearing our friend's voice, and greeted him. Tom moved forward to shake my hand before giving Patty a gentle hug.

"It's good to see you, Tom," I said.

"Wonderful to see you both, too. Have you had breakfast yet?" Tom inquired.

"Yes, we stopped at the diner in Long Lake," I responded.

"Then let's go to my office where we can talk," he offered.

We followed Tom down the hallway into his office. I noticed that he had replaced some of his furniture. Three new oil paintings adorned his walls: one large piece behind his desk, and the others adjacent. The larger one, a painting of the new Loggers' Museum, was magnificent. I spied the name of the artist in the lower right hand corner of the oak frame: J. Mahaffy. What a surprise! Neither John nor Tom had ever mentioned it to me.

"Tom, what a beautiful painting. I didn't know John was creating this oil behind your desk. It's perfect!" I exclaimed.

"He did a great job on it, didn't he? I'm very pleased."

"He's a talented artist, Tom," Patty agreed.

"Marvelous," Tom added. He turned to my wife. "Patty, how are you feeling?"

"I'm doing just great. We're just looking forward to the birth of our child in July."

"I'm so glad to hear it. And this is a pleasant surprise to see you both here," Tom said. "Is there any special reason that brought you here?" he asked, looking at us somewhat hopeful.

We sat down in front of Tom's desk. "Tom, Patty and I have had serious thoughts about your offer of a position with your organization. Is the offer still valid?" I inquired.

A smile beamed across Tom's face. He hesitated for a moment before he responded. "It certainly is, you know that—for both of you."

We discussed at length the reasons for our decision. Tom listened intently. He was clearly jubilant. "How soon can you start?" he asked eagerly.

I found myself taken aback. I really hadn't thought of an actual date. "We have some matters we have to take care of first at our home in Old Forge."

"You won't have to worry about housing. I have a suite of rooms that will exactly suit your needs. It's located on the first floor at the rear of the lodge. It's already furnished and temporarily suitable for the two of you—I mean, the three of you. If you prefer more privacy, we have a few private cottages on the property and one could be provided to you for your growing family. We'll discuss your starting salary later, but I'm sure it will be adequate; you'll have medical and dental benefits, with a retirement plan. How does that sound to you?" He waited anxiously for my reply.

"All this is overwhelming. Your offer is more than generous, I'm sure," I responded happy that our future would feel more financially secure.

"Your housing is in addition to your starting salary. Also I have many contacts available to assist you, Patty, when the new baby arrives. And, Jason, I want you to keep your Old Forge home if you can swing it—perhaps you could rent it during the seasons. And you might even still be able to take care of some of your detective work."

"Oh! You're much too generous, Tom," Patty chimed in.

"You're both a part of my family and never forget that," Tom said as his eyes began to water.

Tom was a sentimental man and he went out of his way to make our contemplated move as easy as possible for us. I felt I should make him aware of the situation I was facing from the Draper threats.

"Tom, are you aware of the prison escape in Michigan regarding Draper who operated the jewelry store west of Tupper Lake?"

"Yes, Lieutenant Doyle has called me personally because he thought Draper might show up here. In fact the entire North Country has been alerted in this region."

"Yes, I'm aware of that. And, as you know, Doyle, Chief Wilson from Old Forge, and me have all been threatened personally."

"Yes, I'm aware of that."

"Naturally, I'm concerned, especially for my wife, our unborn child—they could be in danger, too." I said.

"I agree. It sure is a worry." Then he looked over and saw the conversation could be upsetting to Patty, who had risen and asked to excuse herself to use the restroom. Tom then discussed the duties I would be performing as an employee under his growing Breakshire umbrella. Included would be the security and management of all the properties owned by Tom. There would be no doubt about it. I would be a busy person with a great many responsibilities.

"Jason, I'm aware that Wilt and his men worked very hard on the addition they built on your log home. Maybe you could possibly spend a couple of days a week in Old Forge. I'd try to arrange a suitable working schedule for you—say, four ten-hour days—that would give you three days to go to your home in Old Forge. The rest of the week you and your family would be able to stay here. How does that sound?" He watched for my reaction.

"Tom, that's really wonderful of you." He was such a considerate person. "You realize how much our home means to us."

Patty rejoined us. I was well aware how Tom felt about her and me. Since the deaths of his wife and only son, he had looked upon us as part of his family. He had two nephews, whom I had met, but he hadn't mentioned them lately. I assumed they were busy in their own lives. I did not ask Tom about them because I had come to the conclusion that if he wanted to talk about them he certainly would.

We sat in Tom's office discussing the major change we would be making in our lives. It looked like we might still be able to maintain our home in Old Forge and our many friends in the area—that would definitely be a plus. At this crucial time in our lives, with our baby arriving shortly, this move would definitely improve our financial picture.

Tom went on to explain that after the birth of the baby, if Patty still wanted employment, he would like her to be one of the three hostesses at the lodge, perhaps eventually to take charge of the operation of the kitchen and dining areas. This supervisory position would include the hiring and discharging of employees. He assured Patty she would undergo some on-the-job training to achieve the necessary knowledge she would need to assume the many duties.

"Tom, do you think I'd be able to handle that position?" Patty asked, looking rather overwhelmed. "With the new baby coming, I wouldn't be able to leave my child too soon. And what about day care?"

"Patty, after you go through the proper training, I'd have no hesitation in placing you in that position. After all, you have been involved with the food service business for a long time as a waitress. With your intelligence and willingness to learn, you'll have the opportunity to experience the responsibilities of a supervisor in the field that you are already well acquainted with. Don't worry; everything will work out. You just wait and see." Tom said proudly. "And as far as day care is concerned, there are several women available who I call upon when I need their services for my guests. I see no problem there."

"Tom, it's very kind of you to provide a position for Patty. She won't let you down, believe me," I added.

Tom's face turned a bit sad. "I want you to know that I have no idea how long I'll be around. If my health fails, I do not want to have to close down the lodge. It's been my life. I worked so hard to achieve my goals, and maybe I haven't accomplished everything I set out to do, but I've given it my best. Patty and Jason, I trust you and I trust your judgment. I'm grooming you both to become a part of the Breakshire Lodge family. Eventually perhaps you'll share in the ownership of the lodge, after I'm gone."

"What?" I asked, astonished to hear him talking so gloomily.

"You heard me, Jason! I won't take no for answer," Tom stated adamantly.

"Tom, Patty and I certainly didn't expect this kind of support. Are you certain this is what you want?"

"I think it's time you know: you both are listed in my will. This is all I have to say on this subject for now. My next question to you is when can I expect you to make the move?"

I looked at Patty and she looked at me.

"Patty will have to give John and Lila two weeks' notice. I'd say that we can be here in about three or four weeks. We'll have to get things wrapped up there."

"That'll be fine. I'm looking forward to it. Jason, you're going to be my right-hand man here at the lodge. In a few weeks I'll arrange for a staff meeting and introduce you to everyone. This will take a big load off my shoulders." He smiled widely. "I appreciate the decision you have made to join us here at Lake Placid."

"We both thank you and we'll do our best to live up to the confidence you have bestowed on us, Tom." I returned his smile.

"You're more than welcome. And now, I've taken the liberty of arranging for lunch for the three of us. Maybe you'd like to take a minute to freshen up before. I'll meet you in the dining room in about ten minutes."

When we entered the dining room, Tom was standing at our table by the window. As we reached him, he pulled out a chair to seat Patty, and we took our seats. The waitress, Carmella, appeared at our table to give us the menus and to take our drink order. Patty decided on lemonade while Tom and I ordered hot tea. When she returned with our drinks we placed our food order. Patty ordered the Cobb salad and Tom and I decided on the special of the day, grilled salmon.

"Tom, how many waitresses do you employ here?" Patty inquired, looking around.

"We have a total of twelve full-time waitresses and waiters. Of course, during the busy seasons, and for banquets and weddings, we have a roster of part-time servers on call."

"I'm very impressed, Tom," Patty remarked.

"Yes, Patty, I have been most fortunate to be surrounded by good people. In this business, as you know, good service to the public is essential."

"Most important!" I chimed in.

Our lunches arrived shortly. It appeared that Carmella was an excellent waitress. I could see that Patty was observing with approval the way she served our table in an efficient, deliberate way.

Lunch at the table was quiet, with very little being discussed. We were all deep into our thoughts, me especially wondering what Tom's comment about his health had meant. Patty finally broke the silence by telling Tom how much she was enjoying her salad. Then I thanked him and told him that the chef should be congratulated—the salmon was perfect.

We sat for a few more minutes and talked with Tom over refills of tea to thank him for the confidence and trust that he had placed in us. We assured him that we would begin our plans for our move to Lake Placid as soon as possible. He told us that our suite of rooms would soon be ready for us to occupy and that if there were anything else we needed we were just to let him know.

We finally left for our drive back to Old Forge. Our meeting with Tom had been monumentally important to us. Each still taking it in, we talked very little on the way home. Moving to Lake Placid would be a good new beginning, but it would also be a difficult one.

When we passed Gertie's, the parking area was crammed full of cars and pickup trucks. Gertie and Bob would no doubt be surprised when they heard about the change in our lives. In fact, everyone would be. However, we knew we would try to maintain our log home in the area we loved, Old Forge. People would understand that with the baby due to arrive soon, we had to consider our financial situation. At Lake Placid, Patty's employment in the hostess position would be easier for her, with a set salary instead of relying on tips and not knowing whether we would be able to meet our monthly bills. Hopefully, everything would work out satisfactorily. I would try to explain it to all my friends whom I had made over the years. Several had expended a great deal of time on the addition to our log home. Somehow I would make it up to them. I was determined.

The Kliffside Kennel was just about to close when we arrived to pick up Ruben. I left Patty in the Bronco as I went up the stairs to the office door. As I entered I heard several dogs barking in the back. Lynn must have seen us pull in, as she was already bringing Ruben out. She had to pull hard on the leash that was fastened to his collar to keep him under control because he had become so excited when he saw me standing there.

"Settle down, Ruben," I commanded.

"He's alright, Jason, just excited to see you," Lynn remarked.

"You did a great job, Lynn." I complimented her for how clean and trimmed he was.

"He's a good boy, Jason," Lynn said.

I paid the bill and thanked her, then left the office and put

Ruben in the back of the Bronco after I opened the gate for him.

"Good boy, Ruben," Patty called back to him.

"Ruben looks good, honey. Lynn knows her business."

We backed out of the parking area and headed toward our home after our fruitful trip up north. I was sure glad to be home again.

CHAPTER TWENTY-FIVE

It was late in the afternoon. Luther Johnson, a U.S. Marine Corps veteran from the Star Lake area and a friend of Jason Black, was just coming out of the Star Lake grocery store carrying two paper bags full of groceries, when a redheaded woman who was hurriedly entering the store accidentally bumped into his left arm with sufficient force to cause him to drop one of his bags.

"Oh, I'm sorry, mister," she apologized.

"Don't worry about it. It appears there's nothing broken," Luther replied.

A clerk who saw the mishap came rushing over with a new paper bag. The redhead leaned down and started handing the clerk the items to place in the new bag. Luther was still holding the remaining bag in his right arm. He realized that he had never seen the redheaded woman before. With the bag refilled, the clerk placed it in Luther's left arm. Luther thanked him and turned to address the woman who had run into him.

"Are you okay?" Luther asked.

"I'm okay and I'm so sorry, mister," she replied.

"What's your name?" Luther asked the stranger.

"Hilda," she replied without thinking. Immediately she realized she should have made up a fictitious name.

"My name is Luther. You must not be from these parts, as I've never seen you before."

"We're just tourists passing through. You have a picturesque place," she said hurriedly.

"Whereabouts are you folks staying?" Luther probed further.

"Oh! We're just renting a small place a few miles from here," she answered, knowing that she had already told this man too much.

"Where's that?" Luther asked.

"Not too far from here. Well, I have to get going," she said as she walked away.

Luther watched her as she disappeared down one of the aisles in the store. Not having any perishables in his grocery bags, he decided to wait in his pickup and keep his eye open for the redhead when she left the store. Luther had a strange feeling about this woman. Something wasn't just right, and Luther's sixth sense was activated. He didn't have to wait very long. Hilda came out of the store and looked around. She continued walking briskly down along the second row of parked vehicles. She stopped in front of a maroon-colored Ford sedan and climbed in with her purchases. Luther kept an eye on the Ford as Hilda pulled out of the parking lot and headed west on Route 3. Luther decided to follow her at a safe distance. He waited until she was about a-half-mile down the road before pulling his pickup onto the highway. He didn't want to cause this woman to become suspicious, so he stayed just in sight of the Ford. When the Ford turned at Fine onto the Fine-Edwards Road, Luther slowed his pickup down to a crawl. The road ran along the Oswegatchie River for about eight miles. He continued to follow the car for approximately two-and a-half miles until it pulled into a lane. Luther knew then where Hilda was going—the one small cabin at the end of the lane. He pulled off the road and waited for a few minutes before returning to the Star Lake area and his home.

CHAPTER TWENTY-SIX

When we pulled into our driveway to our log home, a large doe was nibbling on one of our hydrangea plants.

"Jason! Jason, that's our plant she's eating," Patty cried. She had mixed emotions. She loved her flowers but she also loved the deer.

I could see that Patty was getting upset, so I tapped the horn lightly. The doe sauntered off with a portion of the plant in her mouth.

"Darn it," I said. "You can't have anything growing in the yard. Even the plants the so-called experts maintain deer do not consume are bitten down to the ground. I often wonder where they do their research from—possibly a computer?"

"Jason, I work so very hard to keep our plants and flowers looking presentable, and now look at them!" she exclaimed, trying unsuccessfully not to show her frustration.

Patty got out of the Bronco and went directly into the house. I got out and opened the back gate. Ruben leaped out, ran around in two or three circles, and then entered his dog run. I closed the gate and went inside to join Patty, who was still fuming over her injured plants. I could tell that her dander was up, so I tried to remain calm. I went to her, put my arms around her gently, and told her that everything would be fine.

"Try to relax, Patty. Getting upset isn't good for you or the baby. We can always replace the plant life."

"Oh, you're right as usual. I'm sorry, sweetheart, but when I observed our plants being destroyed, I lost my temper. I'm alright now."

Just then the telephone rang. Patty rose to answer it.

"Hello," she said. "It's for you, Jason," she said, handing me the phone.

"I'll take it in the office, Patty. Wait till I pick it up before you hang up."

"Okay, honey," she replied.

I went into the office and picked up my receiver.

"Hello, can I help you?"

"*Semper fi!* Jason, Luther Johnson here," he said excitedly.

"Luther, you ole son-of-a-gun, how are you?"

"Jason, except for a little arthritis, I'm pretty good. Say, Jason, regarding that Draper who escaped from a Michigan prison: what kind of a car is he supposed to be in?" he asked.

"He's supposedly with his redheaded girlfriend in a Mustang. Why do you ask?"

"I was grocery shopping a little while ago in Star Lake, and when I was leaving the store a good-looking redheaded woman walked into me and one of my grocery bags ripped, causing the groceries to spill all over the floor. She was pretty embarrassed."

"There's a lot of redheaded women in this world," I replied. "Why did she appear suspicious to you?"

"Well, there's a little more. She went on shopping inside the store after she told me her name, and I went out to my pickup truck and waited for her to come out."

"I thought you had a black Jeep."

"I do, but I purchased a good used Chevy pickup."

"Well, go on. Is there more?"

"Yes, I had this strange feeling about her—guess you ex-cops call it a sixth sense. Anyways, I followed her at a distance. She was driving a maroon Ford sedan. She proceeded to Fine and then took the road toward Edwards. That's about an eight-mile stretch. She turned off on a lane, which leads to a small rental cabin owned by a fellow from Rochester. I didn't follow her in there; I turned around and headed home."

"What did she say her name was?" I asked. I couldn't help but wonder if this could be Draper's redhead.

"We exchanged names. She seemed like a friendly gal, with fiery red hair and freckles that were becoming to her. Her name is Hilda. She didn't tell me her last name."

"Hilda! Did you say Hilda?" I exclaimed. I could not believe what I had heard. Surely it couldn't be just coincidence.

"That's the name she gave me, Jason."

"Luther, I may owe you a steak dinner. Draper is supposed to be traveling with a Hilda Furman. She has fiery red hair."

"Holy cow! Do you think it could be them in that cabin, Jason?"

"There's a darn good possibility that it could be them. There haven't been any sightings of them anywhere in the country. Have you told anyone else about this, Luther?"

"No one, but you, Jason," he replied.

"It's best not to say anything to anyone else yet. I'll contact the authorities right away!"

"Don't worry I won't say a word."

"Thanks, buddy, for calling me. "Semper fi!"

"Semper fi!"

I couldn't help but believe that Draper had returned to the scene of his criminal activity. Could it really be them? I went to my gun safe, removed my .44 caliber handgun, and checked the ammunition to make sure it was sufficient. I told Patty what was going on and asked her if she'd mind if I used her Jeep. There was no question when it came to the use of her vehicle, but only her concern for my safety.

I went into the office to call Doyle. I asked him to meet me in Tupper Lake on Route 3 at the first shopping center on the right. I told him that it was important and that he should bring about ten troopers, either uniformed or BCI people. And they should bring their weaponry and vests.

"Jason, what's going on?" Jack demanded.

"I think I've found Draper, Jack. I'll give you the facts when I see you. I should be there in about an hour and a half."

"It better be good, Jason."

"Sir, I'd never give you a bum steer! You know me better than that."

I kissed Patty and held her close to me, gently but fiercely.

"Are you sure you have to go? Let the troopers handle it, please," she pleaded.

"Patty, you know I have to be there," I answered firmly.

She evidently saw the determined look in his eyes. "I understand. But please be careful, darling," she said, trying to hold back her tears.

"I will, darling. Keep all the doors locked."

Patty's Jeep had a full tank of gasoline. I headed north on Route 28. Traffic was light and I was too engrossed to even check the speedometer. The white broken lines passed by quickly. Normally I wouldn't be pushing so hurriedly, but the information Luther had shared with me was too important to ignore.

When I arrived in Tupper Lake I turned onto Route 3 and headed west. As I turned into the designated shopping center parking area, I was pleased to observe two BCI cars and two troop cars already waiting. Lieutenant Doyle immediately jumped out of his car to approach the Jeep.

"What's up, Jason? It better be good," he asked, somewhat grimly.

I explained to him about the telephone call I had received from Luther Johnson. Jack listened to every word. He advised me that I wouldn't be able to accompany his detail to the cabin, but I could follow the detail to the intersection of the lane in question where it joined the Fine-Edwards road. He quickly devised the plan to approach the cabin and what the detail would do when they arrived there.

Jack returned to his detail and explained his plan quickly to his men. They lined up behind him and moved out. I fell in behind the last troop car. When we arrived in Fine we pulled off the highway. I remained in the Jeep while Lieutenant Doyle discussed their approach to the cabin. With my window down I could barely overhear the lieutenant mention that once the cabin was surrounded they would use the bullhorn to announce their presence and order the occupant or occupants outside. After the briefing, Jack approached the Jeep.

"Jason, I'm sorry that I can't permit you to join us, but I know you understand why."

"I do, Jack. This information may be nothing at all, but it has to be checked out."

"Yes, it does. Remember, Jason, Draper made threats in that prison cell against us both. If it is him and his girlfriend, he's probably armed, and naturally under those circumstances should be considered extremely dangerous. After we have the cabin surrounded we'll attempt to make contact with them. Hopefully they'll come out, but if they don't we'll give them some tear gas. We didn't have a K-9 available or we would have brought him with us."

"Good luck, Jack," I said tersely.

"Jason, this is one of the reasons I came on the job. I love busting the bad guys and gals."

"Just be careful," I warned him.

The detail moved further down the road and parked off the highway just a short distance from the lane in question. I followed in the Jeep and pulled around the parked troop cars, then turned around so I could view the entrance to the lane.

The grim-faced detail of troopers lined up with their weaponry. From inside the Jeep I could view Jack giving the men their final instructions. I counted nine officers as they filed behind Jack and approached guardedly up the lane. Just before they climbed the knoll I could see them disperse to the left and right. I assumed the cabin was probably just over the knoll, tucked away behind a stand of pine trees. What would the troopers encounter?

I kept my window down in hopes of hearing anything. In a few minutes a voice blared from the bullhorn quite a distance away, just over the knoll.

"This is the state police!" Jack's voice boomed. "We know you are in there. Come outside! We would like to talk with you."

There was silence and then I heard again, "This is the state police! We know you are in there. Come outside immediately! We would like to talk with you. You are surrounded. Come outside immediately!"

CHAPTER TWENTY-SEVEN

Inside the cabin Draper clenched his fists in anger.

"Hilda, did you hear that?" he shouted over to her where she stood at the window in the bedroom looking out.

"Yes, Bernie, I did. Oh, what are we going to do? There are a lot of cops outside." Her voice was tight and shrill.

"Hilda, what did you do at the store, tell the world we were here?"

"I didn't say anything about us or where we were staying. Honest, Bernie, I didn't."

"Damn it! These New York State cops mean business. Son-of-a-----, we're cornered like those Arizona fruit rats."

"Why did I get involved with you in the first place, Bernie?" she lamented loudly.

"Supposedly you fell in love with me, Hilda," Bernie said harshly, picking up his shotgun.

"Bernie, put that gun down," she pleaded with tears forming in her eyes. "I do love you, Bernie." She began to sob.

"Well, love or no love, I'm not going back to that damned cell," he vowed angrily. He leaned forward to kiss Hilda and shut her up.

At that moment, a tear gas projectile came flying through the window.

Without uttering another word, Draper flung the door of the cabin open and began shooting the shotgun in the direction of the troopers. He pumped the action on the shotgun twice before receiving a shot to the head. The shotgun dropped from his hands as he tried to call out to Hilda. Then he fell to the floor in the doorway, flat on his face, dead. Hilda began to scream and sob uncontrollably.

The troopers advanced toward the cabin slowly and cautiously.

Hilda screamed out, "Don't shoot! I'm not armed!"

One trooper stepped over Draper's body to see his open eyes staring off into infinity. He reached down to check for a pulse. The beating had ceased. Another trooper went to Hilda to comfort and apprehend her. She continued to sob and plead as the tears continued to stream down her cheeks.

Other members of the detail began to place yellow tape around the cabin to rope off the crime scene. Lieutenant Doyle called Troop S Headquarters to advise them that the situation at Star Lake had been resolved and to have them contact the medical examiner's office and kindly ask them to send someone to the scene.

CHAPTER TWENTY-EIGHT

After all the gunshots I impatiently waited for someone to tell me what was going on. I found it difficult to continue to stay there, but I did not go against Doyle's request. A few minutes later a trooper walked over the knoll and signaled me to join the detail.

I eagerly jumped out of the Jeep, locked the door, and ran up the knoll. As I approached the cabin I spotted Doyle and several troopers standing near the entrance. They seemed to be speaking to a redheaded woman who was crying hysterically. A man lay in blood on the floor of the cabin's doorway, partially outside the entrance. From my position I could not make a positive identification; however, I was confident it must be Draper. Lieutenant Doyle broke away from the group to walk toward me.

"Jack, is it him?" I asked apprehensively.

"Yes, Jason, it's Draper. After we fired the tear gas, he finally appeared and began to open fire immediately with a shotgun aimed directly at us. Our people returned fire. Draper was shot dead in the heavy exchange of bullets. We had no choice. We have arrested his girlfriend, Hilda Furman, and we'll be turning her over to the feds. Our evidence people have been alerted and are en route along with the medical examiner. They will process the scene." Jack sighed heavily. "It's too bad that it had to end this way, but it did. Furman apparently loved

Draper, but by her association with him she'll undoubtedly be facing some federal charges."

"I don't see how it could have ended any other way, Jack. Draper was determined to avenge the criminal charges he went to prison for, and by his own actions he caused the criminal justice system to respond. Yes, it's over with. He brought it on himself."

"Thank you for contacting us, Jason. Major Roy Garrison is on his way to the scene."

"I don't mind admitting this conclusion is a huge relief to me. And now I had best be on my way. Patty is at home worrying mightily. Please give my regards to the major. Take care of yourself, Jack."

We shook hands. I turned and walked toward the Jeep. As I descended the knoll I found myself silently thanking Luther Johnson for feeling there was something amiss when he dropped his bag of groceries. Luther's sixth sense about Hilda Furman hastily entering and leaving the grocery store paid off in the end. Throughout my career, help from ordinary citizens like Luther had helped me close many cases successfully.

I arrived back at the Jeep knowing a new freedom now that Bernard Draper was no longer around to threaten me. Now my only thought was to return to my home and my wife. I backed the Jeep up and turned toward the highway. I glanced at my watch, turned the radio on, and headed to Tupper Lake and then to Old Forge. Patty, so worried, would be so happy to see me arrive home safe. My foot pressed down on the gas pedal.

When I pulled into the yard of our log home I could see Ruben lying on the porch with his ears standing up straight at full attention. His tail began swishing back and forth as soon as he recognized me. The door opened and my blond haired wife stood smiling in the doorway to greet me, with her arms extended. I was happy to be home.

"Jason, I'm so glad you're home safely. Are you okay, sweetheart? I've been worried sick!" she said, tears silvering in her eyes.

"I'm fine, darling. Draper was shot to death. I wasn't

anywhere near him. He shot at the troopers first and they returned fire. His girlfriend, Hilda Furman, is now under arrest," I informed her as I embraced her trembling body.

"I'm happy you're home, safe and sound," she added, kissing me lovingly on the cheek.

"So am I, darling. Let's go inside." I wanted us to feel more normal. "Say, I'm kind of hungry. I know it's late, but have we got anything to make a sandwich with?"

"I'm sure I can find something."

"That's wonderful, sweetheart, wonderful."

Patty was full of questions about what happened in the Star Lake region. I didn't have much to tell her, except that as far as Bernie Draper was concerned, the threats he had made from his prison cell were now over, with his death. Draper, by his own hand, had brought about his demise when he pulled the trigger on his shotgun.

"Patty, you can relax now. We both can. Draper is gone from our lives."

Patty sighed deeply and offered no comment. We didn't discuss it any further. We were both overjoyed to finally have it come to an end.

CHAPTER TWENTY-NINE

Two weeks went by. The talk around town about the death of Bernard Draper had dwindled, and the talk around town had shifted to the forthcoming wedding of longtime bachelor, Dale Rush. Jim Jenny had rearranged his schedule so he would be able to perform the honor of being best man. They had become very close friends since he had begun his position at the marina.

On Friday evening Dale's bachelor party took place at the Trails End and was attended by many of our mutual friends plus some of his business associates from the Old Forge and Inlet area. I arrived a few minutes after the party had started. The Rhythm Riders with Penny Younger had just finished playing a song. Penny was relating some stories about Dale's early days as a pilot and how he had power-dived over Penny's farm, causing three horses to bolt over a fence and into the waters of a nearby pond. "Do you remember that day, Dale?"

"Indeed, Penny, I do. I'll never forget it. I thought the wings were coming off the plane," Dale responded, his face a little flushed.

The laughter was loud in the banquet room until the booming voice of Wilt Chambers brought everyone to silence.

"The roasting of Dale will now begin," he announced. Several of the men present told stories about Dale in his younger days. They chided him about being too bashful to ask the girls to the high school dances. Another told a tale of Dale being chased by a swarm of bees and how he had had to dive into First Lake to avoid being stung. The bits and pieces from Dale's friends and former students also revealed a young man who had developed into an intelligent gentleman, a trusted friend, and a loyal American who had served his nation in the highest tradition of military service.

Continuing on with the roasting, the crowd broke out into laughter when Jack Falsey told about the time while he was fishing on Fourth Lake and out of the north appeared a red and white seaplane. It was Dale, who had put the plane into a dive at the exact moment that Jack was trying to battle a lake trout. Jack had lost his focus on landing the feisty fish, so when Dale pulled out of the dive, the trout had wiggled free from the hook to find freedom in the blue waters of the lake.

I rose to add my comments, "Dale, all I can say after hearing these tales from your so called friends is thanks to Evelyn for taking you off our hands!" The guests clapped with a resounding cheer.

The roasting lasted for almost an hour. It was all in fun. When Dale got up from the table to give his comments to the group, he first apologized to Jack for causing him to lose the prize trout. Everybody applauded and raised their glasses high to toast and wish their good friend, Dale Rush, the very best in his upcoming marriage to Evelyn O'Brien. After the roasting by his good friends, everyone milled around and enjoyed the remainder of the festivities until the party broke up around eleven.

The next morning, before family and friends, Dale Patrick Rush and Evelyn Christina O'Brien were united in marriage in the St. Olaf Chapel on South Shore Road, by Pastor John O'Connor of Rome, New York, when he pronounced them husband and wife. One of the highlights of the wedding was soloist Rolf Brynilsen singing "I'll Walk With God." Patty and I held hands tightly during the song.

After the ceremony the wedding party formed a line outside the chapel where everyone congratulated the new bride and groom. The newlyweds looked very happy as they greeted their guests warmly in the reception line. The best man, Jim Jenny, and his lovely wife stood alongside the newly married couple, with her brother and his wife from Maine. They had arrived the day before so he could give his sister away at the wedding. Unfortunately her other brother was unable to attend due to the illness of his wife.

When the last guest departed the reception line, we all followed the wedding party to the reception being held across the road at Brynilsen's Viking Village, where Jan and Rolf Brynilsen were to host a delightful buffet. Patty and I sat with Wilt, Jack and Irene Falsey, and Charlie Perkins and his lovely wife, Janet. Our table was next to the bridal party. A designated table was piled high with gifts and cards.

Dale and Evelyn danced gracefully across the wooden dance floor. All eyes were on the handsome couple. After the first dance, several other couples drifted onto the floor to join them. Soon the dance floor began to fill, especially when the band played a waltz. The well-known photographer, Jerry, from Boonville, kept his camera flashing as he took pictures of the festivities.

Around two, servers began to set up the table with covered buffet pans, salads, various covered bowls, condiments, and rolls. The tables were called individually after the serving of the wedding table. Platters of roast beef, ham, scalloped potatoes, baked beans, and mixed vegetables were all piping hot, along with other dishes too numerous to recall. I, of course, found it difficult not to overfill my plate, but Patty tried to exert restraint on hers.

After the meal, the group returned to the dance floor and conversation as the Rhythm Riders returned to the stage to play. It was a gala affair.

At three, the bride and groom proceeded to the table where the five-tier wedding cake awaited them. They cut the first slice together and gave each other a taste. The servers then took over by cutting the rest of the cake and delivering a piece to each of the waiting guests along with hot steaming cups of coffee and decaf.

The reception came to an end around four-thirty in the afternoon. As they left, everyone congratulated the newlyweds and wished them the very best on their marriage.

"Jason, Evelyn looks so beautiful," Patty said admiringly.

"Yes, she's a beautiful woman. And I believe she and Dale will make a great married couple. Like you and me, they love each other very much. I knew that someday the right woman for Dale would come into his life. Well, Patty, that day has arrived and now they're off on their honeymoon. Where do you think they're going?"

"Evelyn did tell me in confidence that they were considering Silverton, Colorado. It's located north of Durango. Evelyn's family owns a mountain retreat near Red Mountain Pass, north of Silverton."

"Really? Dale never mentioned to me that Evelyn's family had property in the west."

"I didn't know it either, Jason. I was surprised to learn of it."

"Oh, so was I. I just hope that they'll both be as happy as we are. I love you Patty."

"I know you do, Jason, and I feel the same way about you." She reached over to clasp my hand.

"I wonder how long they'll be gone," I said.

"Evelyn indicated it might be two weeks," she replied.

"That's good!"

"She confided in me, Jason. Both of them are stressed out from the past winter's snowmobile business, and they just want to relax and rest. The marina is in good hands. Jim Jenny has been placed in charge of operations and is employing two new people from the Finger Lakes region."

"Boy! You certainly know what's going on," I said admiringly.

"I just keep my ears open, Jason. I'm a good listener."

We pulled into the driveway at about five-thirty. Ruben was on guard. His ears shot straight up at attention when he spotted us. I pulled up as close as I could to the dog run. We exited the car, walked over to the run, and went inside along with our dog. Patty stroked his back lovingly. His tail swished back and forth before moving over to me for attention. He was definitely an equal time-pet, not wanting either of us to feel neglected.

Patty and I decided that we would best skip supper because we had so much to eat that afternoon at the wedding reception.

"Patty, it's still difficult to believe Dale is married. I never thought that he would give up his bachelorhood."

"All it takes is the right woman, Jason."

"You're so right about that. I'm so pleased that he found someone. Evelyn is just the right match for him. They have so much in common. Honey, I hope that he is as happy as I am being married to you. I certainly wish both of them every bit of happiness they can muster, especially in the crazy world we live in."

"I agree."

We decided to turn on the television to see if there was a movie that would interest us. We found a light comedy to enjoy until ten o'clock, time to retire.

I let Ruben out for a quick run into the woods. Before long he returned, followed me into the house, and took his place on his air mattress. I returned to Patty in the living room, excited to share with her an idea I had had while waiting for the dog.

"Patty, what do you think? If we rent out our log home, it would give us additional income and we wouldn't have to sell our property. What do you say?" I eagerly watched for her expression.

"What a good idea, Jason!" she replied. "Do you have anyone in particular in mind?"

"I believe that Jim Jenny is looking for a place to rent. He has to commute five days a week to the O'Brien Marina. I'll check with him to see if he may be interested in renting our place. I know if he did rent it he would take care of it as though it was his own. He is a meticulous gentleman." I was eager to reassure her.

"I know he is. That would be wonderful, Jason."

"I'll call him shortly. But first I will have to meet with Wilt and the guys with the news before any rumors start. I'll mention it to Jim Jenny then. No sense in creating any confusion. It's going to be difficult enough to tell them about our new beginning in Lake Placid," I said. I hadn't wanted to mention it prior to the wedding in the event they had any antagonism toward me with our leaving the area. With this decision made, I felt a huge sense of relief and, all of a sudden, was overtaken by exhaustion.

We retreated to the bedroom. We had had so much to think about. After our nightly prayers, sleep overtook us immediately.

CHAPTER THIRTY

The tugging sensation on the foot of the bed aroused us. I quickly looked over at the alarm clock—almost six-thirty. The alarm clock wound down. I nudged Patty and she slowly pushed the covers back and got out of bed.

"Jason, I can't believe we overslept. I'm going to be late. Thank goodness for Ruben. Good boy, Ruben," she said as she leaned over to pet him.

While Patty went to the bathroom to shower and get dressed for work, I let Ruben out for his morning run. I waited by the door for his return. As he bounded back toward the house, I slipped outside to open the dog run gate. He went into the run without hesitation.

When I went back inside, Patty was already picking up her purse and her keys for the Jeep. She quickly kissed me as she rushed out.

"Have a good day, Patty. I'll try to stop in for lunch today," I called after her.

"See you later, dear. I'd best get going," Patty replied.

"Drive carefully."

"I will, Sherlock. Don't worry so much."

I watched her drive toward Route 28. She was soon out of sight. I closed the door and went to the bathroom to shave and shower. The hot water from the pulsating showerhead relaxed my tight back muscles. After the hot shower I turned the lever

213

so I could fully wake up with ice cold water pouncing on my body. I felt like a new man. I grabbed one of our new large bath towels to dry myself off. Nothing like my morning shower to revitalize me.

For breakfast I scrambled two eggs, placed two slices of Texas toast in the toaster, and instead of coffee I decided on a cup of green tea. I poured myself a small glass of cranberry juice, which quenched my early morning thirst.

I had just finished washing the breakfast dishes when the telephone rang.

"Hello," I said.

"Jason, Lieutenant Doyle here."

"Jack, it's good to hear from you. It must be important for you to be calling so early."

"It's very important, Jason. For several days we have been interviewing Hilda Furman, Draper's girlfriend. Believe me, we have learned a great deal from her. She has been candid with us—not only about Draper, but about some other Draper types in Arizona. She's been blowing the whistle on several so-called big shots. I can't go into detail, but I've got some bad news for you!"

"What? What kind of news, Jack?" I asked, concerned.

"Furman told us that Draper was so adamant about causing revenge on us and others that he may have engaged a couple of real bad dudes to carry out the threats if something happened to him."

"Are you kidding?" I was dumbfounded.

"No, damn it, I'm serious."

"Do you have any idea who they are?"

"Only that they are from Phoenix. She saw them once with Draper, but she doesn't know their names. She did indicate that they are Caucasian, both around forty years of age. One of them has a scar that goes from the center of his forehead to the bottom of his right ear lobe. I've contacted the detective division of the Phoenix PD and given them the information. I'm certain they will be able to ID both of them. It is believed that both of them have extensive criminal histories. I was going to contact your buddy, Jack Flynn, but thought that you'd like to do the honors."

"I'll do that this morning, Jack!"

"Be careful, Jason. We have no idea where these bums are at the present time. If I hear anything I'll let you know immediately. In the meantime, we will continue our session with Furman. She has been cooperative, probably looking for a break. Draper really had her on the string with his phony baloney, but I believe she really loved him. From what she told us, I feel she was trying to derail him from his vengeful plans. I'll call you immediately if anything develops. In the meantime, be on guard, at least until we can get a location on these birds," he cautioned.

"I will, Lieutenant. Thanks for calling. Jack, again, thanks for letting me know about Draper's friends."

"Just be careful, Jason. I've already called Chief Todd Wilson and the two local troopers in your area."

"Good."

We hung up. It was too early to contact Jack because of the time difference. I made a mental note to call him later. I went over to the stove and turned on the burner under the teakettle. My mind was now racing with Jack's phone message. I'd have to share the bad news with Patty. Maybe these two people wouldn't carry out the threat for Draper now that he was deceased. Or maybe they would. Frightening to think about!

I went into my office to type up a few bad-check case reports and file them in their respective folders. I cleaned off the desk, ran the vacuum cleaner throughout the house, and I dusted the furniture, trying to keep busy so I wouldn't be too troubled with my thoughts.

I would approach Jim Jenny about the possibility of him renting our property. I was certain there would be no problem with Jim and his family in our home. And I was pretty sure he'd welcome the offer. The long drive to and from the Utica region can wear a person down. And his vehicle was using a great amount of fuel, a costly consideration.

I checked my watch—now eleven-thirty. I placed a call to

Flynn Investigations. The recording came on indicating they were out of the office, but to leave a message. I decided to call back later. Next I called Tom Huston at the Breakshire Lodge. We spoke for a few minutes. Tom advised me that the Loggers' Museum seemed to be well received. He was pleased with the performance of the gift shop. Irene Falsey had selected some excellent items for display that were proving to be very popular with the visitors. But although he was trying to sound upbeat, I detected a note in Tom's voice that upset me. I asked him how he was feeling, but of course he said he was doing just fine. I told him that I'd try to come to the lodge in a few days to discuss my new position. He was obviously pleased, saying he would be looking forward to that.

"Tom, take care."

"You, too, Jason. Please give my regards to Patty."

We said our goodbyes and hung up.

I went outside to check on Ruben, who was inside his doghouse taking a snooze. I went back inside the house, picked up my car keys, and locked the door on my way out. It was just after the noon hour. I climbed into the Bronco, started it up, and let it warm for a few minutes. I then headed toward Route 28, but could not pull out onto the highway because two large semis were coming down the hill headed to Old Forge. After they passed I pulled in behind them.

The parking lot was jammed at John's Diner. Lila's chicken and biscuit special always filled the place. The customers loved her special, which, I had to admit, was one of the best chicken and biscuits in this section of the mountains. The meat was tender and plentiful in sizable pieces that would melt in your mouth, always served piping hot with delicious fluffy biscuits and gravy.

As usual I located a space at the end of the parking area. I had just enough room to pull in. Barely able to get out of the car, I squeezed through the narrow opening. I nodded at Peter, one of the local attorneys, as he was leaving to return to his law office.

I entered the diner and found a seat near the counter. Patty was taking an order at one of the tables and gave me a smile as she passed by. Surprisingly, she was still able to maneuver around the crowded restaurant despite her added weight.

"I'll be with you shortly, Jason," she acknowledged.

There was no need to look at the menu. I had already decided on the weekly special, the popular chicken and biscuits.

I glanced around the diner, but did not see anyone I knew. Either they had eaten already or they were running late.

"I bet I know what you're going to order, my dear," Patty said as she walked up behind me.

"Yes, sweetheart, I'll have the special."

"The chicken is especially tender today and all the biscuits are coming out of the oven golden brown. Would you care for some coleslaw with that? And what would you like to drink?" Patty asked as she wrote down my order.

"Honey, yes, I would like the coleslaw. For drinks, hot green tea and a tall glass of ice-cold water with a lemon wedge.

"You'll love the coleslaw. It's sweetened with a touch of sugar, just the way you like it."

"Sounds good to me, honey," I replied as she scurried off to the kitchen to place my order.

I noticed many new faces in the diner. The tourist season seemed to be well underway. Curiosity about the serene Adirondack region brought people to the mountains with their tents, campers, motor homes, and vehicles to enjoy Mother Nature's scenic beauty so bountiful with its rivers, lakes, and mountain trails. There seemed to be a renewed interest for second homes. I could only hope that the overdevelopment would not painfully alter the atmosphere of my beloved mountain retreat.

My thoughts drifted back to my present predicament. I did not think that this would be a good time to tell Patty the unfortunate news that I had just received from Jack Doyle earlier. I had better wait until evening. I didn't want to upset her at work, especially in her present condition.

Patty appeared with my order. She set the steaming plate of

chicken and biscuits in front of me along with my bowl of coleslaw, a glass of ice water, and a cup of green tea.

"Jason, is there anything else you'd like?"

"No, I can't think of a thing. Everything looks wonderful," I replied as I picked up my fork to begin.

It didn't take me long to finish my lunch. I would have ordered a second plate of chicken and biscuits, but the words of Patty kept echoing in my ears: "Watch your weight, Jason."

I told Patty that I'd see her at home around five-thirty that afternoon. She asked if I had enjoyed my lunch. I assured her that it had indeed been very tasty and asked her to give my compliments to the chef. I then went to the cashier and paid the check while Patty rushed off to take an order. I waved to her as I left the diner.

Walking across the parking lot I met Chief Wilson, who was stopping for his lunch.

"Jason, has Doyle called you with the bad news?" Todd asked.

"Yes, he has. I haven't told Patty yet—thought it best to wait until tonight."

"Good idea. She's got enough on her plate. Don't worry; I won't mention it to her. My people and the two local troopers have been alerted. If anything develops on this end, I'll let you know right away. From what I have gathered from Doyle's conversation, it appears that the two men from Phoenix who worked for Draper occasionally may be the ones to carry out the plot. Doyle was able to establish that information from talking to the detective division of the Phoenix PD. Just be on your guard. I know you will be. The lieutenant is very concerned, too. Although Draper has met his end, there evidently is still danger ahead, especially if these unknowns attempt to carry out his threats. Jack Doyle is presently trying to identify them."

"Chief, I'm going to call my friend, Jack Flynn, the private investigator in Phoenix. I tried to call him earlier, but they were out of the office. Flynn is a former homicide detective, as you know, and he may be able to develop some useful information. No one knows the streets and bars like he does. If he can come up with some names, it'll sure be helpful."

"Definitely a good idea, Jason. Hey, I'd better grab lunch. I'm famished!"

"I'll let you know if I come up with anything, Chief."

"Thanks. See you later."

I continued on to the Bronco, opened the driver's side door, and slid behind the steering wheel. I headed to the post office to pick up the mail.

My post office box contained a sizeable payment for services rendered in the collection of bad checks from the Mountain Bank. The post office staff was busy as usual. Their service to the public was important and most appreciated by all of us. Many of us still enjoyed letter writing.

Before heading back to our log home I decided I had better stop at the garage to have the tire pressure checked, as one tire had appeared down a bit. When I pulled in, Dr. Don was exiting his pickup with a large pizza in hand for his lunch.

"Hi, Dr. Don, how have you been?" I asked.

"Jason, everything is fine. Busy all the time! How's Patty feeling?"

"Fine, Doc, thanks for asking."

"Tell her I was asking."

"I certainly will, Doc."

He rushed past me into his office with the pizza. I took care of putting air in the tire, checked them all with my tire pressure gauge, and put the caps back on. I then replaced the air hose on the hook.

When I looked in the window to say goodbye, Don motioned for me to come and join him.

"Jason, come on in here. I've got plenty of pizza here for the both of us."

"Thanks all the same, but I just finished lunch."

"Okay, maybe next time," he said.

I thanked him for the free air and climbed back into the Bronco to proceed to the supermarket, where I purchased a newspaper and a few groceries. Making my way to the deli I decided to buy some of the lean corned beef for Reuben sandwiches. We already had sauerkraut at home. The deli worker sliced the corned beef nice and thin, the way I liked it. Along with the deli purchase I located a fresh loaf of seedless rye bread on the bottom shelf. It was my plan to surprise Patty with a light meal. I concluded my shopping spree with a few odds and ends, and checked out.

Driving directly home now was a necessity due to the fact that several of my purchases had to be refrigerated. The temperatures had been climbing, and I felt it would not be wise to linger with perishables in the car.

Ruben was standing at attention in his dog run waiting patiently for his master. I turned off the ignition, got out of the Bronco, and went to his dog run to open the gate.

"A little warm, Ruben?" I said to him as I let him out. We evidently were having an unexpected heat wave for mid-June with temperatures almost in the eighties.

The big K-9 took off for the woods as I carried the groceries into the house and placed the perishable items in the refrigerator.

Ruben returned from the woods. I brought him inside with me, as it was cooler in the log home for him. I then turned on two of my ceiling fans and placed his air mattress under the whirling fan blades. I looked over at Ruben and saw that he must be cooling off a little, as he seemed contented. He soon stretched out on his bedding.

I then went into my office to place another call to Jack Flynn in Arizona. Surprisingly his answering machine came on again with the same recording that they were presently out of the office, but to leave a name and number and they would call when they returned after three. Rather than leave a message, I opted to call back later. I went in to clean up before preparing our light dinner.

First, I mixed some Russian dressing for our sandwiches and placed it in the refrigerator to cool. I had purchased some cottage cheese and sliced peaches for our salad plate to accompany the sandwiches. I hoped everything would meet with Patty's approval.

I went into the living room to relax and meditate. How foolish I had been to believe that all was well after Draper's death! My mind was consumed with worry again, not only for Patty in the latter stage of her pregnancy, but that the possibility of being stalked by Draper's lowlife friends would sharply interfere with our planned move to Lake Placid and the new responsibilities I'd be taking on for Tom Huston at the Breakshire Lodge. And if that weren't all, I still did not know what I was going to say to my friends who had worked so hard on the addition for the baby's nursery. Somehow I had to explain to them that my present circumstances left me no choice but to take advantage of this opportunity at Lake Placid in order to meet our financial obligations. Hopefully, they'd understand my dilemma. There was no doubt about it: Patty and I were presently experiencing the dynamics of life's journey. I remember too well as a child my father's struggle to provide for the family.

I tried to clear my mind. I decided that maybe some wood chopping would ease my stress. There is no greater tension reliever than physical exertion. That's what my mom had always told me. The near-eighty temperature was unusually high. I went outdoors to begin my chore and went on to split a cord of wood, which I piled next to the others I had previously split. Sweat ran down my face as I put the axe away and returned indoors. I could feel myself relax. I guess my mom was right again.

With our light dinner set for preparation, I went into the office and decided to try my friend in Phoenix again. It would be just about three there, considering the time difference.

"Flynn Investigations," Ruby Wolkowski's familiar voice answered.

"Ruby, Jason here! I've been trying to get you all day. How are you? Is Jack in, I hope?"

"Jason, we've been in and out of the office all day. Jack and I've been thinking about you. How's Patty feeling? Has the baby been born?" Ruby asked excitedly.

"Not yet Ruby. Probably in a month. We're eagerly waiting; in fact, we're on pins and needles."

"Say hello to Patty for me. Miss you both. Just a moment and I'll get Jack for you."

Jack came on the line. "Okay, Jason, what's the excuse this time? Has a black bear had you up a tree? God, man, I haven't heard from you in a long time," he said jokingly.

"Sorry, Jack. I have to be serious, buddy! By the way, phones work both ways. Anyway, I'm sure you've already heard about Draper's fate?"

Jack's voice became solemn. "Did I hear? I guess I did. Your friend, Lieutenant Jack Doyle, called Jay Goldstein at homicide the same day it happened, and I believe he called again yesterday."

"I assume Jay called you then."

"He stays in touch with me just about every day. Why do you ask?"

"Seeing you're so informed, did you happen to hear about two guys from Phoenix that are believed to be planning on carrying out a contract for the late Mr. Draper?"

"Oh, I know even more than that, Jason: they want you and Doyle eliminated. Draper had made arrangements to have these guys paid several thousand dollars to ensure that the contracts would be carried out even in the event of his death. I just heard about it today. Your timing is amazing. I was going to call you this afternoon, but you beat me to it."

"Who are these bastards, Jack? Do you have any ideas?"

"I hope to have some information later today. I have an idea already, which I have one of my snitches checking out. These two characters are bad news from the get-go. The names I have in mind I'd rather keep to myself until I verify whether or not they are the actual bad guys. Believe me, if they're the ones I'm thinking of, they have the potential in their hearts."

"Jack, I hope your snitch comes up with the right names. You can't blame me for being nervous about it. Draper was clearly irrational to come out of the cabin the way he did shooting at the troopers."

"True. That girlfriend of his should never have gotten tangled up with him. Except for her lady-of-the-night activities, she really wasn't a bad kid. Her father was a clergyman, and after he passed away she started hitting the pickup joints. However, after she met Bernard Draper, the vice squad at the PD never observed her with anyone else, only Draper. My surmise is that his strong personality influenced her to a point where she came under his power. Just look at the mess she's in now."

"I think you're right, Jack. Well, when you verify those names, please call me immediately. I need to know!"

"I'll call you; don't worry. Also, Jay will contact Doyle. If it is the people that I have in mind, one of them has probably violated his parole. Hopefully, the detectives downtown will be able to get them off the street before they can try anything. We'll see what develops."

"Thanks a lot. You know with Patty being pregnant, it's very important for our safety's sake to see these people stopped before they commit any overt act toward us."

"I know, Jason. I know. I'll call you, buddy, as soon as I know anything."

"Okay, take care. Say so long to Ruby for me. Goodbye, Jack." I hung up my receiver.

It was good to have talked with Jack. If anyone could get the identity on those two people, it would be him. When he had been on the department he had had many informants. He knew how to handle all the people he had come in contact with, both the good and the bad. During his years of dedication in the law enforcement arena, the people of Phoenix knew Jack Flynn and he knew them. He had that lovable Irish way about him— almost a stereotypical Irish cop.

I glanced at my watch. The time had passed by quickly that day. Patty would be pulling into the yard in about five minutes. I went into the bathroom, washed my hands, and threw some ice-cold water onto my face. It was refreshing and it reinvigorated me.

With the table already set, I proceeded to prepare our

corned beef sandwiches for dinner. I placed four slices of the rye bread on the cutting board and buttered four sides, then placed our large griddle on the burner to heat. I removed the thinly sliced corned beef from the refrigerator, stacked a few slices of it on the bread, and added sauerkraut to each. After spooning a small amount of Russian dressing I added a slice of Swiss cheese to each and placed the other slice of bread to the top. Now they were ready to be gently heated on the griddle until the flavors blended.

I heard Ruben bark, probably signaling Patty's arrival. I ran to the door to open it for her.

"Hi, sweetheart," I said, putting my arms around her oh-so-gently.

"Sherlock, I'm so glad to be home. The baby was moving around all day," she said as she placed her right hand on her midriff.

"The little kicker's really moving, eh?" I asked happily.

"Lately, quite a bit," she replied, reaching over to place my hand where I could feel the movement.

"That's our baby, honey," I told her proudly.

"Yes, Jason, that's our baby!" she agreed in deep contentment.

"We're having a light dinner tonight, Patty. I hope you don't mind. After that large lunch I had, and I'm sure you had some, too."

"What is it, Jason?" she asked

"You get ready for dinner and then I'll surprise you."

Patty went into the bedroom to change into something comfortable. I heard her go into the bathroom to wash her hands and put her hair down to flow over her shoulders before returning to the kitchen to join me.

In the meantime, I carefully turned the corned beef sandwiches and placed our peach and cottage cheese salads on the table, along with a small bowl of extra Russian dressing, if needed.

"Sherlock, the Reuben sandwiches look wonderful!" she offered as she sat herself.

"Not to brag, but the sandwiches do look tempting, even if I say so myself," I agreed.

We enjoyed our light dinner, and Patty thanked me for coming up with this tasty treat. She then rose from the table to prepare our two cups of decaf green tea. When she returned I told her that I had some news to share with her.

"What is it, Jason?" she asked, evidently noting something was amiss.

"Patty, I really hate to tell you this, but we may still be in danger." I finally was able to blurt it out.

"Wha--what do you mean, Jason?" Patty asked, visibly upset by my statement.

"I mean that Draper, that b-----d, more or less has initiated a contract to bring harm to those responsible for his capture. Here we thought it was over with his death, but evidently there may still be a problem. I don't know yet. Doyle and Flynn are trying to get to the bottom of these threats. In the meantime, we have to be cautious."

"Oh, no!" she said as tears welled in her eyes. "I just can't believe it. Why do we have to be always targeted like this?"

"I wish I knew, honey. I guess it's the luck of the draw. Maybe one could consider it a part of this culture of violence. I wish I had the answers. Criminal conduct does seem to be spreading throughout every segment of society. Depending on who knows what, a child can determine which path he or she will pursue. Take, for example, Draper: he may have started out with honorable intentions, but somewhere along the way he got sidetracked and greed overtook his reasoning. It's a complex subject, Patty. Any street cop out among the public every day could tell you that."

"I understand, but what else can we do to ensure our safety?" she asked dejectedly.

"There is a possibility that whoever is involved could be identified and apprehended before even arriving here. I talked to Jack Flynn and Ruby this afternoon. Jack, of course, is constantly in touch with the detectives at the Phoenix PD, and he already has talked to one of his snitches to determine who these people could possibly be. Apparently Draper paid a sum of money to carry out his threats in the event that something were to happen to him, and now that he's no longer with us, who knows? We have no idea at this point. Just stay alert, Patty. That's all we can do right now."

I told her to go sit in the living room with her knitting while I washed what few dishes there were to do, and I would be in shortly to join her.

After I did up the dishes and cleaned the kitchen, I asked her if she would like to join Ruben and me for a walk to the woods. We took a leisurely stroll while holding hands and stopping occasionally for a warm embrace.

"I know, Patty, that we will miss Old Forge, but we've got to make this move we're contemplating a positive one. We'll come back to visit and check on our property when we can. If Jim and his wife decide on renting our place, we won't have a worry at all. They'll take care of it as though it was their own. I'm a pretty good judge of people."

"They're fine folks, Jason. I agree with you on that."

"Yes, they certainly are. I'll talk with him during the week."

"When are you planning on telling the fellows about our plans?" she asked.

"I'm planning on meeting them for a mid-morning breakfast when I go to Utica next week. I'll set it up with Wilt and he'll pass the word to them. Wilt realizes the strain we're going through. Don't worry, Patty; everything will work out alright. You'll see! I'm going to call Jack Flynn tomorrow to see if he's heard anything further about the identification of Draper's hit men. I don't know who Jack's snitch is. He didn't tell me. All I know is that he possesses an uncanny ability to ferret out information that some of his counterparts can't even begin to acquire."

"Jack is very clever, Jason—and Sherlock, you are, too," she added.

"Flattery will get you anywhere, Patty."

"Look, honey! Ruben's found a playmate. The chippie is

trying to trick him."

As he sniffed around a brush pile, a fast-moving chipmunk brushed by Ruben's nose and ran into the pile, almost daring our K-9 to pursue him. The chase turned out to be in vain. Ruben lost.

We walked back to our log home. The sun was setting in the west over the mountain. Bright reds blended with the cloud cover and displayed a beautiful mural in the sky: Mother Nature at her best. The peace and tranquility of this beauty was most welcome to both Patty and me.

Patty went inside with Ruben while I stopped by the Jeep and Bronco to check the oil and windshield-washer fluids. I also checked each of the tires with the pressure gauge; all were fine except the right front one on the Bronco.

When I went inside, Patty asked me, with a bit of worry, why I had taken so long. I explained to her that I had checked a few things on each of our vehicles. After I washed my hands in the sink, I joined Patty in the living room and we selected a couple of tapes to listen to. When the music started to play, I turned the volume down so we could really relax. We sat next to each other on the davenport until it was time to go to bed. Before I entered the bedroom, I let Ruben out for a quick run. He returned shortly. The security light went on and illuminated the front yard.

Patty had already brushed her teeth and was cuddled up in the middle of our bed. I noticed she was wearing a lighter nightgown, nice and loose, as the temperature had remained warm.

"Are you going to read for a while?" she asked sleepily.

"Not tonight, honey. I'm bushed. All that we have going on just tires me out thinking about it," I replied. As I leaned over to kiss her on the forehead, I discovered that she had already drifted off into dreamland. It wasn't very long before I joined her.

The ringing of the alarm clock woke me out of my deep sleep. I reached over toward Patty, but she had already left our warm bed to take her shower in the bathroom. I looked at the clock: five-twenty. Now that I was somewhat awake, I pushed the covers back and slid out of bed. I knew that after the baby was born we'd both be taking turns getting up every few hours to care for our little sweetheart.

I reached over for my favorite faded blue jeans, which I felt comfortable wearing as long as I didn't have a special meeting or mission to attend to, along with a t-shirt that I selected from the bottom drawer of my dresser. I noticed there were only two left in the drawer, which was a signal to me that it was time to do the washing, one of my specific chores around the house, given that Patty was working full-time. I slipped one over my head just as my lovely wife came into the bedroom.

"Patty, I'll be doing the laundry today, honey. Do you have anything to add to it?"

"No, I already put everything in the bag behind the bathroom door. And please don't forget to check the basket."

"I'll be certain to take them with me when I leave," I promised. "By the way, have you made a decision on whether we'll be using disposable or cloth diapers?"

"I think the only way to go with our move will probably be disposable; if that's alright with you?"

"That'll be fine, hon," I agreed.

"I've got to leave, dearest. We've been unusually busy for this time of the year lately, early tourists I guess. Lila had to call two part-time waitresses yesterday to give us a hand. Besides, we will be having our regulars. John set up some tables outside to take care of the overflow."

"Listen, Patty, I want you to take it a little easy. I don't want you to overdo, especially this far along in your pregnancy. Do you hear me?" I asked adamantly.

"Sherlock, don't worry so much. Believe me, if I was having any difficulty I'd come home and rest. But I feel great. When we move to Lake Placid, I promise I'll take it easy until the baby is born."

"Promise?"

"I promise, darling," she answered.

Patty came over to me for a quick kiss goodbye. She then

grabbed her purse and headed for the door to leave for work.

There was no doubt about it: Patty was a dedicated employee and a wonderful wife. John and Lila considered her a part of their family and valued her highly as an employee and a friend. I knew it would be difficult for them to replace her when she told them she would be leaving, but I also knew they would understand. Both John and Lila were aware of what Patty had had to endure in her first marriage, wed to a man who had become so abusive. Even though they would be saddened to lose her, they would rejoice in her good fortune.

After a hurried breakfast I found myself growing anxious as I waited to hear from Jack Flynn. Because of the time difference, I had to wait until eleven to place a call to Flynn Investigations in Phoenix. Just before that hour I dialed the number. After several rings, just as I was about to hang up, Ruby answered, somewhat out of breath.

"Flynn Investigations," she said, sounding rushed.

"Ruby, good morning from the Adirondacks. Jason here." I tried to keep my tone light.

"Good morning, Jason. How are you? Hearing from you twice in a week could start a rumor." She chuckled.

"I have to talk with Jack. Is he in yet?" I asked.

"I'm looking out the window and he's just pulling in. He's been really busy since you talked with him. He called me at home early this morning and wanted me to check on something for him. Why don't I have him call you right back?" Ruby asked.

"Thanks, Ruby. I'll be waiting right here at home," I responded, hoping he would have some information.

It wasn't long before the telephone rang.

"Is this the Jason Black who served with me in the US Marine Corps, now the all-seeing eye of the Adirondack Mountains? I've been up all night working for you, my friend."

"Hello, Jack. You're feisty for being up so early."

"Jason, I mean it—I haven't slept all night. I've been digging for information that might save your life. Before I called you I had to have a cup of strong black coffee."

"Let's cut to the chase, Jack. What have you learned?" I asked anxiously.

"These two characters are bad guys. They're the ones I suspected. One has violated his parole and the other is the likely perpetrator in a homicide case here in south Phoenix. Apparently he went into a fast food restaurant and shot the manager while the man was pleading for his life. The victim, in his thirties, was going to school full-time, married, with two children and a third on the way—a really great guy. It happened just last week."

I felt a stone in my chest. "Wow! Bad isn't the word for it. I'd say ruthless. Got a name for these guys?"

"Well, what you'll find interesting is that they both formerly worked the freight docks for Draper, and both served hard time in the state prison at Florence. Their names are Charles Kelts, age 41 and Taco Jones, age 47, addresses unknown, except a former shared address of 22 Bacon Lane, Mesa, Arizona. Draper must have promised them big money. We don't know who the payoff man is as yet. With the assistance of the detectives from the PD, I was able to learn that these two birds paid cash for a 1983 Ford Van. It has a temporary plate on it. Don't know the plate number, but the van is a combination yellow and black—black on the bottom and yellow on the top."

"Any information about whether they are armed or not?" I asked.

"I have no definite information except both are known to carry knives. One of my snitches informed me early this morning that they have already left the Phoenix area for New York."

"Did your snitch happen to mention when they left or where they were headed in New York?"

"No idea, Jason, but I will tell you right now: they are bad and they're headed east. If you can, I'd have Patty stay secretly at a friend's house until this is over with. I feel strongly that Kelts and Jones are going to try to fulfill the contract they had with Draper, even though Draper is dead. You've got to be careful, Jason. Both of them are stalkers, and are the type that will lay in wait for the right opportunity to carry out their plans on their intended targets."

My friend's words had my heart pumping hard. "Jack, I owe you. I deeply appreciate your furnishing me with these facts. Patty and I both do."

"Listen, I know you'd do the same for me if it was the other way around. Look what you did for me by coming out to help on my case when I called on you. That's what friends are for. Oh, and I called Jay Goldstein and discussed the case with him. He went on to tell me that he would call Major Garrison and Lieutenant Doyle at Troop S to give him all this information. Just wanted to let you know."

"That's great, Jack. Jay's a good man."

"Well, good friend, keep me posted if you hear anything more."

"Jason, you owe me 24 hours of sleep. Don't worry—if I hear anything else, I'll give you a call immediately," he assured me. "Take care, buddy, Semper fi."

"Semper fi." I responded.

"Just as I was ready to call Lieutenant Doyle, the phone rang.

"Hello, Wilt here," the caller announced.

"Hi, Wilt. It's been a while. I'm glad you called. Would you be able to meet me with the fellows for breakfast at the Pancake House in the morning?" I was looking forward to the opportunity to tell my friends the news about our move.

"What time would be convenient?" he asked.

"About eight, if possible," I replied.

Wilt and I talked briefly about his involvement with the Loggers' Museum. He indicated that the museum had already generated a great deal of interest and that Tom Huston's concept for it was an excellent one. It brought out the historical threads of an industry that had been so important to our area's economy, both past and present. He spoke with great excitement about his contribution to this project.

"Wilt, I have to commend you for assisting Tom with your

vast knowledge of logging and the components that make up the industry."

"Thanks, Jason. It's my life, and I'm so glad to be involved in this project. For your information, I'm in the process of carving out two black bears to be placed at the entrance to the Loggers' Museum."

"That's wonderful, Wilt." I could tell by Wilt's voice how happy he was with his involvement.

I didn't want to upset Wilt by bringing up the threats of Bernard Draper and the information that had been developed about the two hit men en route from Phoenix. I'd wait until we met at breakfast.

After Wilt's call I dialed Jack Doyle.

"Lieutenant Doyle speaking," he said. I couldn't mistake his Irish brogue.

"Jack, how are you? I just called to share some news with you," I said.

"Just got off the phone with Captain Silverstein from Phoenix. He told me all about the two ex-cons and the black and yellow van. They sound like a couple of bad apples. The captain indicated they are the potential hit men. Apparently Draper was completely serious about his intentions to bring us harm. These two bums are his insurance policy to carry out his revenge. Listen, I'm on edge about this. The background on these people spells violence in every sense of the word."

"I agree. I talked with Jack Flynn this morning. He advised me to have Patty stay with a friend until this matter is taken care of. I'm not taking any chances, especially with her being pregnant. I'll be at the house."

"Not alone, you won't!" he exclaimed.

"What are you talking about?" I replied.

"Jason, I know that I cannot tell you what to do in your own home, but I think it would be wise to have someone else there with you under these circumstances. I know, too, that when you were on the job you liked to do it your way, but with your wife expecting, you'd better think twice on this one," he warned.

"I understand what you're saying, Jack. But this thing has got to end," I said adamantly.

"I'm thinking of Patty and your child that will be born, they both will need you, buddy. I know you'd like to take both of these b-----ds on, but as your friend I'm hoping that you'll be prudent and carefully think about the strategy you will be undertaking. Remember, they have to commit an overt act toward you first before you can legally respond," he reminded me, although he, of course, knew I was aware of all the rules.

"I'll go this far, Jack Doyle. I'll arrange for Patty to stay with her former landlady, with whom she stayed before we were married. She'll be safe there. I will be at our log home at night. I'll have Ruben with me—a great guard dog. My vehicle will be parked in the yard as usual. I'll keep the security lights off during the hours of darkness. I have night-time vision binoculars and a loaded Browning semi-automatic 12 gauge-shotgun, which will be fully loaded with slugs and double-0 buckshot. If any intruders show up, I'll call 911. And that's the deal, Jack," I said adamantly.

"I can see that there's no negotiating with you, Jason, so I'll concur with your demands. But you damned well better call 911 if intruders try to enter your home!"

"I will, Jack, I promise."

I glanced at my watch and asked Jack to keep me posted. We said our goodbyes and hung up.

Jack's words resounded over and over. He was right. I should have someone else with me in the house. But, why? We didn't even know for certain if the two men, Kelts and Jones, were headed toward Saranac, where Jack Doyle was located, or to our area. With the information about the two would-be killers, precautions were necessary and immediate. Chief Todd Wilson, his staff, and the local troopers would be continually scanning the area and checking all the hotels, motels, and campgrounds. They would be on the lookout for the 1983 Ford Van, black and yellow, displaying a temporary registration plate. With the intensity of their efforts, I felt fairly confident that everything was being done that could be to insure our security. I got up from my desk and went into the kitchen. I decided in order to keep myself calm, it would be best to keep busy with my chores.

The blue bag of laundry was full. I reached underneath the cabinet and took out the soap and the bleach. I placed them in the laundry basket and took them out to the Bronco. I opened the rear window and placed the laundry bag along with the laundry basket, soap, and bleach in the back.

With the house locked up and Ruben pacing back and forth in his dog run, I climbed into the Bronco, drove toward the highway, and headed toward Old Forge. When I pulled into the parking lot of the laundromat, two pickups were just leaving with their laundry baskets placed in the back of their trucks, enabling me to find a parking space near the entrance door. I turned the ignition off and proceeded to remove the laundry from the rear and into the nearly empty laundromat. There was quiet music playing in the background. I selected two machines and sorted the laundry to colored and whites, then added the soap to each and the bleach to the dispenser for the whites. I placed the quarters in the slot and pushed the start button. I heard the water start to flow as soon as I closed the lids. I decided that I would not go to John's Diner for lunch. In fact, it wouldn't hurt me to skip it entirely. The five pounds I had gained recently wasn't very healthy. And with all the bad news, I really wasn't very hungry now anyway.

The washer cycle would allow me enough time for a quick trip to the post office to pick up the mail. To my disappointment, the box was empty. However, I was reminded that I would have to pick up a change of address form prior to our move to Lake Placid—just one of the many items to be added to my Things-to-do-list. I went inside the office to say hello to the postmaster and the staff. They were busy as usual. We exchanged pleasantries before I returned to the laundromat.

When I arrived I found that my parking space was occupied, so I pulled into another close by. I went inside, and luckily the two washers were just completing the last spin cycle. I put the laundry into the dryers along with a dryer sheet for each. A rack with some news magazines enticed me to stay while waiting for the laundry to dry.

I began to read an editorial, only to find my concentration interrupted by my memory of the annoying threats that Draper had made from his prison cell. How could any of us have imagined that the demise of Draper would unleash a backup plan to carry out his sinister plot? That even in death he would try to avenge his arrest for running his large scale smuggling operation of drugs, untaxed cigarettes, whiskey, and other illegal activities, which had provided him a lucrative lifestyle?

When the dryers clicked off, my thoughts returned to the duties at hand. I removed the dried laundry, hung some of the items on hangers, folded the others into neat stacks, and carefully placed them into the laundry basket. I nodded to the others doing their laundry, went out to the Bronco to load it with the clean clothes, and drove home.

Ruben barked when I exited the Bronco. I carried the laundry basket inside, then hung the garments to be ironed in the corner of the closet and the folded pieces in their dresser drawers.

I called Harriet Stone, Patty's former landlady, intending to ask her about caring for Patty during this dangerous time.

"Hello, Harriet. Jason Black here. Do you have a minute to talk with me?" I asked our good friend.

"Hi, stranger. How have you been, Jason? I bet you are both so happy with the baby coming soon. Of course I always have time for you," she replied.

"We've been thriving, Harriet. Yes, we are very happy about the future event. But I have a favor to ask of you."

"What is it Jason?"

"Would you mind taking in a boarder for a week or two? I can't go into the details, but I'd like Patty to stay with you for a while until a matter is resolved."

"Jason Black, Patty is like a daughter to me. She can move in today! She'll be good company for me."

"Oh, thank you so much, Harriet."

"Will Patty be coming tonight, Jason?"

"I was thinking about tomorrow evening, if possible. In fact, I haven't discussed it with her yet."

"That'll be fine, Jason. You know, when my husband was alive I used to complain about his slippers being underfoot all the time and that he was always missing his car keys. But, Jason, I'd give up everything to have him with me. His passing was a big loss."

"I know exactly what you mean, Harriet. He was a fine gentleman."

"He certainly was."

Harriet and I chatted a few minutes longer. She told me to come over with Patty the next evening, and that she was going to bake a batch of jelly-ginger cookies. I told her I would look forward to that.

My conversation with Harriet had relieved my anxiety somewhat. I felt that Patty would be safe with her, especially during the night.

CHAPTER THIRTY-ONE

Near Mansfield, Ohio, a 1983 Ford van bearing a cardboard like license plate was pulled in next to a drugstore, occupying a space at the end of the parking lot, partially hidden between two large trucks. The two occupants of the van were Charles Kelts and Taco Jones from the Mesa, Arizona area. The individuals were in their forties, Caucasian, heavily tattooed, both with shaved heads. Taco Jones had a large earring dangling from his left lobe.

They had been driving constantly, taking turns at the wheel of the yellow and black Ford van. At midnight they had pulled in between the two parked trucks to catch some much needed sleep. They had just awakened.

"Hey! Charlie, I'm tired. And I still can't believe that our pal Draper is dead!" he said in between yawns.

"Believe it, Taco. Why in the hell do you think we're here? With him dead we have to take care of a couple of New York State cops—one retired pig and the other that still totes his badge. We can't get the money Draper offered until we take care of them."

"Charlie, maybe we should head back to Arizona. These troopers in New York are tough."

"Who told you that stuff?"

"Well, Draper's six foot under, isn't he? And I hadn't thought of what could be going on with Hilda. She must be

237

telling the cops everything."

"You wanna chicken out, get the hell out of the van right now!"

"Aw, Charlie, half of that $200,000 is mine. No, I'm not leaving."

"Taco, straighten up then! We can't collect the money until the job is done. Remember, all we need to collect the money is a newspaper article that those particular cops are no longer with us."

"Charlie, I'm with ya, but I don't like it."

"You're either with me or not. It's a long ways back to Mesa."

"I'm with ya."

CHAPTER THIRTY-TWO

After my phone calls, I took Ruben for a walk, then prepared a special dinner for Patty and me. Meatloaf with gravy was the main entrée, along with slivered buttered carrots, mashed potatoes, pickled beets, and corn bread. Patty arrived home from the diner at her usual time.

"Hello Sherlock, I'm so glad to be home! We had another really busy day."

I went over to Patty to embrace her. Her long blond hair flowed on her shoulders. "Honey, you must be tired. Let me take your jacket."

I assisted her in removing it. She went into the bathroom to freshen up, then returned to the kitchen. I seated her at the table and lit our two candles.

"Sherlock, you're fussing too much," she said, looking up to me.

"Honey, you work very hard, and it's the least I can do." I served Patty and then I sat down to join her. The meatloaf was even tastier than I had hoped. Sliced mushrooms in the gravy added an excellent touch. The real mashed potatoes were fluffy and went well with the meatloaf.

Not wanting to put it off any longer, I asked Patty to join me in the living room with our decaf as I had an important issue to discuss with her. I carried both cups in on a tray and set them on the coffee table.

She looked up at me with a puzzled expression. "What's going on, Jason?"

"Please try not to get too upset, dear. But I have to tell you this. Evidently, we're not out of the woods on Draper's threats as yet. According to Jack Doyle, Draper had made arrangements with someone to carry out his revenge in the event of his demise."

She gasped. "I don't believe it! What are you saying! It can't be true," she responded as her body trembled uncontrollably.

"I'm sorry, dearest, it is!"

"Jason, we can't live like this," she exclaimed, trying to regain her composure.

"I know, Patty. That's why I have come up with a plan. Although I have no way of knowing if the threats would actually materialize, I felt it would be a good idea for you to stay with Harriet for a little while, therefore I have already taken the liberty to ask her if it would be all right."

"I don't care who you called, I'm not leaving," she flashed back angrily.

"Patty, please try to understand. It's not only your safety that concerns me, but you have to consider the safety of our child," I explained soothingly.

Through a barrage of tears, she sobbed, "Jason, I'm not leaving!" she said, firmly.

As I had anticipated her rejection of my proposal, she began to relent when she saw how fully determined I was. She finally agreed and went in to call Harriet to thank her.

While she was gone, my thoughts drifted back to the day when I had seen the maroon car pull up to our house and then back out of our driveway. Could that have been Draper and Furman? I probably would never know, but I decided to check with Jack Doyle to determine if Hilda Furman had ever mentioned it in any of her statements to the investigators. Just how close had I been to having an encounter at that time? That's why it was imperative for Patty to be somewhere safer than our home.

While I began to clear the table and take care of the kitchen duty, Patty went into the bedroom to ready the necessary items she would take to Harriet's. She packed just a few things, for she knew I would be available to bring her anything she might have forgotten.

"Jason, will anyone be with you here at the house?" she asked with a worried look on her face. "I just hate to leave you here alone."

I didn't want to tell her that I was planning on just Ruben and myself. "I'm working on it, Patty. Don't worry, it's being taken care of." I would never want to intentionally lie to Patty, but I felt it was necessary due to this late stage of her pregnancy. I was only thinking of her safety and welfare.

I reminded Patty that Lieutenant Doyle had contacted Chief Todd Wilson and the local troopers to alert them of any impending dangers to Todd or me. Having this knowledge, and sharing it with her, relieved some of the strain I had been experiencing. I did not regard myself a hero in any sense of the word, but having always been an independent individual, I would have to deal with it by myself.

When we finished our chores, we decided to take Ruben for a walk into the woods together. Although the chippies were playing in the underbrush, for some reason Ruben never left our side. He continued to heel just behind us. It was as though he sensed our troubled mood. I could not explain his behavior tonight, but he appeared to be very protective.

CHAPTER THIRTY-THREE

Near Silver Creek, New York, Kelts and Jones had pulled the 1983 Ford van into a remote area off the main highway. They had acquired several cans of black spray paint and were now applying it over the yellow portion of the van, perhaps assuming the police were on the alert for the yellow and black vehicle. They had decided that this quick paint job was a necessity. Not only would the van be black, but they had stolen a set of license plates and had installed them on the vehicle. Kelts began ranting over a paint stain on his favorite jeans.

"Charlie, quit your bitching about the paint."

"Shut up, Taco. I don't wanna hear your mouth. I just want to do what we have to do up north and get the hell out of this state."

"I know we have to get the job done if we want the money. I just can't believe Draper's dead."

"You keep saying that. Get over it. Believe it. These state cops don't fool around. So, Taco, you've got to do as I say. This should be an easy hit. We've got the map that Draper sent us. According to his note he was in this ex-copper's driveway."

"That took guts!"

"Yeah! Draper had guts, but look what happened to him!"

"Let's get this paint job done. It'll have to dry in the sun this afternoon. We won't hit the road until after dark.

CHAPTER THIRTY-FOUR

The next morning, I arrived at the Pancake House at a little after nine. Wilt's big Dodge was parked on the north side of the diner. I knew it would be difficult for me to face my friends this morning with the news of our move. We were a close-knit group, and I wondered how they would accept it.

When I opened the door I observed my friends seated at a large table.

"Good morning, Jason. Come on over and join us," Wilt called out as the rest of the group turned to look.

They were all here: Wilt, Jim, Jack, even Charlie, who had taken the time from his log run to join us. We all decided on the special, pancakes with two eggs. Some opted for bacon or sausage with theirs. We all ordered coffee.

While we waited for our food to arrive we conversed about generalities. Of course, all asked about Patty, how she was feeling, and if the baby was still expected on the due date. I decided I had best wait until we finished our breakfast before I shared the news with them. As I looked around the table at my friends, they all appeared cheerful, yet I had the distinct feeling that they sensed this get-together had a specific purpose. I realized my feeling probably only arose from the guilt I had because I was aware of the hours of labor they had expended on the addition for our baby's nursery and our home.

Two waitresses appeared at our table with large trays,

delivering to each of us an attractive plate of steaming hot food. Kathy, one of the two, returned to refill our coffees. It did not take long for our hungry group to clean our plates of the light and fluffy pancakes.

"That was sure tasty!" a voice from the other end of the table said.

"You can say that again. That bacon certainly was crisp, just the way I like it," Jack Falsey added.

"I agree," Charlie chimed in.

"Fellas, I'd like another order, but I'm trying to watch my weight. It was excellent," Wilt jokingly added while patting his mouth with his napkin.

Kathy again returned with the coffee for those who still wanted more.

I could wait no longer. Now would be the time I would have to break the news to my close friends. It would not be easy, but it had to be done. I cleared my throat loudly to get their attention. The table fell silent as they all looked my way.

"Gentlemen—and I do mean gentlemen, for that you are and also my closest friends—I have asked you here this morning to share with you some news that will be difficult for me to relate. First of all I want to thank you from the bottom of my heart for taking time out of your busy schedules and your lives to build the addition on my log home. You all gave of your time unselfishly—putting in many hours of your own time to the project—possessing special talents when it comes to carpentry. The addition is beautiful and heartfelt. In my career with the state I met many people from all sectors of our society, from the rich to poor, the downtrodden to the intellectual. Gentlemen, you are a unique group and represent very well the cross-section of our great Adirondack Park and across our country. You as individuals have carved out a life of your own and each of you can stand up to the best."

I looked around and noticed the dubious expression on some of their faces. I continued, "I do hope what I'm about to say will never affect our relationship. Patty and I look at you as part of our family. We know each other well. Our memories are many. The respect we possess for one another is well known. But, I must tell you, gentlemen, I have been offered a personnel and security position with the Breakshire Lodge in Lake Placid, and I have accepted it."

A surprised quiet fell over the group, but no one uttered a word.

"This came at a time when you had completed the nursery for our newborn baby. So you see why it was so very difficult for us to make this decision. However, this move will give me the opportunity to make a decent salary, which will allow us to pay for the work you did on the nursery and possibly still be able to keep our Old Forge home. Jim, I was going to call you privately to see if you might be interested in renting our log home, as I understand you'd like to reside closer to the marina. If you like, we can discuss it before we leave here this morning."

"Yes, Jason, I suppose I would," Jim replied, looking around, rather bewildered.

"Thanks, Jim. I have a few more things to say before we have our get-together," I said.

"Please do not take this as an insult, but my intention will be to compensate all of you for your tireless efforts on the project. This is the only way I can live with myself. Rest assured we are planning to keep our log home."

It felt only right that I should reveal at this time also the new threat that hung over the men responsible for Draper's arrest. "The threats we thought had ended with Draper's demise may still be a danger. Evidently he had made arrangements prior to his death that if anything happened to him, someone else would complete his mission for revenge. Supposedly there are two ex-cons that have been hired by someone unknown at this time. Needless to say, I am concerned."

Wilt immediately spoke up. "Jason, if you need any help, let us know. You know we're here for you."

"I will, Wilt. I have a strategy I've been toying with. Keep this quiet, but Patty will be staying in a safe place until this is over with. I'm not going into details, but believe me, I'm working on a plan. By the way, the police in the area have been alerted."

"Jason, do you have any idea what kind of vehicle they are driving?" one of the group queried.

"All I can tell you is that it's supposed to be a 1983 Ford yellow and black van. I can't believe they're going to come into our area, probably knowing that the authorities will be looking for it. That's all I know for now. I would appreciate it if you fellows would keep this information under your hat. But keep your eyes and ears open."

"We will, Jason, and we'll keep it quiet, too."

We talked for a while longer. Everyone seemed pleased with my new job offer, knowing that with our baby coming the additional income would be needed for added expenses. They wished me luck on our forthcoming move, but expressed concern over the renewed threats and our safety. I told them that Patty would still be working at the diner for now and that we were planning to make the move in a few weeks.

Knowing the fellows as I did, I could sense that they were pleased for us, but that they were genuinely sorry about our moving away. I told them that we had decided that it would be a significant new beginning—a new opportunity, and a new baby.

After the others left, Jim lingered. We sat back down to discuss his renting of the log home.

"Jason, I have to admit that, for myself, I'm sorry that you're making this move to Lake Placid, but I can understand your reasons. More important right now, regarding the threats that you and the trooper have received, is there anything I can do to assist you in any way?"

"Jim, I appreciate your concern. Just keep your eyes open and let Chief Wilson or me know about any observations you may make. Fortunately we have heard about it in advance, so we can be prepared."

"I see your point," he said.

"That's all I can ask of you, Jim. Now as far as renting our log home is concerned, we will be leaving it furnished."

We negotiated what we both considered a fair and equitable price for the rent. I knew that houses and camps rented for much more, especially furnished, but I was taking into consideration the effort Jim had put in on the new addition. Of course by renting our home, we would no longer have the luxury of weekend usage, but occasionally we could stay at one of our local motels.

"Jason, are you sure? Seems kind of low for such a nice home, and one that's furnished, too." He seemed somewhat overwhelmed.

"For you, Jim, that's my price."

"Well, thanks, Jason. It's a deal." He grinned with delight.

"Good. Then it's all set. I'll let you know when we're making the move."

Jim left the restaurant to head north to Old Forge. I talked with the owner, telling him how much we had enjoyed breakfast, and thanked him for allowing us to conduct our meeting. I paid the check and left.

Things seemed to be falling into place. Our log home would be rented, allowing us to keep owning it; Patty would be safe with Harriet; and I would start putting my strategy into operation. Doyle had offered—almost demanded—that he assign a man to be with me in the house, but I politely rebuffed the offer by promising my well-meaning friend that if anything should transpire I would dial 911 immediately to call for assistance. I was determined to do things my way. Listening to the advice of others in the past hadn't always worked.

I concluded that our breakfast meeting had gone well, as I had not noticed any hostility from my friends regarding our decision to leave Old Forge for a new home. They realized that the decision was based on finances rather than a desire to leave the place we loved so much.

I decided to stop at the post office even though it was still a little early. I pulled in and picked up the mail. When I passed John's Diner, I saw Patty's Jeep parked in the rear of the lot. My eyes searched for any vans in the area; I recognized two parked on the street, both belonging to locals. I didn't stop at the diner because I thought it best to go directly home to check on Ruben.

The big K-9 was pacing back and forth in his dog run. I pulled up close to the gate and got out to see him. When I opened the gate, Ruben came running over to me and rubbed his head against my leg. I patted his back and head.

"Good boy, Ruben," I said.

He barked once as I went into the house to make myself a cup of green tea. While the water heated, I went to the gun safe to remove my Browning semi-automatic twelve-gauge shotgun. I checked it over closely. I was definitely not a gun nut, but unfortunately when a segment of society threatened one's existence, an individual had to be prepared with the proper weapon for defending one's life and home. In my case I was faced with two potential killers. During my life before I had become a trooper, I had learned at an early age from my father how to respect and handle firearms, and after that, of course, use of them was part of my training as a marine. In my time with the troopers, one of the many attributes that had been extremely important had been the use of firearms and how to handle them. Fortunately, during my time of service in the troop, I had never had to discharge a firearm except at the paper targets attached to a frame for range qualifications every year.

CHAPTER THIRTY-FIVE

The solid black van that had been traveling the back roads near Rochester had just experienced a blown right rear tire. Charles Kelts had all he could do to control the steering wheel. Taco Jones had his hand on the safety bar with a tight grip.

He hollered out, "What? What the hell is going on, Charlie? We're all over the road!"

The road surface was sandy and slippery.

"I...I'm doing the best I can. A f---ing tire must have blown!"

The van, its black paint still tacky, skidded off the road into a shallow ditch. Both men got out to see the right rear tire in shreds, partially off the rim.

"Taco, get the jack out of the back and I'll get the spare tire ready," the driver ordered.

"Son-of—a-------. It's always me that has to do the dirty work! How come?" his companion said angrily.

"Because I said so, dummy!" Charlie shouted back.

Taco, rather fearful of Charlie's wrath, complied with his fellow killer's demand.

It took about half an hour to change the tire. Charlie threw the old shredded one in the back of the van and put the jack away. The van's left wheels were in a slight culvert. Charlie climbed back into the van, while Taco watched from outside. The left rear tire started spinning. Taco ran back to the rear to push with everything he had. The tires spun, but finally the van surged ahead as Charlie was able to drive onto the roadway. Taco climbed into the passenger side and the killers continued on their way.

"Taco, glad to see you're good for something!" Charlie taunted him.

"What do you mean by that?" Taco snarled.

"You've got a lot of push."

On their way again, the two discussed their future plans. They would take care of the private detective first and then go after the copper. What they didn't know was the surprise that lay in wait for them.

CHAPTER THIRTY-SIX

With Patty secured at Harriet's, I waited in tight patience for something to happen. During the day I tried to carry on some of my usual activities, make frequent calls to Patty to let her know all was well, and take brief naps so sleep would not deter my vigil in the darkness. But for three nights I sat in my leather recliner in the pitch blackness of my home. The only light was outdoors; I had dimmed, but it still illuminated the only two windows to which an intruder could gain access. I had never before experienced the little noises that occur when one is alone in the house, especially in the dark waiting for something to happen. Ruben was by my side; reluctantly, but out of necessity, I had muzzled him to prevent any barking that would alert unwanted visitors. My chair was situated far enough from the window so I could not be seen. I kept my loaded semi-automatic shotgun close by.

I tried to get my sleep during the daytime, but it was difficult. I hoped I was getting a sufficient amount so I would not fall asleep during my watch.

At approximately three in the morning of the fourth night, with Ruben close by as I stood up to get a glass of water, I glanced toward the window and observed two shadows. Ruben lurched ahead, but I held him back by grabbing his collar. The K-9 was still strong, despite his age.

"Settle down, boy," I whispered. "Hush!" I stroked his

251

back. With my own body on full alert, I could barely make out two men bent over by the windows. I had intentionally left both windows unlocked. From my distance I was able to distinguish something in each of their hands. It appeared to be either a pry bar or a knife. I didn't detect a firearm, for which I was grateful.

I had seen so many gunshot wounds during my career: people either murdered or wounded. I felt in my heart that the shooting of people should never happen in a civilized society. I believed that even when differences could not be rectified by use of negotiation or compromise, violence should not be a recourse. Yet here I was ready to resort to the very method I so abhorred.

During my career I had been assigned to several stakeouts, but here I was alone. I had the shotgun in my hands aimed in the direction of the window. I forced myself to wait until the intruders entered. Before the first night of my wait, I had moved several pieces of furniture into the bedroom. Both windows were now slowly being pushed upward. If they had a flashlight, the men didn't use it; as far as I could tell, they were carrying only the objects in their hands. I quickly removed the muzzle from Ruben, still holding him with one hand on the leash. Both men were now inside. I snapped the light on just as I released Ruben—completely taking the two men by surprise. Ruben leapt into action, flying into the air like a propelled rocket. He knocked one down with a crash to the floor. The other made a dash for the window.

"On the floor next to your buddy, you b-----d, or you're dead!" I shouted as I rushed over to him with my shotgun pointed at him.

He quickly lay down on the floor next to the bigger man who was attempting to hold off Ruben, wielding a knife at him, but he howled with pain as Ruben caught him in the throat, jaws pressing firmly to hold the villain down.

The man screamed out as best he could, "Get this animal off me!"

I kept my shotgun pointed menacingly toward them.

"Don't shoot, don't shoot!" one screamed out.

"How much are you being paid to carry out Draper's dirty work?" I asked harshly.

Neither spoke a word; they just continued to tremble. Ruben had straddled the larger man, who continued to plead with me to call off the dog. I held the leash firmly while I dialed 911 to notify them to send assistance. While my K-9 kept the larger man under control, I walked over to the other lying there. I reached down, brought him to his feet, and pinned him against the wall. I kicked his knife, lying on the floor, out of the way. The other's knife had slid under the table nearby.

"I'm making a citizens arrest and turning you over to the police. They'll be here shortly." Neither uttered a word as Ruben growled ferociously as he stood over them.

"I could have shot you both. This is my home. If I ever see either of you again, I will not be as hospitable as I have been today," I continued with a cold hatred as I trained the shotgun on them. I heard sirens wailing as the police approached.

I walked over to unlock the door. The first man through the door was Chief Wilson with two of his men.

"Are you okay, Jason?" he asked with great concern.

"Yes, Chief," I answered. "Thanks for your fast response."

I went over to the men and repeated, "I am making a citizen's arrest and turning you both over to the Town of Webb Police Chief, Todd Wilson."

Chief Wilson and one of his men took them into custody, cuffing them, and reading them their rights, while the troopers who had followed the chief taped off the crime scene.

The apprehended criminals were indeed identified as Charles Kelts and Taco Jones from Mesa, Arizona. All I could do was sincerely hope it was over this time. I was exhausted, but relieved at the same time. I thanked God with my soul's appreciation that I hadn't had to use deadly physical force on either of them. If they had resisted it would have been a much different conclusion. I knew that Ruben's role had been essential. Now perhaps the tentacles of Draper would cease forever when it came to Patty and me. We just wanted to live in peace.

The chief, with one of his officers, removed Kelts and Jones to the local police station for interviewing and processing. The trooper contacted zone headquarters to send evidence personnel to the scene for the completion of the search: photos, dusting for prints, and the removal of the perimeter tapes.

I took a few minutes to hug and thank Ruben for his assistance. Before I locked up the log home, including the two windows where the criminals had entered, and placed Ruben in his dog run. "You're a good boy, Ruben. What would I have done without you?" I said, petting his head and giving him two dog biscuits.

Despite my fatigue, I then proceeded to the local police department, where I submitted two sworn affidavits to the Webb police.

As I was leaving, Doyle, who must have been in with the interviewers, rushed down the steps to stop me.

"Jason, may I see you a moment?" he asked kindly.

"Of course, Jack," I said, turning toward him.

"Jason, I have to hand it to you. You never cease to amaze me. Kelts and Jones told us that they were sure they were going to die. You and your K-9 scared the hell out of them. They're still shaking."

"Jack, no offense, but I'd rather not discuss it right now. I put everything in my sworn statements. It was a tense situation—and they're right: they're lucky to be alive."

"Well, I just want you to know we all appreciate the action you took. I probably would have shot them both when they entered my home, but who knows? No one in law enforcement really wants to shoot another human being. Your dog had Kelts convinced not to move a muscle or he'd have more than a hold."

I didn't want to hurt Jack's feelings, but I was exhausted and anxious to get on my way. "Jack, I'm glad it's finally over. This time I hope it's for good. Luckily you have them in tow now. They're a couple of bad hombres, the worst of the worse. I'd personally like to take Kelts out behind the barn and teach him some proper etiquette. But, Jack, I'd best be going now. I haven't talked with Patty yet. I want to be sure to see her before she hears any rumors," I explained.

"I understand. Give her my regards, Jason. What an ordeal for you both! How's she feeling anyway?"

"Amazingly good. The baby's due soon."

"Okay, papa!"

We shook hands, said our goodbyes, and I departed. I looked at my watch: 10:15. This was a good time to stop at the diner to see Patty who was busy waiting on a few customers. I tried to explain as best I could the breaking into of our home, the capture of the two would-be assassins who were now under arrest and, I promised I would give her all the details at home later.

"Honey, it's now safe for you to return home," I assured her as I gave her a kiss on the cheek. I couldn't wait until I had my Patty home with me again.

Trying to hold back tears of joy, she replied, "I can't tell you how happy I am." She rushed from behind the counter to give me a big hug.

"I know. We'll be all right now. Take care, dear, and I'll see you tonight." I waved to Lila as I left the diner.

I then stopped at the post office before driving home. When I returned home I realized I was about to collapse from my four nights without sleep. I called Harriet Stone to tell her that everything appeared to be back to normal finally, and that I would have Patty call her later to explain all the details. Harriet expressed her deep relief. She also mentioned that she had just finished baking some molasses cookies and if I'd come over she'd share them with us.

"Harriet, when Patty comes to your house to pick up her things, maybe you could put a couple of them in bag for me," I said. "I'd like that."

"A couple? Why, shucks, Jason, I'll have Patty bring you a half dozen," she said.

"Great! I guess Ruben deserves one, too."

I thanked Harriet for letting Patty stay with her and for the cookies she would be sending over. She was a kind and charitable lady. Her offer of the gift for my sweet tooth helped me feel more normal again.

I looked outside toward the woods from the same windows the two intruders had entered. I reached over to ensure both windows were locked. I noticed I had some cleaning to do, with the fingerprint dust still on the glass and the smudges left on the furniture from the lifted fingerprint powder.

I continued to gaze out at the tall trees and the mountain before me. I was deep in my thoughts, remembering the hikes that Patty, Ruben, and I had taken during all four seasons. I recalled our canoe trips before we were married, and the snowmobile rides in the frigid temperatures of the Adirondacks during the frosty winter days as we took in all the wonders of Mother Nature deep in the woods. The occasional caw of the crow, the screech of the loons in the middle of the nights— these were all bits and pieces that were so much a part of our life together.

Would our move to Lake Placid in a few weeks change the lifestyle that we had grown so accustomed to in Old Forge, where our true love for the land had thrived and so many friends surrounded us? Our woods and the friends we had made here would be so many miles away. My tired mind began working overtime. I reminded myself that Lake Placid was an integral part of the Adirondack Park and there must certainly be wonderful people there, too. One of them, for sure, was our good friend, Tom Huston. In my heart, I knew there were good people all throughout this great land of ours. I had met so many.

I went into the kitchen and took the glass cleaner out of the cabinet along with some paper towels. Returning to the windows, I cleaned them inside and out. It felt good to wipe away all signs of the intruders. I then ran the vacuum cleaner and tidied up the house.

My eyes burned from lack of sleep, but I didn't want to lie

down, for fear that I might fall into deep sleep. Instead I went into the office and shuffled some paperwork on the desk. It was just past four when I reached for the telephone to dial Tom Huston's private number.

"Breakshire Lodge, Tom Huston speaking."

"Good afternoon, Tom. Jason Black here."

"Jason, I just heard the news on the radio. Your name was mentioned," he said enthusiastically.

"Yes, we had a little excitement here at the house. I'll tell you all about it when I see you. What's important is that it looks like that Draper matter may finally be over. But I've called to see how you're feeling, Tom. How are you?" I asked, concerned for my friend.

"I'm a little tired, but since the doctor has me on a new medicine, I believe I'm feeling better, Jason."

"I'm happy to hear that."

"Keep in mind that the suite of rooms for you and Patty and the baby is all ready for you to occupy. I've had our cleaning staff go through it and I've replaced the furniture. It's roomy and I'm certain it will be to your liking. Were you able to rent your Old Forge home?"

"Yes, Tom, I was. I believe you've met Jim Jenny, who is employed by Dale at the marina. He's a very fine gentleman and I know that he'll take good care of our home."

"That's fine, Jason. I know you and Patty will miss the area, but I'm so pleased that you have accepted my offer."

"As you know, I did have reservations about it, Tom, but it is a challenge that I welcome. I truly believe that we'll get along well."

"I know we will. My door is always open to you. And, to show my good faith, I have a surprise for you, a company vehicle. I'm sure you'll like it. I drove it from the dealer. It's loaded with everything. There are no limitations. You and Patty can use it anytime for personal trips. It's at your disposal."

I was astounded. "Tom, you're much too kind to me. You didn't have to go to that expense. I love my old Bronco."

"You can keep your Bronco, but if you do use it for work, just keep track of the miles. But, as it stands, the vehicle is for you and Patty. Jason, you are going to be representing the Breakshire Lodge, and of course you'll be meeting many of our guests, many of whom occasionally may need a ride; therefore, I felt it only right you should have the proper vehicle as a representative of the lodge," he said firmly.

"Yes, you're right, Tom. How can I ever thank you for all you've done?"

We talked for a few minutes more before he was interrupted by another incoming call. I quickly told him that we would be seeing him shortly, then hung up.

I was so eager to see Patty that I went outside to take Ruben for a short walk until she came home. The afternoon was an ideal Adirondack day in June surrounded by the mountain greenery and ferns that were coming to life. Just as we returned to wait for her on the porch, I heard the familiar sound of the Jeep's engine and the beep of the horn. Patty had arrived. I was on my feet as Ruben ran from the porch to greet her. I walked toward her to give her a gentle welcome home hug. I had missed her so much. Our lips met and we kissed each other warmly as Ruben pranced happily around.

"Jason, are you all right? I never want to be away from you that long again!" she exclaimed. "The phone calls were appreciated, but just not the same."

"I'm okay, Patty, and those two bums are locked up. You would have been proud of Ruben: he came through like a champ."

"I'm proud of both of you. That was taking such a chance, you waiting all alone for them," she replied with tears forming in her eyes.

"Honey, it's alright. I have to admit, especially when they were coming through the window, I had all I could do to hold Ruben back until they were inside. We had to act fast. If they'd had firearms it probably would have been more difficult, but that semiautomatic of mine was a convincer."

"Let's hope it is the end of this nightmare," she responded.

"I believe it is. Ruben was spectacular. He's still strong and fast. His jaws are powerful, and Kelts found it out."

"It's been a tiring time, Jason, probably because I've been so worried about you and the danger that you were in. I'm glad it's finally over," she added. With a huge sigh of relief she laid her head on my chest.

"Patty, I've got an idea. I know we're both exhausted, but rather than preparing dinner and cleaning up, why don't you freshen up and we'll go to Drew's for some dinner tonight? What do you think?" I asked.

"Good idea. Give me a few minutes to change and I'll be ready. We so seldom go out," she said excitedly. "It'll be a celebration."

"Honey, we can go out anytime you'd like. Just say the word," I responded.

Patty disappeared into the bathroom. In a few minutes she came out of the bedroom dressed in a blue denim maternity outfit.

"You look stunning, my dear," I remarked.

"Even without a waistline?" Patty asked, teasing.

"To me, you are more beautiful than ever," I replied. "I love you, Patty, more than you'll ever know."

"The feeling is very mutual. And I could keep kissing you forever, but we'd better get going now before we change our minds about going out." Patty smiled as she reached for a wrap as the evening temperature had cooled.

On the way out to the Bronco I looked over into the dog run. Ruben was in his doghouse with his head tucked between his front paws.

"Be a good dog, Ruben. We'll be back in a while," I hollered over to him as we walked by.

I helped Patty into the passenger side, closed her door, went around to the driver's side, and slid behind the steering wheel to start the car. I drove slowly out of the drive to avoid the two potholes that had developed on the roadway, as I didn't want to bounce Patty.

"I'll have to remember to fill those in, Patty," I remarked.

"You'd better, before I give birth right here in the driveway. Only kidding, Sherlock."

On the way to Drew's I related to her my conversation with Tom Huston in which he had informed me that the suite was now ready with new furnishings, and how we would have a company car at our disposal.

"What do you think of that? Aren't you happy?" I glanced over to catch her expression.

She grasped my arm. "Yes, it all sounds great. But I'm still apprehensive, because you know how much we love the Old Forge region and the people. It's going to be hard on both of us for a while until we get used to the Placid area."

Her response reminded me how deeply she felt about our move. "I know, Patty, but we'll adjust and we'll do just fine. With Jim Jenny renting our home and the money from him coming in monthly, we'll be able to compensate Wilt and the fellows that helped him on the addition."

"That will be wonderful, Jason. You know I do think we'll eventually be better off," she agreed.

"Definitely, sweetheart. And we have to keep in mind that no one is going to subsidize our incomes for us. We have to make our own way in this complex society. That's another consideration when making the decision to reside inside the Blue Line of the park. The generations that were born inside the park have had to work hard to be able to survive here without industry to provide job opportunities. They have either created a way to make a living wage or have had to leave the area."

"True, Jason. We both see every day how hard people here have adapted because of their love for the area."

"It's definitely so, Patty."

"By the way, what did you tell Tom about when we will be leaving here?"

"About three weeks. We'll load everything that we need in both vehicles. I'll ask Wilt and Jack to bring up our snowmobiles later. I'm going to leave the canoe for Jim Jenny and his wife to use until we need it. Because we're renting the log home furnished, the physical move will be fairly easy on us."

"You're a sweetheart, Jason," she remarked, "You think of everything."

"Hon, I'm just trying to make it easier on you."

The parking area at Drew's Restaurant had one space left. I pulled in between a pickup and a sports car. I turned the Bronco off, got out, and went around to Patty's side to open the door for her. The fading sunlight caught her at just the right angle.

"Patty, you look absolutely radiant in the late sunlight. It's simply fantastic! It must be true what they say about the glow of motherhood!"

"Quit spoofing me, sweetheart! I know how I look. I have a mirror," she added.

"It won't be long before you're a mother and back to your old trim self."

"We're looking forward to that, aren't we, Jason?"

"That's for sure—but you know I do mean it when I say you're beautiful in your pregnancy."

When we walked into Drew's Restaurant, Paula, Mike's wife, was there to greet us with her warm and friendly smile. She led us to an open booth and placed the menus on the table.

We took a few minutes to look the menu over.

"What looks good to you, Patty?"

"Everything, sweetheart, but I believe I'll have the small steak with a side of mushrooms, baked potato, and the veggie—and, of course, the salad," she responded as she folded the menu.

"That sounds good to me, too. I guess I'll join you."

Paula soon brought our two glasses of ice water with lemon. She took our orders and left. Patty and I both asked to have the leafy salad served before our meals, and Paula promptly brought it to the table.

While we ate our salads, we discussed the numerous things that had to be accomplished before our move. The telephone and power companies were first on our list to notify. Then we'd need change of address forms to be made out and submitted. Our banking accounts had to be changed, along with other notifications. We both realized it was somewhat involved in order to move from one locality to another. We agreed that we would systematically initiate the changes in order of priority and make a Things-to-do list so we would not forget anything.

Paula returned with our dinners. The two steaks were sizzling and everything was piping hot, just the way we liked it. Before we began our meal I said a blessing thanking God for the gifts we were about to receive, and then we proceeded to enjoy our delicious dinner. The steak was tender and cooked to a perfect medium rare.

Paula stopped by and inquired, "Is everything alright, folks?"

"Everything is delicious, Paula. Kindly inform Chef Michael that we're enjoying dinner very much," I said sincerely.

"I will, Jason. Patty, you're looking well. When is the baby due?" she asked, turning to her.

"In a few weeks, Paula," Patty said, wearing a proud smile.

"I wish you both the very best," she said as she left our table to take another order.

As I looked around the room, I realized that there were no familiar faces, which was very unusual: a sure sign that new residents were moving into the area as new homes and camps were being constructed throughout the Adirondack Park. With the new growth it would only be a matter of time before changes would arise and decisions would have to be made that would affect all of us living inside the Blue Line. Right now I would just have to wait and see. I firmly believed that taking on my new position at the Breakshire Lodge would be a smart move for us. I could only hope that the many friends we had in Old Forge would remain steadfast for years to come. They were all good solid Adirondackers who unselfishly had given their all for Patty and me in the completion of our addition. How could we ever forget their generosity? I knew we would not.

Chef Michael stopped by the table and Patty and I both told him how much we were enjoying the cuisine. He smiled and moved on to another table. We ordered two cups of decaf, but although tempted by the list of desserts, we decided on none.

After paying our check, we left the restaurant and walked over to the Bronco. I noticed the right rear tire was soft. We climbed in and drove to the gas station just outside of Inlet. I got out and put some air into the tire. I realized I'd have to keep watch of the tire; if it continued to lose air, Dr. Don would be getting a visit. On the way home two large does and a fawn ran directly across the highway in front of us— fortunately, several yards ahead.

The dark of night had arrived. Our headlights reflected off the eyes of the occasional animal who lined both sides of Route 28. The majority of the eyes belonged to the local deer population. I kept my speed down in order to be able to stop the Bronco immediately if a deer or two decided to dash across the highway in front of us. In my many years as a member of the state police, I had investigated numerous deer car accidents; some had endangered human lives, not to speak of the costly damage to the vehicles, and usually the deer had died.

When we arrived home, I assisted Patty into the house and then let Ruben out for a run into the woods. The K-9 returned shortly, following me inside. Patty had gone into the bedroom to change into something comfortable. She soon appeared in the doorway wearing her maroon robe, loosely belted, and joined me on the davenport.

We decided to watch a movie on television. Patty quickly became engrossed in her knitting, but I found it difficult to enjoy the movie, as I was unable to relax. Something gnawed at me as I reflected on the recent capture of the two hired killers. If Draper had enough funds to hire two hit men, what was to prevent someone from hiring others to complete the task? I had been so jubilant about their arrest, but now I was beginning to foresee possible future threats. I decided to call

Jack Doyle first thing in the morning to voice my fears.

"Jason, didn't you hear me? I asked you a question," Patty asked, puzzled.

"Oh, Patty, I'm sorry. I must have been engrossed in the movie," I answered, not wanting to upset her with my thoughts. "What was it, dear?"

"I was just going to ask you if you're ready for bed? With all the excitement, I'm really exhausted. And our child has been active," she said, reaching over for my hand to place it on her tummy.

"I see—I mean, I feel—exactly what you mean, honey. You go on in and I'll be with you shortly," I assured her.

Patty rose and placed her knitting in the basket. I knew she needed to go to bed, as she was still working hard and had to get up early.

I continued to sit on the couch with my thoughts. I hoped I would be able to sleep that night. I wondered when this nightmare would end. With a sigh I rose to fulfill my nightly chores, letting Ruben out for his walk, securing the home, and turning off the lights. Then I gratefully joined my sleeping wife.

CHAPTER THIRTY-SEVEN

I was awakened by the annoying sound of the alarm to find Patty already in the shower preparing for another busy day at the diner. It wasn't long before she was ready to leave. This was the first time that I was actually pleased to watch her back out, as I was deeply anxious to contact Lt. Doyle, even if it meant catching him at home before he went to his office. His home number was unlisted, but he had shared it with me in the event of an emergency, which I felt this was.

I poured myself another cup of coffee, went into my office to look up his number, and dialed. A sleepy voice finally answered, "Hello."

"Jack, I'm truly sorry to bother you so early, but I feel that this is important. I rolled and tossed all night. Here's my fear— if someone has the resources to hire hit men to avenge Draper's incarceration, what's to stop them from hiring more?"

"Calm down! Calm down, Jason. I'm way ahead of you," he replied consolingly. "We're already working on that angle."

"What do you mean?" I asked, taken aback.

"We haven't released any information on their capture to the national press. Here's what's going on: Kelts remains mute; however, Taco Jones appears to be close to cooperating with us. We're trying to find out who is calling the shots, and we feel that we're getting close. I'm sorry that I didn't inform you sooner; I really should have. Now, try to relax a little. Your old buddy is on top of this, with a little help from Jay Silverstein of the Phoenix PD."

I felt some of my tense muscles relax. "I should have known better, Jack. But with Patty expecting, you can imagine the inner turmoil that I've been suffering."

"Believe me when I say I understand what you must be going through. I guarantee that I will call you immediately when we identify Draper's contact. We feel that we're getting very close to solving this case. You take it easy, Jason; I'll stay in touch."

I hung up feeling somewhat relieved. I realized I should have known better. The old adage of "being brothers for life" doesn't cease upon retirement from the troopers. No one messes with the world of law enforcement. It's an ingrained unwritten code: never harm a police officer or their families, or else you will face the consequences.

Now that my mind was clearer, I could focus better. With our move to Lake Placid being a short ways off, I decided to clean out some old papers, magazines and old files for the refuse containers after breakfast. Ruben was out in the dog run. My call to Jack Doyle had given me some hope.

CHAPTER THIRTY-EIGHT

At Troop S Headquarters, Lieutenant Jack Doyle was wasting no time in furthering his inquiry into the matter of the late Draper and the acts carried out by Charles Kelts and Taco Jones. Kelts had chosen to remain mute, and not talking about anything. Taco Jones of Mesa, Arizona, had a different agenda.

It was 10:00 a.m. when Doyle and Senior Investigator Carl Griffin joined Taco Jones in the interview room. Doyle and Griffin were both masterful interrogators, both dedicated to the state troopers, both fine examples of law-enforcement officers.

Taco Jones, age 40, of Cactus Road, Mesa, Arizona sat at the end of a large table. He was permitted to smoke, at his request. A pitcher of ice water and several plastic glasses waited nearby.

Information gathered by Jay Silverstein of the Phoenix PD revealed that Taco was from a large family and had quit school when he was sixteen. Born in Phoenix, he had a record of juvenile arrests, and his arrest as an adult had led to him serving time in several Arizona correctional facilities. Lieutenant Doyle began the interview.

"Good morning, Mr. Jones. As you know, my name is Jack Doyle. I would like you to meet Senior Investigator Carl Griffin. We are both members of the Bureau of Criminal

Investigation, and we are here this morning to talk with you for a while concerning your recent activities in the Adirondacks."

"Hello, Mr. Jones. I'm sorry to meet you under these circumstances," Griffin said.

He sat in a chair near the interviewee.

"Me, too, sir," Taco answered, submissively looking away from Griffin's intense stare.

"We're not here to harm you, Taco—by the way, you don't mind if I address you as Taco?"

"No, that's my name, Taco Jones," the interviewee responded uncertainly.

Lieutenant Jack Doyle, sitting across from Griffin, made some entries into his notebook, listening intently as Griffin continued.

"Taco, have you ever been to New York State before?"

"No, sir, this is my first time."

"What was the purpose of your visit to our state?" Griffin asked, keeping his eyes on the shaken man.

"Charlie Kelts asked me if I'd like to make some money. Charlie told me that he had to go to New York to put a scare into some people."

"Taco, I believe you came to New York to do a little more than just scare someone. Tell us the real purpose for your visit. You must understand that we know a great deal about you and Mr. Kelts. Both of you have extensive records and, Taco, I want you to listen closely to what I have to say. You have already had a break in this matter. When you and Kelts entered Jason Black's home with the intent to cause deadly physical harm to him and his family, he had the right to take appropriate action, and kill you. I want you to know right now that if it had been my dwelling, we wouldn't be sitting in this room today, because you'd be in another place."

"What place is that?" Taco asked, seeming bewildered.

"The morgue," Griffin replied harshly.

Taco visibly shivered. "Wha--what's in it for me if I tell you what I know?"

Griffin's voice seemed to soften. "I can't make any

promises, Taco. But I definitely would be able to tell the district attorney that you cooperated. You understand, no, I'm not into making deals, Taco. I'm in no position to. It's up to you. You see, we can find out from other sources who's behind the arrangements to pay you and Kelts for your dirty deeds. We're dead serious. We're not going to fool around with you." His statement conveyed an ominous threat.

Taco's complexion paled to a ghost's. Griffin looked over at Doyle and caught his expression.

"Lieutenant Doyle, do you have something you'd like to say to Taco?"

"Yes, Senior Griffin, I do," he replied pushing his chair back. *"Taco, I've been sitting here listening to you and Senior Griffin. I'm appalled to hear that you and your friend, Kelts, came to our area with evil in your hearts. It's up to you, Taco: you can cooperate, or you can sit in jail, which you're going to do anyways. This matter is serious, and if you think for one moment that we're joking with you, you'd better think again."*

"Mr. Griffin told me that you people cannot make deals, but that if I tell you all I know you tell the district attorney of my cooperation," Taco replied, visibly shaken.

"That's what he said, Taco. Keeping your rights in mind, would you be willing to give us a sworn statement as to your participation in this crime?" Doyle asked.

"I--I'll give you a statement," Taco declared with a trembling voice. *"Yeah. A statement."*

"Senior Griffin, why don't you take Mr. Jones to your office for the statement?" Lieutenant Doyle suggested.

"Mr. Jones, we'll go to my office and you can tell me what you know," Griffin said firmly. He requested a uniformed trooper to take Jones to the BCI area of the headquarters.

CHAPTER THIRTY-NINE

As I finished cleaning up the dishes I had used for my noontime lunch of franks and barbecued beans, little did I know that Taco Jones, one of the men who had entered our log home, was about to give a sworn statement to Senior Investigator Carl Griffin of the BCI.

Just as I put the final dish away, the phone rang. I rushed into my office and answered it.

"Hello, Jason Black here," I said.

"Jason, Doyle here. Glad I caught you at home. I have some good news to share with you. About twenty minutes ago, Taco Jones subscribed to a sworn statement concerning his full participation in this crime. The main reason I called you was the fact that Jones knew all along who Draper's contact person was. It's a disbarred lawyer from Phoenix, name of Warren McCandless, age about 50. The Phoenix PD is picking him up this afternoon. At last, I believe you and Patty can relax and rest assured that the Draper mess is finally closed for keeps."

I didn't know what to feel. "I sure in the hell hope so," I said. "It's been plaguing Patty and me more than you'll ever know. But one thing I still can't understand why he would continue this vendetta after Draper's demise?"

"It seems that McCandless was heavily invested in the Draper organization: a silent partner, part of the reason for his disbarment, I guess that was his motive. I'll tell you more when I get all the facts,"

"Probably that's it. By the way, we owe you a big steak, Jack!"

"We'll see about that. Anyway, that's the scoop. As you know, Draper possessed a split personality. He could have been a star in our society, but the darker side took over and instead he went down the path of self-destruction."

"Jack Doyle, I've known you a long time, and your efforts in this particular case went beyond what is required. Speaking for Patty and myself, please accept a big thanks for you and your staff."

After saying goodbye, I stood up and stretched out fully. Then I looked at my watch and realized I had time to thaw the small pot roast in the freezer by defrosting it in the microwave. I wanted to prepare it for a special dinner and surprise Patty, along with the good news that Jack Doyle had related to me. It was truly a night to celebrate. How glad I was that I hadn't had to shoot the two intruders. Ruben had made a good partner and I wouldn't forget him; when it came to giving out plaudits, the retired K-9 would receive two of his favorite biscuits instead of one. Russ Slingerland, his former handler, would certainly be proud of Ruben's actions in the apprehension of Kelts and Jones.

I coated the thawed roast with a mixture of flour, pepper, and a dash of garlic salt. I added a small amount of oil to the Dutch oven to let it heat before browning the roast. I also put some sliced onions to brown into the pot just before adding some water, then covered it tightly to simmer slowly.

Approximately two hours later I added the cut-up potatoes and carrots. It wasn't long before the aroma of the pot roast wafted throughout the log home. Because of Patty's pregnancy I did not add wine to the process, as I normally would have.

With dinner well on the way I proceeded to set the table. My inner self was jubilant with the news from Doyle. I planned to share the celebratory news with Patty during dinner.

Ruben began to bark loudly. I looked outside and saw the red Jeep pull up near the dog run. Patty was home. She got out of the vehicle and went over to the dog run to go inside and pat his head. Patty loved Ruben just as much as I did. When she left the run and headed to the rear door, I opened the door and greeted her with a gentle embrace.

"I'm happy to be home, Jason. We had a busy day at the diner. The special was chicken and biscuits again, always sure to bring out the customers." She paused. "Mmm—something smells good. You must have prepared the pot roast for dinner," she exclaimed on her way over to the stove to take a peek. She lifted the cover, took a spoonful, and carefully sipped the simmering liquid. "That tastes great, Jason," she said with true praise.

"Honey, I'm glad you like it, I said with pride. "I still have to thicken it a little, of course."

"What a nice surprise. Okay, sweetheart, I'll go in and freshen up a little," Patty said, giving me a peck on the cheek as she passed by on her way to the bedroom.

By the time Patty returned I had our dinner ready for serving. I wanted to blurt out the good news, but I decided to wait until after dinner.

"I'm ready to be spoiled, Jason," she said, walking over to her chair.

"Oh, you are, are you? I'll spoil you," I replied, pulling her chair out for her.

"Jason, the baby was sure busy today. Kicking up a storm."

"It won't be long, July 15th, darling, before the baby will be born and we'll be three instead of two," I remarked, full of happiness at the thought.

With Patty seated and ready to eat, I went over to the Dutch oven, removed the pot roast, and laid it on a platter. I sliced several portions of roast and surrounded them with vegetables, then filled the gravy bowl and went back to the table. I fixed our plates and added two small serving dishes of coleslaw. The rolls that I had taken from the freezer earlier were now warmed, so I served Patty an opened buttered one.

"Your pot roast is so tasty and tender, darling. I love the hint of garlic and onion. And the vegetables are cooked just right. Oh, I love you, Jason; you can prepare dinner for me anytime you want to," she said, flirtatiously.

"Thanks, babe. I'm pleased the way it turned out myself. That was a good cut of meat. And as you know, Patty, simmering it slowly brings out the flavor. This is exceptionally good tonight," I agreed.

"You can say that again. And I'm looking forward to a nice cup of green tea with you after we finish."

"I figured that you might, so I'm way ahead of you. The teakettle is already on a slow burner."

After our delicious meal we settled down with our green tea and oatmeal cookies. I thought this was the appropriate time to share the good news with her.

"Honey, I have an important surprise for you tonight," I said, trying to contain my excitement.

"What might that be, Jason?" she asked.

I didn't respond right away, not knowing where or how to begin. The room was silent for a few moments.

"Well, I received a call earlier today from Lieutenant Doyle. Are you ready for this?"

"Jason, tell me. What is it?" she asked somewhat apprehensively.

"It seems that one of the men that entered our home, Taco Jones, has decided to tell the police everything in a sworn statement about the plan to seek revenge against those responsible for leading to Draper's capture."

"That's great, Jason! Do you mean to tell me that we really won't have to worry anymore about retaliation from those evil people?" she inquired anxiously. "I hope this time it's really over."

"That's correct. Doyle also informed me that Draper's contact person was a Warren McCandless, a disbarred attorney: evidently he was invested in Draper's organization. Now that he's under arrest, I truly believe that this is the end of the Draper matter forever. How do you feel about it, Patty?" I asked.

"Oh, honey, that's such good news. It takes so much

pressure off us."

"Yes, dear, we'll have a more relaxed environment to raise our child without the worry," I agreed.

"Have you told anyone else as yet?" she asked.

"No, I've only shared it with you, so far. I wanted you to be the first to know."

"That's real good news, honey. I'm happy about it." She smiled fully. "And I also have some good news. I didn't tell you at dinner, but I have a little surprise for you!"

"What would that be, my dear?"

"Guess," she said with a chuckle.

"I haven't a clue. You've got me: what's the surprise?" I asked, eager for her answer.

"I know that you've wanted to visit the Loggers' Museum, and I'd like to see it myself before the baby's born. Lila has given me the day off tomorrow. I thought you'd like to visit there before our move and our new duties," she said, watching for my reaction.

"That's wonderful of Lila. And you definitely can use a break from work," I suggested. "How come? The diner has been so busy lately."

"One of the waitresses volunteered to cover for me. That was really nice of her. My only wish is that she could have given us a little more notice."

"No problem at all. I'm very flexible right now. Business hasn't picked up yet," I explained.

"I can pack a picnic basket and take the cooler along with us, or we could find some place on the road. I can get up a little early in the morning and make a small salad and put together some cold cuts and those nice soft rolls. How does that sound?" she offered happily.

"Patty, I think that's a great idea. But I don't want you doing so much. Let's find some place to eat on the road, okay?" I asked.

"Fine with me," she answered approvingly.

"This trip will not only give us the opportunity to tour the museum, but also to enjoy some time to relax after the strain we've been under."

"Come here, you big lug!" she commanded playfully as she grabbed me to give me a big hug and a kiss on the cheek.

With our plans settled we moved into the living room to play some music. We sat on the davenport close to each other before retiring around ten. Although Patty would not have to rise for her morning shift, we still wanted to get an early start for our trip. She got ready for bed while I tended to my regular duties, letting the dog out and locking up, before joining her in the bedroom where she was already engaged in reading a book on newborns. I pulled down the bed covers and started to read our local newspaper.

It wasn't long before Patty fell off to sleep. I slid out of bed to go around to her side, remove her book, and place it on the night stand. I covered up her shoulders and gently kissed her on the forehead. I then went out to check on Ruben, who was also in a deep sleep. I got back into bed to read some more, but found it was difficult to keep my eyes open. It wasn't long before I joined my family in the land of sleep.

CHAPTER FORTY

I was awakened by a noise from the kitchen. Still groggy from my deep sleep, I called out, "Patty, are you okay?"

"I'm alright, honey. I just dropped a pan," she answered. "Sorry if I woke you," she apologized. "I guess I'm getting a bit clumsy,"

"You didn't do it on purpose, did you?" I chided.

"Honest, honey, it just slipped out of my hands," she explained.

"Patty, did you let Ruben out for his run this morning?" I asked as I swung my legs out of bed.

"Yes, when I first got up. He returned to his dog run and is lying in his doghouse watching a couple of crows."

"I can hear them out there, always cawing. They're sort of a pain, especially in the early morning hours."

"I agree, honey. Do you want coffee or green tea?"

"I'd better have coffee this morning, darling. Did you shower already?"

"Yes, I did."

"I'll shower before I have my coffee, so give me ten minutes, babe."

I rushed into the bathroom, disrobed, and went into the shower. The hot water felt good on my spine. I reached up and adjusted the showerhead into the pulsating position. I turned the shower to hot and let the pelting water work my back. I could feel the muscles relax. I shouted to Patty, "Honey, boy, does this shower feel good!"

There was a moment of silence and then I heard, "Sherlock, that shower head was a very good investment. And now are you about ready for your coffee?"

"I'll be out in a couple of minutes, sweetheart."

I turned off the shower after my cold rinse, wrapped the fluffy bath towel around my waist, and headed to the bedroom. I finished drying and quickly dressed, not wanting to lollygag too long. We had a good day ahead of us, hopefully.

I quickly dried and combed my hair before joining Patty in the kitchen, where she was already pouring my coffee. I went over to give her a little kiss on her cheek.

"Jason, didn't you shave? I felt your whiskers when you kissed me!" she exclaimed in surprise.

"I'm going to use my electric razor after I have my coffee," I explained.

"Do you want me to scramble you an egg with a slice of toast?"

"Good idea," I answered between sips of my hot coffee.

"Why don't you shave after you have your coffee? While you're shaving I'll prepare your breakfast."

"Swell. I'll only be a minute. I haven't used this electric shaver in a long time."

I took the last swallow of coffee and returned to the bathroom. I preferred my regular razor for shaving, but today I just felt like trying my electric razor for a change. To my surprise it worked better than I'd expected. I rubbed my hand over my face. Nice and smooth with no stubbles.

The scrambled eggs and one slice of whole-wheat toast were waiting for me when I came out. Patty had poached herself one egg and put it on a slice of toasted wheat bread. After we ate we quickly finished cleaning up the kitchen together; Patty washed the dishes while I put everything away and tidied up the area. I placed a call to Lynn at the kennel to ask if she would be able to give Ruben a bath, explaining that we would be back late in the afternoon to pick him up. She assured me that there would be no problem and would look forward to seeing him.

Shortly after nine we pulled out of the yard and headed the Bronco northward toward Inlet. I checked over the house closely before departing. Ruben was sitting in the back. It was timely for Ruben to visit Lynn at her kennels, and while there he would enjoy a good bath and some grooming.

I pulled up in front of the kennel and turned the Bronco off. I got out, opened the rear gate, and Ruben jumped to the ground to follow me. I snapped his leash onto his collar and we went up the stairs and inside to find Lynn sitting at her desk.

"Hello, Jason. How have you and Patty been? Ruben looks good. I'll be glad to get him bathed and trimmed up a bit," she said.

"We're doing just fine. Yes, a bath and whatever grooming you feel necessary would be fine. And as I said, we'll be gone for just the day, so we'll pick him up late this afternoon."

"Have a good trip, and say hello to Patty for me. When's the baby due?"

"Just a few weeks now."

"Oh, I'm so happy for you two having a sweet little baby."

I thanked Lynn warmly and told Ruben to be a good boy as I left the kennel.

We drove north through Inlet and continued on toward Blue Mountain. There was a medium flow of traffic. Between Blue Mountain and Long Lake I noticed a photographer with a tripod. It appeared he was taking a landscape photograph of a declining group of trees that continued to the water's edge of Long Lake.

"Patty, did you see the photographer back there?" I asked after passing him.

"Yes, he seemed occupied looking toward the lake. It was a beautiful scene."

"Maybe he is taking it for a calendar," I surmised.

"Could be. Every so often we have photographers stop by the diner. I don't mean the tourist type, but professionals."

"Honey, this is the perfect place on earth to click the

cameras professionally or for your own personal enjoyment," I commented.

When we drove by Gertie's Diner we could see that the parking area was full with cars and trucks. We decided that we'd stop on our way back to Old Forge, knowing that she would probably be too busy to visit now, judging from the number of vehicles in the lot.

It was almost noon when we pulled up to the Loggers' Museum. We noticed right away from the crowds that Tom Huston's vision had materialized into something very special. I looked around and spied Wilt's truck parked next to Jack Falsey's pickup truck. I proceeded to pull up beside Wilt's vehicle to park.

I climbed out and went around to Patty's side to open the door for her.

"Thank you, honey. You're always so thoughtful," she said.

Suddenly I noticed a puzzling sight. "Do you see the smoke rising over there?" I asked.

"Hmm. Maybe they're preparing the beef barbecue. I remember now that Wilt stopped by the diner one day last week and mentioned that they might try to have a barbecue here today, Jason. I had completely forgotten until I just smelled the wonderful aroma," she explained.

"It sure is wonderful! You know, we're just in time for lunch. What a treat!" I exclaimed. "Shall we eat now, or do you want to go through the museum first?"

"Whatever you decide will be okay with me," she responded. "Unfortunately, I'm always hungry now."

We decided to have lunch, so proceeded inside the building where the buffet was being served. We walked over to the area where tables and chairs were set up. Several people were already partaking of the reasonably priced buffet lunch. The aroma of the barbecued beef permeated the air, definitely a good draw for the hungry public. Background music added to the ambience.

We picked out a table, then made our way to the serving

line where two young men wearing whites were serving the barbecue, coleslaw, and baked beans. Patty, ahead of me in line, held her tray as one of the servers ladled a generous portion of barbecue onto a large grilled roll, along with a side of coleslaw and baked beans. I received the same and also served myself two dill pickles. Patty returned to the table and I joined her after paying the woman at the register.

"This is very tasty," Patty assured me, as she had already sampled hers.

"Hmmm! Delicious! The beef is tender, and I detect a hickory flavor in the sauce," I agreed emphatically.

"So do I. It's a wonderful lunch. I hope they can keep up this quality."

After we finished our sandwiches, we approached the young men on the serving line to tell them how much we had enjoyed their barbecued beef.

Patty and I spent the remainder of the afternoon touring the museum to view the many interesting displays. The guides that we talked with were informative and answered our inquiries intelligently. Evidently they were well informed on their subject matter. When we approached the gift shop we found both Jack and Irene Falsey stocking some miniature lumberjack dolls on the shelves.

"Hello, Jack and Irene. You look as though you both are busy," I said in greeting. "Irene, I'm surprised that you're still here. I thought you were just going to be involved in the initial position as an adviser until a permanent individual was appointed."

"You're right. But she's still moving into the area, so I volunteered to fill in for her until she was settled," she explained.

"How are these lumberjack dolls selling?" I asked.

"They've been selling well, Jason," Irene said with satisfaction.

"Jason, how many can I wrap up for you?" Jack asked half-jokingly.

"I'll tell you what, Jack: we'll take two of them."

"You see that, Irene? I told you I could make a sale for you."

"That you did, Jack," Irene said with a chuckle as she handed Jack two lumberjack dolls for wrapping.

"Jason, as you both probably know, a percentage of the sale price goes into the special fund set aside for families of lumberjacks," Irene told us.

"Yes, we're aware of that. It's for a very good cause," I replied.

"You're so right," Jack agreed.

"Say, have you seen Wilt around today? We don't want to miss him," I inquired.

"I saw him around earlier. He's here, but who knows where? You'll run into him somewhere, I'm sure."

While Jack and I conversed some more, Irene and Patty chatted about the imminent birth of our baby.

"Irene, we thought this would be a good time to tour the museum, because we're going to be busy for a while with all the changes in our lives: the move, the new job and, above all, our new baby," I heard her say.

"That was a good idea, Patty. You're right; it will be a busy time for you both," she said, knowingly.

We wished Irene and Jack the best, then left the gift shop. We continued our tour of the many displays while looking for Wilt and any other familiar faces. Just as we were about ready to complete our tour of the museum, we heard a booming voice behind us that we knew so well.

"Hey! Patty and Jason, wait up! Thanks for stopping by today," Wilt almost roared while trying to catch up with us.

We turned around and there he was: Wilt, dressed in his lumberjack garb, with a hat shoved into his trouser pocket. Bright red suspenders set his outfit off well.

"Wilt, aren't you a little warm in that attire?" Patty inquired teasingly.

"Shucks no, Patty and Jason. Well, it might be a bit warm, but the spectators keep their cameras busy snapping pictures."

"I have to give you a great deal of credit, Wilt. Tom

certainly selected the right man to head up the museum. Your experience is unsurpassed," I said.

"Aw, come on, Jason. Any of our seasoned timber people could handle this position," he replied, turning almost as red as his suspenders.

"No, I mean it, Wilt. It just goes to show you that Tom Huston knows people."

"Jason, if it wasn't for you introducing me to Mr. Huston I wouldn't be in charge of this project today. It was a brilliant idea he had to keep the spirit of the logging theme alive and well. You'd be surprised to know how many people this museum, even though it's new, has drawn to its front door. Some of them may be just curious tourists, but many timber folks from all over the northeast have also visited here. We are adding to the displays every week. And there's even the possibility that we may keep it open during the winter season on a trial basis. You know, even when the snow sets in, the logging industry keeps on plugging along!"

"That's true, Wilt. I hope this museum and the programs associated with it will be here for years to come. They'll help educate the present generation and future generations about every facet of the timber industry that's played such an economic role in the development of this area."

"Well put, Jason." Wilt nodded in agreement.

Before we left the museum we talked with Wilt for a few more minutes about our plans for our future with the baby's arrival and our move. He again expressed his sadness at our need to leave the area but made clear he understood the reasons that had gone into making our decision. He gave us each a bear hug as we said our goodbyes.

As we walked to the car, Patty told me she had had a long talk with Lila about her departure from the diner. They had agreed that she would stay two weeks before our move to Lake Placid. I knew I would be continuing my investigative work, which had slowed down considerably except for a few check cases and some civil processes that still were waiting to be served. I planned to continue some of my detective work when we moved as well, with Tom Huston's permission to be away from the lodge for brief periods in the event any of the cases needed my personal attention. I was sure he would be understanding in taking into consideration my needs, knowing I would never take advantage of his generosity. The drive home seemed longer than the drive up. It wasn't long before Patty dozed off leaving me alone with my thoughts.

It was late afternoon when we finally arrived at the kennel to pick up Ruben. Patty woke as soon as the car stopped at the kennel.

"Jason, have you enough money to pay Lynn?" Patty asked sleepily.

"Yes, honey, I'm sure I do," I answered.

"Tell her I said hello, and tell her I'll be in to say goodbye before we leave."

"I will," I assured her.

I got out and went up the stairs. When I reached the front door I heard that familiar bark as I turned the knob. Evidently Lynn had seen us pull up out front, as she had the well-groomed Ruben ready for his ride home.

"How was your trip, Jason?" she asked.

"Very nice, Lynn. We both enjoyed it. I recommend visiting the Loggers' Museum. Has Ruben been a good boy?"

"He's always a good dog, but he does seem to pace a lot when he's here. He must miss you and Patty. Oh, I clipped his nails while he was here; I hope that's okay."

"Glad you did, Lynn. How much do I owe you?"

"I have your bill right here," she said as she placed it on the counter.

"Are you sure that's all, Lynn?" I asked as I reached for my wallet.

"That's fine, Jason. You have been a good customer for a long time. We're going to miss you folks and Ruben," she said sincerely.

"You'll be interested to learn I've rented our home to Jim Jenny, who has a couple of dogs. You can be sure I'll tell him about your fine service, Lynn."

"Thank you, Jason. I'd appreciate that."

I looked over at Ruben, whose tail was thumping noisily against the floor. He was anxious to leave.

"Say hello to Patty for me," she said, as she handed me the leash.

"I will. She said she would stop in to say goodbye before our move."

Ruben lunged ahead of me as we headed toward the rear of the Bronco. I opened it and he bolted into the car.

"Ruben, have you been a good dog?" Patty asked lovingly.

He let out a bark as he leaned forward toward her. His large jaws opened wide in his excitement to be with us again.

"Settle down, big boy," I commanded, trying to get him to calm down.

When we pulled into the driveway of our log home a sense of sadness fell over me. *Am I doing the right thing by accepting the personnel and security job in Lake Placid?* I asked myself.

I realized it could go either way. Here we were in Old Forge, the place we loved and wanted to be. Here was my lovely wife, pregnant with our child. It had been a big decision. Had I made a mistake by not trying to find a position here where we were so happy? The opportunity at Lake Placid had come along and seemed to be the answer to our financial dilemma. Hopefully we had made the right choice. Only time would tell. Right now the birth of our new baby was the most important consideration.

"Honey, what's the matter? You look worried," she asked.

"Everything's alright honey, just thinking to myself," I responded trying to smile.

Patty looked over at me with concern as if she were able to read my thoughts. "Everything will work out Jason. You wait and see," she said reassuringly.

"I know, darling, I know."

I got out from the Bronco to open Patty's door. She reached for her purse before exiting the car. I walked her to the door and unlocked it for her, then returned to the car to let the playful Ruben out.

"Not now, Ruben, not now," I said firmly, leading him to his dog run.

I opened the gate and he went inside. When I joined Patty in the living room, she had already started knitting.

"Do you need any help, sweetheart?" she asked as I walked in.

"No problem, babe," I replied.

While she was busy I went into the office to find the light blinking on the answering machine. I played the messages from the callers: one from Tom Huston and the other from Dale. I called Tom right away, as it had been a while since I had last talked to him.

"Breakshire Lodge. May I help you?" the courteous desk clerk answered.

"Mr. Huston, please. Jason Black calling."

"Just a moment, sir, I'll ring his office."

My future employer's voice came on the line. "Jason, glad you called. How are you and Patty doing?"

"Better, Tom. It looks like that Draper matter has been resolved successfully. I'll give you a complete rundown when I see you in person. We certainly were living under a strain. We took some time off for a little R & R today, a trip to the Loggers' Museum. It was relaxing for us both. But that's enough about me. How have you been feeling? I would have called sooner, but we've really been engrossed by this Draper threat," I explained.

"I'm very glad to hear about your safety! I'm quite tired most of the time, but the doctor just tells me to get more rest. It's good you could get away for a day. And I'm happy to remind you that everything is ready for you—your furnished suite, your job—just waiting for you to arrive. When do you plan to make the move?" he inquired.

"Tom, be certain to follow the doctor's orders! As for us, I believe we can move in about three weeks. We've rented our log home to Jim Jenny and his wife, completely furnished. That's one thing we won't have to worry about."

"That sounds good. Now, I want you to keep in mind that it's fine with me for you to maintain your private investigative work as well. Jason, you are well known throughout the mountains inside the Blue Line, and it's important for you to continue your P.I. work, when required. You have many contacts."

His words reassured me. "Well, Tom, I appreciate your understanding and I thank you for allowing me to be able to pursue my activity in the event I'm called on to do so."

"Jason, you're like a son to me, and don't ever forget it."

"Thank you, Tom. I'm honored."

"Do you need any help in your moving arrangements?" he asked.

"No, Tom, everything's being take care of at this end by the gang down here, but thank you for asking," I replied.

"You've got good friends, Jason," he acknowledged.

"Yes, we're very fortunate to have such loyal friends."

"You're right. Please be sure to tell them they're always welcome here," he added.

"Thank you, Tom. You're most generous."

"Well, that's all for now. Give Patty my love. I'm looking forward to seeing you soon."

"I will tell her. Take care, Tom."

Patty came into the office just as I hung up.

"Honey, that was Tom. He sends his love to you."

"How's he feeling?" she asked.

"He told me that he's still very tired most of the time and that his doctor wants him to get more rest."

"He should. Honey, I worry about him. He's a wonderful person, very caring and considerate for others. Very seldom do you come across a person with those attributes."

"I know, Patty, you're right. And how are you feeling, my dear, after that long ride?"

"I feel pretty good. The baby's moving around more than ever. Remember that I see the doctor day after tomorrow. He's going to give me the name of a doctor in Saranac Lake that he recommends."

"That's good, honey. You may have mentioned it before. I'm glad that you'll have your doctor's referral. I wonder if you already met him when you were in the Saranac Lake Hospital."

"I may have. Don't forget I've got to give Lila at least two weeks' notice then we'll need at least a week to get all our clothes and things ready that we'll need to take with us," she stated firmly.

"Tom assured me everything is ready. We really won't need to take a lot of things from our cabinets. We'll just take our clothes, my case files, some of our office equipment, and the baby's crib and things for the nursery: and of course, anything else we'll need. While we're on the subject, have you come up with any more ideas for names?" I asked playfully.

"You know I have a list of names written down. My favorite for a boy is still Jason, and if it should be a girl, now I'm leaning toward Deborah Anne. What do you think, dear?"

"I'm not too certain about the first, but I will go along with your suggestion, if that's what you like."

"I'll be glad to have everything ready before the little one arrives," Patty said as she placed her hand on her rounded belly.

I walked over and carefully embraced her. She looked beautiful. We kissed each other warmly.

"Jason, I love you so much," she said looking up into my eyes.

"I love you, too, sweetheart."

Patty went into the living room to return to her knitting and I returned to my office. Looking around the room I tried to determine what to do with some of the pictures and plaques. I decided to pack them all in a large box and put them in the storage area at the Breakshire Lodge until I saw how much room we would have. So many of them brought back memories of my trooper days: the daily routine patrols, the interaction with the citizenry of each community that I had been honored to serve, my public appearances before various organizations, and my visits to the schools in my districts for safety lectures to school-bus drivers. What a journey it had been! My numerous investigations could fill volumes. In my opinion, there was simply no other profession in the world that could compare to it. Pulling my mind back to the task at hand, I decided I had better return Dale's telephone call.

He answered his phone on the third ring. "Jason, how have you been? I thought I'd better check in to see how things are progressing with your move."

"Good, Dale. I was just talking with Tom Huston for a few minutes."

"How is Tom, Jason? He looked kind of pale the last time we met."

"He told me that he's been pretty tired and that his doctor has recommended more rest. He's apparently keeping a good eye on his general health," I explained.

"Maybe he just expended too much of his energy on his Loggers' Museum. Hopefully when you get up there, you can relieve him of some of his responsibilities," he added.

"I'll do my best. I'm sure I'll have a lot to learn, but I'm looking forward to the challenge."

"Aw, come on, Jason. You won't have any trouble. Don't sell yourself short. But back to the move: what's the plan?"

"Dale, Wilt's getting a crew together to help us with the move. He'll be using his truck. It is scheduled in about three weeks. I'll call you on the definite date and time. Would you mind driving Patty's Jeep up to there?" I asked.

"Certainly, I'll be glad to! Is that all you want?"

"Wilt's got a large truck, but Jack Falsey's van will also be available if needed for boxes and clothes," I added.

"It sounds like everything is pretty well-covered. I'll wait for further instructions." He chuckled.

"Thanks, Dale, and say hello to your lovely wife."

"I will, Jason. You do the same."

I knew I had better call Jack, Charlie, and Jim with the tentative date, but I decided to wait till the next day. I went in to join Patty in the living room, but found her fast asleep. I carefully covered her with an afghan so as not to wake her. Clearly it had been a long day for her.

I went outside to let Ruben go for a run to the woods. I hoped he would have no trouble adapting to his new home in Lake Placid. I watched him from a distance as he sniffed around some brush piles looking for chippies before he raced back to me. I leaned down to pet him before we entered our home. When I peeked into the living room I found Patty still asleep. Not wanting to disturb her, I returned to my office.

CHAPTER FORTY-ONE

The next three weeks were a flurry of activities. Patty gave her two weeks' notice to John and Lila, who were saddened to see her leave, but wished her well with all their hearts. I took care of change of addresses to the post office and all our banks and business contacts. Each day passed swiftly. After Patty stopped working at the diner, we packed box after box of clothing, nursery items, books, and the odds and ends that we had elected to take with us. Unwanted items were put into separate boxes to be donated to the local church. In spite of the fact that we thought we had eliminated many items, we ended up with more boxes to take than we had anticipated.

In the midst of all this activity, somehow our friends and acquaintances managed to hold a farewell celebration at the firehouse, as there were too many well-wishers to fit into any of the restaurants. The food was catered and the Rhythm Riders provided music. Beautifully wrapped gifts of all sizes were piled atop a table for our new baby. How could we ever thank our community for their overwhelming response? I felt fairly sure the large turnout was because of the many people Patty had met at the diner. Their speeches were brief but sincere. It was fully evident to me that my wife Patty—the pretty blond waitress—would be surely missed. And, no doubt about it, we'd miss all the Old Forge folks, too.

Finally, the day of the move arrived. For some reason, the

weatherman cooperated and we were blessed with a cool, but sunshiny day. The crew—Wilt, Dale, Charlie, Jack, and Jim—arrived at the log home at seven. The hustle and bustle of this well organized group took about four hours before the caravan left on its way to our new residence at Lake Placid. I turned over my set of keys to Jim Jenny, who would be moving into our log home in about a week.

With the help of the efficient housekeeping staff, it didn't take long before we were settled successfully into our new suite of rooms. Before the moving crew left, we all joined Tom in the restaurant for a special buffet that he had had his chef prepare. It was set up in a small, separate dining room for privacy. The table had a large bowl of garden salad, steaming trays of fried chicken and roast beef, mashed potatoes, gravy, mixed vegetables, and all the extras for our hungry group. Conversation remained at a minimum as we all enjoyed the well-prepared food.

As we finished with coffee and dessert, Tom joined us at the table. I heartily thanked him and his staff for their efforts.

Tom rose to address the group. "I want to welcome you all to the Breakshire Lodge. But to Patty and Jason, I'm glad to say, welcome to your new home." He walked over to Patty to give her a warm embrace.

"Thank you, Tom, for everything," she said, tearing up.

"I know you are all tired from your efforts today and that you're ready for the long drive home. I'll make this short. Gentlemen, I know you are dear friends of Patty and Jason, and I consider you all my friends, too. You and your families are always welcome here at the lodge." He smiled fully at everyone in the group.

Wilt stood up and said with all sincerity, "Tom, speaking for all of us, we thank you for the wonderful buffet and for your kind remarks. We consider you our good friend and we ask you to watch over our buddy, Jason, and his wonderful wife, Patty."

"Wilt, and all of you, you can count on that. I thank you for your friendship. Being an owner of a lodge is a time-consuming position, but with friends like you, it is also rewarding. Please visit often," Tom urged. "Well, I'll excuse myself now. Travel well." With that he left the room.

Dale broke the silence that followed. "As much as we'd like to stay, we had better think about leaving. It is a long drive home," he said as he reluctantly looked at his watch.

Patty and I emotionally thanked our friends as they rose to leave. I had a difficult time holding back the tears, and Patty was absolutely unable to do so, reaching into her pocket several times for tissues. We promised we would keep in touch and that they would be the first to know when the baby arrived. We walked out to the parking lot with our friends and waved as they left. I loaned Patty my handkerchief to try to dry her eyes.

CHAPTER FORTY-TWO

Adjusting to our new surroundings went smoothly. I began to learn the ins and outs of the running of the lodge, and Patty occupied herself with rearranging our comfortable suite to suit our tastes and accommodate the arrival of the baby.

Then on the morning around two Patty softly nudged my shoulder. "Jason, I--I think I'm ready to go to the hospital. I'm having some sharp pains," she whispered urgently.

I sprang out of bed. "Really?" I asked, trying to remain calm. "So it's time! I'll call the hospital."

"And I'll get dressed and finish putting a few things into my suitcase."

I called the Saranac Lake Hospital, quickly dressed, helped Patty put on a jacket, and ran outside to the Bronco to drive it to the side entrance where Patty was waiting for me with her small suitcase. The drive to the hospital didn't take too long, as there was no traffic on the road.

When we arrived at the emergency entrance, two nurses were already waiting with a wheelchair. The labor pains were becoming more frequent.

Patty, seeing the distressed look on my face, reached over for my hand as they prepared to wheel her away. "Jason, don't worry. I'll be all right, dear," she assured me.

"I know you will," I answered as I leaned down to give her a kiss on the forehead.

I was instructed to go to the waiting room as I had opted not to be present during the delivery. They told me that I would be informed. There was no one else in the room. I was so nervous that I began to pace back and forth. Time stretched to eternity before her doctor, wearing scrubs, came through the door with a big smile. I glanced at my watch: six-thirty.

"Mr. Black, I am happy to inform you that you are the proud father of a healthy baby boy weighing seven pounds and twelve ounces. Congratulations! Mother is doing fine. She's resting now, but a nurse will let you know as soon as you can see your wife and baby," he said as he shook my hand.

With a joy that almost overwhelmed me, I continued to pace for what seemed a long, long time before the door opened again. This time it was a nurse who entered. "Mr. Black, congratulations. Will you follow me, please?"

"Yes, certainly," I said, my words sounding strange from my dry throat. I realized I had forgotten even to take a drink of water for many hours. I followed her to the room where Patty awaited me, with our tiny son in her arms. She looked somewhat pale, but when I entered the room her face seemed full of light.

"Jason, darling, I'd like you to meet, Jason Black, the second."

I approached almost in awe. He was wrapped in a small soft blanket and he wore on his head a little hat Patty had knitted for him. His eyes were closed and he appeared to be sleeping. Patty was holding him so very gently. I kissed her on the forehead, and she took one of my fingers and drew it down to the baby's hand.

"Honey, he is beautiful," I said, not able to take my gaze away from the miracle before me. "Our son."

I soon returned to the hospital to pick up my wife and child and bring them to our home at the Breakshire Lodge. I had immediately made several telephone calls to inform all our friends of the blessed event. Wilt had sent three dozen red roses from the moving group to Patty and the baby. I had sent a box of the best cigars to Lila to be passed out to our friends and, Patty's loyal customers and for those who weren't smokers, a large box of chocolates. The same day little Jason was born, Tom Huston had presented us with a beautiful new rocking horse for our baby boy, explaining, "I know I'm a little premature, but I wanted to give him his first horse."

"You're very thoughtful, Tom," I had told him gratefully. "We thank you for the rocking horse and for everything you've done for us."

"My pleasure," Tom had said with satisfaction before excusing himself to return to his busy office.

We soon adjusted to the routine of our new responsibilities of the early morning feedings that had led to a lack of sleep.

I adapted to my duties at the lodge, spending a great deal of time with Tom, who I was sad to see become frailer. However, he continued to claim that he was feeling as well as could be expected, and he worked many hours every day. Over the next few weeks, I was able to relieve him of some of his responsibilities to employees and guests. I found myself enjoying the interesting, diverse work. Ruben was enjoying his kennel life and was exercising daily by running back and forth in the large fenced area provided for the guests of the lodge.

The fears that we had experienced prior to our departure from our home fortunately proved to be groundless. I was happily busy with my new position, Patty had fallen in love with being a full-time mother, little Jason was growing and thriving, and Ruben was acquiring new friends daily as guests' canines joined him in the kennel area.

Our new beginning in the high peaks of the Adirondacks could only be called successful. The people we met were all friendly and helpful as they welcomed us to their community. Already we had a strong sense of fitting in and belonging.

"Jason," Patty said to me one bright autumn morning as she held our sleepy son in her arms. "I'm so glad we made the right decision and came to Lake Placid."

Looking at her with love in my heart, I could only smile and nod and fully agree.